Simple Truth

Carol Bodensteiner

Simple Truth

Carol Bodensteiner

Rising Sun Press
Des Moines, Iowa

This is a work of fiction. Names, characters, organizations, places, events, and incidents are either products of the author's imagination or are used fictitiously.

Rising Sun Press
Des Moines, Iowa

ISBN: 1981745386
ISBN-13: 9781981745388
ISBN 978-0-9797997-9-2 (ebook)

Cover design by Jenny Quinlan

Printed in the United States of America

Also by Carol Bodensteiner

Non-Fiction
Growing Up Country: Memories of an Iowa Farm Girl

Fiction
Go Away Home

For Hannah and Eliza

"Neutrality helps the oppressor, never the victim. Silence encourages the tormentor, never the tormented."
—Elie Wiesel
©The Nobel Foundation.

Chapter 1

A crisis isn't by definition a bad thing. Depends on whose crisis it is. Which side you're on. And how you handle it.

Only a few think about a crisis that way. Public-relations counselors among them, Angela thought as she hoisted the first of her two suitcases into the trunk. If she did her job right, her clients came out looking good. This particular crisis looked like it could also be good for her. Really good.

Boosting the second suitcase with her knee, she managed to get it loaded, too. She laughed as she thought about how she'd packed the night before. Each blouse she'd looked at, she'd thought, *Well, maybe,* and added it to the stack. Same with blazers, skirts, slacks. Spring weather compounded the clothing problem. April in Iowa could be warm, as it was today, or freezing cold. No one in their right mind needed this many clothes for a couple of weeks. That was what her dad always said when they loaded up for family vacations. Since she was driving, though, it didn't matter how much she took. That was always her mother's response. Angela favored her mother on this one.

Her luggage stowed, she took in the view one last time. To the east, the golden dome of the state capitol dominated the view. Directly to the west, the Des Moines skyline spread out along the river. Within three blocks she had her choice of restaurants, bars, and one-of-a-kind boutique shops. Her apartment building was full of young professionals like herself, drawn to the area for these amenities and more just across the river. Sherborn-Watts, the marketing agency where she'd worked for the past five years, stood only a dozen blocks farther west, nestled among the downtown high rises. Walkable on nice days. At the moment Angela noted dark clouds gathering and knew she needed to get going.

For the next three or four months, her view would be considerably different. *Probably not a building tall enough to block a sunrise in Hammond,* she mused. She imagined her restaurant options in the small town where she was going would be seriously limited. When she'd met her friend Jess for a going-away dinner the night before, Jess had encouraged Angela to share a second dragon roll.

"Better enjoy it now," Jess urged. "I bet you won't find anything as good as this in Hammond."

"Probably won't have such good company, either." Angela had smiled and toasted their friendship with a sip of merlot.

Angela enjoyed spending time with her friends, but there hadn't been a man in the picture for a while. The long hours she spent at work had driven the last one away. He had no problem concentrating on his own career, but he made light of her work dedication to a point that seriously annoyed her. Maybe she didn't spend enough time nurturing him. She worried about that for about a half hour after they broke up. Then felt only relief he'd gone. She could only imagine how much jabbing she'd have had to take from him about spending months away on client business.

The town of Hammond and her client, Barton Packing—a meat-packing plant—lay three hours away if she drove fast. She took one last look around her neighborhood and blew a kiss at her apartment. She'd miss the new home she'd had for only a few months and was still decorating. The deep, rich forest-green paint on the living room walls was so new she could still smell it when she came home at night. It looked perfect, though, especially with the purple couch she'd bought because she loved it at first sight. She'd have changed the walls before giving up the couch.

Plants weren't her thing, but she did have one pathetic Christmas cactus that looked more like Charlie Brown's Christmas tree. It needed little tending, but Jess had promised to check on it from time to time as long as Angela didn't blame her if it breathed its last on her watch.

Well, she wouldn't get there if she didn't start, as her dad said. She slid behind the wheel, turned the radio to a classical jazz station, and headed to the I-235 north on-ramp. She still couldn't believe her good fortune.

Before Barton Packing came her way, she'd juggled six accounts at Sherborn-Watts, doing most of the work herself. Account people who were assigned to work on one big account dismissed her clients as "Angela's cats and dogs," a tag that gained traction after she'd picked up the animal-shelter account. There was more prestige working on the big-name accounts, but she'd always felt she learned more, faster managing different accounts in different categories at the same time. At least that was how she'd positioned the reality that she hadn't been given a shot at a big client yet.

This account—one that came with a promotion to supervisor and a salary bump to acknowledge the increased responsibility—confirmed that at thirty-one years of age, she was ready to handle an important account. And do it on her own. More or less. At least outside the day-to-day supervision of the Sherborn-Watts offices and her boss, Dave Wilstat. The idea alternately thrilled and scared the bejesus out of her.

She'd been on the road less than ten minutes when her cell phone rang. She pushed the steering-wheel button to activate the call hands-free and mute the radio.

"Hi, Mom. I just got on the freeway. I was going to call you in a few minutes." She checked her mirrors. "No, this is fine. Hardly any traffic. How's Dad doing? Is he sleeping? Uh-huh. Good."

In her mind's eye, Angela could see her mother curled up in a chair on the sun porch, the cream-colored afghan wrapped around her shoulders, redbud trees blooming raspberry sherbet outside the windows. These Sunday-afternoon calls were a welcome opportunity to connect and decompress.

Two years ago, when he was only fifty-eight years old, Angela's father had been diagnosed with early-onset Alzheimer's disease. Within a few months of the diagnosis, he'd had to cut back his hours teaching at the community college. It was unlikely he'd be able to teach at all this fall. Angela's mother, a pediatric nurse at the county hospital, struggled to manage work, house, and care for her husband. Even though they had reasonably good insurance, it didn't compensate for the loss of his full salary. Over her mother's objections, Angela sent money from each paycheck to help with her parents' expenses. Sometimes she managed a spa gift certificate so her mother could really relax. The pay bump that came with this assignment meant she could help even more.

"You should save the money for the down payment on a house," her mother had protested. "You've been talking about that for five years."

"I want to do this, Mom," she'd responded. She hadn't said that a house would always be there but her father wouldn't.

Her mother had finally acquiesced, her voice thick with emotion. They hadn't talked of it since.

Now Angela said, "I should be in Hammond by six. Maybe a little later. I hope before the rain." She noted the storm clouds blackening as they talked. "Yes, I'm a little anxious about the job." She shared her concerns, admitting to her mother what she couldn't say to anyone at the office. Was she experienced enough? Could she handle it on her own? Would her limited knowledge of Barton Packing's business make them regret the decision?

Her mother didn't understand much about public relations, but she'd always had the utmost confidence in Angela. Bolstered by their conversation, Angela finally signed off.

By this time, Angela had left the urban landscape behind and faced miles of open fields in the rolling hills of central Iowa. The farm landscape felt foreign yet familiar. She'd grown up in a small town in southwest Iowa. Though it was the county seat, just over 1,500 people called Corning home. Even those who lived in town had roots in farming. Angela's grandparents had farmed right outside of town, and she had walked to their house after school each day, staying there until her parents came home from work.

Despite her upbringing, Angela didn't think about farming on a regular basis. Living in the city, it was easy to forget how much of the state continued to depend on agriculture. Now that she was in the country, though, she began her typical "windshield survey" of the crops, storing up tidbits to share with her dad. Corn had emerged enough in some fields to show rows, while other fields had yet to be planted. It tickled her to see calves born that spring cavorting in fields of grass.

Since the Alzheimer's settled in, farming was the one thing her dad seemed to remember clearly, even though he hadn't lived on the farm since he was eighteen. Or at least he remembered his connection to farming at the times he and Angela talked. Whether he retained anything the two of them discussed long enough to pass it along, she didn't know. Last Christmas, she had given him a scale-model John Deere tractor like the one he had driven on the farm. Every time she came home, he told her another story about the tractor. The memories were so rich she'd begun writing them down.

She spotted another livestock confinement building close to the interstate. The farther north she drove, the more she saw. The building could have housed either hogs or poultry; she was never sure which. If poultry, the facility may have been a supplier to Barton Packing.

A privately held company, Barton Packing was not required to disclose much, and it didn't. A product-recall crisis two months ago that forced the company to take back product from stores in three states had convinced the normally closemouthed company to consider outside public-relations counsel. It was fortunate that only a dozen people reported getting ill and none of those died. Sherborn-Watts was the obvious choice to help Barton, since the agency already handled its advertising.

Dave had asked her to do research to prepare him for the meeting with the Barton executives who came to Des Moines to discuss the problem. Only at the last minute had he called her to the conference room to meet with Barton's CEO, Nick Barton, and his chief operations officer, Gordon Ryker.

It had quickly become clear that Barton and Ryker were not on the same page when it came to using public relations to help solve their problems. In a very uncharacteristic move, Dave sat back and let her take the lead in a wide-ranging discussion of the roles a public-relations agency could provide: responding to reporters' questions, arranging interviews, preparing spokespeople, identifying ways to rebuild relationships with customers, and to build stronger relationships with people in the community. Overall, they would work to rebuild trust with Barton Packing customers, to ensure that employees were confident in their future with the company, and to reassure the community of Hammond that the company would continue to be a strong, stable part of the town.

Given that she hadn't prepared for that role, she thought she did pretty well. But when Nick Barton ended the meeting abruptly and Dave asked her to leave, she was confused, anxious, and a little miffed. She'd done her best, but Dave left her twisting in the wind. If they didn't get the account, he could hardly blame her.

Angela's surprise could not have been greater when Dave told her Nick Barton not only wanted her on the account but also wanted her to work at the Barton office in Hammond for a few months. Among the deciding factors: Angela's fluency in Spanish and her skill with the media.

Recalling the meeting, which had taken place only a week ago, she said, "Smart move, Angela." She smiled, thinking about the foresight she'd shown in leaving high-school French behind to minor in Spanish in college. She'd thought Spanish would have broader application. Here was validation.

The downside of this gig was leaving her life in Des Moines even for a few months. For approximately the hundredth time, she scrolled through her mental calendar. The timing on this trip actually worked pretty well, all things considered.

The Broadway series at the Des Moines Civic Center, for which she had season tickets, was coming to a close. The last musical, *Kinky Boots*, was next weekend. No way would she miss that. Cyndi Lauper's lyrics had topped her playlist as soon as the musical came out. She and Jess had been looking forward to it for months. The tune for "Sex Is in the Heel" popped into her head, so she turned off the radio and tapped the beat on the steering wheel as she sang along, dancing in her mind, glad that no one could hear her squeaky soprano.

Once she exited the interstate, it took another hour to reach Hammond. Home to roughly two thousand residents, Hammond was like any number of small Iowa towns. Blink and you'd miss it. Still, size was relative. Corning, where she grew up, had felt big until she went to college in Ames. And Corning was smaller than Hammond. Ames had felt big until she took a job in Des Moines. The bigger the city she lived in, the more insignificant the smaller towns became in her mind.

At last, she reached Hammond. The rain still held off, though the clouds had grown seriously black and from time to time she heard a rumble of thunder. She checked her watch. From the south edge of Hammond to the north—three to four minutes.

She pointed her car toward the Cozy Inn, the better of the two motels in town. Locally owned and run, the Cozy Inn would have fit right in with the retro 1950s and '60s motels she and her parents had stayed in on a family road trip across Route 66.

As she unlocked her room door, lightning flashed and thunder rumbled as the storm clouds rolled directly overhead. She meant to get all her things inside before the rain started, but when her eyes fell on the green-and-gold floral polyester spread covering the queen-size bed, she stood still and surveyed the room with a groan. The furnishings were far less than she had expected. She lifted her nose and sniffed. The room smelled smoke-free, though, a fact that made up for a lot in her book.

Oh, would she miss her apartment. Maybe she'd bring her own chenille bedspread on her next trip up. And her grandmother's old-fashioned multicolored afghan. She wrapped that afghan around herself every night when she cocooned on the purple couch to read or watch TV.

For all its downsides, the motel room had one plus. It constituted the one longer-term residence room in all of Hammond. So said the motel manager. A tiny kitchenette offered the luxuries of a cooktop, a microwave, and a small refrigerator. A small circular table offered an alternative to eating at the desk.

A crack of lightning brought her back to her senses. She wheeled her first suitcase in and ran back immediately to get the other. It took three trips to get everything she had in the car. No sooner had she closed the door behind her than a booming clap of thunder made her jump and the rain let loose. She pulled open the curtains to watch the storm and laughed. She'd arrived safe and dry. Crisis avoided.

Chapter 2

At 7:20 a.m. on Monday, Angela drove a mile north of Hammond to Barton Packing, pulled into the management parking lot as instructed, and navigated around rain-filled ruts in the gravel until she found an open space.

The plant complex was far larger than she'd imagined. Surrounded by farm fields planted with corn or soybeans, the plant was a windowless concrete-block structure sprawling across an area the size of six city blocks.

On the south side, trucks transporting live birds lined up at the docks. On the north side, refrigerated semis stood ready to be loaded with boxes of processed poultry for delivery to customers. Black tanker cars stretched along a railroad spur in front of the plant. Rust seeped through the white paint on a water tower looming over the plant, bleeding down, tarnishing the name "Barton Packing" written on the side of the tower. The overall effect conveyed neglect, not a favorable image for the media, she thought, though the gray skies may have dampened her mood.

The two-story office section of the building stood out, because it had windows. Flagpoles near large glass doors flew the American flag, a POW/MIA flag, and a flag with the Barton Packing logo, an incongruous white seagull in flight.

Accustomed to the time it took her to drive, park, and make it to the agency offices in Des Moines (she could walk there faster), she'd automatically allowed the same amount of time in Hammond. But now she was a ridiculously early.

She passed twenty minutes responding to email messages from the team members who'd taken over her other accounts and now reported to her, then put away her phone and grabbed her umbrella. Mud puddles and high heels weren't a good match, but she reached the sidewalk without damage and marched into the lobby, consciously working to convey more confidence than she felt.

A trim middle-aged woman with platinum hair moussed into spikes greeted her.

"I'm Liz Corwith, Mr. Barton's assistant. I've been expecting you."

The woman wore oversized glasses with plastic tortoise-shell rims. Combined with the platinum hair, they pulled off a funky librarian look.

"It's my pleasure, Ms. Corwith." Angela smiled. "I hope I'm not too early."

"I was more worried you were going to be on time." Smile lines crinkled at the corners of her eyes. "Around here, early is the same as on time. On time is late. We have a full schedule for you today. This way." She took off down a hallway at a brisk clip. Over her shoulder, she added, "And call me Liz."

As they walked, she pointed out the coffee machine and bathrooms. "The important stuff," she said. The hallway opened into a cluster of spartan cubicles in the center of a room ringed by equally mundane offices.

The cubicle walls were gray fabric. The industrial carpet would have been modern in the 1980s. The white walls needed a fresh coat of paint. It didn't appear that Barton Packing's profits found their way into fancy offices.

"You can put your things here." Liz gestured to an empty cubicle. "I'll give you a quick office tour and then Mr. Ryker will give you a tour of the plant. We should have told you that. You're not really dressed for it." She gestured to Angela's pumps.

"I have a pair of flats in the car?"

"You'll need them."

They headed back to the lobby so Angela could run out to retrieve her flats. She'd put considerable thought into choosing her outfit for the day. Given all the options she had to choose from, she felt a little foolish to have her first choice be wrong. Yet if everyone moved as fast as Liz, Angela knew she'd be wise to keep flat shoes close by.

After Angela stowed her shoes and briefcase in the cubicle, Liz continued the orientation, briskly walking her past more unremarkable offices and conference rooms; then they stopped at Liz's desk, where she retrieved a schedule outlining Angela's day. A quick glance revealed meetings with the company attorney, HR, and the sales manager.

"I'll point out their offices as we walk," Liz said. "This is Mr. Barton's office." She indicated the door nearest her desk. "You'll meet with him this afternoon. Any time you need to see him, check with me, and I'll get you on his calendar. Keep in mind he's frequently out of the office, particularly in the afternoon."

"Will do, Ms. Corwith," Angela said. "Liz."

* * *

After the rapid-fire office tour, Angela had twenty minutes before the plant tour, so she returned to her desk to settle in. With pushpins, she secured a small mirror with a neon-green plastic rim to the wall above the phone. A media mirror, she called it. A reminder to smile when she talked on the phone. She slid a bag of peanut M&M's in the drawer. Her ever-present and oh-so-useful "Stresstabs." The bowlful she kept in her office at Sherborn-Watts provided relief to many of her coworkers.

From the bottom of her purse, she fished out a river stone. A gift from her public-relations mentor, the smooth gray rock had "Integrity" engraved on one side, the letters painted black.

She cradled the stone in her palm, rubbing her finger across the letters as she remembered an exchange she'd had while still studying at Iowa State. Home for the weekend, she'd arranged to meet her mother at a community art show. In the course of the afternoon, a local man she knew only by sight came up to her.

"Your mother tells me you're studying public relations," he'd said.

"I am," she affirmed, euphoric to be so close to realizing her dream. "I graduate in May."

"My niece thought about going into public relations, but it would never work," he said. "She couldn't lie."

Angela was dumbstruck. To her core, Angela believed in telling the truth. To her core, she believed a public-relations professional was honest and aboveboard in dealing with the media, the client, the public. The man had moved on, leaving Angela to wish she'd delivered a snappy comeback to his insult to her intended profession.

She placed the stone on her desk next to the phone. Even though she wouldn't be in Hammond long, these few items gave her a sense of belonging.

Before heading out to meet Gordon Ryker, she checked herself out in the media mirror. Blessed with flawless, almost porcelain-pale skin, she wore little makeup. Eyeliner, blush, and lipstick were enough to pull her look together.

She also refreshed her memory of Gordon. She'd met him only the one time, but she had clear memories. A short, powerfully built man with buzz-cut graying hair, Gordon had a jawline sharp enough to chisel granite. And he wore a large Harley-Davidson belt buckle with his suit. Though he'd had been with Barton Packing for twenty-five years, he seldom showed up in any of her advance research of the company's online presence. No doubt due to his opposition to working with the media, antipathy he hadn't been shy about sharing during the meeting. While she preferred clients more open to the media, she'd always been able to bring them around. She felt confident she could persuade him, too.

She ran her fingers through her thick auburn hair and called it good. She was as prepared for the upcoming tour as she could get. Then she remembered the real reason she had the media mirror. She smiled.

Chapter 3

When Angela arrived at the conference room ten minutes early, Gordon was already there, waiting. Good thing she'd taken Liz's comment to heart. She noticed that he was wearing the same Harley-Davidson belt buckle today. As she crossed the room, she felt him scan her from head to foot. His gray eyes caused adrenaline to flood her body, and her breath caught in her chest. Yet she didn't hesitate.

"It's good to see you again, Gordon," she said, extending her hand.

When they met at the office, he'd shaken her hand using a grip hard enough to be painful. Yet his smile had been friendly enough. Unconsciously, Angela now flexed the fingers of her right hand.

"Morning, Angela," he said. "We'll get you a smock and hard hat, so your suit will be fine. But you'll have to be careful in those shoes."

She exhaled. He'd been assessing her in the context of a plant tour. Nothing more. "They have low heels."

"It's the soles," he said. "The floors are wet. We hose down after each shift, and one shift a day we close down the entire line to clean top to bottom. Without a tread, you can slip."

Angela glanced down at her flats. The smooth soles hadn't crossed her mind. Now she felt more foolish. A pencil skirt? High heels? In a packing plant? She must have been in outer space when she dressed that morning. She met his gaze. "Of course. I'll bring in better shoes tomorrow."

He led her to a closet at the end of a hallway; it was filled with smocks and hard hats. "You need these anytime you're in the plant." He handed her a white lab coat, which was several sizes too large. "If they're not dirty, hang them back up when you come out."

The hard hat bore the nicks of years of use and took some adjusting before it fit snugly on her head. "Anything else?" she asked, feeling self-conscious in the roomy lab coat and hard hat.

"We're good to go," he said, then opened the door next to the closet. Angela followed him onto a small metal catwalk overlooking the plant floor a story below.

Angela gripped the railing, steadying herself against a wave of vertigo. She knew the offices connected to the plant, but she found it vaguely disorienting to make such a complete transition from an unremarkable office environment on one side of the wall to assembly lines transporting disassembled chickens on the other.

To prepare for this assignment, she'd read about packing plants in general. As the nation's largest producer of hogs and eggs, Iowa had many such facilities. She'd also watched YouTube videos posted by animal-rights groups, videos purported to reveal the horrors of packing plants. Finally, she'd dug out everything she could find on Barton Packing. So she'd felt she knew what to expect, but the reality was different. The magnitude of such an operation didn't show on the videos.

Workers clad in knee-high rubber boots and waterproof clothing—aprons, coats, some with hoods—stood shoulder to shoulder on raised platforms next to conveyors carrying chicken carcasses suspended by their legs. With nets covering their hair, it was hard to tell with a cursory glance whether a worker was male or female.

Birds moved along the gleaming conveyor at a mind-numbing pace.

"Up to three thousand per hour," Gordon said, pride in his voice.

Angela was so focused on taking in the scene before her this was the first comment she registered.

"Remarkable," she said. "How can they keep up?"

"They each have one job. If they pay attention, it's no problem."

"Not like Lucy and Ethel in the chocolate factory?" she asked with a smile.

Gordon dismissed her with a snort. "Falling behind here has consequences."

She hadn't expected her comment to be taken seriously. But if he was always so serious, she better be, too. She focused on the line. Despite the speed, the workers stole glances their way. Their actions appeared so practiced and mechanical they barely needed to attend to what they did. Or perhaps the appearance of any outsider was too appealing not to note. In either case, she hoped the distraction wasn't dangerous.

"I presume they're trained for this?"

"They're trained whenever they take on a new job. We assign people to different jobs from day to day so they don't get repetitive-motion injuries." Gordon stepped away from the rail. "We'll start at the dock where the trucks are unloading live birds so you can track the whole system." He headed down the steps.

The platform and steps were made of a metal grid with treads to prevent slipping, yet Angela clung to the handrail, watching each step, as she took in Gordon's running commentary on poultry processing. The plant floor was wet, as he'd warned her it would be. As Angela hurried to keep up, the wisdom of rubber-soled shoes was immediately apparent, and she wished she still had a handrail to clutch.

Gordon paused before opening the large door that led to the kill floor. "We don't usually include this area on tours. But Nick felt you needed to see the whole operation."

Angela nodded. Conceptually, she understood there were two separate parts of the processing operation. There was the kill floor, where live birds were slaughtered, stripped of feathers, and gutted. Then there was everything else—carcasses were cooled, cleaned, cut into parts, packaged, put into cold storage. She knew that many people, while happy to include meat in their meals, were reluctant to think about how that meat made it to their dinner plates. Research told her that consumers often achieved a total disconnect between the packages of beef, pork, and poultry they picked up in grocery stores and the living animals the meat had once been.

Angela herself was not one of these people. In addition to having grandparents who farmed, she had other relatives and friends who lived on farms. Whenever she visited, she helped her cousins with their chores. Sometimes she fed the chickens; sometimes she collected eggs. Once she'd even been there when they butchered chickens, wielding a knife as she learned how to cut up a carcass. The process stank for sure, but it was over quickly. And her aunt made the most incredible fried chicken.

"Let's go," she said, confident she knew what waited.

She was wrong.

Trucks piled high with wire crates packed with live birds were backed up to the unloading dock. The rank smell of dust, manure, and blood blanketed the dock, and Angela felt the acrid air settle over her. Instinctively, she covered her mouth and nose with her hand. "Oh, my god," she gasped.

"You all right?" Gordon asked.

Hand still tight across her mouth, she looked up and saw he appeared to be trying not to laugh. She dropped her hand to her side.

"I'm fine," she said, and forced herself to take in the scene.

All those working in the area wore dust masks and hair covers; Angela wished she had such protection, too. She glanced at Gordon out of the corner of her eye. He appeared unaffected by the smell. Was that why he hadn't given her a mask? As men pulled the crates off the trucks, others workers wearing heavy gloves and long canvas aprons reached in, grabbed birds, and hooked their feet to a conveyor line. Once the birds were head down, they ceased to struggle and hung motionless as they moved into a stainless-steel chute spattered with blood. This was nothing at all like butchering chickens with her cousins.

Nothing. At. All.

She pointed to the birds being channeled into the chute, where a razor-sharp blade waited. "Do they feel that?"

"Not a thing. The birds get an electric shock before the blade slices their necks. Packing plants are improving in humane livestock treatment all the time."

Angela's nostrils flared, her jaws clamped tight, and she fought the overpowering urge to step away. Out of the corner of her eye, she saw Gordon look at her again. Did he expect her to faint, or throw up, or run?

Steeling herself to keep watching, Angela absorbed his words without allowing emotion to intrude. If he hoped for a reaction because he thought a woman couldn't handle it, she wouldn't give him the satisfaction.

Breathing through her mouth, she fired questions at him. How long were the birds in the trucks? Did these workers work in this area all the time? What about breaks? How much training? Were there injuries? Gordon responded with the confidence of more than two decades in the business. Even if she found it difficult to read him, she had to admit he really was a wealth of knowledge. She respected that.

As they talked, she watched the workers on the dock and in the kill room. All men. All Latino and black. The men on the kill floor performed their tasks with precision, their clothing smeared with manure and blood. She saw them look at Gordon and her, all the while maintaining the rhythm of grabbing birds out of crates and hanging them on the conveyor line without ever missing a beat or a hook. They didn't talk; she imagined the intense, unrelenting work left no time for chatting.

From time to time, Angela caught the eyes of one of the men and offered a smile. The most she got in return was a blank stare, a reaction that left her feeling uneasy. Whatever they felt or thought, they weren't sharing it with her.

The killing blade left chicken heads dangling by a shred of skin, blood streaming from the nearly decapitated birds, before the carcasses were dipped into a tank of scalding water to loosen their feathers. Out of the tank, the carcasses moved through a device with whirling rubber fingers that stripped off the feathers. For the first time, the birds looked less like something once living and more like what she picked up at the meat counter.

As Gordon responded to Angela's questions, she felt him open up, offering more information than she asked for. She relaxed, too. All her preparation before coming to Hammond, the hours spent reading about the poultry industry and Barton Packing, had paid off. Although they stayed in the kill room less than fifteen minutes, it felt far longer. By the time they walked out, Angela believed she'd gained some measure of respect in Gordon's mind. She was beginning to get a sense of his style. Liking Gordon wasn't part of her job, and he didn't need to like her, either. If they respected each other, that was enough.

The farther away from the kill floor, the farther she moved from blood, filth, and death, the easier the tour became.

Gordon mentioned again that all work areas were hosed down regularly. There was still an odor, but it was more antiseptic, more sterile. Angela felt tension in her neck as she realized she was still on guard, still holding her breath. She exhaled, rolling her shoulders as discreetly as she could.

She shivered and was glad to have the smock cover the goose bumps rising on her arms. From where they stood, in addition to a long stretch of conveyor, Angela could see stations where workers took carcasses and cut them into parts on machines that looked something like the table saw her father used for woodworking. A dangerous piece of equipment her father unfailingly warned her to give a wide berth.

"That's one of the new machines we put in a year ago. State of the art. Really speeds things up," Gordon said.

With surgical precision, a worker grabbed a whole chicken and fed it into the blade, cutting the carcass down the backbone, then repositioning to separate the hindquarters, repositioning again to cut leg from thigh, tossing parts into bins other workers wheeled away as soon as they were filled.

As they watched, the man running the saw tossed a chicken quarter toward a nearby bin. And missed. Another worker reached down, grabbed the carcass off the floor, and tossed it on top of the full bin.

"Five-second rule?" Angela joked.

"There are rules for handling dropped product. And that's not it." Gordon's voice grew hard. "Wait here." He strode over to the line supervisor.

Angela cringed. Of course they cared about sanitation. They'd just experienced a recall. How silly could she be? Over the plant noise, Angela could hear nothing Gordon and the other men were saying, but by the gestures and expressions on the men's faces, she could tell it wasn't pleasant. Eyes all along the assembly line followed the exchange.

In a few minutes he returned. "Let's move on."

"It should have been discarded, right?" Angela asked.

"If it's cleaned, it's OK."

His nonchalant tone took Angela by surprise. "Really? Not thrown away?"

Hearing the disbelief in her voice, his tone changed to one of concern. "We send out nothing but clean product," he assured her. "We don't have to learn that lesson twice."

She wanted to ask more about the dropped product, but she followed his lead. "Don't they get cold?" She indicated the people standing by the conveyor.

"They're working. They don't have time to be cold."

Angela rubbed her arms. They might not be cold, but she was. Like those working on the kill floor, these people were predominately Latino and black. A handful were Asian; fewer were white. In this part of the plant, there were many women, too.

In the meeting at Sherborn-Watts, Nick Barton had called her Spanish fluency a plus, but he hadn't mentioned the need for any other languages. "I expected the Latino employees, but not so many blacks and Asians."

"Most are refugees from Africa and Burma. We hire more refugees all the time. They arrive in other states but move to Iowa when they hear about the jobs here."

"Do they speak English?" she asked.

"You don't have to know much English to gut a bird."

Was he joking? She read nothing in his face. "Probably not," she said, trying to match his tone. "But I imagine there's lots of information that has to get shared."

"Depends how long they've been in the US. Most know enough to get along."

For several minutes, they stood and watched as each person performed a single task: removing the lungs, sorting the giblets, rendering whole birds into parts. Some tasks—like gutting the bird—were automated. Yet once the guts were extracted, someone still had to sort out the gizzard and liver. Angela was glad that wasn't her job.

The speed with which the people on the line performed their tasks was impressive. The efficiency of the system demanded admiration, and Gordon spoke with obvious satisfaction as he explained that the faster "the product" moved through processing, the fresher the outcome. Immersed in a topic he clearly knew well, he no longer spoke with his earlier guarded defensiveness. Sometimes he even smiled. When they stopped at a point where they could see several operations simultaneously, he brought up her reason for being at Barton Packing.

"Nick and I talked about news releases you might do. We employ more people than any other company. And the company's been growing. So it matters that we're in business. He figured you'd have ideas already, too."

What Gordon said reinforced what he'd said earlier. She'd hoped for more. "Dave and I did some brainstorming," she said. "Topics like how Barton Packing supports the community in general, programs you have to support specific local organizations, that sort of thing. I'd like to hear about those. Then, from a trade media standpoint, we can look at innovations in processing." She waited for him to offer examples. When he didn't, she probed. "Does Barton Packing do anything differently from other plants?" she asked.

"We upgrade the line when it makes economic sense. Those machines we saw earlier. That's an example. It's all about the bottom line. There's not a big margin in this business. Pennies per pound. The faster we work, the better."

"I see how speed benefits the company. What I'm looking for is how that speed benefits the customer." Line speed, she'd read, was a plus for the company but a negative for the workers, contributing to repetitive-motion injuries and accidents caused by fatigue.

"I'll think on that," he said.

"I will, too," she said. "You've talked about a number of things during the tour that could have promise. I'll give those some thought and get back to you."

She wondered if it was also possible that speed might have had something to do with the contamination that led to the recall.

"I've read everything I could find on the recall," she said. "I know it was salmonella, but the articles didn't specify how it happened." She looked at Gordon expectantly.

"We clean the line at least once a day. But the cleaning crew didn't do it well enough. There was product buildup, and bacteria grew."

"I see." The next question she intended to ask was the question the media always had, What had they done to ensure the problem didn't happen again? But Gordon had flagged a man who was holding a clipboard and talking with two other men.

"Hey, Al. Come here. I want you to meet someone." The man acknowledged him with a wave.

"I'd like to talk more about that when you have a moment," Angela said.

Gordon shrugged. "It's history. We've taken care of it. Now, I want you to meet Al Duarte. He's a shift supervisor. From El Salvador."

Duarte wore a chambray shirt and dark-blue pants with knee-high rubber boots and a blue hair covering but none of the other waterproof clothing worn by those on the line. Angela could hear Duarte and the men with him speaking Spanish. Now might be the time to put her own language skills to work, though in the presence of native Spanish speakers, she felt self-conscious. The truth was, she seldom spoke Spanish with native speakers.

As Duarte walked toward them, she took in his high cheekbones and aquiline nose, which reminded her of classical sculptures. His skin was darker than most Latino men she'd met, and thick black eyebrows slashed above deep-set dark-chocolate eyes, creating a look of stormy intensity.

Gordon introduced her. "This is Angela Darrah, our new PR person."

Duarte responded in English wrapped in a rich Spanish accent.

"Good morning, Ms. Darrah." He extended a hand, warm in spite of the cold room. "I am pleased to meet you."

She responded, *"Buenos dias, Al. Encantada de conocerte."*

A small smile carved a dimple in Duarte's cheek, and Angela wondered if it surprised him that she spoke Spanish.

"The workers know their place in Hammond. Al can tell you about that as well as anyone," Gordon added.

Her eyes darted from Gordon to Duarte. "Their place." Did he realize how that sounded? She caught no reaction in Duarte's eyes. Maybe he did not understand.

"She's going to make us look good," Gordon added. "She might need to talk to you from time to time."

"Yes, sir," Duarte said.

"Gracias. Voy a estar en contacto pronto," she said. For Gordon's benefit, she translated. "I told him I'll be in touch soon."

"You don't have to pull out the Spanish for Al. He's been in the US for years," Gordon said. "Some of the equipment improvements we made two years ago were on his recommendation."

"Oh..." She looked from Duarte to Gordon. "I thought..." Gordon's mouth curved in a smile. Or was it a smirk? She forced herself to meet Duarte's eyes. "I misunderstood."

Now the dimple was firmly etched by his smile. *"De nada,"* he said. *"Cualquier cosa para usted, señorita Darrah."*

He looked at Gordon. "I told her, anything for her."

Was he making fun of her? Angela felt even more awkward.

"Let me know when you want to get together, Ms. Darrah."

"I will," she responded.

"Is that all, Mr. Ryker?" Duarte asked.

"That's it," Gordon said, and Duarte returned to the line.

She chewed the inside of her lower lip. Why had she assumed Duarte couldn't speak English? Though her Spanish fluency was one reason Barton Packing had hired her, Gordon hadn't said Duarte couldn't. She'd jumped to that conclusion on her own. Foolish, for sure.

"I'll get in touch with him soon," she said, and changed the subject. "Where does the product go from here?"

"Storage and shipping are the last part of the tour." Gordon took her to an area where the product was packed and labeled for individual customers. The boxes then moved on to be flash frozen and stored or to be shipped immediately as fresh product. He pushed open a heavy door and led her into a refrigerated room.

Shocked by the sudden temperature drop, Angela squeaked, "Holy moly!" Her breath crystalized ahead of her, and she rubbed her hands together, then tucked them under her arms for warmth. The thin layer of her lab coat was little protection from the sharp cold.

Gordon strode past boxes of product stored in long rows on pallets stacked so high she couldn't see over their tops. Men clad in heavy coats, hats with earflaps, and gloves drove forklifts, negotiating the alleys as they stacked boxes of product or moved them to refrigerated trucks at the loading dock.

"It's a maze in here, isn't it?" she said.

"Could be."

He explained the FIFO—first in, first out—system that ensured product spent the least amount of time in storage before being shipped. Customers choosing a package of legs, thighs, or breasts at the grocery store could be eating chicken only a few days from the time it was slaughtered.

Angela pulled the lab coat closer around her. "Gives new meaning to 'fresh frozen,'" she said.

"Seen enough?"

"For now, yes. I appreciate the tour."

Back in the office hallway, she handed over the hard hat and thin lab coat. "Gordon? When we met at Sherborn-Watts, you mentioned the influx of immigrants moving to Hammond. I didn't give it much thought then, but I couldn't help but notice now that the workforce in the plant is almost anything but white."

"Ninety percent."

"That's more than I expected. Aren't there local people who want these jobs?"

"We hire as many locals as we can. A good half of our employees are from around here. But we need more workers than the local market can provide. And we get them."

The logistics of finding, recruiting, and training so many people was more than Angela could get her head around just then. "I have an appointment with HR next. I'll get info from them," she said. "Then I know I'll need to talk to you more."

"Talk to Al. He knows how the plant runs. Then clear whatever he tells you with me. He doesn't understand the full business reality."

"I will. We touched on the recall, but I'll need more background to answer media questions and move stories in a positive direction for the company. Is there a good time to talk about it?"

"I have a meeting with Nick. I'll bring it up with him." Without waiting for a response, he turned and was gone.

She looked at her watch. She'd hoped to have a few minutes in her cubicle to capture first impressions about the plant, but that would have to wait till after her next meeting.

It was close to noon before she made it back to her cubicle. The plant tour remained vivid in her mind, and she easily slipped into noting impressions and listing questions for follow-up.

Gordon's words "full business reality" came to mind. Everything he'd said related to production efficiency, pounds processed, profit margin. Unless she asked a specific question, he didn't talk about the people who kept the plant running.

What about the workers she'd made eye contact with? They hadn't responded to her smiles. Had they thought she was patronizing them? She knew she hadn't been. But what had she been trying to do? Identify with them in some way? Was that possible? She doubted she had much in common with them.

Al Duarte could be the key to helping her get to know people in the plant. Granted, assuming that someone didn't speak English or would prefer she spoke Spanish wasn't the best way to start a new relationship. She'd have to fix that.

People in the plant could help her understand from their perspective how the salmonella outbreak happened. Even more important, she thought, in light of the product she'd seen picked up off the floor. She knew that salmonella and *E. coli* were spread through dirty conditions and that deaths and hospitalization caused by salmonella in food hit the headlines every year. Salmonella lived in the gut of chickens, so if the chicken wasn't cleaned or cooked properly, the bacteria could continue to exist. She imagined that chicken on her dinner plate and squirmed. Knowing too much about how chicken got to the supermarket meat case had its disadvantages.

Twice she picked up the phone to call Dave, but then put it down. She stood and looked across the neighboring cubicles. No one occupied the adjacent desks at the moment, but she still felt exposed. She texted a request to talk. He responded in under a minute, and she headed to the parking lot.

The sun had burned off the early-morning rain clouds, leaving the interior of her car comfortably warm. She cracked the windows and hit Dave's number, then balanced a notebook against the steering wheel and put her phone on speaker when he answered.

"How's it going?" he asked.

At the sound of Dave's voice, Angela suddenly felt the tension she'd carried all morning. New client. New environment. High expectations. "It's been a full day. And it's only noon."

"What's it like there?"

An odd earthy smell permeated the car, and she wrinkled her nose. Looking toward the plant, she saw the flags by the entrance billow in her direction. Did the smell carry into town?

"First thing, I took an orientation tour with Mr. Barton's secretary, Liz. I like her. Then Gordon Ryker took me through the plant. That was the biggest chunk of time and the most fascinating. Gordon reiterated what they said in our offices. That they want some news releases. I probed on topics. He didn't give me much, but what you and I talked about is a place to start."

As she outlined her discussion with Gordon, she sniffed again. The source of the smell was closer. Definitely in the car. She scanned the floor of the front seats. Had she forgotten to throw out a fast-food bag?

"I'm a little worried," she said. "Maybe they don't intend to do anything substantial." The idea that her first big client opportunity could come down to a few news releases filled her with dismay. She frowned. As the space warmed up, the odor became more pronounced. And unpleasant. She lifted her feet and looked at the soles of her shoes. Maybe she'd stepped in something. They appeared clean enough, so it couldn't be that. She squirmed around and looked in the back seat. Nothing she could see. She faced forward again and focused on her boss's voice.

"That doesn't make much sense," Dave was saying. "They've invested in having you there. Your instincts are good. With what you've told me, you can look for ways to broaden what they're doing. You were on the right track asking about community impact. You can identify people around town who could be allies."

In block letters, Angela wrote *allies* in her notebook.

"He loosen up at all during the tour?"

"For a while, I thought he had. After we left the kill floor."

"He took you on the kill floor?"

"Uh-huh. He watched me all the while. Pretty sure he expected me to puke. Or run." That smell. She grabbed a lock of hair and brought it under her nose. Oh, yuck. It wasn't the air or her shoes; it was her. *She* smelled like the kill floor. She glanced at the clock, wondering if she could get to the motel and shower before her meeting with Nick.

"I knew you could take it. Actually, taking someone on the kill floor is a sign of trust."

"You think?"

"That's the worst they've got. It's why they don't want any activist groups in there. They're not making cupcakes."

"He's a puzzle, though. Sometimes he makes a joke. Or what I think is a joke. But when I respond in kind, he's all business. He's guarded in what he shares. I can't read him."

"You'll figure it out. Have you talked with Nick one on one yet?"

"This afternoon."

Taking the lead with someone like Nick, doing it without a team from the agency, gave her pause. The idea of managing a big account was exciting, but the reality was more terrifying. Dave must have sensed her concern.

"Nobody expects you to have all the answers, Angela," he said. "Keep asking questions. Keep making contacts. If you want this job to be more than window dressing, it's up to you to make it happen. Yes?"

Angela nodded as though he could see her.

The half hour Angela spent on the phone with Dave gave her a shot of confidence. She looked at her watch again, sniffed at her shirt. Oh, man, she wished she had time for a shower. But the extremely efficient Liz Corwith had set up introductory meetings all day. Not even time to swing by the convenience store for a prepackaged sandwich. She threw everything into her briefcase and headed back to the office.

Chapter 4

When Angela arrived at 2:45 p.m. for her 3:00 p.m. appointment, Liz looked up from her keyboard and said, "Right on time."

"We aim to please." Angela smiled.

"Go on in." She made a hitchhiking gesture with her thumb at the double doors behind her. "He's expecting you."

After tapping firmly on the door, Angela stepped into one of the largest offices she'd ever seen. A mahogany desk looking as though it belonged in a furniture showroom dominated one end of the room. Books lined shelves behind the desk, and while she couldn't see titles, she recognized the clean white covers and minimal graphics of two by Malcolm Gladwell.

"Come in, Angela." Nick's voice drew her to a conference table at the other end of the office. He laid his glasses on the table as he stood to greet her. "Have a seat." He gestured to the comfortable chairs around the table. "Would you like something to drink? Water? Pop? If you want coffee, I can have Liz bring some in."

"Water, please," Angela said.

As he took two bottles from a small refrigerator, she slid into a chair, hoping she looked more comfortable than she felt. Nick Barton had a commanding presence not diminished in the least by preparing glasses and ice. He was every bit as handsome as she remembered. With a full head of wavy silver hair, he looked anything but his sixty-plus years. Angela remembered thinking at their first meeting that he would have looked even younger except that his smile didn't reach all the way to his eyes.

Angela scanned the room. Paintings of seascapes and seagulls lined one wall. Near those paintings were pictures of Nick and a willowy woman with short blond hair on a sailboat. In one he rested a hand on her hip as he steered the boat and she looked at him, her chin tilted up, caught in the middle of a laugh. In all the photos they seemed easy with each other, as though they genuinely enjoyed their time together. On another wall were pictures of Barton posed with rows of men in front of poultry-industry banners.

Turning back to Nick, she realized he'd been watching her take in the office.

"I'm curious about the seagulls," she said quickly.

"What about them?"

"You have a seagull in your logo. And in all these paintings. It seems an unusual choice for an Iowa company."

"That's my wife's doing." He nodded toward the woman on the sailboat. "Maggie's always been a fan of the ocean, and seagulls are her favorite bird. When we were starting up, she thought it would be a way to make the company stand out. She was right. Everyone asks."

He turned his attention from Angela to the paintings lining the walls. "Whenever we vacationed by the ocean, she collected paintings by local artists. Anything with seagulls in it. She even painted some herself. The one behind the desk is hers."

Nick's voice trailed off as his eyes lingered on the painting of a seagull perched on a piling at the end of a wharf, a smooth sea extending to the horizon. The seagull appeared ready to take to the air, another seagull winging toward it.

"It's lovely," Angela said. Though Nick referred to his wife in the present tense, Angela knew Mrs. Barton had died almost two years ago. "She was talented."

"I always thought so." He made a point of looking at his watch, then picked up gunmetal-gray wire-rimmed bifocals and settled them back on his nose. "I'm interested in your initial reactions," he said. "First impressions from your first day."

He wanted to change the subject. Should she express her sympathy anyway? She took the easy way out. She began telling him about her meetings and the plant tour.

Nick interrupted. "Did Gordon take you in the kill area?"

"Yes."

"I didn't think it necessary, but he insisted."

Angela tilted her head, recalling her conversation with Gordon. She was certain he'd said touring that part of the plant was Nick's idea. Why would he shift the responsibility to his boss? "I'm glad I got the whole picture," she said. "Though I wondered how people could do such a job all day, every day."

"It's not for anyone without stamina. The job requires strength, but the least skill. Some start there, then move into the plant; others wash out. A few are best suited to that job and stay."

She thought about that for a moment. What did it take to be "suited" to a job like that? Beyond the physical demands of lifting crates and birds all day, how did one stomach sending thousands of living creatures to their deaths?

"This was my first tour of a packing plant. It's impressive how fast it goes. How many birds move through every hour. Really, it's amazing."

"That surprises most people. Over the years, we've had a few customers tour the plant, and it's a selling feature for them. Really emphasizes the 'fresh' message."

"Have plant tours been part of your postrecall communication?"

Nick leaned back, resting his elbows on the chair arms and steepling his hands. "The logistics of getting people here would be problematic."

She brought up the idea of videos as a vehicle to meet that challenge and to communicate the company's commitment to cleanliness and freshness to customers and the media. The idea intrigued him, so they spent some time on the topic. They could also use portions of the video in employee recruitment and training, two other needs she'd picked up on during the plant tour. Since it couldn't hire enough people locally, Barton Packing recruited from other states to meet the need for six hundred workers. Video made great sense.

"Gordon told me about immigrants and refugees," she said, moving to another topic. "I hadn't realized refugees were such a significant source of labor."

"There's a good communication network in the various refugee communities. Once they know we have jobs, they come to us. Their paperwork is in order, so that makes things easier."

Angela looked up from making a note. "Paperwork?"

"Green cards. Work visas. We ensure people have the legal right to work in the US. Ever since ICE raided the Postville plant, all employers have been more careful. Refugees have been vetted by the government, so we know they have the right paperwork."

Angela nodded, remembering news stories about the Immigration and Customs Enforcement raid that ended in arrests and the owners on trial. "I understand the majority of Barton employees aren't refugees, though."

"Correct. We recruit heavily from the southwestern states. With all our workers, we use the government E-Verify program to ensure they can work legally."

Another new term. She added *E-Verify* to her "get smart" reading list.

"Gordon also told me a little about the recall," she said. "He said the cleaning crew wasn't as thorough as they needed to be. I'd like your thoughts on the recall."

Nick massaged a tic in his cheek with his fingertips as he thought. She'd noticed that tic during the meeting in the agency office and wondered if he'd always had it.

"We've been talking about the diversity in the plant. In part, a communication breakdown led to the salmonella problem," he said.

Angela waited. If communication was the problem, it was critical she help fix it. But better communication wasn't a solution if the underlying problems weren't fixed. Finally, she prompted, "How so?"

"This isn't something we share outside these offices, Angela."

"I understand." She conveyed her commitment to confidentiality through her gaze, then added, "I won't share anything without your approval."

Nick studied her as though trying to decide if he could trust her. Finally, he continued. "As Gordon told you, the crew let waste build up and contaminate product on a line. Plus, the cleaning crew didn't use the right chemicals for sanitizing."

She recalled Gordon's comment that employees didn't need much English to gut a chicken. Reading container labels probably required a lot of English. Or were the labels also in Spanish? But were the people who did the cleaning Latino, or African, or Asian?

"I expect there are lots of ways cleaning could go wrong. Wrong chemicals, inadequate cleaning procedures, training. Probably some I don't even know about," she said.

"It could have been worse. Some of the chemicals are toxic."

A frown creased her forehead. "Toxic chemicals are stored with food-safe chemicals?"

"Not anymore."

That was a relief. "What kind of training do employees have for cleaning? Are there language requirements for the crews? I can imagine that with your diverse workforce, there would be a range of language abilities."

"Gordon can give you the details."

She chuckled to herself as she made a note to ask Gordon about training again. Nick had commented during their first meeting at the agency that the language of a packing plant could be rough. She'd understood him to mean the words could be coarse.

She expected he hadn't meant interpersonal communication. Now that Angela knew Gordon wasn't the most forthcoming person, she realized she would have to work on that language, too.

"What steps did you take to make sure it doesn't happen again? That's what the media always want to know."

"We took responsibility. Recalled the bad product and destroyed it. Compensated the grocery stores. Gave them reduced prices to restock. We've always treated our customers fairly."

"What about changes in the plant?"

"We segregated cleaning chemicals into a separate area, as I mentioned. We let the original crew go, and we hired a new crew. Started fresh. That was Gordon's recommendation. The recall cost us hundreds of thousands of dollars, and people have to be held responsible." He folded his arms across his chest. The muscles in his jaw tightened. The tic palpitated. "With the steps we've taken, we're confident it won't happen again." His tone was brusque. "And I want you to help with the image of the company going forward."

Angela scanned her notes and moved the conversation in a new direction. "Perfect. Let's start at the beginning. Tell me who you see as your most important audiences."

Without hesitating, Nick responded. "It's always been the customer. Get them. Provide good product. Keep them happy."

Over the next several minutes, Nick outlined the steps he'd taken since the recall to reassure customers. Prior to the recall, he'd ceded most customer relationships to Gordon while he saw even their best customers only once or twice a year. They went on to discuss regulatory officials, industry associations, suppliers, employees, the community. Any of which could be concerned about the company as a result of the recall.

"I'm sure you're not the first business to muddle through and then think how to do it better next time. Lucky for agencies like ours," she said.

"So true." He chuckled. "I'm surprised you didn't mention the media."

"I should have," she admitted. "Who are you wanting to reach?"

"Truth be told, I don't want to reach anyone. I only want the media to stop calling us."

Angela laughed at his candor. "An interesting goal," she said. "Not so easy to achieve. If you don't respond to the media, they see you as a challenge, with the possibility that you're hiding a big story. If you do respond, they may become more interested because you're a good source when they need a story."

"So what's the answer?"

"You're better off being open with the media than not. If you build relationships with reporters, being open and honest, when there's a crisis—"

"They'll let you off the hook," he interjected. The twinkle in his eye told her he was joking.

"No." She grinned and shook her head. "They won't let you off the hook. But they're more likely to give you the benefit of the doubt. So which reporters, exactly, do you want to go away?"

Nick's answer came down to local media. Since the company handled the recall professionally and worked well with customers, trade-media interest trailed off quickly.

"I expect the recall gave local media an entrée into the company they didn't have before." Angela tapped the end of her pen on her notebook as she thought. "Did you communicate regularly with your employees during the crisis? Or reach out to town leaders?"

"Not really. A mistake?"

"No irreparable harm done, but when reporters can't get to the source, they talk to people around the source. People closest to you can be your biggest allies and supporters. Or the opposite."

"So where do we go from here?"

Angela tapped her pen on her notebook as she considered an approach much broader than the original assignment. He'd hired her to get them back on track with customers and to manage the media by making them go away. The better approach was more comprehensive. "I know you brought me in for some specific tasks, including news releases. But I think there's more we can do. Are you open to that?"

"I can't see why not," Nick agreed.

Her eyes fell on the poultry-industry photos on the wall. "Have you looked at how other plants have handled issues like these?"

Nick shook his head.

"I'll get our research department to get some background on that. I expect you're already doing many right things. We need to talk about those things proactively. That's why you brought me here, right?"

He pulled out a handkerchief and cleaned his glasses. When the glasses were back in place, he said, "Let me give that some thought. In the meantime, what can we do now?"

She recapped the points Gordon suggested: company growth, number of jobs, economic impact. Then she explained why reporters might view releases on those topics as puff pieces or even regard them negatively, as attempts by the company to avoid the real news. After brief discussion, Nick approved Gordon's approach. While these releases weren't the best, she acknowledged they moved the process forward. Any news releases were progress for a company that had seemed devoted to never doing any.

"All right, we have a plan." Angela smiled at Nick as she closed her notebook. "I'll have draft releases for you and Gordon to look at by early next week."

* * *

Back in her motel room that evening, Angela shucked off every piece of clothing she'd worn that day and secured it all in a plastic bag, hoping a dry cleaner could get the smell out. Already she missed the stacked washer and dryer in her apartment. Then she let a hot shower and the motel's spring-fresh-scented soap wash the kill floor off her body and out of her hair as events of the day scrolled through her mind.

For a first day, things had gone pretty well. The plant tour was eye opening. The meeting with Nick was successful—stimulating, even. The discussion of audiences had helped clarify where she should spend her time.

She had learned a lot, but each thing she learned uncovered new things to explore, things like employee training and rules governing product dropped on the floor. That was what she liked about agency work. Always something new.

Sitting on the edge of the bed, towel drying her hair, she acknowledged Gordon would be a puzzle to decipher. And that the one glitch in the day had been with the Latino floor supervisor. Her attempt to connect with him had fallen flat. A bridge to be mended.

She thought about the men on the kill floor and wondered about the impact on a person so intimately involved with death each day. Had those men expected her to be repulsed, as Gordon apparently had? Did the smell of blood and manure stay with them even after they washed, a stain under their skin?

Her stomach growled, reminding her she'd skipped lunch in favor of talking to Dave. Her food options were underwhelming: find a restaurant and eat alone, get a prewrapped sandwich or a slice of pizza from the convenience store, eat the yogurt and fruit she'd stocked in her fridge from the Economart grocery south of town. Besides being whipped, she wanted to begin drafting releases. Yogurt it was.

Chapter 5

"Angela. I have these for you." The receptionist waved pink "while you were out" call slips above her head as Angela passed through the lobby at the end of the next day.

Casting an envious look at the exit, Angela veered back to the desk. Her brain already felt as though it might explode from information overload. After another day of back-to-back meetings, she had so many notes to make sense of and so many company reports to read, she knew her workday would extend into a work evening.

Angela scanned the slips. All the calls were from Trevor McKay, a reporter with the *Elbridge Times*. Call dates spanned more than a week. "Did he say it was urgent?" she asked.

"He calls pretty often."

"Do you know if Gordon called him back?"

The lights on the phone lit up, and the receptionist shook her head, peered at Angela through Coke-bottle-thick glasses, and mouthed "round file" as she pointed to the wastebasket, then picked up the receiver.

She didn't know why she asked. She'd learned that even during the recall they had sent out only one news release, refused all interviews, and ordered the receptionist to tell any reporter who called to say, "No one's available." She had nearly choked when she heard that.

Even if this reporter's calls weren't urgent, Angela could see no good coming from ignoring him. A call back moved to the top of her to-do list for the morning. But first, she would do some digging on him. Back in her cubicle, she flipped open her laptop. Facebook gave her nothing, but she found him on LinkedIn.

McKay's profile listed a journalism degree from the University of Iowa, though not the year. His picture presented a slight young man with a crooked yet engaging smile and shaggy red hair. He might have done himself a favor if he'd gotten a haircut before having the picture taken.

Since the *Elbridge Times* didn't have an online edition, she headed for the Hammond library, a newer building and one of the only places in town where she could be assured of reliable Wi-Fi, a tip Liz had shared during the orientation tour. Since then, Angela had experienced her own challenges with Hammond's unreliable tech: infuriatingly slow Wi-Fi at the motel and dropped cell-phone calls even in town. "Gotta love small-town living," she muttered as she walked up the library steps.

The two women staffing the library were thrilled to have someone new walk through their doors. The women—their name tags identified them as Helen and Martha—oriented Angela not only to the library but also to the highs and lows of the town.

Helen, a woman with a thin face and a pinched mouth, lamented the tattered state of Main Street. "It's been taken over by those foreigners," she said, locking eyes with Angela, tilting her chin up, and speaking in an I-don't-care-who-hears-me way. "Most people do their shopping in Mason City these days," she added.

Then Martha, an older woman with a pleasant smile, outlined the efforts they were making at the library to help new families by providing information on city services and supporting the school, which was now half populated by children who spoke English as a second language.

"We close at 8:00 p.m.," Helen reminded Angela as she pointed her to the shelves lined with newspapers representing several counties. A glance at the clock behind the desk showed she still had an hour.

Angela carried the entire stack of *Elbridge Times* issues to a table and was soon lost in thought as she flipped from front to back of each copy. Trevor McKay had bylines in all of them, mostly human-interest stories. Each story included unexpected and fascinating tidbits about the interviewee, and Angela found herself enjoying both the writing style and the people she met through the articles.

"Looking for something in particular?" A male voice interrupted her thoughts.

"I'm fine," she said without glancing up. She neither needed nor wanted to spend more time with the library staff.

"I work for the *Times*," the voice said.

At that, Angela raised her head and found Trevor McKay looking at her, a copy of the *Des Moines Register* in one hand, a notebook and pencil in the other. The sprinkle of freckles across his nose hadn't been visible in the LinkedIn picture, but they fit with blue eyes straight out of a baby-food commercial. His reddish hair still looked as though it needed a cut.

"Trevor McKay, correct? I was just reading some of your writing." She tapped a finger on the article in front of her, then extended a hand. "I'm Angela Darrah with Sherborn-Watts."

"Pleased to meet you, Ms. Darrah." He shook her hand. "I hear you're the new PR person at Barton." He tilted his head in the direction of the women at the front desk.

Angela glanced at the women, who made no effort to disguise their curiosity. Apparently they were the information desk for everything.

"Do you have a few minutes?" McKay slid out a chair without waiting for a response. "I've been hoping to talk with someone at Barton Packing."

"I intended to call you in the morning."

"Did you really?" His tone said he didn't believe her.

"Yes, I did. Why wouldn't I?"

"I've been calling the Barton office; it's what they always tell me."

"Ah. I see." She regrouped. "Well, this is my job. I answer media calls. But I'm the new kid on the block. I thought I'd look at some of your work before we talked. I enjoyed reading the profiles. You write well."

"I think most people have interesting stories to tell, if you give them a chance. That's why I've been trying to reach Mr. Barton. I'd really like to do a profile on him."

He didn't waste time getting to what he wanted. She deflected. "Mr. Barton isn't the type to have the spotlight on himself."

"I've heard he's a humble man. But this would be the perfect time for a story, don't you think?"

"In what way?"

"A profile of Mr. Barton could show how they're getting back on track since the recall."

Clearly he wasn't looking simply for his usual human-interest story. This was a reporter to keep an eye on. "Recalls are regrettable, but they aren't uncommon," she said. "They've addressed the problem and are moving forward."

"Yes. But the court of public opinion and all that. A profile would show they don't have anything to hide." His tone changed from persistent to aggressive.

Angela relaxed her voice and let a small smile diffuse the tension. "Trevor, Barton Packing has taken steps to deal with the recall. They value their relationship with customers and regret the problems this caused." It was classic crisis-communication messaging. "And they're working to make sure the problem won't happen again."

McKay flipped to a clean page in his notebook and jotted a few lines without even looking at the paper. "Could you tell me what those steps are? How the company has dealt with the recall?"

"This isn't an interview, is it?" She pointed at his notebook.

"To help my memory."

"In any case, I can't comment on the recall. As I said, I'm new." She spread her hands helplessly. She'd promised to keep what Nick told her confidential. And she would. "Are you on a deadline for a story?"

"My deadline is Thursdays."

He hadn't said he *had* to have this story by Thursday. So he was fishing. "There are some things your readers might be interested in about the company," she said. "But I can't give you a story for this week."

McKay's face fell.

"In the meantime"—Angela dug in her purse and pulled out a business card—"here's my card. It has my cell number on it. When you call, I'll get back to you. I promise."

McKay studied the card for a moment. "Sherborn-Watts is one of the big guns. Some would say bringing in a PR person says they have concerns."

Alarm bells jangled in Angela's brain. She sure didn't want the agency to become the story. Nor to have the hiring of an agency cast a shadow on Barton's intentions.

"No surprise. Sherborn-Watts has handled advertising for Barton Packing for some time, so they knew us. With the increased media interest of late, the company simply wants to make sure they're communicating well on all fronts."

"I suppose." He looked at her card again before slipping it into his shirt pocket. "I've taken enough of your time." He flashed a boy-next-door smile and stood. "I'll be in touch, Ms. Darrah."

"Angela is fine." She smiled. "I look forward to working with you."

He nodded. "I know there are lots of good stories at Barton, Angela."

She watched him walk out the door and noticed that the two librarians kept an eye on them both. When she touched her fingers to her forehead in a small salute, they looked sheepish. She turned her attention back to the *Elbridge Times*, reading McKay's articles with heightened interest. McKay may have been reporting for only a couple of years, but he was persistent and knew how to get people to talk to him. She wouldn't discount him.

Chapter 6

Angela arrived in the break room fifteen minutes before she was scheduled to meet Duarte. He wasn't there, nor was anyone else. Harsh fluorescent lights reflected on stainless-steel tables and metal chairs. Concrete-block walls felt jail-cell stark, despite the speckled paint finish. Nothing in the room was inviting.

She put her notepad and pencil on a table in the corner and went to the vending machine to get a cold drink. As a bottle clunked through the dispenser, the door to the plant opened and five men crowded in. Three were Latino. She looked at them, her face open, friendly, expectant, anticipating one would be the man she was to meet. All the men wore heavy work boots, aprons, and coats, with nets covering their hair; none acknowledged her with more than a curious glance, so she took her water and returned to the corner. The men filled chairs at a table across the room, speaking in a mixture of Spanish and English.

She'd come to this meeting armed with a wealth of statistics from HR: numbers of employees, breakdown by ethnicity, payroll and benefits, turnover, along with a rough sense of how these figures compared to the packing industry as a whole. She also had happened across an article on the ICE raid on the Agriprocessors plant in 2008. In that raid, nearly four hundred workers were charged with document fraud; the plant was shut down and the owners prosecuted. One owner was still in prison.

No wonder Nick stressed that all Barton Packing employees had legal papers. It didn't matter who they were or where they came from; if they checked out through the government system, the company was in the clear.

When Angela had asked about employee training, HR sent her back to Gordon, who reminded her to talk with Duarte first. She was finding that getting information on the simplest things could take all day. Perhaps it would get easier as she came to know the company and her sources better. In her meeting with Duarte, she hoped to finally get the specific information she needed on employee training. She also hoped to put the awkwardness of their first meeting in the plant behind her.

A steady flow of workers came and went from the break room. Each time the door opened, Angela looked up, expecting Duarte. She made eye contact and smiled at everyone. As the tables in the break room filled, she realized this must be a shift break, and she wondered if she should give up her space.

Her phone vibrated with a text from the account manager who'd taken over the animal shelter account in her absence. He wanted her approval of the dog he'd chosen for the noon show on the leading Des Moines–area TV station. She'd been particularly proud to get a regular placement on that show because the animals they featured were almost always adopted within the day. This dog was a lovely—and no doubt lively—sheltie. As she OK'd the choice with a caution about making sure the dog wasn't too unruly, Angela felt homesick. She missed the dogs, the way their eyes lit up and their tails wagged when they were removed from the cages. She'd never considered herself a dog person, but if her apartment allowed pets, she'd now be tempted. With an assignment like this one in Hammond, though, she was better off without a dog.

"*Señorita* Darrah?" An accent-rich baritone voice broke her concentration.

Angela looked up, recognized the floor supervisor at once (as soon as she saw him, she wondered how she could have ever doubted she would), and hurried to stand, extending a hand in greeting. "Al. I didn't see you come in." His hand was as warm as it had been in the plant. How did he manage given the cold he worked in every day? She gestured to the table. "Is this OK?"

"As good as anyplace." He pulled out a chair and sat, leaning back and crossing an ankle over his knee. He opened a Coke and took a drink. Today, the heavy, arched eyebrows looked amused. "*Mi nombre es* Alvaro. Mr. Ryker is the only one who calls me Al."

Oh, for pity's sake, she thought. Getting his name wrong compounded the problem. Even if it wasn't her fault.

"Alvaro." She repeated the name, rolling the *r* across her tongue. "Thank you for telling me."

He was even more attractive than she'd remembered, and younger. Somewhere close to her age, she guessed. In spite of the generic, loose-fitting work clothes, she could tell he was fit. The dark skin, aquiline nose, and brooding eyebrows implied Aztec or Incan heritage.

"I appreciate your time," she said, centering her notebook in front of her. She briefly thought about simply ignoring her misstep in the plant. Yet if she did, that rough patch would always be out there, at least in her mind.

"Before we get to business, I want to apologize for . . . for the way I handled our first meeting." She felt contrite and hoped it showed. "Nick—Mr. Barton—suggested speaking Spanish would be helpful. I assumed . . ."

"You assumed I would not speak English?"

"Gordon said you were from El Salvador . . ."

"Ah." He nodded thoughtfully. "You assumed someone from El Salvador would not speak English."

"Yes, I'm sorry. I did make an assumption—about the plant and people working here."

"Even people from El Salvador, even people who work in a packing plant, can learn English." The thick black eyebrows hunched like storm clouds. "Given enough time."

Feeling the paper cut of sarcasm, Angela cringed. "I didn't mean it that way."

The corners of his mouth curled in a micro smile. "I hear it often since I came here. Maybe gringos think we can't speak English because they can't speak Spanish."

"You speak English well. My Spanish isn't nearly as good as your English." She flushed. "I suppose that sounded condescending, too. I didn't mean it to."

What was the matter with her? Everything she said was off, while everything he said made her defensive. She was trying so hard. She hadn't felt this way since . . . Megan Jeffries popped into her mind. She hadn't thought of Megan, one of the popular girls in sixth grade, in years. Angela had really wanted to be her friend, but Megan challenged everything Angela said or did. Even when Angela knew she was right. When Angela was wrong, it was worse. Angela had whined to her father, who made it clear that whatever was going on probably wasn't about her.

"You don't know what's going on in Megan's life," he had said. "She might have troubles you don't know. And you can't make someone like you. You be you, and either they'll like you or they won't. But you'll have been true to yourself."

Just as she wanted Megan to like her, she wanted this man to like her. She stared at her notes again simply to avoid looking at him. She took a drink of the water and finally met his eyes with a shy smile. "I've stepped in it, haven't I?"

"Stepped in it?" His eyebrows knit into a frown of confusion.

"It means getting into a predicament, a problem, one not easy to get out of. It's a common phrase around here, maybe because of the farms. Literally, it means stepping in, um, manure."

"I see." The dimple carved deep when he laughed. "I'll remember that."

She shared the laugh. It helped to learn he didn't know everything about English.

"Anyway, I'm embarrassed," she said.

"No hay problema." He perched the Coke bottle on his knee, where it balanced rock still.

"I'm curious, Alvaro. How did you come to Barton Packing?" Angela hadn't intended to ask about him personally, but she realized this was what she most wanted to know. She'd never considered El Salvador a source of immigrant labor.

"Mr. Barton heard me present a paper at the ASEE conference."

"A-C?"

"The American Society for Engineering Education. ASEE. I presented a research paper I wrote at Iowa State. How to adapt production-line equipment for greater efficiency." Alvaro's face was animated. "Mr. Barton was on the ASEE board and he invited me to visit Barton Packing."

"That's right. Gordon said they adopted some of the new equipment on your recommendation. So you went to Iowa State? I did, too."

"What did you study?" he asked. He drank from the Coke bottle, then balanced it again on his knee.

"Journalism, public relations, Spanish, business. Everything to prepare me for a job like I have now." She guessed he was in his early thirties, plus or minus. Within a year or two of her. The way he balanced a bottle like that made her think of guys she met in college. She wondered if they'd hung out at any of the same campus bars.

A devilish glint lit up his eyes. "School Spanish. I thought so. You speak Spanish like a gringo."

"Yeah." She accepted the friendly jab with a smile. "Because I am." She peppered questions back to him. "Why did you choose Iowa? How did you even know to come here? And why leave El Salvador?"

"I came on a student visa. After I graduated with a degree in engineering, I got an H-1B visa and have worked at Barton Packing since."

Alvaro glanced at the break room clock. "I only have a little time. Mr. Ryker said you wanted to talk to me. What about?"

They'd gotten way off track, and she spoke quickly to catch up. "As he said, I'm here to do public relations for Barton Packing. I'm coming up to speed on the company as fast as I can, and he sent me to you to learn how the plant works. Since my company was hired because of the recall, I'm starting with that. What's your take on what happened?"

The Coke bottle slipped off Alvaro's knee, the sudden movement startled Angela, and she reached out at the same time that he grabbed it and rebalanced it on his knee.

"Good save," she said.

He nodded and continued as though nothing had happened. "The recall. There were many factors. The chemicals were all stored in the one room and the cleaning crew took the wrong one by accident."

"How did that happen?"

"The worker, we thought he could read the labels. It turned out he could not. He had memorized the colors on the labels and where the barrels were in the storeroom."

"So it was the employee's fault."

"Yes and no. It is true, the employee could not read the labels, but the training did not discover that. Then, when someone put the barrels in different places, it became a problem."

"I understand the chemicals are stored in different places now, so that's some help, but not if people can't read the labels. When I toured the plant, I was struck by how diverse the workforce is and wondered whether everyone spoke English."

"Many languages are spoken here," he affirmed. "The Somalis and Chin—"

"Chin?"

"Refugees from Myanmar. They have lived in the United States a while. Many of the Somalis speak English. Fewer Chin do. They help each other."

"And the Latinos? I suppose that's easier since you speak Spanish."

"You think all the Latinos who work here are immigrants and speak only Spanish?"

His comment stopped her. That was exactly what she thought. If not directly from Latin America, they at least had migrated from the Southwest and spoke English as a second language.

"Some have lived in Hammond their whole lives. They were born here and raised here and speak English. Many of those who come from outside Iowa for the jobs have also lived in the country their whole lives."

"Point taken. I did assume otherwise. And I try not to assume," she said, though she caught herself doing it with uncomfortable frequency. She pushed her hair back from her face. "So how do you handle training? If people don't all speak the same language?"

"We use the ones who speak English to tell the others."

"Sort of like the telephone game."

"Telephone game?"

"A game we played as kids. One person whispers something to the next person in line, who whispers what they heard to the next person. And so on. Usually the last person to get the message has it all wrong. It can be hysterical."

Alvaro did not look amused as he shifted in his chair and set the pop bottle on the table. "I see. It can happen. It is not always funny."

"I'm sure it's not."

"Has the company hired translators?"

"From time to time. But not so many people in Hammond speak Chin or Somali."

"I imagine," she said. Belatedly, she picked up his undertone. She searched his face. "You're teasing."

He grinned.

She shook her head and chuckled at his joke. And at herself. She knew she could be overly serious. "It was also how the cleaning was done, correct? I understand the crew didn't do a thorough job?"

"It is important to clean quickly for the next shift."

His answer didn't address her question. "But they were not thorough?"

"They needed to get the job done." Alvaro rubbed a drop of condensation off the bottle. "Speed is important."

"I could see that when I took the tour. Doing the job well must also be important, though, right?" She looked to him for confirmation.

"They are both important. They did it as well as they could in the time they had."

His response suggested that in the scheme of things speed held more value than being thorough. She continued.

"How have the cleaning procedures and training changed since then?"

"We trained a new crew. We organized the chemical-storage area to make things clearer. We stressed the need to do the job well and on time. The line supervisors watch more closely."

"Are they given more time to do the job? Or was another person added to the crew?"

"I suggested these things, but Mr. Ryker believes the actions we have taken are sufficient."

"What do you think?"

"Time will tell."

His answers indicated he wasn't convinced, but she elected not to ask again. He'd already sidestepped the question twice. "How was the language problem addressed?" she asked.

"It could be better. People who really know each language would help."

"However, as you pointed out, not many in Hammond speak Chin." She stared into the distance as she thought. "But someone speaks at least some of each language, right?"

"Enough for telephone." He grinned.

Again he looked at the clock. "I have only a few minutes. Do you have more questions?"

"A page full." She gestured to her notebook. "For the moment, I am most curious how people wind up here? It's hard to believe people would come all this way to work in meat packing."

Alvaro looked at her with a curious expression. "They go where they must to take care of their families. The jobs are hard, but the pay is better than they can get in their home countries . . . or most places in the United States. Also, the company recruits them."

A woman stuck her head through the plant door. "Alvaro. They need you in here."

"I have to get back to work." He drained the last of the Coke and stood.

Angela stood, too. "Thanks for your time, Alvaro. I'll contact you about meeting again."

"*Cualquier cosa para usted, señorita* Darrah. Anything for you." He put the empty bottle in a recycling bin.

His Spanish was as warm as his hands, and the comment felt very much like flirting. She gave a little wave and watched him disappear into the plant.

He'd challenged her, embarrassed her, teased her. Even so, she was glad Gordon had sent her in Alvaro's direction; working with him would be far more interesting than working with Gordon.

Chapter 7

When she arrived in Hammond, Angela's major focus had been on where she'd stay and on her short commute to and from Barton Packing. She'd given only a cursory glance at homes and businesses as she drove through town. At first look, they appeared typical of any rural town, but walking down Main Street after her third day of work, she was getting a different view.

While storefronts attested to a present-day population expanding beyond the original German and Norwegian immigrants who founded Hammond after the Civil War, the pride and optimism with which the town was built a century and a half ago lay obscured under chipping layers of paint.

Angela counted at least four colors peeling around a store window displaying christening and *quinceañera* gowns. The awning shielding one store window from the setting sun drooped sadly to one side. A small sign in an empty storefront touted last year's sauerkraut festival, the only vestige she'd seen of the town's northern European heritage. Sheets of paper obscured the windows of another store. A small sign over a door farther down the street advertised beer and pizza. None of the storefronts looked welcoming, and Angela did not go into any of them.

Stopping to read the posters in one window, she found announcements of bands and dances hung side by side with a flyer listing indications of abuse and encouraging women in dangerous relationships to seek help.

Widening her view, she took in all the two- and three-story buildings on both sides of the street. It looked as though apartments occupied the second floors. Curtains draped many windows and plants lined some windowsills. The library parking lot up the hill afforded a back-alley view of these buildings. From the elevated height, she'd seen satellite dishes sprouting like weeds from the roofs. She wondered if storekeepers lived above the shops now as they did 150 years ago.

Her great-grandparents had been shopkeepers when they came to Iowa from France, arriving in southwest Iowa at about the same time French Icarians chose to establish a utopian community in the area. Living above the general store they owned, her grandparents had worked long hours and opened the store whenever needed, even in the middle of the night. When Angela was a child, the stories of her ancestors had felt like remnants of a long-gone time. But now, looking at these buildings, she connected her own immigrant past to the present.

Angela walked both sides of the street of the three-block-long business district and stood considering whether the bar with the pizza sign might be the place for supper. She wasn't wild about eating in a bar alone, though. Ever since college, when going to a bar meant looking for a date, she couldn't go in one without feeling as though she was either on display or doing the looking herself. Well, she had to eat somewhere. As she stepped off the curb, she heard a man call her name.

Surprised, she looked over her shoulder. A half block away, Alvaro Duarte waved at her. She smiled and stepped back onto the sidewalk.

Dressed in blue jeans and a red-and-gold T-shirt sporting a small ISU logo, he looked more like a college student than a packing-plant supervisor. As he neared, she spotted a tattoo winding down a well-defined left bicep and ending above his elbow. Though the T-shirt sleeve covered much of the tattoo, the ink made him seem tough. Had she seen him walking toward her on campus, she'd have looked twice, maybe offered an interested smile. Had she seen him walking toward her at night on a Des Moines street, she'd have crossed to the other side. Or looked for the safety of numbers.

"*¿Que pasa?*" he said.

"Alvaro." She was taken aback. Why he was speaking Spanish now, when her last attempt had fallen short? And when he'd called her on her assumption that he didn't speak English?

He smiled and repeated, "*¿Que pasa?*"

She shook her head in confusion. "I'm sorry, I didn't think you'd want to speak Spanish. I mean, after our last . . . my assumption . . . my accent?"

"I was hard on you."

"I was only trying to . . . ," she began to explain, but stopped. "I was trying," she concluded.

"I understand." He rubbed the back of his neck.

Although he looked weary, his kindness put her at ease. She knew what a long workday felt like. "It's OK." She smiled. "I'm over it if you are. *¿De acuerdo?*"

"Agreed."

"*Bueno,*" she said, delighted to see the dimple show up with his smile. "*Y mi nombre es Angela.*"

"Angela," he said. "*Anhela.*" He repeated her name the Spanish way, with a soft *a*, a silent *g*. The Spanish pronunciation came through silky and gentle. Enjoying the sound of her name, she leaned in. In the past, the sound of her name had made her cringe. It started when grade-school boys had taunted her, drawing out the *a* with a repulsive nasal twang. She could hear their voices squealing "Angie," or even worse, "Ang."

"I was going to get something to eat. Want to join me?" She pointed to the bar across the street.

"Do you like Mexican? Eduardo's is the best in Iowa." He gestured toward a storefront she'd walked past without recognizing it as a restaurant.

"If you recommend it, I'm in. I've eaten way too much pizza lately."

In minutes they were seated at one of the nine chrome-trimmed tables in the small restaurant that appeared a cross between a Mexican café and a 1950s diner. Chairs with red plastic upholstery matched retro tables topped with napkin dispensers and yellow plastic salt and pepper shakers. Paintings of calla lilies and adobe buildings in desert landscapes adorned the walls. The counter dividing the dining area from the kitchen held a cash register and fishbowls full of different kinds of candy for sale at twenty-five cents apiece.

"*Buenas tardes*, Alvaro. *¿Cómo estás?*" An older man with dark hair and silver sideburns brought menus, a basket of chips, and a bowl of salsa.

"*Muy bien, amigo*," Alvaro said. "Eduardo, this is Angela Darrah. Angela, this is Eduardo Gonzales. He and his wife, Maria, own this restaurant." He waved to a woman working in the kitchen. "*Hola*, Maria."

"*Mucho gusto.*" Angela shook the man's hand. "I'm new in town. Alvaro says your place is the best in Iowa."

The old man rested a hand on Alvaro's shoulder. "We pay him to say it."

"I do not take money for the truth," Alvaro said.

Only later would she realize that Alvaro had switched to English when he introduced her. And even though she greeted Eduardo in Spanish, both she and Eduardo then spoke in English. A courtesy? Because it was easy? An expectation? Because she had a gringo accent? Hammond presented the first real opportunity, outside of school-related activities, that she'd had to interact with native Spanish speakers, and yet she held back.

Angela scanned the menu but closed it without choosing. "Bring me what you like best," she said, handing Eduardo the menu. "I'm here on a new adventure, so this is part of it. And a Diet Coke."

Eduardo beamed. "Maria will prepare something you will like."

"You made a friend," Alvaro said after Eduardo returned to the kitchen.

"Do you think?"

"I know. Eduardo is famous. He and Maria ran a restaurant in San Antonio before coming here. You can read about them." He pointed to a framed newspaper article hanging on the wall next to the cash register.

"How did he come to Hammond?" Angela asked.

"An opportunity," Alvaro said. "It's the same for everyone."

"What are your plans? Will you stay?"

"My visa expires at the end of the year. Then I am back to El Salvador."

"Do you go home often?" She dipped a chip in salsa rich with cilantro.

"No. It is almost eight years."

"That's a long time. Couldn't you have gone back, even for a visit?"

"My mother said it's better for me to stay here."

"Still, eight years. I can't imagine."

Eduardo set a glass of cola and a straw on the table in front of Angela. He brought a bottle of Coke for Alvaro.

"Why a bottle for you?" she asked when Eduardo left.

"Mexican Coca-Cola," he explained. "American pop is for gringos."

"I didn't know there was such a thing." She turned the bottle to read the label. "It looks the same. What's the difference?"

"Mexican Coke is made with real sugar. Not like the American stuff."

"I'll try it next time," she said. "Now, back to the eight years."

"I came here to learn, so I could do more for my family. Now is time for me to go back. My mother and sister, they need me."

"You must miss them."

"My sister Eva is grown up while I am gone." He drained a third of the Coke. "I do miss them."

She scanned his face. "I hear a 'but' in there. Have you thought about staying? Could you stay?"

"I've lived here a long time. My home is there and here, too."

"You mentioned your mother and sister. What about your father?"

The heavy eyebrows settled lower. "My father died when I was six," he said at last.

"I'm so sorry, Alvaro."

"He was killed in the civil war."

"He was a soldier?"

"A civilian. Wrong place, wrong time."

"That is tragic." Instinctively, Angela reached across the table and laid her hand on his. The sight of her pale skin, such a dramatic contrast to his rich umber color, held her gaze. She forced herself to look up. "How sad for your family."

A look of distress moved across Alvaro's face as he pulled his hand away. "Our food is here," he said, sliding silverware out of the way as Eduardo delivered the hot plates. "What did Maria make us tonight?"

"*Guisado de puerco,*" Eduardo responded.

"I don't know that one," Angela said.

"Similar to *carnitas,*" he explained. "Diced pork, lots of seasoning. Maria used chili verde since it's Alvaro's favorite. We also make it with red sauce."

"It smells delicious."

"You will like it, I know," Alvaro affirmed. "Thank Maria for us."

The explanation of the dishes offered a welcome break. For her, at least, and maybe for Alvaro. Had her touch been welcome or presumptuous? Had she comforted or offended?

Perhaps in El Salvador, a woman would not touch a man that way. She pushed the moment to the back of her mind.

"I can't wait to get started." She picked up her fork, ready to dig in.

But Alvaro did not begin to eat. Instead, he bowed his head and crossed himself.

Caught off guard, Angela was unsure what to do. Public displays of faith were completely outside her Lutheran church upbringing. During college, she had stopped attending church services. Now she went only when she visited her parents. She put her fork back on the table and folded her hands in her lap, waiting for him to finish. Her family's mealtime prayer popped into her head, so with eyes wide open, she repeated the blessing to herself.

Completing his prayer, Alvaro crossed himself again and picked up his fork. "Taste it," he urged.

She thought about saying something about the prayer, but talking about faith was as unfamiliar to her as praying in a restaurant.

"Oh, it's excellent," she exclaimed after sampling the pork.

Alvaro nodded. "It is the best I have eaten in Iowa."

"I would never have guessed based on the outside of the restaurant." Realizing her comment could have been offensive, she glanced behind her and was glad to see Eduardo out of hearing range. "I find myself making so many assumptions. And being so wrong." She defended herself. "It's my public-relations background. Image is important. It's why I'm here. To help with Barton Packing's image."

"It is more important what is inside than how it looks outside. No?"

"Yes, that's true. But more people would try this place out if the outside were more inviting. Surely you didn't find places like this in Ames."

"If you knew where to look." He shrugged. "But, see. There is plenty of business."

Indeed, the tables had all filled as they talked and people were taking carryout bags from the counter. Angela noticed most of the patrons were white.

"Do the people you work with at the plant come here?"

"Some do. If they have family here, they eat at home. Even the men who are here alone don't eat out much. They send most of what they earn to their families."

Angela considered that. "Do you send money home, too?"

"Yes," he responded. "Even when I was in college, I had a job and sent what I could home. I had a scholarship, so that helped. With this job, I can send more."

"I'm impressed," she said. "I had a scholarship, too, and a job, but it never covered everything. My parents helped me a lot."

She thought about her parents and how she was helping them now. She didn't feel comfortable sharing that, though she couldn't have said why.

"Like most American kids, I think."

"We are not all the same, either." She took another bite, chewing it thoroughly. She felt awkward asking this because he was a client. But because he was a client, it was relevant. "I need to know: Is my accent really so bad?"

"You sound like someone who doesn't speak Spanish often." He spoke lightly as he added, "And you are easy to tease."

Again his comments felt like flirting, and she laughed, feeling the same push and pull of attraction she'd experienced at their last meeting. To hide the flush she felt on her cheeks, she gazed down at her plate as she moved the fork around to get the next bite. She took it in her mouth and chewed it slowly. "This is really good. I'm glad you saved me from another slice of pizza." She wiped her lips. Before his flirting went further, she needed to get them back on business. "If it's OK, I'd like to ask some of the questions I didn't have time for when we met at the plant. OK?"

He shrugged. "Sure."

Over the next hour, she led him into a wide-ranging discussion of how Barton employees assimilated into Hammond. They finished eating long before they finished talking. One thing he remarked on caught her attention.

"The housing you mentioned the company arranges for new employees. Can you tell me where it is? I drove around but I didn't see apartment buildings."

"We can walk to some when we finish here. If you want."

"Really? We can walk? I expected apartment buildings to be farther away. On the edge of town, at least." She knew the sun would set in an hour or so. "I don't want to rush, but I would like to see them."

"It is not all apartment buildings. Some are houses, and they are not far."

"Let's go, then," she said.

While they settled up with Eduardo at the cash register, Angela scanned the framed article Alvaro had pointed to earlier, a piece by her newest media contact, Trevor McKay. Eduardo and Maria were indeed famous. They'd won awards for the restaurant they'd owned in San Antonio, and this Iowa location had been cited by the *Elbridge Times* as best Mexican restaurant in three counties.

Outside the restaurant, Alvaro led her to houses only three blocks from Main Street. One was a smallish story-and-a-half frame house with peeling white paint, a torn screen door, and broken slats in the shutters. An enclosed porch and at least one other room were clumsily cobbled onto the original structure. The corner of another room jutted out the back, barely visible from the street. Weeds sprouted through cracks in the sidewalk and grew ragged around the foundation. A yellow dog slept on the porch next to two bulging trash bags. Piles of dog poop dotted the overgrown lawn.

Angela couldn't conceal her disbelief at the state of disrepair. "Really? This is housing Barton Packing arranges for new employees?"

"There are other houses around town," he said. "Like this one."

In the face of such a run-down structure, she hardly knew what to say. "Does a family live here?"

He pointed to the roof. "Count the satellite dishes."

Angela looked up. She could see four of the silver disks from where she stood. What she'd thought to be a single-family house had apparently been divided up into at least four apartments. From the positioning of the satellite dishes, it looked like even the enclosed porch was someone's home. A line of cars and trucks behind the house made the backyard look like a used-car lot.

She turned to Alvaro. "How many do you think live here?"

"Four, five, maybe more. Some are not married, or they come alone because it is not possible to bring their families."

"What about families? Where do they live?" she asked.

He led her up the street and stopped at a lot crowded with two single-wide trailer homes with blue siding and white trim. "These are for families," he said.

Angela was relieved to note that each trailer had only one satellite dish. Wooden decks attached to the sides of the trailers held lawn chairs. One had a picnic table. A bicycle with a tire missing leaned against the base of an ash tree. Behind the trailers were a pickup truck and a couple of cars.

There were such places in the town where she grew up. Run-down houses where poorer families lived. Lindy had lived in a house like that, she remembered. A stick-thin girl who wore too-big jeans and a plaid blouse to class nearly every day, Lindy had moved to Corning with her family during Angela's third-grade year. Some of the girls teased Lindy about always wearing the same thing until Lindy punched one of them in the nose. She was suspended for two days for fighting, but the teasing stopped. Such a bold action horrified and fascinated Angela. She walked home with Lindy the first day she returned to class. The two stood on the sidewalk in front of a house just like these. Lindy didn't invite her in. Within a month, Lindy wasn't in class anymore. Angela's parents had told her the family moved away.

"I had something different in mind," she admitted. "Apartment buildings. Duplexes. Quadplexes." She hesitated to say more lest her words offend him. Maybe he considered this good housing.

"They are glad to have a place to stay."

"So how does the housing work?"

"The company pays the first month's rent. After that, the employee pays."

"Do they stay after the month?"

"Some do and some don't."

Angela peeked at Alvaro out of the corner of her eye. She sensed they were both being careful about what they said.

"There are other houses if you'd like to see them."

"I would."

Over the course of the next hour, they walked to a half dozen houses, all with similar appearances. Old houses converted into crowded apartments, all in need of maintenance.

"We look for other places for the workers to live, but there are not many. It's a small town."

"We? You and Gordon?"

"No. Father Burke, the priest at Saint Catherine's."

"I'm meeting people around town over the next couple of weeks. Sounds as though Father Burke should be on my list."

"I help there two nights a week. I will introduce you."

"It's a deal. Just say when."

After he left her at her car on Main Street, Angela drove past the houses he'd shown her. She tried to put herself in the shoes of the people living there. A month of free rent was a definite plus. If someone was trying a job that didn't pan out, they weren't saddled with a deposit or a lease. But if many employees didn't work out, the company was shouldering a significant expense it'd never recoup.

Well-kept homes with tidy yards filled the same blocks as the run-down houses. That made her think about how others in the community might perceive this housing. She doubted neighbors were happy with deteriorating houses next door, while town leaders might consider it a plus that properties weren't abandoned. Apartment owners might not appreciate Barton being in competition for renters. No doubt there were other angles she hadn't discovered yet.

Her first thought had been that a housing program like this was a good story. Now, having seen the properties, she wasn't so sure. Who was responsible for property upkeep? Perhaps, as Alvaro said, there simply weren't many options in Hammond. Or maybe he didn't think there was anything that could be done. Or maybe he was doing whatever he could in working with Father Burke to find other accommodations.

Questions abounded.

Chapter 8

TGIF. Finally. Angela giggled through a mouthful of tooth-paste. She was so eager to get out of Hammond and back to Des Moines she felt giddy. The week had gone fast enough, but coming back to this outdated motel room every night was depressing. She looked at her feet clad in satin slippers. She couldn't wait to sink her bare toes into the chenille rug in front of her bathroom sink, to be barefoot from the moment she walked through her apartment door. The carpet in the motel looked mostly OK, but she couldn't be certain. She always wore slippers. After wiping her mouth, she used the hand towel to rub flecks of toothpaste off the mirror. Unnecessary in a rent-ed room, yet the small action made her feel like the unfamiliar space was hers.

As she stuffed dirty clothes in a bag, she laughed out loud, realizing she actually looked forward to doing the laundry.

She checked inside her purse for her ticket to the sold-out performance of *Kinky Boots* at the Civic Center. She hummed the tune to "The History of Wrong Guys," a favorite with Angela and her friends because they'd all been there at least once. Invariably, when one of them spotted a guy of interest, someone in the group began humming the tune. Bought months before this gig in Hammond came up, the tickets were too good to give away.

She'd leave Hammond early so she wouldn't be late getting back to Des Moines for the performance.

At the door she scanned the room one last time, knowing she wouldn't be back before leaving town. Even though she would return in forty-eight hours, the only things she left behind were a novel someone at work had passed her way because they both liked fantasy and three containers of blueberry-flavored Greek yogurt in the refrigerator.

For the first time that week, she didn't have meetings scheduled at Barton Packing. So she filled the morning reworking the releases on company growth that she'd talked with her boss about the night before. The content still felt like puff pieces to her, but it was the best topic they had. The only other potential newsworthy topic she'd uncovered so far—Barton's program to provide a month of free rent—had its problems. When she'd described the condition of the houses, Dave had laughed, told her it sounded like places he'd lived in his college days. Not a picture to put in front of the media, she'd insisted. He'd challenged her to work out the pros and cons. That was one of the things she liked most about his mentoring style. Because he gave her space to think through the issues herself, she'd gotten better at crafting messages, often on the fly.

Early that afternoon, Angela drove back to Main Street. She'd walked right by the Mexican restaurant Wednesday night and not seen it. What else had she overlooked? She pulled into a spot a few doors down from a storefront Alvaro had said was a Chin grocery. This was a store she'd assumed was out of business because the windows were covered with eight-by-ten sheets of yellowing paper. The door's windows were similarly blocked.

Looking again, her eyes fell on a piece of paper taped in the upper-right-hand corner of the window, lettered with the words "Asian Store."

She thought about going into the store, but the flimsy sheets of paper held her back. The fully covered window communicated exclusion as effectively as steel bars or a brick wall.

Instead of getting out, she remained sitting in her car, staring at the storefront, as she reflected on what she knew about the Chin working at the plant.

The vast majority were men. According to the Barton HR director, the Chin women were mostly stay-at-home moms with a good number of children. Like the Somalis, the Chin were secondary migrants, settling first in another part of the US, then coming to Hammond, a handful at first, more as the community established.

Barton Packing looked favorably on the Chin as employees. They had the right paperwork. They worked hard. Their lack of English was seldom an issue.

"Have there been particular problems with the Chin?" Angela had asked the HR director.

The woman thought for a moment before answering, "Well. A worker lost part of his hand in one of the machines. That didn't have anything to do with his being Chin, though."

When Angela gasped, her hands and fingers curling reflexively into her armpits, the woman added, "It was terribly unfortunate, but sometimes accidents happen. Let me assure you that happened quite a while ago. We haven't had such a problem since."

Angela found it hard to release the spasms in her clenched fists. "What responsibility does the company have when something like that happens?"

"Well, thank goodness it doesn't happen often. Of course we cover the hospital bills. We also make a payment to the employee to compensate for the accident."

"What happened to him then? I can't imagine he could come back to work."

"No. Of course he doesn't work here anymore," the HR manager had said, and then changed the subject.

At that moment, a Chin woman came down the street with two children trailing close to her skirt. The petite woman balanced another child on her hip, shifting the child from side to side to offset her pregnant belly. The mother herded her children up the steps and into the store. Angela thought of the man with a mutilated hand as she tucked her own fingers safely under her thighs.

As she contemplated going into the store, she realized this was really the first time she saw herself as different, in the minority, felt the unease someone who didn't look like everyone else around them might feel. What would it be like to face this every day with every store you entered? Did you wonder if clerks would be friendly? Or if you would be greeted with suspicion and skepticism? Would you be able to find what you came for or scurry out embarrassed and ashamed because no one understood you?

Don't overthink it, Darrah, Angela chided herself. *What's the worst that could happen?* She got out of the car and crossed the sidewalk. She climbed the first of the store's concrete steps and reached out to open the door just as two Asian women came out, laughing, talking in a language she assumed was Chin.

Angela smiled and said, "Hello." The women's smiles evaporated and their faces grew guarded as they crowded past without speaking. Talking in low tones, they hurried away. When they glanced back and saw her looking at them, they walked faster. Angela backed off the steps, away from the door. Maybe she'd go in another time.

The experience unsettled her. She returned to the car, abandoning the thought of exploring more of Main Street. Her phone pinged with new messages she was only too happy to take. After a while, she checked the time; a quick stop at the bank ATM, and she'd be off for Des Moines.

* * *

Angela pulled into the Hammond State Bank parking lot expecting to sail through the drive-through only to find a line of cars queued up for the one machine. "Rats," she muttered. Who'd have thought the bank would be so popular on a Friday afternoon? She checked her watch. Still time to get to *Kinky Boots*.

A car parked near the bank entrance pulled out and Angela swung in, grabbed her purse, and ran in to use the lobby ATM. It had to be faster than the drive-through. She was surprised to see the lobby looked like hotel check-in during a convention. Customers three deep waited at each of the teller windows and at the ATM.

She resigned herself to the end of the ATM line, encouraged that the teenage girl at the machine already had cash in hand. Behind the girl, a lanky man sporting a sweat-stained John Deere cap cleared his throat and checked his phone twice in ten seconds. A middle-aged woman with graying hair so tightly curled it made her look like a poodle had her head buried in her purse and didn't look up as Angela joined the queue.

"I didn't expect this," Angela commented to the poodle woman. "Busy place."

"Always is on payday," the poodle woman muttered, still digging in her handbag. "And I bet we're the only ones in here who speak English."

The woman's tone surprised Angela. The librarian's comments were the closest she'd come to hearing that kind of prejudice in Hammond, though admittedly she hadn't been a lot of places.

Angela uttered a noncommittal, "Hmm," and looked at the crowd in the teller lines more closely. Most were Latino. Some were black. Somalis from the plant, she guessed. Though she knew that the Somalis commuted to Hammond every day from Waterloo, a drive of about forty minutes, maybe it was easier to get their checks cashed here. She heard Spanish; she also heard English. Maybe they were all associated with the plant. Maybe they weren't.

"Sally tells me . . ." The woman finally raised her head, absorbed Angela's tailored slacks, stylish silk blouse, and chic gold jewelry, and continued speaking in a voice loud enough to be heard halfway across the lobby. "Sally's a teller." She poked her head toward the counter and spoke with palpable animosity. "Every payday, Sally says those people from the plant come in here and get money orders to send back to Mexico."

Prickling with embarrassment, Angela glanced around, hoping no one had heard the woman, hoping no one thought she was the one who'd said it. She looked with yearning at the ATM. John Deere Cap was taking an inordinate amount of time. She checked her watch and finally said, "It's what the bank is for."

The woman leaned closer, as though the two were friends. Angela edged away and stared fixedly at her phone, but the woman continued. "Do they ever learn English?" She answered her own question. "Not that Sally can tell."

Angela looked again at the tellers and the lines. The tellers were all white women; she wondered which one was Sally.

"You're not from around here, are you?" the woman persisted. "Hammond used to be a really nice town before all this." She dismissed the customers with a curled lip. "Still is if you can stay away from the coloreds. I bet you hesitated to even come in here when you saw this crowd. Where do you work?"

Angela knew she should say something—in defense of the people in the bank, of Barton Packing. That was her job, but she didn't know how this all could escalate. While her stomach hurt to keep quiet, the thought of a scene causing public-relations blowback made her throat lock.

Finally, she said, "I'm an account manager with Sherborn-Watts. In Des Moines." An answer. A truth. Yet also words that distanced her from the targets of the woman's venom. John Deere Cap left, and she pointed to the ATM. "Your turn."

"Finally."

To Angela's relief, the woman finished her transaction and left without acknowledging Angela again. Back in her car, Angela reached for the ignition and saw her hand trembling, felt her heart racing. The encounter with the woman in the bank felt like a hit and run, an accident in which she'd barely escaped injury. Already she regretted her cowardly sidestep of not saying something direct to stand up for the people the woman attacked.

As she backed out, she spotted Alvaro going into the bank. He saw her at the same time and waved. She returned the wave and smiled, sorry she didn't have time to stop and chat. Selfishly, she wished the woman in the bank could see her acknowledge him.

Hammond receded in her rearview mirror, but the woman in the bank would not let go. She'd have turned that ill will on Angela as easily as she did everyone else in the bank. Except that Angela was white. And wore nice clothes. The woman judged her and Angela passed. And that shamed Angela. As did her unwillingness to be associated with the very people she was in Hammond to represent.

Did the woman's anger rain on every Hispanic person? Every black person? Every person who wasn't white? What about the fact that Hispanics had lived in Hammond for decades? And why was she angry anyway? The Barton employees didn't harm her, did they? Angela built the argument that all the Barton employees actually helped the woman—that their paychecks helped Hammond thrive. Then she remembered the woman's comment about the paychecks buying money orders that were sent to Mexico.

Some of the Latino and black people in the bank must have heard the woman's comments. They couldn't have avoided it; she talked so loudly. For Angela, walking into the Chin store was an idle experiment, a brief excursion into the unfamiliar. Immigrants might face discomfort, confusion, or embarrassment every day. Did they ever get used to it?

In Hammond, every other person she saw on the streets was a different race or ethnicity than she. Her hometown could not have been more different. All of the people in her classes at school, at church, in Girl Scouts, had been white. Until she was in college, she'd had almost no interactions with people of color.

Even then, her relationships with anyone nonwhite had never reached a friend level. Now she saw how limited her experiences had been.

She was furious, and sad, and completely caught up in imaginary arguments with this woman. It took most of the first hour of straight, almost empty roads for Angela to become rational. No doubt the woman reflected the opinions of others in Hammond, a fact Angela did not like but needed to accept. And deal with. She added the bank president to her list of people to talk with in the next week, whether Nick Barton wanted her to or not. Yet even making a list of positive actions didn't erase the troubling thoughts.

She knew she judged others unfairly. She'd done that with Alvaro. So was she any different than that woman? That was what really bothered her.

"Rats!" she screamed, and hammered a fist on the steering wheel.

Chapter 9

The next Wednesday morning, Angela arrived at Nick Barton's office with more than she'd promised. She brought the two news releases and a memo offering preliminary observations on PR opportunities for the company. She also came with heightened awareness of diversity.

The experience with the woman at the bank had made her really look at her own environment. Over the weekend in Des Moines, she saw diversity she'd never noted before. Nearly all of the staff at a popular deli where she joined a friend for breakfast were Latino, a fact she hadn't before taken the time to see. For the first time, she consciously thought about the fact that there was not a single person of color who worked at Sherborn-Watts. When she asked Dave about that, he said they'd seldom had any person of color apply and none that had were qualified. She'd always thought him to be gender blind, so she had no basis for questioning if he was also color blind. But she began to wonder.

Over drinks after the show, Angela laid out the situations she'd seen to her friend Jess, replaying both the bank encounter and her hesitation to go into the Chin store.

"Was I overreacting?" she asked about the bank.

Jess shrugged. "On the one hand, the woman was rude. Talking so loud like that. On the other hand, she had a point about speaking English."

Angela frowned. It surprised her to hear Jess suggest everyone should speak English. "Have you ever been in a place where you were the minority?"

"I've traveled overseas, Germany and France. I always feel as though I need to be able to do basic business in the local language."

"But you don't speak the local language all the time, right?"

"No." Jess laughed. "I admit I'm always glad to find someone who speaks English. It takes the pressure off."

"Pressure." Angela nodded. "That's what it is. Based on expectations. Theirs or our own." She sipped from her glass of cabernet. "I know I felt pressure standing outside the Asian store." She snickered. "I was such a coward."

They continued to talk for another hour, mostly about their life experiences with diverse groups. It was the first such conversation Angela had ever been part of.

The weekend had invigorated her. She'd opened her eyes and her mind. That always felt good. She channeled her newfound energy into crafting the releases she gave to Nick that morning. Because of her encounter with the woman in the bank, she'd worked in statistics about how each dollar spent multiplied throughout a community. These figures gave the releases weight. She set aside her concerns that the releases would be seen as fluff, trusting that the media would be pleased to get something from a company that historically had given them nothing.

Nick approved the general content of the releases but objected to being the person quoted. Though a news release didn't automatically generate an interview, it could happen, positioning him to respond to more media inquiries. "What about Gordon?" he suggested.

She shifted in her chair. From what she'd seen, Gordon would be a problematic spokesperson. In the short time she'd been there, she'd seen Gordon be blunt to the point of rude, speak in borderline racist terms, and flat-out refuse to answer questions. She could hardly imagine him as a spokesperson.

Angela and Dave had talked over the pros and cons of three spokespeople: Nick, Gordon, and herself.

"There are pros and cons with Gordon. Gordon is"—she searched for tact—"inclined to speak without considering how his words may be heard."

"He can be direct," Nick agreed.

Direct didn't come close to encompassing all the problems, Angela thought. "We'd work with whoever was the spokesperson to make sure they were prepared."

She went on to talk about media training. Again, she brought up Trevor McKay's interest in an interview, particularly a profile piece. As she talked, another person came to mind, someone who could be both spokesperson and subject for a profile. Alvaro was smart. He'd look good on camera. He knew the plant. As a Latino, he would be a progressive face and voice for the company. She'd enjoy coaching him for the spokesperson role.

"Here's another spokesperson thought," she said. "What about Alvaro?"

"Alvaro?" Nick didn't register the name.

"Alvaro Duarte. He's a plant supervisor. You hired him after hearing him present at an engineering conference. Gordon directed me to use him as a contact for things related to the plant."

"Ah, yes. He is a bright young man. We helped him get a work visa." Nick leaned back in his chair, looking off into middle distance as he brought Alvaro to mind. "I recall Gordon had hesitations at the time."

"Why was that?" Angela hoped for more insight into both Gordon and Alvaro.

"He thought a college kid would wash out fast. But Duarte was a hard worker. Took anything Gordon threw at

him. And I expect he threw plenty." Nick smiled as he remembered. "I kept closer track of Duarte at first, but once
he won Gordon over, I stepped back. I knew the boy was a
success when Gordon promoted him to floor supervisor." He
leaned forward. "Hmm. Hadn't thought about him in a while.
I should check in. His visa must expire in a year or so."

"The end of this year, he tells me." It pleased her to hear
Nick talk about Alvaro in such a positive manner.

"Then why would we use him as a spokesperson?"

"Not for all situations, but he could be someone for the
profile piece McKay wants to do." Intuitively, she'd liked the
idea of a story on Alvaro, but she quickly realized she'd let her
personal feelings get ahead of her professional objectivity. She'd
jumped on the idea of Alvaro as spokesperson without thinking
through all the angles. A plant supervisor commenting on company growth? Not a good idea.

She backpedaled. "I spoke too fast. Alvaro couldn't speak
to the recall. That's still on the reporter's mind, and it would no
doubt come up."

"Still?"

Hearing impatience sharpen Nick's voice, Angela wondered if she'd overstepped. He was so easy to talk with she'd let
herself get sloppy. "It was big news. It threatened a company
vital to the life of this town and the state. It is possible the media
cling to the recall because it's the only concrete thing they have.
If we give them other things, they *may* let go of the recall. That's
what we hope will happen."

She returned to the point that started the discussion. "OK.
In terms of a spokesperson, you've said you don't want to be in
that role."

"And I understand your concern about Gordon."

"Which leaves me," she acquiesced.

Nick brought the papers together into a pile. "I'll read the
releases with that change in mind."

She moved to the next topic on her agenda, handing him a list of town leaders she'd met and thought might make good partners with Barton Packing.

"I didn't set out to meet these people, but Hammond is a small town, and I met people as I walked around," she said. "Eduardo Gonzales and his wife, for instance. They own a restaurant on Main Street where I had dinner. They're not the business leaders I originally had in mind, but I believe they could be allies."

Nick read the memo twice. "Good. I'll put together a list of others you need to talk with."

He'd said yes to her recommendation. Angela could hardly wait to tell Dave. Representing such an important client on her own offered challenges, yet she found the experience exhilarating. Reacting, responding, counseling a CEO on the fly, having the entire responsibility in the moment felt just as rewarding as she'd imagined it would be. Nick was such a contrast to Gordon. Nick was open to new ideas and discussion, while Gordon remained wary. And unpredictable. Even with Nick, she had to be careful, though. She'd remember that.

As she gathered up her notes, she thought of something else she wanted to ask him. "Do you have time for another question, Nick? A personal one?"

"You may ask; we'll see if I answer," he said, amusement in his tone.

"I don't understand. Why do you resist speaking on behalf of your own company?"

"Occasionally, I spoke at industry events, but it wasn't personal. And honestly? Maggie propped me up before every interview."

"Your wife?" She looked at the pictures of industry meetings on the wall. When he didn't answer, she looked back at him.

Nick's jaw tightened and red splotches bloomed across his cheeks. The wire-rimmed glasses didn't hide the glistening in his eyes. He swallowed as though his throat was raw, and a raspy sound escaped his lips.

Dismayed, Angela couldn't think what to do. She'd never lost someone close to her.

"Nick, I . . ."

The obituary hadn't given Maggie Barton's cause of death. The two years since her passing seemed like a long time. But maybe it seemed so only to her.

The muscles in Nick's jaw worked, as though he were chewing up the grief and swallowing it all over again. He blinked twice before offering a bleak smile; then he went to the refrigerator and pulled out a bottle of water. "The plans we had . . . It hasn't gotten easier." He drained half the bottle in a long gulp.

"I'm so sorry."

"I've joined a travel group and started to visit the places we planned to. She wanted that. That's been more interesting than I thought it would be, but then memories come back, and I lose her all over again."

He reached for the news releases but stopped short of picking them up. "I'll look these over tonight. Liz will find a time when we can talk again."

"Of course." Angela gathered her papers and left. At the door, she glanced back. Nick stood silhouetted against the window, the expanse of Barton Packing rooftops warming in the late-April sun laid out before him. Her dad used to say, "You don't know what you've got till it's gone." Maybe Nick Barton felt that way.

Chapter 10

After meeting with Nick, she took a chance and sought out Gordon in his office. Seeing her at the door, he motioned her in as he continued to talk, the phone clamped between his ear and shoulder. She pantomimed that she could come back, but he waved her to the chair across from his desk.

Angela took the empty chair and waited. As he talked, her eyes were drawn to a wall lined with pictures, and she got up for a closer look.

Motorcycles and military were the general themes. A good-looking, serious young man in a Marines dress uniform stared out from one. In a smaller photo the same young man dressed in mottled brown camouflage lounged next to a vehicle in rough desert terrain, cradling an assault rifle in his arms as gently as if it were a baby. In another photo grizzled men wearing a mixture of camouflage and denim straddled motorcycles. Their T-shirts sported American flags and slogans like "Freedom Isn't Free." Some wore helmets; most did not. Each motorcycle flew an American flag. She looked closer and saw Gordon astride one of the bikes.

These men looked like one of the motorcycle honor guards that attended the funerals of service members killed in Iraq and Afghanistan, funerals that had been all too frequent after 9/11.

Now the Harley-Davidson belt buckle Gordon wore every day made sense.

She remembered the day she'd come upon one of these funerals. Among the townspeople who'd gathered to mourn was a small group of demonstrators from Westboro Baptist Church chanting, "God hates fags" and "Thank God for AIDS." The Westboro church made a name for itself demonstrating at the funerals of soldiers, pointing to soldier deaths as proof that God hated homosexuality. One of the demonstrators had been a teenage boy who shouted with arms raised, hands balled into fists, his lips curled back, his face contorted with hate.

That boy could have been one of the bullies in her high school, the ones who taunted her lab partner Marty, a boy everyone knew to be gay. One day, she'd heard them spit out invectives—homo, queer, fag—at Marty as they passed him in the hallway. One of them punched Marty hard on the shoulder. Marty put his head down and kept walking.

In lab, she asked him, "Why don't you say something? Or tell someone?"

"It would only make them get even."

Angela thought about reporting the boys to the principal. But she convinced herself Marty was right. It would only have made the boys want to get back at him. But in her heart, she'd known she should have spoken up, should have said something.

At the funeral the Patriot Guard Riders had stood between the demonstrators and the family. They hadn't been able to stop the shouts, but at the least the family had known they had people standing with them. A flare of shame ignited in Angela's chest and spread to her face. She wished she'd been there for Marty.

The telephone receiver clicked back in the cradle, drawing her back to the moment. Angela brushed a hand across her cheek, feeling the heat of memory that must still show.

"That took longer than I expected," Gordon said.

"No problem. You're a patriot rider?" she asked over her shoulder.

"I ride with a unit from Hammond."

"So you were in the military?"

"Marines."

The way he stood, back straight, shoulders squared, balanced on his feet, hands clasped behind his back, he could still be in the service. Take twenty-five years off, and he could be the young Marine in the picture on the wall.

"It's impressive what you do. I happened through a town last year when a soldier was being buried. I think every last person in town turned out." She pointed to the young man in the photo. "Is this your son?"

"Yes. Jason did a tour in Iraq and one in Afghanistan."

"You must be proud to have him follow in your footsteps," she said. "Is he still in the service?"

"He was injured by an IED. He lives with us now."

"How awful! Will he be able to return to the Marines?"

"No. That's over for him. But he's getting involved with other injured vets." Gordon hooked a thumb behind the Harley buckle. "There wasn't much action when I did my tour. He saw enough for both of us. I ride because of him."

He turned abruptly and returned to his desk. "What did you want to see me about?"

She'd touched another delicate subject. With Nick and now Gordon. She sat and retrieved her notebook but didn't open it right away. "Your son is brave," she said quietly. "Please thank him for me."

He looked at her with tight eyes. "I will."

She pulled out the news releases and opened the notebook to a blank page. "Nick and I talked about the news releases I gave you drafts of. He wants me to be spokesperson for these releases. But he did say he's had you in mind for that role."

Gordon registered pleased surprise. "He did?"

"Yes. He said a company leader needs to be able to talk with a range of people inside the company and out. He alluded to your experience but didn't give me details. What's that been like?"

He loosened up as he continued to talk about his experiences with employees, customers, and community groups.

As Angela made notes of the man's many engagements, she began to think he might be able to handle spokesperson responsibilities after all.

When he paused, she asked, "Have you ever been interviewed by the media? Maybe in your role with the patriot riders?"

"Once or twice," he snapped.

"How did it go?"

"Fine." His chiseled jaw turned to granite.

Amazing. One word about the media, and he reverted to his closemouthed self.

"Of course, it isn't all about the media," she said.

"Damn right."

She sucked in a little breath as the death-defying roller coaster of Gordon's reactions took her breath away again. OK, forget that. Hiding such an innate hostility toward the media would be no easy task. She clenched her teeth and coached herself to keep smiling. Then ask questions.

"Gordon, getting stories in the press helps change attitudes about the recall. Can you help me understand what your resistance is? If you're the spokesperson, it'll be important to deal with the media."

His eyes landed on a spot over Angela's left shoulder. She couldn't read anything in his face, and after a minute passed, she wondered if he'd respond at all.

Finally, he spoke, his voice hard and flat. "It's none of their business."

Irritation flashed behind her eyes. She could agree. She could disagree. She could tell him that whatever Nick wanted, Nick got, and these releases were what Nick wanted. Working with this guy was flat-out *hard*.

She took a couple of deep, measured breaths, which really wasn't easy to do while holding the smile in place. She handed him the releases, and they agreed she'd incorporate any changes he and Nick suggested.

Leaving would have been the easy thing, but then she'd just have to come back later. She decided to ask him about the employee housing. "There's one other thing: the housing program the company has for new employees."

"How did you hear about that?"

There was no denying the suspicious growl in his tone. If she could have figured out a way to end the meeting right there, she would have. Stuck, she kept her response light. "I've been keeping my ears open for possible stories to feed the media." Her gut told her not to bring Alvaro into it.

"What do you want to know?" He picked up a pencil and began weaving it between his fingers.

"I heard the first month of rent is free. Making sure employees have housing. It's a story that would interest the media."

"It's not a good idea. The housing's all handled by a Chicago company." He hooked his thumb behind his buckle again and continued to work the pencil with his other hand.

She watched the pencil, mesmerized. Shaking her head and tearing away her eyes, she turned to a fresh page in her notebook.

"So which part does Barton handle?" she asked.

"We let employees know about housing options. We pay the first month's rent. Then it's all between them and the management company."

Angela tilted her head. Now she was glad she had asked. She'd been going down a wrong path in thinking about the housing. "That's different than I'd understood. And it's actually a relief. The houses could use some TLC. Who hires the management company?"

Gordon stopped working the pencil, frowned, and ran his hand over the bristle of his close-cropped hair. "I never asked.

I suppose the company that owns the properties. You'd have to go to HR for anything else." He leaned forward. "All I know is they're glad to have a roof over their heads. Is that all?"

"Yes." She stood. "Oh, I met with Alvaro. As you suggested. We had a productive conversation. But we only got started. I'll be talking with him again."

"I know." A nanosecond smile flashed through his gray eyes, a smile that said there was nothing she could do in Hammond that he wouldn't know about.

She did not tell him she and Alvaro had had dinner together or that Alvaro had shown her company housing. Her skin prickled at the thought that he'd tell her he knew that already, too.

* * *

In her motel room that night, Angela sat cross-legged on the bed and forked into her mouth the most tender chunks of carnitas with chili verde she'd ever eaten. She wished Eduardo and Maria were open for breakfast. She also wished she could enjoy the meal with Alvaro. He was the closest thing to a friend she had in Hammond.

The conversation with Nick Barton had sent her back to a file of background articles she'd brought with her from Des Moines. The file lay open on her lap, Maggie Barton's obituary on top. The list of Mrs. Barton's activities was impressive: management of community fundraisers to support the library and fire department, service on the Faith Lutheran Church council, longtime membership with the American Association of University Women, which she'd joined after graduating magna cum laude from Wartburg College. An intelligent woman to complement a successful husband. She'd doted on her husband, the obit said, planning vacations and traveling with him as often as she could. While the obituary didn't list a cause of death, people were encouraged to send memorials to Saint Catherine's Hospice. Maybe cancer.

Angela wondered if Nick had been thinking about retirement. Who knew what plans the two of them may have had? Obituaries were like holiday letters, emphasizing a life's accomplishments while leaving the reader to wonder what pain had been left out.

She wished she knew someone to ask, but her contacts were few. Liz and Gordon would certainly know, but they hadn't left any personal doors open to make her feel comfortable asking them. And she didn't want to appear to be prying. The only other possibility was Alvaro. She could see no downside to asking him. She'd have called him right then if she'd had his cell number.

She licked traces of chili verde from the corners of her mouth and felt herself flush as Alvaro's lips came to mind. She traced her own mouth with her tongue, and her breath quickened as hot sensations raced through her core. She laughed, the feelings of desire so unexpected, so delicious, so inappropriate. Perhaps better she did not have his number, she thought as she licked each fork tine clean. Not a client. Never. No.

Chapter 11

Angela glanced in her rearview mirror. The motorcycle that had roared up behind her three blocks ago was still there. As she followed Alvaro into the parking lot at Saint Catherine's, she expected the cyclist to drive by. Instead, the rider followed. She took one of the few empty places in the parking lot, while the motorcyclist pulled into the space reserved for the parish priest.

She climbed out of her car, locked the doors, and joined Alvaro.

"That takes nerve." She tilted her head at the motorcycle. "I wonder if someone will tell him to move?"

Without responding, Alvaro headed toward the cyclist. She didn't think it was their place to confront the man, but Angela followed anyway.

Clad in black leathers and black construction boots, the cyclist was a bulky man, easily in his fifties, who almost made the Harley look small. He shut off the motorcycle, knocked down the kickstand, and dismounted. Hanging his helmet on the handlebar, the man ran his fingers through a mass of curly black hair streaked with gray. He turned and headed toward them, unzipping his jacket. Only then did Angela see the clerical collar.

"He's the *priest?*" She chided Alvaro with a look. Every clergyman Angela knew looked the part: mild mannered, professionally dressed, at peace and spreading peace. "You could have told me about the motorcycle," she whispered.

"I said you'd be surprised." He grinned. "Hola, Padre. This is Angela Darrah, who I told you about."

"Pleased to meet you, Angela." He held out his hand. "I'm Tom Burke, priest here at Saint Catherine's." Deeply tanned creases on the priest's face attested to ample time recently on the bike, even though it was still spring.

"I encounter something that surprises me every day," she responded, feeling genuinely welcomed by the priest's deep voice and open smile. "Alvaro has told me a few things about the church. I look forward to learning more."

"My pleasure. Let's start downstairs." The priest gestured toward a small door at the side of the church.

"I will be with the boys," Alvaro said, heading up the front steps.

"We'll come by your classroom when we finish," the priest called after him. "This way," he said to Angela, leading her down a set of narrow basement stairs.

"You're an unlikely looking priest," Angela said.

The priest's hearty laugh matched his size. "I wear the collar to reassure my older parishioners I haven't gone totally down the road to hell when I wheel my bike out of the garage. The teenagers think an old guy like me riding a motorcycle is cool. The immigrant community"—he shrugged his shoulders—"they don't know quite what to make of me at first."

At the bottom of the steps, Father Burke stopped with his hand on the doorknob, lowered his voice, and leaned toward Angela. "The truth is, riding makes me feel like I'm living the whole 'Born to be Wild' vibe. Free. No obligations. When I take off, I leave all my problems behind."

He opened the door to a large room sectioned into smaller rooms by collapsible walls. Groups of adults and children clustered around the tables that filled the basement. Even the crowded parking lot had not prepared her for so many people in the church.

The basement hummed with chatter that included a range of languages and accents. The aroma of food cooking permeated the air. Alvaro had told her a meal drew many to the church whether they took classes or not.

"We have day care and after-school programs five days a week," the priest explained. "Adult English classes a couple of times a week." He stopped by a table where Latino men and women hunched over books, puzzling out words.

"*Buenas tardes,* Maria. Good afternoon." The priest spoke with one of the women first in Spanish, then repeated his comment in English. "*¿Cómo estás?* How are you?"

"*Muy bien,* Padre. I am well, Father." She hesitated before adding the more difficult, "*Estoy aprendiendo.* I am learning."

"*Bien!*"

The woman beamed.

"Learning English seems like a steep mountain to climb, yet they do it." Father Burke turned to Angela. "I know I'm only supposed to speak to them in English. But I have a confession: I'm studying Spanish through a computer program, and this reinforces it for me, too."

Angela found his open honesty refreshing. "I expect they get plenty of total immersion. Are you learning Chin, too?"

"Now there's a mountain I haven't tackled yet. We reach out to the Chin families, but they've been more reluctant. There's a group in Des Moines that works with Burmese immigrants. We hope we can get some help from them."

"If it would help, I could contact them when I'm in Des Moines next, or someone from my agency could." Angela's stomach growled. She clapped a hand to her middle. "How rude!"

Burke responded with another laugh and an invitation. "You must join us for supper."

"Why, thank you. It does smell tasty." She took in the space, teeming with activity. "It must be a challenge keeping everything organized."

"I have a lot of help."

"From the looks of this and what you describe, all of Saint Catherine's must be involved."

"It's been better lately, but it hasn't always been a smooth path."

"How so?"

"Like a lot of churches, Saint Catherine's mission used to involve sending money overseas. Write the check. Feel good. Actually, I thought overseas mission work might be for me. But then, four years ago, I was assigned here."

"You were disappointed?"

"At first I was. But God had a lesson for me. In being humble. In trusting his plan. When we saw people right in our own town who needed help, it became more complicated. Some parishioners were eager to get involved right away. Take Linda over there." He pointed to a slim woman wearing jeans and a sweatshirt sporting the Hammond school's Mighty Oaks mascot. With her long blond hair secured in a ponytail and large brown-plastic-rimmed glasses, the woman looked more like a teenager than a teacher. "She teaches in the local grade school, then comes here three nights a week to teach adults English. She knows the children pick up languages faster, but if the parents aren't literate in English, their children will have a hard time succeeding and there is more discord in the homes."

"I'm impressed. That's a real time commitment."

"The more people who teach, the more manageable the task." He surveyed the room and then turned to Angela. "Perhaps you would consider teaching a class? Alvaro thought you'd be interested in helping, and we can always use more hands."

"He thinks so, huh? I don't know how I could. I'm only in town for a short while. A couple of months." She backed off mentally before realizing she'd taken an actual step back.

"That's enough time to start."

"Besides, I've never taught before."

"Ah." The priest appeared to consider what she'd said. "Well, think about it. Money doesn't fill every need. We need people, too, but only people who want to serve."

He moved a few feet away from the class and Angela followed, feeling strangely disappointed in herself.

Father Burke ushered her into a small windowless room that might once have been a storage closet but now served as a small library. "We can talk here for a few minutes." They settled into two metal folding chairs that were more utilitarian than comfortable. "We are fortunate many do want to help. Some in the congregation aren't yet convinced."

"Why not?" Angela hoped he would add some context to what she'd experienced in the bank.

"Lots of reasons. Personal prejudices come into play. And history. Many parishioners had family who worked in the packing plant at some point. Or they did themselves. Maybe a high school or college summer job."

A summer job in the plant? Angela's most challenging summer job had been waitressing at a food stand at the county fair. For six solid hours each night, she'd never stopped moving. The money had been good but the work exhausting. She imagined working at the fair was a day at the beach compared to a day in a packing plant. That was a job she didn't want to try, especially if Gordon Ryker was the one throwing work her way.

She asked, "Gordon Ryker . . . you know him?"

The priest nodded. "It is because of him we serve chicken so often. A donation from Barton Packing."

"Really? I didn't know the company did that." It surprised her Gordon hadn't mentioned it when she'd asked about programs Barton had with local organizations.

"For some time now."

"I'll ask him about it next time I see him." It was the perfect topic for a news release. Given his involvement, maybe Gordon would even be spokesperson. "Gordon says local people don't really want the jobs. Do you agree?"

Father Burke considered the question. "It's complicated. When he says 'local' people, he may be referring to local white people. The plant jobs are hard, and it's true many white people don't line up for them. Particularly those who remember how the pay used to be when the plant was unionized. They believe if people of color—citizens or new immigrants—weren't here and willing to work for less, then wages would be higher."

"Is that true?"

"It may or may not be. But this is nothing new. History tells us immigrants fill a lot of lower-paying jobs or any job, really, that Americans who've been here longer don't want to do. In New York in the early nineteenth century, it was Irish and Italian immigrants. If the available workforce is plentiful, companies can pay less. At the Postville plant, it was eastern Europeans who'd come to work, as well as Latinos. Here it's Latinos and Somalis. And now Chin.

"The first Latinos who came to Hammond to work in the plant arrived more than thirty years ago. Before Nick Barton took over the plant. So they are 'local' now, compared to the immigrants you see here."

"The unions helped with the pay, didn't they?"

"They did for a while. I don't know all that history. Someone at the company could fill you in, I expect. There's not a union now," Father Burke continued. "Politics also come into play. Everyone hears the rhetoric about undocumented workers. Securing the border. Building walls. Some folks don't believe we should help anyone who isn't here legally."

"That's something I'm curious about." She glanced back to ensure the door was closed. "Are they here legally?" She'd absorbed so many news stories on immigrants that she found herself wondering that very thing when she saw people of color, particularly Latinos. It annoyed her that legal status was one of her first thoughts, but that was simply a fact.

"It's not for me to say. Besides, legal status isn't really the issue, as I see it. We deal with the reality in front of us. These people are here, so we care for them. As well as we can."

"How does Barton Packing help?"

"The food donation is useful, but I think they could do more."

"Like what?"

"Barton Packing is always bringing in more people. Sometimes busloads at a time. How are they supposed to get along when they arrive? Many speak limited English, even those who have lived a long time in the US. They have families in El Salvador. Guatemala. Texas. Mexico. They send most of what they earn back home. They live here on a shoestring. The things Barton Packing does are mainly a public-relations fix. No offense intended," he hastened to add.

"None taken," she said. "Please continue."

"The people we serve here are citizens, they're people with green cards who are working on English, they're immigrants new to the country, and they're kids trying to catch up in school. The only concrete aid is the chicken, and that comes about once a quarter. We appreciate every box, but it's nothing we can count on. The churches can only do so much."

She could tell the priest was frustrated, but Barton Packing couldn't be expected to handle all those needs, could it? "They do provide housing," she said in her client's defense.

Father Burke shook his head. "A company store is what that is."

"A company store?"

"A postslavery term. Tenant farmers, loggers, miners, railroad workers—they all had to buy everything from the store the landowner set up. It was the only place they could buy on credit, but the cost was so high they wound up owing more than they earned. So they were never able to get out of debt, let alone get ahead. In the end, they owed their souls to the company store, as an old song went."

The houses could use some maintenance, but the priest's assessment felt a little unfair. The housing Barton arranged provided a real benefit to employees. She said, "I know some of the houses aren't very attractive, but there's limited housing in Hammond."

"It's more than that. The rent is so steep. People come to us for help when they can't make the payments."

"I don't know about rent rates, only that Barton Packing pays for the first month. Afterward, everything is handled by a management company."

"Is that right? I didn't know," he said.

Hearing about the programs implemented throughout the week at Saint Catherine's, seeing the basement full of people hungry for learning and food, watching the teachers and cooks and helpers who took on the responsibility as volunteers, Angela couldn't imagine how they could do more. How could a church, even in such a small community, possibly be responsible for everything? Maybe Barton could do more to help its employees.

The priest's comments echoed in her head. *We deal with the reality in front of us. These people are here.*

Father Burke looked at the wall clock. "Alvaro is finishing up with his class now. It's in the sanctuary, the one place we hope the older boys will be more quiet. I'll take you there, and then we'll all come back down to eat."

When he opened the door, the aroma of toasted Parmesan cheese wafting through the air made her mouth water. "I appreciate your input, Father," Angela said as he ushered her past a window where women scooped lasagna onto plates and added garlic bread as a line formed.

"Please join us. No one leaves here hungry."

"That's kind of you. I'd be happy to pay for my meal."

"No need."

She dug a ten-dollar bill out of her purse. "To help someone," she insisted. Her father always pulled out his wallet when they went through a potluck line at their church. She pressed the bill into his hand. He didn't refuse.

"Over supper, I'll introduce you to Linda," he said. "She can answer your questions about teaching."

She smiled. She didn't have questions about teaching. Yet he'd planted a seed, and even in the past few minutes, the idea had grown into a tiny plant of possibility.

"We can always use more English teachers," he said. "Even for a month."

Halfway up a set of stairs, she asked, "Father Burke? When you get on your motorcycle, are you trying to get away from all this?"

The priest looked back at her. "We all may wonder at some point whether we can escape what we have to do. But when I'm out on my bike, I hear God assure me that together anything is possible. I always come back ready to dive back in." He climbed a few more steps and spoke again. "I think you'd enjoy working with us."

Angela smiled; the man was unstoppable. Optimistic in a way she expected encouraged parishioners to get involved. His sincere persistence and the genuine need of the people he served made her feel needed.

* * *

Talking with the priest helped her begin to pull apart the tangled threads of how Iowans talked about immigrants and jobs. In the articles she'd read, she assumed the people quoted saying that immigrants were taking "their jobs" were white, based on their names. When someone said, "Local people didn't want those jobs," they seemed to mean that white people didn't want those jobs. Plenty of people of color did take the jobs. She quickly figured out that "local" equaled "white."

Yet "local" didn't necessarily mean "white" in towns dominated by packing plants. These towns had a vastly different demographic mix. In these towns, people of color made up as much as half the population. Many had lived in these towns for decades, possibly were born and raised in them.

Yet at some point in the larger conversation across the country, it appeared all people of color were lumped under the umbrella of "immigrants" simply based on the color of their skin. She'd found another term—foreign-born—that helped tease apart the meaning of "immigrant." While "foreign-born" could accurately describe a certain segment of people, it failed to consider citizenship or legal documents. It seemed no label was entirely accurate and any label glossed over a complicated subject.

She spent a good hour that night sorting out the interconnectedness of the issues. When she finally decided to stop thinking about it for the night, she knew her understanding still wasn't entirely clear or even necessarily accurate in all respects, but she was beginning to get a sense of the situation. How to communicate that clearly, accurately, and concisely remained to be figured out.

She felt she'd made a significant step simply in realizing that her own thinking and the way she spoke on the topic were jumbled. She thought of Alvaro, and it occurred to her that ditching all labels might be the best route. He was a person.

Chapter 12

"I appreciate how you've helped me meet with employees," Angela said as they straightened up the small room after their last employee discussion group.

"Cualquier cosa para usted." Alvaro repeated. "Anything for you" had become a running joke.

"You probably didn't know what you were signing up for when Gordon made you my plant contact."

He shrugged. "It makes the days different."

"You've worked magic to get me time with people. And make the time productive." She'd proposed small-group meetings with employees without realizing how complicated it was to pull people off the line. Asking them to give up their breaks was unfair, never mind that fifteen minutes was barely time to introduce everyone and explain the purpose, let alone get answers to her many questions.

Alvaro had helped by explaining the purpose of the meetings ahead of time and figuring out a way to pull each group off the line for a half hour. She'd brought boxes of donuts and paid for drinks, small tokens to compensate the employees for their time. Gordon gave grudging support to the effort, though he expressed doubt she'd get anything useful out of them.

Ultimately, she learned more than the answers to her questions, as responses touched on the plant, history, culture, religion, and family life.

The first group included those who had each worked at Barton Packing for fifteen to twenty years. In the group were two white men. The other six were Hispanic men and women.

"The packing plant was a prime job everyone wanted," said Jack, a burly man who drove a forklift and planned to retire at the end of the year. He'd been at the plant for twenty-seven years. "When I started here, I made sixteen dollars an hour." He looked around the table and added, "I still make that." He laughed heartily and the others joined him.

Angela expected he'd told that story more than once. "How does that happen?" she asked.

"Oh, hell. People think the lower wages are because the immigrants work for cheap. But that's not all of it. When the company went out of business and Barton took over, he forced the union out. He slashed wages, and what could we do? We took the jobs even though we earned half as much. At least we had work."

A sturdy Latino named Jorge related that he came to Iowa from Arizona when he was sixteen because relatives told him about the jobs. "When I got my first paycheck, I couldn't believe it was so much money. I do not complain about the work. I have a house and a family."

Jack chimed in again. "Sure, the immigrants will take lower wages, but I don't blame them. All they wanna do is support their families. Just like me. You won't find harder workers than these guys." He nodded to the others.

None of them disputed the hard work and long hours. They wore their ability to handle it as a badge of honor.

"They hired a white boy right out of high school," said Jorge with a snort. "We knew he wouldn't last."

"Not even a week," Jack confirmed with a dismissive head shake.

"One thing is that we don't want our children to work here," said Maria, who came in wearing three gloves on her right hand for warmth but only two on her left so she retained flexibility with the knife. After she removed the gloves, she rubbed her hands incessantly as she talked. "We want our kids to go to high school and college. They will come back to Hammond and start other businesses."

Angela noticed that everyone nodded in agreement with Maria's statement. She wondered how many families were able to achieve that dream.

Alvaro translated for Mariana, who spoke mostly Spanish.

"I know if I learned English," she said, "I could have more opportunities, but I cannot take the time for classes. My husband used to work here, but he's ill. So I must work every hour I can."

Each group revealed some new aspect of plant life. The most challenging meeting was with the Somali men. The barrier there was religious custom rather than language. For this group, Alvaro suggested he should do the talking. Angela could be there to observe, but not talk.

"It is as it should be. No?" he teased when she objected to this subservient role.

"You better be joking." She stabbed him with a visual dart. She acquiesced when he explained that many of the men were Muslims who customarily did not talk directly with women who weren't family members.

Unused to avoiding people's eyes as they talked, Angela fidgeted. She pulled at a thread in her cuff, doodled in the margins of her notebook, spotted a stain on her slacks. But she became so engaged with what people were saying she gradually relaxed into the role of note taker.

The youngest and most vocal of the Somalis was Mahad, a wiry young man of medium height with a triangular face and deep-set black eyes. Mahad came to the United States as a ten-year-old with his parents in 1995 and spoke English well.

When Alvaro asked about challenges they faced, the conversation moved immediately to having time for prayer.

"We only need ten minutes," Mahad said. "To take off the apron, pray, and return."

"Four times we pray in our homes. Only one time we pray here. And they say we don't have the time," another man added.

"When we first came here, it was not a problem for us to leave the line for this short time," Mahad explained. "Now it is."

A group of Muslim women they met with later—a group Angela took the lead in questioning—reinforced the men's concerns. Faiza, a woman with a round face and expressive eyes, said, "If I stop my prayer time, everything is hard for me." Other women bobbed heads in agreement. When Angela probed into how their lives were made harder, the women's answers revealed that prayer was so integral to their lives that everyday tasks like cooking and interacting with family members, even how they felt about themselves, were "off" if they did not pray regularly.

This unfamiliar culture had fascinated Angela. She had thought of how Alvaro prayed before meals. And how awkward that felt to her the first time they ate together. Would his day be disrupted if he didn't pray?

Over supper with Alvaro at Eduardo's, Angela revisited the comments the Muslims made about prayer.

"Did I understand it right? Were they able to pray before and now they can't?" She cut off a bite of chile relleno while he answered.

"They can pray, but depending on the shift, it may not be possible to let someone go," he explained. "It is up to the shift supervisor to decide."

"I can understand that, but Mahad made it sound like it was about more. Did something change?"

A frown made Alvaro look older and especially serious. "It has been a while. I am trying to remember." He concentrated. "Two years ago, I think, Mr. Ryker made a new system where employees get points if they do something wrong. If they get enough points, they can be fired."

"Sounds similar to how getting too many points can cost you your driver's license. Do the points go away after a time?"

"I do not know about that."

"What does that have to do with the prayers?"

"Supervisors must approve if an employee leaves the line during a shift. Some supervisors say a worker can leave, but he will get a point on his record."

Angela frowned. "That seems harsh." She knew little about the Islamic faith, but from what she'd read, she knew regular prayer went beyond religious beliefs. It became ingrained as part of a Muslim's lifestyle, as the Muslim women had described. "How often does someone get points for prayer?"

He shrugged. "I don't know. It is not a problem on all shifts or with all employees or with all supervisors."

"I imagine that inconsistency would cause anxiety. Have you ever given an employee points for going to prayer?"

"No. To have someone leave the line for a few minutes is not a problem."

"Where do people go to pray?" she asked.

"They use the room where we store chemicals."

She imagined that for a moment. "Not exactly a spiritual place. Or private."

"It is quiet and near the line. That is all they have asked."

"Hmm."

The conversation made her wonder about religious freedom. Were companies required to provide a prayer space and give people time off to use it?

Alvaro straightened up. "Mr. Ryker just came in."

She looked over her shoulder. Gordon headed to their table. "Hi, Gordon." She smiled.

"I see you found the best Mexican food in town," he said.

"Alvaro introduced me. It really is good." Given their conversation, his appearance was timely. "Would you like to join us?"

"No time. I'm getting carryout," he said. "I see they've got it ready."

"OK. I'll catch you at the office."

Gordon left as abruptly as he'd arrived.

"He's an interesting guy," Angela said.

"I don't think I've ever seen him in here before," Alvaro said.

"I'm actually glad he didn't join us. I've had enough of work talk." She slid her empty plate to the side. After spending her days in the plant, where most of the staff she interacted with were as old as her parents and where she always felt she had to keep her professional guard up, Angela enjoyed spending time with someone her own age. Sure, he was a client, but their collaborating made him seem more like one of the team at Sherborn-Watts.

"What will you do when you get back to El Salvador?" she asked.

"I will eat. My mother is waiting to fix me *pupusas.*"

"It will be strange, don't you think?"

"Eating pupusas strange?" He looked at her with a dead solemn face. "I do not think she forgets how to make them."

She laughed. He took pleasure in pretending he did not understand, even though she knew he did. "You know what I mean. To be in El Salvador after so many years? You've lived your whole adult life in the United States."

His attention turned inward. "It is true. I can only say I do not know. I am pulled from both sides. I miss my family. But that is changing, too. My sister Eva was eleven when I left. Now she is married with a baby. I have never met her husband. My mother sends letters and pictures. We Skype once a week." The yearning tone of his voice whispered nostalgia.

"Would you live with them when you go back?"

"For a while. They would not have room to take me in for a long time. Mama lives with Eva. And I don't know about a job."

"You said you wanted to create jobs for a lot of people. Could you start your own company, or would you have to work for someone else to subsidize it?"

"You have many questions and I have few answers."

"True." She smiled. "Please let me know if I'm overstepping. You are so good with the children at Saint Catherine's. Do you see yourself doing something with kids in El Salvador?"

"I would like the kids to have opportunities as I had. To learn. Maybe to come north. My high-school teacher Mr. Morales looked after me. He saw I was good in school, so he kept me after school every day to study. And did not let me walk home alone. If he did not, I could be in a gang now." The excitement faded from his voice. "Or I could be like my father. In the wrong place and dead."

"I understand." She sought to return the discussion to a happier place. "But you could start a class or help kids find ways to go to school?"

"I would have to make money. That is why I got the engineering degree."

"Your degree prepared you for many things. Not only a packing plant. Engineers are valuable everywhere. What does your town need? What do the people need? There must be other people trying to make El Salvador better? People you could work with?"

"You make me wonder if I am thinking too narrow."

"Let's brainstorm," Angela said. "What do you like about what you have here? If you know what it is, maybe you can make it happen there, too."

"Can I borrow a piece of paper?"

She tore out several sheets from the notebook she kept in her purse. "I don't need them back."

He grinned as he began to draw a chart.

She saw he labeled columns *US Pro, US Con, ES Pro, ES Con*. He wrote something in the US Pro column and then immediately erased it.

"What was that?" she asked. "The first thing you thought of for why you like it here?"

"It does not matter," he said, his dark eyes unreadable.

"It all matters," Angela insisted. "What was it?"

Seconds passed before he said, "It is safe here."

"Oh," she said, thrown by the unexpected response. She searched his face. To live in fear, she simply couldn't imagine. Without reason, she was intensely afraid for him. And for his family. The emotions must have shown on her face, because he tapped his pencil on the table to get her attention.

"Hey," he said. "It's all right."

She forced a smile. "I think you should put safety on the list anyway."

"If you say so, boss."

As they continued talking, he put ideas in columns, his engineering mind bringing order to a problem with many questions and few answers.

Chapter 13

A few days later, Angela sought out Gordon to follow up on the salary history and Muslim prayer questions. She related Jack's experience of making essentially the same wage now as he did twenty-seven years ago.

"When Nick took over the plant, he pushed out the union. He had to," Gordon explained. "The union had negotiated such high wages and benefits there was no way Nick could still make a profit."

"Why would people agree to such a salary cut?"

"They had a choice: job or no job. They knew the work. They wanted to live in Hammond. The whole town wanted that plant open. Nick made it happen."

"But shouldn't wages be higher now?"

"We're competitive with the industry. We have to go farther to recruit, but we can always find people who want jobs."

She pursued the question of time for Muslim employees to pray.

"We give them a place for it, and we don't stand in their way."

"Is it true they might be penalized with points for leaving the line?"

"Everybody has a choice. We're running a business here. We have to keep the line running. If they don't want to do it, they can find another job."

His answers sounded harsh. Yes, the "business" was processing chicken; it was also people. Jack, whose pay had been flat for twenty-seven years. Maria, who never stopped rubbing her hands to get them warm. Mahad and Faiza, who needed fifteen minutes of prayer to make the day right. She couldn't get their faces out of her head. Was this the "full business reality" Gordon had referred to during the tour on her first day?

* * *

The more she thought about Father Burke's request that she teach a class at Saint Catherine's, the more intrigued she became. It wasn't why she'd come to Hammond, but it would give her something useful to fill her evenings. When she told Dave about the opportunity, he encouraged her.

"It'll help you understand the town better, and you may make helpful connections," he said.

Facing her first class, Angela wondered if she'd made a terrible mistake. She peeked around the end of one of the collapsible walls that formed her classroom and not for the first time considered sneaking out of the church before classes started. She'd never taught English before. She'd never taught any kind of class to children. Adults, sure. Coaching adults, she was fine. But kids?

Beyond the divider, six boys and two girls crowded around a child-sized table. They were eight or nine years old, maybe ten. These kids would be helpful connections? Yeah, right.

She'd slept little the night before, and all day at Barton Packing she'd been able to think of little except this class. She'd outlined the hour, identified the key teaching points, practiced what she'd say over and over, putting as much effort into preparing for her eight students as she ever had for a client meeting.

She peeked in the room again. Two minutes until the classes started.

A tap on her shoulder drew her around.

"Don't tell me you're hiding," Linda said. The elementary-school teacher Angela had met on her first visit to Saint Catherine's had taught her the basics of teaching English as a second language with such enthusiasm that Angela had begun to think she could actually do it. Now she wasn't so sure.

"Don't make me do this," she pleaded. "I'm not ready."

"You are more than ready," Linda insisted. "Besides, they're sponges. Whatever you say will be helpful. It's all English to them." She grinned.

Linda's joke sailed right by Angela's anxiety. "What if they hate me?"

"Oh, please. It's a handful of eight-year-olds." Linda grasped Angela's shoulders and held her at arm's length. She shook her head, her ponytail whipping from side to side. "If you care about them—and I know you do—they'll love you."

"I don't know . . ." Angela cast a doubtful eye toward the kids.

"You'll be fine. Now get on in there." Linda nudged her toward the classroom. "I have to get to my class."

Angela inhaled Linda's courage, adopted what she hoped was a confident look, and marched to the one solid wall of the classroom, largely covered by a whiteboard. On each side of the whiteboard hung line drawings of cats, dogs, horses, apples, loaves of bread, and glasses of milk. Each picture bore the English word for the item portrayed. Each picture had been colored by children. Presumably an assignment from the teacher who'd had the class before.

At the front of the class, she turned to the kids, who stared at her with dark, eager eyes. She amped up her smile another hundred watts.

"Hello." She spoke more loudly than necessary. "My name is . . . Angela." She wrote her name on the whiteboard.

Someone sounded out the letters as she wrote. She glanced over her shoulder. The voice belonged to a bony-thin boy with round features and serious pitch-black eyes.

"Well done," she said. Abandoning her script, she sat down so they were all at eye level. "What is your name?" she asked the boy who had sounded out her name.

"Emilio."

"I'm pleased to meet you, Emilio." Angela shook his hand. "Now I'd like to meet the rest of you." She turned to a girl squirming in her chair. "My name is Angela. What is your name?"

The girl teetered on the edge of the seat. "Mi name es Sofia."

"Hello, Sofia." Angela shook the girl's hand. "It is nice to meet you." In her excitement, the girl tipped off the chair.

Angela reached out and caught her. "Careful there," she said, righting chair and child.

Around the table she went. Some of the children looked puzzled. She touched her chest. "My name is Angela. Angela," she repeated. Twice she switched to Spanish. "*¿Cómo es su nombre?* What is your name?"

It was as simple as that. They introduced themselves. She shook each child's hand. She wrote each name on the whiteboard. Emilio. Sofia. Manuel. Juan. Maria. Ramon. Carlos. Jorge.

They counted from one to ten. Named objects like ball, cat, and dog, and spoke simple sentences. Colored pictures. They all smiled a lot. The children were quick to learn and so keen to please, clamoring to be the first to answer, sparring for crayons, correcting each other's mistakes, not always kindly but with great enthusiasm.

Linda poked her head into Angela's space. "About finished?" she asked.

Angela looked at her watch; the hour was over. So soon.

She clapped her hands twice and the kids looked up from their coloring. "Are you hungry?" she asked. They knew what that meant. "*Bien trabajo.* Good job. Now go." She shooed them out and they fled, absorbed into the crowd gathering for supper.

Only Emilio remained. "You can go, too." She pointed him toward the food line. He continued to color the picture of a horse. "Do you want to stay, Emilio?" she asked. He colored faster.

"Looks like it went well," Linda said.

"Yes, it was fun. Exhilarating." She exhaled with her hand over her heart. "Exhausting."

Emilio finished his drawing and followed the other kids. Once all the children were gone, Angela began to pick up crayons, slotting them into a plastic Folgers coffee container. The adrenaline that had jacked her up earlier drained away. She straightened up, hands on hips, arching her back.

"I'm whipped," she admitted. "But I didn't realize it until this minute. What happened to the teacher before me? Did she die of exhaustion?" She laughed.

Linda returned the laughter as she pushed the folding panels back to the walls. "You'll get used to it. It's a new class. You're the first teacher."

"Wow. I really am impressed now. The kids are so quick."

"Most of them go to the local school. I overheard you send them off, speaking Spanish."

"Every once in a while, I slipped some in," Angela acknowledged. She slid chairs under the table as they talked. "It made things go smoother when they didn't get what I was saying."

"The more English they hear, the faster they pick it up. When you speak Spanish to them, it tells them they don't have to speak English all the time. So they don't."

"Then why did Father Burke think it was important I speak Spanish when he talked me into this gig?"

"It's not critical, but it can help. Particularly with the parents. It's harder for them to pick up English." Linda pushed the last chairs up to the table. "And you know you don't have to do all this cleaning up. The kids can help."

"I guess I never thought about asking them."

"Not *asking*." Linda grinned. "*Telling*. Any kid will get out of work if they can. You need to tell them it's part of their responsibility. Unless you want to be cleaning up after them forever."

"I didn't think of that."

"You must not work with kids much."

"I confess. First time," Angela admitted.

"You did great. I was keeping an ear on your class. You'll catch on." Linda threw a friendly arm around Angela's shoulders. "Are you eating here? Want to get supper?"

"Sure." Angela scanned the now-tidy space. As they were about to leave, she noticed Emilio standing behind Linda.

"Emilio," she said. "I thought you were going to eat. Are you waiting for me?"

He looked at her shyly and didn't speak.

"On second thought, go ahead, Linda. I'll catch up."

She pulled out a chair and beckoned the boy to join her. "Come. Sit, Emilio." Angela pulled out a second chair.

He did not speak.

"Where is your family?" she asked.

Throughout the class, the boy had shown a better command of English than anyone else in the group. Now, he appeared not to understand. His eyes darted past her and then back. He looked confused. For a second, she thought he might bolt. Ignoring Linda's advice about English, she switched to Spanish.

"*¿Dónde están tus padres?* Where are your parents?"

Again his eyes darted away. He seemed afraid, but she couldn't imagine why.

Finally, he answered, "They are not here. *Pero mi madre está en camino.*"

"Oh, you're waiting for her." She smiled, relieved to understand at last. "Are you hungry? *¿Tienes hambre?*"

He nodded.

"Your mother can join us when she gets here."

She took him by the hand, and they joined the queue waiting to fill plates. Though the boy had been talkative in class, now he stood silent, looking toward the door every few seconds. She'd made him uncomfortable, and she didn't know how to continue the conversation. They found places to sit, and he began eating as soon as they sat down. She persisted in asking questions.

"How old are you?"

"Diez."

"In English, please."

"Ten."

"Do you have brothers and sisters?"

"Sí. Dos hermanos y dos hermanas."

She considered asking for English again, but let it pass. "Do they come here for classes, too?"

"No están aquí."

"Do they come sometimes?"

He looked at her as though she was the one who did not understand. He scooped an overly large helping of enchilada into his mouth.

Lost in translation, she thought. She was exhausted, but she tried yet again.

"This is good, isn't it?" she said.

He pushed another forkful into his mouth.

She stifled a sigh. Maybe he was as tired as she was. It was easier for her simply to eat, too, so she didn't ask any more questions and kept her eyes on her plate, occasionally glancing at the boy. During the class, he'd acted with confidence that made him seem older than ten, but now his small frame made him look younger, more vulnerable.

"Hola, Emilio. Angela. ¿Que pasa?"

Emilio looked up. Delight transformed his face when he saw Alvaro approaching.

"Hola, Alvaro!" Emilio raised a fist. Alvaro balanced a glass of milk on his plate and obliged with a fist bump.

As happy to see Alvaro as Emilio was, she gestured to the chair next to Emilio. "Join us if you don't have other plans."

"Thanks." Alvaro settled in. He positioned his plate and glass, then closed his eyes and crossed himself.

While the first time she'd seen him pray before a meal had made her uncomfortable, she now realized saying grace before eating was as much a part of him as the dimple in his cheek. She admired his devotion.

"Emilio is in my class," she said when he began to eat. "Since his parents aren't here yet, we're getting to know each other."

Alvaro stopped, fork halfway to his mouth. His eyes squinted, sending a clear message of caution.

"What?" she asked.

Alvaro turned to Emilio. "The boys are going out to play basketball." He pointed toward a group at the next table. "Are you going, too?"

"Yes." The boy's face lit up with enthusiasm. "I am good," he said to Angela.

"I bet you are." She smiled. He was such a cute little boy. So eager. And once again, he understood English just fine.

"Go on out. Take your plate to the kitchen first," Alvaro ordered.

"OK." Emilio pushed a last bite into his mouth, gulped down the rest of his milk, and grabbed his plate and silverware. *"Adios, maestra."* He smiled shyly at Angela. Then he took off for the kitchen.

"No running in church, Emilio," Alvaro said. "You know that."

"Comprendo." Emilio saluted Alvaro. He exaggerated a slow-motion run, watching Alvaro with a grin. When his foot hit the first step of the stairs to the parking lot, he took one more look at Alvaro, laughed out loud, and ran.

"He's a good boy," Alvaro said.

"I know. He's really smart. He already knows much more English than the other kids his age. Maybe he should be in a more advanced class."

"He picks it up fast. He'll be good for the others."

"I was glad you showed up when you did. He was OK in class, but he clammed up when it was just the two of us. So, thank you." She captured a piece of lettuce with her fork. "I made it through one class, and I thought it went OK. But now I wonder. Maybe I'm not cut out for working with kids."

"Are you always perfect at what you do? Even the first time?"

She grinned. "No. But I think I should be."

"You'll be fine. With Emilio, too."

"Why did you look at me that way? And why did you send him away?"

"You need to know about him."

She cocked her head. "That sounds serious."

"Emilio came here only a couple of months ago. From Honduras."

"With his family?"

"He came with some other boys. His mother believed he would be safer here than in Honduras. She paid a *coyotaje*, a human smuggler, to bring him as far as the border."

"But he said his mother was coming," she said.

He shook his head. "He says that sometimes. He hopes she will come, but I do not think so."

She stopped eating and tried to absorb the idea of a child as young as Emilio traveling with strangers all the way from Central America to the United States. She remembered the anxiety of being separated from her parents the first time they sent her to eastern Iowa to spend a week on her aunt and uncle's farm. Even though she'd been eleven years old, she'd grown so homesick her parents wound up coming for her early.

"Where does he live?"

"Emilio is living with the Muñoz family until his hearing. Cesar Muñoz is his uncle."

"A hearing for what?"

"To decide what happens next."

"You mean he might have to go back?"

Alvaro nodded. "Or he might be able to stay. I do not know how it works."

The anxiety she felt earlier intensified. In the past, she'd skimmed over articles about immigration issues. From time to time, she'd thought through how she would counsel the various sides of an issue if the governor or Iowa's congressional delegation were her client. What messages would she craft for them? An academic exercise, since Sherborn-Watts did not take on politicians as clients. But this business of children coming to the US alone, this wasn't something she'd read about. No, this involved a real child. The boy with the impish smile and daring sense of humor who'd just sat with her and shared a meal.

In her reading, she hadn't separated immigrant children from immigrant adults. She had not imagined children making the trek of thousands of dangerous miles alone. If she'd visualized anyone traveling alone, the person was seventeen or eighteen or older. Not nine or ten. Not a child like Emilio.

She tried to imagine Emilio's mother. What would it take for a mother to send her ten-year-old thousands of miles away on his own? Could she sleep at night wondering what had happened to him? Along the way? In Iowa?

Chapter 14

"Father Burke was delighted you agreed to donate chicken every month for the church meal program," Angela reported, sharing the compliment equally between Nick and Gordon when they met in Nick's office that morning. "He's grateful for your generosity. He asked me to tell you to come for supper whenever you have time. As a small thank-you," Angela added.

"Credit to Gordon," Nick said. "It was his idea to make quarterly donations."

"He already thanked me," Gordon said. "After church on Sunday."

"You attend Saint Catherine's?" Angela asked.

"Since I was born," Gordon said.

She fought to keep the surprise off her face. Why hadn't he said anything before?

Earlier, when she brought up the idea of a regular donation, Gordon had growled, "You think we're made out of money?" But Nick had liked the idea and overruled his right-hand man.

However, both men had dug in their heels when she suggested getting the story out to the media. Nick because he and his wife believed donations should be anonymous, given without an ulterior motive; Gordon because he believed once everyone knew you gave to one, other churches would want a handout, too. She couldn't refute either argument.

Still, their resistance stymied her. She'd been so certain it was exactly the kind of thing they'd said they wanted. Reluctantly, she had given up on the idea.

Balking at her suggestion to offer more frequent donations made even less sense now that she knew Gordon was a church member. "Well, the invitation's open if you want to see how your donation is being used." She moved on. "I've talked with the influencers you recommended. And gathered historical info from HR and others in Barton Packing."

"What's your takeaway from that?" Nick asked.

She outlined the two points of view. The business community knew Hammond would be hard pressed to survive without the packing company. Because of that, Barton could continue as it had been with little involvement in the community. Meanwhile, organizations like the hospital and school were hard pressed by the dramatic increase in people using their services. They looked to Barton to take a leading role in helping to figure out solutions.

While Nick appeared to consider both viewpoints, Gordon sank back in his chair, arms folded across his chest, a bored look on his face. The man could be congenial, even show a level of polish in his interactions. Or he could be the polar opposite. The problem was predicting which Gordon she would get. She focused her eye contact and energy on Nick.

"Some passionately support newcomers; others wish things would go back to the way they were before. Though I doubt anyone really expects the immigrants to go away."

"Did anyone offer ideas or solutions?" Nick asked.

"Or are they just complaining?" Gordon asked.

Angela clenched her teeth as she absorbed the sneer in Gordon's voice. He really knew how to push her buttons. Who did he think was supposed to solve this problem? Everyone had a stake. She elected not to answer his question directly.

"Barton Packing is one of the major employers in Hammond with a diverse workforce. Anyone could reasonably look to you for leadership," she said.

She handed the men copies of a memo outlining the results of her research into immigration history and the interviews
she'd had with governmental and NGO sources in Des Moines.
They scanned the memo as she summarized findings relevant to
Hammond.

"Your recommendation?" Nick asked when she finished.

"Dave and I believe it will be useful to benchmark what
other Iowa plants and communities are doing. It's likely everyone is doing something. With varying degrees of success. With
that information we can shape specific recommendations for
Barton Packing."

"For more money, I suppose," Gordon interjected.

His sarcastic comment got to her. "I'm already here," she
said. "You need to . . ." Belatedly, she saw the smirk behind his
gray eyes. He'd thrown out bait and she'd taken it like a hungry
trout. She swallowed her last words.

"Gordon," Nick said, his voice weary. He rubbed his eyes
with his fingertips, lifting his glasses without taking them off. He re-
positioned the glasses before continuing. He turned to her. "Angela,
you're trying to take us places we aren't sure we want to go."

Angela's teeth clenched. Nick spoke kindly, but his words
raised her ire. Truthfully, if all they wanted was news releases—
which they often wouldn't let her send out—she didn't need to
uproot her life and live in Hammond. Nasty retorts crowded behind her teeth, but she bit them back. Her job was to get along
with everyone.

Just get along. It was the advice she heard from her teachers,
from her mother, and, in a multitude of ways, from Dave about
her job. *Avoid bad feelings,* they said. *Keep the peace,* they said. To her
it always felt as though they meant, *Don't say what you really mean.*
She knew she was being petty, that she should try to be more
diplomatic and breach the gap to find common ground, but right
now, she was frustrated.

She centered her breathing and spoke to Nick. "Nick," she
said. "Everything I've heard from people"—she pointed to the

document she'd given them—"indicates Barton Packing has an opportunity to move beyond the recall and gain goodwill. Yes, there's a cost to implementing some of the programs, but there could also be a significant return on that investment in terms of goodwill with the community and employees. There are probably as many ways to go forward as there are people in Hammond with an opinion. Which would be everyone."

Nick laughed. "No doubt she's right about that. Eh, Gordon?"

Gordon snorted a laugh, his granite-cutting jaw still set tight and hard.

"Nick, of course you can always choose to do nothing. But I expect you grew the company in part by learning what other people did and improving on it. So doesn't it make sense to do the same thing here?"

Nick's attention drifted toward the wall of seagull prints. Without being obvious, Angela peeked at Gordon; his eyes were trained on Nick. Unlike previous times when Nick appeared to be lost in thought, this time she could see the man actively considering. He lifted his chin, tapped an index finger on the table, and finally turned back to them.

"I'll call the plants in Columbus Junction, Waterloo, and Ottumwa this week to let them know you'll be in touch," he said.

"What about Postville?" Gordon asked.

Angela's head whipped in his direction. She couldn't help it. He'd been undercutting everything she said, yet as soon as Nick made a decision, he was on board, even offering more. The man knew when to cut his losses, that was for sure.

"Three communities will give us a good base to work from," Angela said. She could be a gracious winner.

"Let's go with those," Nick said.

Only when she was out in the hall after the meeting did she let loose with a double fist pump.

Chapter 15

Her delight was short lived. Less than a week later, Gordon slapped a copy of the *Times-Herald* down on her desk.

"What's this?" he asked, standing inches away, his stance radiating blast-furnace heat.

Angela slid her chair back as she reached for the newspaper and scanned the headlines, spotting at once the object of Gordon's wrath.

"Barton Packing and Saint Catherine's team up to feed hungry."

Since the *Times-Herald*, published biweekly, was more a shopper than a news source and wasn't online, she hadn't seen the issue yet. She usually read it in the library or found a copy in the break room.

"I thought we had decided not to do a release," he said.

"We didn't do one," she said as she speed-read through the article. "The reporter got this story on his own."

"Oh, really?" Sarcasm dripped like molten steel off Gordon's lips. "Then how do you explain this quote?" He jammed a finger at the middle of the article.

She read where he pointed, a sick lump forming in her gut. The words were hers.

"I did talk to the reporter. He said he was working on a story and he wanted a quote from Nick. I thought I diverted him."

Angela pushed her chair back, distancing herself from the heat of his anger.

"You thought. Did you consider saying anything to me? To Nick?"

She had thought about telling Nick and Gordon right after the reporter called. But she'd thought she had it handled.

He glared at her. "You must be happy now."

"Why?"

"You got your way."

Gordon stormed out of her cubicle, leaving the newspaper on her desk.

Angela put her hand flat against her chest, her heart beating like a kettledrum.

On the whole, the article was positive. Exactly what she'd have wished for if she'd been able to put out the release she'd recommended. Two photos made the story stand out: one of Saint Catherine's parishioners serving meals of chicken enchiladas, the other of a child at the head of a long table full of adults and children eagerly chowing down. The quote the reporter attributed to her was something she'd said, and while she wished it had been left out, it wasn't damaging.

Her mistake was not telling the reporter flat-out that what she said was on background. Reporters didn't ask if they could quote you. He'd assumed that unless she specifically established otherwise, anything she said could be used as a quote. A rookie mistake. She could kick herself. She headed up to Barton's office. Better to take her lumps sooner rather than later.

Liz had a twinkle in her eye when she said sotto voce, "You sure stirred it up now."

"Is he angry?" Angela lifted her eyes toward Barton's door.

"Gordon's angry. That's enough." The phone rang and Liz reached for the receiver. "Go on in."

Angela tapped on the open door and peered in. Nick was on the phone, and he didn't look mad. To the contrary, he was smiling. That is, until he spotted her. Then he grew sober.

"You've seen the paper this morning," she said as soon as he put the phone down.

"Gordon made sure I did." Nick leaned back in his chair. He didn't invite her to sit.

She anchored her feet in front of his desk. "I want to explain—"

"You gave a quote to the reporter. Even though we expressly said we didn't want a story."

Unlike Gordon's explosive anger, Nick's displeasure came through in a narrowing of his eyes, a tightness in his voice. She sensed disappointment, too, and Angela realized that hurt her worse.

"It was a mistake on my part. When the reporter called, he wanted a quote from you, but I told him you didn't make the contribution for publicity. I told him you did it because it was the right thing to do."

"As your quote says."

She flushed. Dropped her eyes to the plush maroon carpet. Swallowed. Forced herself to look up again. "It was my mistake for not ensuring he knew my comments weren't for publication. I won't make that mistake again."

"Uh-huh," Nick said. "So you got the story you wanted."

The skin on her arms prickled. "I didn't do this to undercut you."

"Gordon thinks you did."

"Well, he's wrong." Hot tears burned the backs of her eyelids, and she blinked hard to keep them from falling. "Do you think I did this on purpose?"

If Nick agreed with Gordon on this, she was done. She would leave whether Dave said she should or not. Her reputation was everything to her.

She tilted her chin up and asked again, "Do you think I did this on purpose?" She felt his eyes take her measure, and she did not waver. His answer decided her future.

"When Gordon came to me, I wasn't sure. But now that I see you, no. I do not."

The relief she felt on hearing his answer pushed the tears to overflow. She dipped her head and bit her lip hard; crying was unacceptable. She forced a gravelly voiced "Thank you."

He stood and took the newspaper to the conference table. "Let's talk about this article." He gestured her to a seat. "It got people's attention. I've taken half a dozen calls this morning. Gordon has had as many."

"What are they saying?"

"All compliments. Congratulations on a fine article. Thanks for stepping up. Things like that."

With each comment, Angela felt relief fill her lungs. "What did *you* think of the article?"

Nick's face relaxed. "I was disturbed when I found Gordon waiting for me, showing me the article before I could even sit down."

"I get it. The article was unexpected," Angela said. She looked at him with a small feeling of hope. "But it was a good surprise. Yes?"

He didn't let her off the hook. "Gordon wasn't wrong. He says he's gotten two calls from other churches." He allowed a small smile. "But we'll manage the requests. Knowing you didn't intentionally go against our wishes, I have to admit that all in all, it's a good article, Angela. You were right about the idea."

"Thank you, Nick." She knew she was forgiven, but she also knew she had fences to mend with Gordon. Big fences. She sought Nick's help. "Gordon was pretty upset. Any suggestions on how I make it right with him?"

"Tell him what you told me. You learned from the experience and will do it better next time. He'll appreciate that. The last couple of years haven't gone like he expected. Like either of us expected."

Angela presumed he was talking about his wife's death. How that affected Gordon, she didn't know. "What were your expectations?" she asked. "I hope that's not too presumptuous to ask," she hastened to add.

"No. It's a reasonable question."

He went to the refrigerator, brought back bottles of water, and handed one to her.

"Maggie and I planned to retire. We'd been talking about it for years. The company was in good shape, and we thought it was time for me to step away." Talking about the plans he'd made with his wife brought a moment of lightness to his voice.

"Gordon said you'd revitalized the company entirely. How could you step away? Would you sell?"

"Lots of possibilities. Before Maggie's death, Gordon had already been running the day-to-day with little input from me. I make myself scarce as often as I can to give him breathing room. He was our choice to take over when Maggie and I stepped out entirely, and he knew the plan. Then Maggie . . ." He exhaled heavily. "When she . . . died . . . everything came to a stop in my mind. I always appreciated Maggie. It wasn't until she was gone that I realized how much I relied on her. To help me think things through. To make decisions."

"I can only imagine how hard it was for you. I gather you've been more involved in the company since she passed away. Has that been good for you?"

"It's given me something to focus on. Something to keep me productive. But it wasn't what I wanted. We wanted to travel, and I still do. The bank has a travel club that I've joined."

"How has Gordon responded to you engaging again?"

"I try not to get in his way, but I know I don't do things the way he does."

"I expect he doesn't do some things the way you would, either."

He smiled. "No. But that's to be expected."

Liz tapped on the door to remind Nick of his next appointment.

When Angela left Nick's office, she headed downstairs to see Gordon. Nick's counsel for getting back on even footing with his COO made sense. She was glad she'd asked. She shook her head. Even with that, she looked forward to facing Gordon about as much as getting a root canal.

Chapter 16

In spare moments, Angela searched the internet for articles about children traveling alone across the border. There was a lot to read and more articles being published all the time. She was surprised to learn that for decades thousands of children had been coming to the United States on their own. What had been a steady stream of children had become a flood as 2014 unfolded and gang violence exploded in Central America. Yet the journey to the US border could take months and was fraught with danger. Children hopped moving trains, hid to escape gangs, went days without food, and were forced to carry drugs across the border. Both girls and boys endured physical and sexual abuse at the hands of the coyotajes hired to bring them north. A chill ran through her spine as she thought of how scary it must be for a child to endure such hardship. She thought about how desperate Emilio's mother must have been to take such a chance with his life.

Emilio was ten. That was what he'd told her that first class, at least. But Angela wondered if that was true. In a later class, she'd used questions about age to work on both numbers and sentence structure. She had asked Emilio, "How old are you?"

He'd responded, "I am eight."

She smiled. "I thought you were ten."

The boy pushed back in his chair. Confusion skittered across his face. Then it was gone, replaced by a sly grin.

"I forget. I am ten," he said. Then he looked at the boy beside him. "No, I am twelve. Maybe fourteen." He laughed. "How old am I?" he asked the others.

"You are twelve," said one girl.

"You are nine," the boy chimed in. "I think."

Another girl stopped wiggling, put a finger to her chin, and surveyed Emilio with great seriousness. "Hmm. You are sixty-seven?" The class had dissolved into giggles.

"My, that would be old." Angela played along. "Do you know anyone that old?"

The little girl had looked at Angela and said just as seriously, "You?"

She hadn't thought much of it at the time since Emilio was always an outgoing teaser, but later she had wondered. He could look alternately younger and older. He played as often with the younger children as he did with the older boys.

In the classroom, he led the group in English skills. Even though Emilio had landed in the United States only a couple of months ago knowing only a handful of English words, he learned at an amazing speed. He was in school every weekday and would be for another month, into June. Angela was envious of his language ability, as she still had to consciously think through many translations.

After every class—often in the middle of classes—she adjusted her lesson plans, inspired by the children's chatter. Soccer ruled Juan's life, so they learned verbs like "run," "jump," "leap," "score," and nouns like "ball," "field," "goal." "Tip," "chair," "fall," "balance," "active," "quiet" all rose from Sofia's inability to sit still. As Linda suggested, the kids were sponges and Angela found she loved teaching them.

Early on, Emilio became a special resource for her. She asked how he knew what to do in school when he didn't understand what the teachers said. He told her he watched what the other kids did and then he did the same. He listened really hard. He watched TV. It helped that he was fearless in using new words and phrases. She almost laughed out loud during one class when she heard him mutter to himself, "What *were* you thinking?"

He charmed his way into her heart, and she could hardly look at him without feeling a tug of sadness, wondering what would become of him.

One day after class, she caught up with Father Burke as he closed up the sanctuary after classes that week.

"We have never had a child like Emilio in Hammond before, at least that I'm aware of," Father Burke said. "Catholic Charities works on refugee resettlement, but not with immigrants."

"Can he stay with the Muñoz family?"

"I've talked with Cesar Muñoz. He says they can't keep him. Not for the long term." The priest closed the last window in the sanctuary and moved toward the heavy oak doors of the one-hundred-year-old building.

"Surely they'll figure out a way to keep him."

"Easier for us to say, no doubt." Father Burke's tolerant smile held a rebuke so gentle Angela almost missed it. "Cesar and Camila have five children of their own. And I've heard he's had some unexpected financial challenges with his business."

"If Emilio can't stay there, then what will happen?" She followed him down to the basement.

"I don't know. From what I understand, a sponsor is a temporary step. The goal is for the child to get legal status, but I don't know how that happens. Even beyond what is done legally, the whole situation is politicized. Some people want all the children sent back because they came illegally. Others believe we should take them in because it is the humane thing to do."

Angela spotted Emilio sitting with a group of boys, all of them eating supper. "I wonder if anyone trying to send these kids back knows even one of them personally."

"It's always simple when we keep ourselves at a distance."

Angela saw his comment as honest, if not easy. She and Father Burke stood in silence. Once you knew one of these children, she thought, once you looked into their faces and knew them by name, then, no. It was not easy.

* * *

That night she called Dave.

"Dave, do you know an immigration attorney I could talk with?"

"Not off the top of my head, but it can't be hard to find one. Why do you ask?"

"The boy I told you about—Emilio—the one in my class. He came from Honduras to the US."

"I was reading about those kids. He's lucky he's alive."

"For sure. I'm trying to figure out what options he has."

"Isn't he with some relative now? That's what news stories say usually happens."

"For now, he's living with an uncle, but he may not be able to stay there."

"How does this fit into your work for Barton?"

"It doesn't. I know it's not my job, but this is a little boy. I figured maybe I could find out some things that would be helpful."

Silence filled the air.

"You know you aren't going to be in Hammond long. Maybe only another six weeks," he finally said.

"While I'm here, I'll do what I can." She spoke into another silence. "You know it was your advice I get involved. So I'm involved."

"I suggested you get involved to help you do the job for Barton."

"Working at Saint Catherine's has been useful in that way, but I can't help but worry about what's going to happen to this boy."

"The agency won't cover the cost of an attorney," he said. "And I worry you're getting so involved in this you're taking your eye off the job."

Miffed at his resistance, she responded testily. "I was only asking. If you don't know an attorney, I'm sure I can find one. Forget I asked."

"Calm down, Angela. I'll ask our attorney if he can recommend someone."

Chapter 17

The tables in the basement of Saint Catherine's were already beginning to empty a couple of weeks later when Angela and Alvaro picked up plates of chicken tacos with salads and sat down to eat.

"How are the calls going?" Alvaro asked. With the tip of his fork, he pulled a bit of chicken out of the taco and slid it to the side.

"OK. Mostly. Nick's contacts in the other plant towns have been helpful, but I can't help but feel I'm getting the company PR line and not much else."

They'd been eating supper together at the church regularly after classes. Other nights they met at Eduardo's. Their conversations covered a range of topics, and she'd grown to appreciate his perspective on the work she did for Barton.

She nibbled at the salad. "Are you familiar with Impressionist paintings?"

"Some." He paused, then suggested, "Monet?"

"Yes. You know how the pictures are soft, a little blurry? What I'm getting from these calls is like that. People tell me what I ask, but I feel as though the overall picture is a romanticized version of reality."

"Like your public-relations releases." Alvaro continued to poke around in the taco. "It is the picture you want people to see."

She hadn't made that connection, but he was right. "OK. I suppose there's some truth in that." She noticed he'd barely eaten any of his meal. "You're not hungry?"

"Not so much for chicken."

"We have had a lot of it lately. Now that Barton Packing sends a donation regularly, it's the meat of choice."

He pushed the plate away.

"You're always hungry. Don't you feel well?"

"Maybe I will not feel well later."

"That doesn't make sense."

He said nothing. She shrugged and continued to eat. "Donations like this are exactly the kind of thing the company should be doing."

"Maybe not so much." He crossed his arms, and the T-shirt sleeves stretched against his biceps. For the first time she saw that the river tattooed on his bicep flowed through a mountain valley.

"You sound so cynical. What's up?"

He leaned forward, elbows on the table, hands hiding his mouth. He spoke under his breath. "It didn't cost anything. They gave old product."

His comment sent a jolt of electricity to her gut. She stopped eating. "What do you mean?"

He leaned farther forward. "A pallet was in the warehouse too long. Past the expiration date. Mr. Ryker said to send it."

"That's not right, is it?" She'd never heard of such a thing. Angela drank milk a few days past the expiration date if it passed the smell test. It was fine. Most of the time. She bought meat right at the expiration date and either cooked it right away or froze it. Her friend Cassie, on the other hand, was rabid about expiration dates, throwing out any food that sat in her refrigerator more than a few days. She wouldn't buy food with an expiration date less than a week out. Cassie said Angela had a cast-iron stomach. Angela thought Cassie was paranoid.

Yet Angela figured expiration dates were on food for a reason. If she chose to ignore the expiration dates herself, it was her own choice.

What was Gordon thinking, sending out expired product after Barton Packing had had a recall? Did Nick know about it? Shouldn't Father Burke know? The church might not want to accept the donation. For sure it would change the way the volunteers thought about using the chicken. Her mind swam with the implications. Was this why Gordon didn't want to talk to the media?

She looked at the half-eaten taco on her plate, substantially less appealing than it had been two minutes ago. "Wouldn't people in the plant know?"

"They all know. Mr. Ryker had one of the men change dates on the packages."

"No!" Angela responded out of shock. A couple sitting farther down the table looked their direction. She lowered her voice. "Isn't that against the law?"

"Jose did what he was told. He got points when Mr. Ryker found out the product was expired. He could not risk more."

"Shouldn't you say something?" she asked.

"Mr. Ryker told Jose the chicken is fine. That it is frozen the whole time, so it is still good."

"You have to say something. You can't let this pass."

He leaned back, his dark eyes hooded, arms folded again across his chest.

She knew that closed-off, stubborn, don't-push-me look. She sat back and folded her arms across her own chest, sinking into silence as she absorbed Alvaro's comments. Jose got points for not managing inventory correctly. OK. But to get more points if he refused to do something dishonest? That was so wrong. How far past expiration was the chicken? If Gordon had the date changed one time, what was to say it hadn't been changed before? What if someone was to become ill? It was clear now why Gordon didn't want to publicize the donations. Someone needed to do something. But who?

"OK," she said. "I can see why you wouldn't want to confront Gordon."

"It would not be good."

"And I can't go over his head to Nick. But we still have to do something." She thought for a few more moments. "I'll talk to my PR boss," she said at last. He nodded.

She picked up both their plates and took them to the waste bin. Neither of them cared to eat any more.

When she returned to the table, Alvaro said, "Why don't you go to the towns yourself? It is not so far."

"What?" She focused on him again. "I don't understand."

"If you want to know about the other plant towns, why don't you go see them yourself?"

Go herself? She thought of her first days in Hammond. The research she'd done before she came to northeast Iowa gave her one picture. What she saw when she drove through town gave her a slightly different view. The reality when she walked Main Street, read the store signs, saw the multitude of satellite dishes on what should have been single-family homes, worked in the church basement brought the picture into focus in the harsh, gritty light of day. Why not go?

"Actually, that's a good idea, Alvaro."

It was also an idea that made her hesitate. She was fine talking with the company owners and chamber executives. The hesitation arose when she thought about the next layer— minority-owned businesses, clerks, and others who might be minorities. Even though she spoke Spanish, as soon as they saw her, a wall went up, their smiles became hesitant, their words guarded. Only time and familiarity got them past those early rough spots, let trust take root and grow. On a one-day visit, there wasn't time to build those relationships.

When Alvaro accompanied her, he made an immediate connection with people, like when he had introduced her to

Eduardo and Maria. But it was more than that. He knew things it would never dawn on her to think about or question. Like the multiple satellite dishes.

"You could come along," she said on impulse.

His eyes narrowed. "You're joking."

"I'm serious. You see things I don't. Plus, you're a reality check for me. And you have instant credibility with people I'd have to spend weeks with working to build relationships. Come on. What do you say?"

"I can't take time off from work unless it is vacation."

"You shouldn't have to use vacation. If you're willing to go, I'll talk with Nick. I bet he'd see what a good idea this is. You would be paid for your time like I am."

Well, probably not exactly like she was. She had no idea what Alvaro earned working for Barton Packing, but she was reasonably certain he wasn't compensated at the $125-an-hour rate Sherborn-Watts charged for her time.

"I'm going to ask." She smiled. Then she frowned. She realized that in her enthusiasm she may have been guilty of assuming again. She added, "Unless you don't want to go."

He thought for a moment, then leaned forward, arms folded on the table. "OK, Angela. But I will talk with Mr. Ryker."

"Let me talk to my Sherborn-Watts boss first, to be certain he's on board with a trip like this and with you participating. If he does, we can coordinate conversations with Nick and Gordon. OK?"

He held up a fist. She bumped it. They had a plan.

* * *

When she called Dave Wilstat the next morning, she had two things on her mind: product expiration dates and the research field trip. Once she explained her reasoning, he approved the research trip plan without hesitation.

"Good initiative, Angela," he said. "If Nick has any concerns, let me know and I'll call him."

Regarding the expiration-date issue, he saw her point but was less concerned than she'd expected him to be.

"We don't know," he said. "Maybe it was expired by only one day. And if it was frozen the entire time, what Gordon said was probably right, especially knowing the church would use it right away." But he agreed that she was right that it would be a problem if word got out to the media or the public.

"I'll have the research department dig into the rules about product expiration," he said. "Don't take this any further until we know what ground we're standing on. We can't go to Nick or Gordon on hearsay and innuendo."

"Alvaro's trustworthy," she responded. But she left the situation in his hands.

* * *

Nick saw the logic of both the research and including Alvaro and gave the go-ahead. Then Angela met with Gordon to get his thoughts on the people she'd arranged to meet with, a short meeting that went smoothly, even though thoughts about how he'd manipulated the expiration dates never left her mind. At least until the end of the meeting.

As she was getting ready to leave, he said, "This is outside Al's job, you know. You aren't doing him any favors getting him to do your work for you."

"He's not doing my job," she blurted, responding too quickly, too defensively. Then she saw the flicker of satisfaction in his eyes. Again, she'd risen to his bait. In an attempt to recover, she said, "Alvaro will be a real asset on this trip."

"I'm sure." Gordon's gray eyes tracked over her like a buyer appraising livestock. "Yep. Al's endowed with all sorts of assets I imagine you'd find useful."

The implication burned her cheeks. She arched her neck, returned his stare for two full seconds, then left.

Afterward, the scene played over and over in her mind as she drove back to the motel, and with each rerun her anger intensified and she gripped the steering wheel more tightly. Though she'd briefed Dave every step of the way, she did not tell him about the exchange with Gordon. Dave had said the packing business was rough. This was her client, and she'd deal with it. She detoured to the convenience store, where she bought a bag of peanut M&M's. Under normal stress, she ate just three. Tonight, she ate the whole bag.

Chapter 18

Angela sat cross-legged on the bed, a notebook on one knee, her phone—on speaker—balanced on the other. It was early evening, and she planned to leave a message for Claudia Schiffler, the immigration attorney referred by the Sherborn-Watts legal counsel.

Schiffler worked at Standing for Justice, a nonprofit group operating nationwide to provide legal services at no cost to immigrants. Prior to joining the nonprofit, Schiffler led the immigration department at one of the biggest law firms in the state, building a reputation as someone who never shied away from expressing her views to the media. Given the high-power—and no doubt high-paid—position she'd held, Schiffler's move to a nonprofit struck Angela as a bold, and slightly odd, move.

A quick online search of her name turned up more than a thousand hits. Internet images showed Schiffler to be a trim woman with a mass of curly red hair, high chiseled cheekbones, and a thin, pointed nose. In every picture, the woman exuded energy and confidence, features anyone facing an immigration challenge would surely welcome.

When Schiffler answered on the first ring, Angela nearly knocked the phone off her knee in her haste to respond.

"I'm trying to understand the rules for children coming to the US from Central America," Angela explained once she'd introduced herself. "The ones coming in by themselves."

"In general or specifically?" The woman got to the point, a feature Angela appreciated. The free legal service might apply only to immigrants, but even if it extended to her, Angela wanted to be respectful of the attorney's time.

"Specifically. There's a boy from Honduras who landed in . . . a northeast Iowa town."

"What's his situation?"

"He's been here for a couple of months. He's living with his aunt and uncle." Angela provided as much detail as she could, stopping short of using names. She hadn't retained the woman, hoped she wouldn't have to, so she didn't know if client confidentiality applied.

She came to her point. "My question is, what happens to this boy? If he can't stay with his sponsor? If we find another sponsor, can he stay in the US?"

"Having a sponsor doesn't guarantee anything. Let me walk you through the process. If the border patrol catches an unaccompanied minor at the border, the child is immediately placed in deportation proceedings."

"I'm not certain, but I believe this boy turned himself in to the border agents," Angela explained.

"Some do that when they have family waiting for them. Getting into the legal system is the first step to staying in the country legally. Others try to slip through and stay under the immigration radar, especially if the family members they hope to join are undocumented, too," Schiffler said. "Then if the child is in the system, children can either be released to a sponsor—it sounds like your boy is in that group—or they stay in an Office of Refugee Resettlement shelter while they wait for a court date. To avoid deportation, the two most common options for unaccompanied minors are asylum and the Special Immigrant Juvenile status visa—an SIJ."

"This boy was in danger in Honduras," Angela explained, scribbling fast while she tried to keep up. "From the gangs. His mother sent him here to save him. So wouldn't he be able to get asylum?"

"Asylum is difficult," the attorney said. "To get asylum, you have to show past persecution or a well-founded fear of future persecution based on race, religion, nationality, political opinion, or membership in a particular social group. So far, US courts seldom recognize gang violence as a reason to grant asylum. Beyond that, it's particularly difficult to gain asylum in this district."

"Why's that?"

"Hard to say. The law is the same nationally, but the courts interpret it differently. The Chicago district, which includes Iowa, only approves 14 percent of the asylum requests; the San Francisco district approves 84 percent."

Angela chuckled. "Maybe our boy should move to California."

"We recommend kids go there if they have relatives in the district." Schiffler responded seriously to the comment Angela made half in jest.

"I was kidding," Angela said.

"I wasn't," Schiffler responded. "Here in Iowa, your boy could have better success trying for SIJS. It's for children who've been abused, abandoned, or neglected by one or both parents. But they can't be reunited with a parent because of those same reasons."

"But he wasn't any of those things. His mother sent him here to protect him."

"In the eyes of the court, you could make the argument that she abandoned him when she sent him away. Putting him a position where he experienced the trauma of the trip could constitute abuse and neglect."

"I don't like the idea, but I see your point," Angela said, thinking again of how desperate Emilio's mother must have been to put her son in such danger. "What happens if he doesn't qualify for asylum or SIJS?"

"Most of those children are eventually deported. Does your child have an attorney representing him?"

"I don't know. Does it matter?"

"He's got a better chance if he's represented. According to the statistics, only 33 percent of juveniles come to court with an attorney, but 77 percent of children with legal representation are allowed to remain in the United States. Nine out of ten of the children who come without representation are ordered deported." She added, "In any case, it's important the child doesn't miss a hearing date. Any missed hearing date triggers an automatic deportation order."

"Harsh," Angela said.

"It's the rule. The judges have strict procedures they must follow in these cases."

For a half hour, Angela continued to ask questions and Schiffler answered, explaining the process, circling back to earlier points, explaining again. When she glanced at her watch and saw how much time she'd taken, Angela realized she should wrap it up.

"I appreciate your time, Claudia. This is all so confusing," she said. "I wonder how anyone, let alone children, knows what to do? Is there a charge for any of your services?"

"No. We provide legal representation at no cost, so I do consultations like this all the time. If you have more questions, don't hesitate to call or email," she said. "We all want to help these children."

After the call ended, Angela flopped back on the bed, her head jammed with the information Schiffler had provided. During the call, there'd been time only to gather the information, none to think about what it all meant. But now reactions flooded in. Harsh. Unfair. Arbitrary. She scanned the pages of notes. No single word covered the situation Emilio faced.

Incomprehensible. Impossible. The whole situation felt so . . . overwhelming. It made Angela's stomach ache.

Dwelling in the negative didn't help. She sat up and reached in her purse for M&M's as she scanned the notes again. It didn't take long to see the positives. Schiffler was an invaluable asset more than willing to help. Angela knew she could and would assimilate all the new terminology quickly. She wasn't alone. Father Burke and Alvaro would help. So Emilio wasn't alone. The biggest positive? They had hope. Hope was what she'd share with Father Burke before she and Alvaro left town on Thursday.

Chapter 19

Angela pulled up in front of a quadplex on the south side of Hammond. Mature trees lined the residential street that included a range of well-kept multifamily units. As soon as she got out of the car, the scent of lilacs surrounded her, drawing her attention to a spectacular hedgerow of bushes with deep-purple, pale-lavender, and pure-white lilac blossoms in full bloom.

The bushes reminded her of her parents' home. They'd planted three lilacs directly under Angela's bedroom window when she was a child. Each spring, she opened her bedroom windows and let her dreams drift on the fragrant night air.

She detoured off the sidewalk, tiptoed through grass heavy with dew, cupped blossoms the color of amethysts in her hands, and buried her face in the lilac scent. Closing her eyes, she breathed deeply, then opened her eyes. Heaven.

She reluctantly left the flowers and went to ring the doorbell.

"You are early." Alvaro's voice came down from the balcony above the lilac bushes. "Come up."

She headed up the stairs and peeked in the open door. Alvaro was nowhere to be seen.

"Hello," she called.

"I am ready in five minutes," he responded. "Come in."

She stepped into a small living room decorated with furniture and accessories that were obviously secondhand but presented an overall picture that looked comfortable and surprisingly well coordinated. A brown faux-leather sofa. An overstuffed chair upholstered in forest-green brocade. Copies of *Popular Mechanics* and *Men's Health* lay on a trunk repurposed as a coffee table. Also on the trunk, a dish of gold-wrapped Werther's caramels. She bent over to grab a couple and then thought better. At the end of the sofa were two hand weights. Those biceps didn't happen by accident.

"Coffee in the kitchen," Alvaro called.

"Thanks," she responded. He must have expected her to come in because coffee cups and packets of sweetener sat on the counter next to the Mr. Coffee. The sweetener was a nice touch since she knew he drank his without. He also had a thermos on the counter. The kitchen was spotless. The countertops cleared and cleaned. Not even a dirty spoon in the stainless-steel sink. Few men she knew were so tidy.

She fixed herself a cup and wandered back into the living room, gravitating to the bookshelf, an über-modern structure concocted of PVC pipe and closet racks. Engineering books—mostly college texts—filled one shelf. An eclectic mix of novels by science-fiction writers lined another. Isaac Asimov. Douglas Adams. Kurt Vonnegut. And two volumes of *The Hunger Games*.

Angela had read *The Hunger Games* trilogy and seen the movies. Her thoughts returned to the moment in that dystopian future world when Katniss takes her sister's place in an annual lottery that chooses one young boy or girl from each colony and pits them against each other in a fight to the death. Angela was inspired by the way Katniss always stepped up to help others, throughout all three books.

"Ready," Alvaro said, dropping his bag on the sofa.

"You've read *The Hunger Games?*" she asked, taking her cup back to the kitchen. She almost put it in the sink to be washed later, considered better, and washed and dried it.

"One only." He emptied the coffeepot into the thermos and handed it to Angela, then pocketed packets of sweetener. "I thought we could take our own."

"A good idea, but we can expense everything," she said.

"Expense?"

"Have you ever had an expense account?"

"I don't know what it is, so I must not have."

"Didn't Gordon tell you what you could spend on the trip?"

His blank look said no. She knew she could submit her own expenses, but she hadn't thought about him. She'd assumed he'd be covered, too.

"I have my own money," he said.

"But you don't have to pay for the trip. Or rather, we do, but we get reimbursed by Barton Packing."

A look more like concern than doubt filled his eyes.

"I know we do," she insisted. "Don't worry about it. I'll keep the receipts for both of us, and we'll figure it out when we get back."

"I have money in case," he said, and then returned to their earlier discussion about the books. "I was most interested in the societies they set up. The fight to the death was intended to keep each society hating the other, but instead brought some of the fighters together."

"If they lived long enough to get to know each other."

"It made me think of the gangs in El Salvador." Alvaro grabbed his bag and a coat. "Ready?"

"It's warm. I don't think you'll need the coat," she said.

He laughed. "I am always cold in Iowa."

"OK. Might as well; we have the car." She headed down the stairs as Alvaro locked the door and followed.

"Have you seen much of Iowa?" she asked when they were out of Hammond. She'd set Waterloo as the destination in her GPS so she could think of other things while she drove.

"When I was at ISU, we went to Iowa City or Cedar Falls if there was a football game. Not many other places, though. Will we see where you are from?"

"Not even close," she said. "I'm from southwest Iowa. The fields look much the same as this, though. Lots of corn and soybeans." She pointed to the door pocket. "There's an Iowa map in there if you want to see."

He found the map and opened it across his lap. "What do your parents do?"

"My mother is a nurse. My dad taught history at the community college until a couple of years ago when he got sick." Her voice quavered as she told him about the Alzheimer's disease and how fast it had gotten worse, reducing the hours he could teach until now, when it might not be possible for him to teach at all

"I'm sorry, Angela. Your mother still works?"

"She has to, but Dad requires more and more care. It's hard to be so far away. But you know that." She forced a more upbeat tone to her voice. By comparison, she had it better than he. At least she still had her father. At least she could still see her parents. "I get home at least once a month. Since my dad got sick, I go more often. At least, I did before this job in Hammond." It took a good five hours each way to make the drive now.

She lapsed into thought and was grateful Alvaro let her. Before her dad got sick, she'd talked with her parents on Saturday mornings; now she called more frequently. Her mother tried to keep the conversations light and often diverted Angela's concerns about them to questions about how her job was going and whether she was dating anyone, a question asked more frequently after she turned thirty. When she was in high school, her parents had both advised her to wait: wait until she knew who she was, until she was established. Now that she was thirty-one, her mother focused more on spurring her to date someone. Angela had her own list of requirements: smart, funny, college educated, good looking.

She glanced at Alvaro. He met all those requirements, though she was reasonably certain her parents were not thinking Latino. If asked, she would not have said Latino, either. Assuming a white man was not a factor of prejudice or bias, simply the reality of where she grew up and the people she saw around her.

An adopted Korean girl was the only person of color in the southwest Iowa town where she'd grown up. Even though the university in Ames diligently recruited a more diverse student body, the campus population remained more than 75 percent white. Des Moines, where she lived now, had a demographic makeup similar to the university. It was entirely possible to live in Iowa and have nothing more than glancing contact with people of other races and ethnicities if you didn't actively seek deeper relationships.

Gordon's inappropriate comment flashed into her mind; she pushed it away and reached for the coffee.

Alvaro held two fingers on the map, tracking their progress. "Postville is not far," he observed.

"It's not on our list."

"I have heard about the plant there," he said.

"Everyone has," Angela said. "It was big news."

"It isn't so far out of the way."

"We have appointments in Waterloo. And have to get to Washington tonight."

"I calculated it. We could drive through. If we don't stay more than an hour, we can still get where we need to be. We're out. Why not go there, too?"

He could have been one of the kids in her class, he pleaded with such sincerity. She relented.

"Can you reprogram the GPS?" She pointed to the monitor. "Tap the menu and—"

"Can I reprogram a GPS?" He shook his head with disbelief and unhooked the monitor from the dashboard. "I am the engineer. You drive." He checked the map again. "Look for a county road in one mile. Turn left there."

* * *

Postville was in the hilly "little Switzerland" area of northeast Iowa. It did not take overly long to get to Postville, but the drive took them into an entirely different landscape, and Alvaro stopped looking at the map to focus on the scenery.

"These are not mountains like home, *pero son colinas muy hermosas,*" Alvaro said.

Angela smiled. He'd slipped into Spanish without even realizing it. "They are beautiful," she agreed.

When they reached Postville, they drove down several streets and past the Agriprocessors plant. The plant was still owned by Orthodox Jews and still butchered kosher. A good many Jews lived in the town. Making no particular attempt to integrate with the rest of the town's residents, they ran their own school and kept largely to themselves, even though many had lived there for years.

Twice, Angela and Alvaro saw groups of Jews wearing their black suits and hats, with the long curled sideburns reaching their shoulders. She could hardly imagine people looking more out of place walking through a rural Iowa town.

Finally, Angela parked the car, and they walked around the center of town.

"Let's go in here," Alvaro said when they came to a shoe store. "I need laces for my work boots."

"Seriously?" Angela asked. "You want to go shopping?"

"It is only a moment."

A bell jangled as Angela opened the door of a small store smelling of leather and shoe polish and crowded with shelves lined with shoeboxes. Morning sun poured through the front windows, illuminating dust motes in the still air and casting shadows on chairs. Alvaro headed down an aisle displaying shoelaces, polishes, and stockings as Angela stepped up to the counter. The store appeared empty, but within a few moments, a plump woman wearing wire-rimmed glasses and holding a pair of work boots emerged from a back room. She greeted Angela with a smile.

"I'll be with you in a moment," she said, then raised her voice and called to Alvaro. "Can I help you?"

"I can find it," he said as he scanned the shelves.

"I didn't see him come in," she said, tilting her head toward Alvaro as she set the boots on the counter next to other work shoes and a pair of Birkenstocks. "Someone's coming to pick these up shortly," she explained as though Angela had asked. She looked across the store to where Alvaro stood. "Let me know if you need anything," she called out.

He acknowledged her with a wave.

"Now, what can I do for you?" she asked Angela.

"We're passing through and decided to stretch our legs," Angela said. "Looks like business is healthy." She gestured to the shoes and piles of clothes by the sewing machine.

"We do pretty well here. Shoe repair and mending clothes takes most of our time. We sell Red Wing Shoes. Got real comfortable women's shoes, too. If you're interested. We also take care of shoe repair here. I take mending home at night because I can't get it all done during the day."

"You must do a good job." She'd only intended to pass a little time until Alvaro found what he wanted, but the woman appeared eager to talk. "I'm from Des Moines," Angela said. "And more recently Hammond. I'm doing research on towns with packing plants. If you have a moment, might I ask some questions?" She extended her hand. "My name is Angela Darrah."

"I'm Marty." The woman wiped her hand on her jeans before touching Angela's hand. "Boot oil," she explained. "We always polish shoes that come in for repair."

The bell over the door jangled again and a thin woman with the weathered complexion of someone who spent a lot of time in the sun entered and walked right up to the counter.

"Hey, Donna," the store clerk greeted her. "I've got your man's boots right here. I'll ring them up in a second." She nodded at Angela. "Angela here is from Des Moines. Doing research on something or other."

"You found the right person. Marty knows as much as anyone," Donna said.

Donna looked like half the women in Angela's hometown, women who made gardens, put three meals a day on the table, and thrived on collecting and distributing town gossip. Wearing capri pants and a plaid shirt, the woman had mussed brown hair. A smudge of flour at her temple suggested she'd been baking that morning. Angela took advantage of having two people to talk with.

"How's business in town in general?" she asked.

"Not bad. Not like it used to be, though," Marty said as her head swiveled toward Alvaro again.

At first a distraction, what was now obvious surveillance began to irritate Angela. "Oh? How so?"

Marty brought her attention back to Angela. "A lot of the businesses we used to have—movie theater, bowling alley, dance hall—they've all closed. People go to Decorah."

"The people who work in the plant have to shop somewhere," Angela probed. "Grocery stores. Gas stations. It looks as though the storefronts along here are mostly full."

"Well, sure, we have those, and there's those Mexican stores. And there's a couple of restaurants."

Donna chimed in. "There's stores selling dresses for those parties Mexicans have for teenage girls. Those dresses look like something out of the fifties. Could as well have picked up something at the thrift store," she clucked. "No normal person would want the clothes they sell. Any of us have to go out of town to get what we need."

"That's why we stock Red Wing Shoes," Marty said. "Everybody needs those." She wiped her hands on her jeans again. "Excuse me. I need to see what he wants."

Donna watched as the shopkeeper approached Alvaro, then leaned closer to Angela. "Can't be too careful with them," she said. "They'll steal you blind while you're standing there looking at them."

Angela's skin prickled. "Them?"

"Those Mexicans." She bobbed her head toward Alvaro. "Like him."

Ever since her experience at the bank, Angela had imagined a dozen things she would have, could have, should have said. The sharpest retorts bubbled to her lips. But she reminded herself her job was to make friends, not enemies. She swallowed and spoke calmly. "Alvaro is from El Salvador. And he is a friend of mine."

"Well." The ruddy color of Donna's face deepened to brick, and she huffed. "How was I supposed to know?"

You might have asked, Angela thought. *Or you might have chosen not to assume the worst.* She felt a tiny bit better because she'd said something, though not nearly as much as she wished she had. She turned abruptly and walked to Alvaro. "We need to go."

"I'm ready." Alvaro handed two pair of shoelaces and a bottle of leather waterproofing to the storekeeper. "I'll take these."

They followed Marty to the counter, where she rang up the items and put everything in a brown paper bag she slid across the counter. "Thank you," she said as she handed back change from the twenty-dollar bill Alvaro gave her.

"Thank you, ma'am." He pocketed the change and picked up the bag.

Marty said, "You come back anytime."

Angela kept quiet. She'd said all she intended to.

The door wasn't closed behind them when Angela heard Marty say, "He was one of the good ones."

Alvaro strode toward the car without speaking, but Angela caught up and put a hand on his arm to stop him.

"Did you hear them?"

"Yes."

"I'm sorry."

"It wasn't you."

"I feel like I should have said more."

"You are wise to keep quiet." He climbed into the passenger seat and tossed the bag of shoe supplies into the back seat.

Angela selected the address of their appointment in Waterloo on the GPS and headed out of town. South and west. "It surprises me any Latinos shop there."

"They don't have many choices." He opened the map on his lap again and began to trace routes from Postville to Waterloo. "The shopkeeper was OK."

"But she watched you like she was sure you'd steal something at any second. I was embarrassed for you."

He shrugged. "She must have had shoplifters. It was the same in Apopa in El Salvador. The shopkeepers watched us kids when we came in. Did you find out anything useful to our research?"

She obliged his desire to move the conversation along, yet her edgy feeling of irritation remained. "We didn't get far. More tone than substance," she said, and filled him in on the conversation. She paused. "Is it quality of life? Or resistance to change? Who knows? The type of businesses may have changed even if there hadn't been the demographic change. We passed a Walmart on the way into town. Walmart killed Main Street in many small towns."

Alvaro broke into her monologue. "Do you have a notepad?"

"In the glove box. Why?"

"I will write down what you said."

"Good idea. There's a pen in there, too."

He found the paper and drew columns, making tidy notes as she'd seen him do before.

After writing for a few moments, he suggested, "Maybe they should consider themselves lucky Latinos opened stores? Eh?"

"If they could be made to see it," she said. After a few moments, she mused, "Follow the money."

"What do you mean?"

"People are motivated by money. By what's in their own financial interest. If something benefits their pocketbook, they are more likely to support it. If they see it hurts them financially, they are more likely to oppose it."

"I still do not understand 'follow the money.'"

"It means that when something happens that doesn't seem right, it's always a good idea to see who's putting the money into making it happen or to see who gains most from the outcome. If you follow the money, you find the motivation."

"I see."

Angela could see the wheels turning as Alvaro digested what she'd said.

"In El Salvador I do not know of such a saying." He added more notes to his list.

For a while they drove in silence, though from time to time, she looked at him. "Don't you get mad about what people say about you? Or what they infer about you?"

"They are ignorant. I feel sorry for them."

"You are remarkably calm."

"I am lucky to be here to study and to work. Soon I will leave. What is gained by confronting them?"

"I keep asking myself that," she admitted as she massaged her shoulder blade above her heart. She'd felt an actual pang when he said he would leave soon. "My job is to get along with everyone and help everyone get along with each other. But sometimes it seems wrong. I know I don't like the way it makes me feel."

* * *

Angela's plan included talking with people from the packing plants and the chamber in each town. They'd pick up "person on the street" interviews if the opportunity arose.

As the county seat of Black Hawk County, Waterloo was substantially larger and more ethnically diverse than Hammond. Major area employers included Tyson Foods, Deere & Company, the University of Northern Iowa, and two hospitals.

At Tyson, the VP of human resources, a pleasant, soft-spoken woman in her forties, took them to a window looking out over the plant floor, where workers deboned hog carcasses.

"What a good idea. People can see a lot without going in," Angela observed, already thinking about the possibilities for such a window at Barton.

"We don't let anyone but employees into the plant, so it's useful when we have customers visit. We also bring trade media here."

"Consumer media, too?"

"Not since I've been here."

Angela asked a number of other questions about how the company worked with the media and interacted with the community in general, then turned to Alvaro. "What questions do you have?"

"Working on hogs would be harder than chickens because of the size," Alvaro said. "How do you manage that?"

"We're mindful of the effects of repetitive motion, as you no doubt are," she said. "We have a set schedule for moving people from job to job to lessen the possibility of injuries. It's all based on research done at this plant before Tyson acquired it."

"They were progressive to do research like that," Angela said.

The woman smiled. "They were encouraged to be progressive. OSHA levied a large fine on the company because of the number of repetitive-motion injuries incurred when line speed increased. To mitigate the fine, the company agreed to do a study on how line speed contributed to repetitive-motion injuries and how to reduce injuries. As a result, the company implemented significant changes in this plant. The results were shared with everyone in the industry."

Ethnic diversity at the plant was similar to Barton. In spite of the larger population base of Waterloo, this plant also recruited employees from outside the state.

"It doesn't surprise me," said the young man who met them at the chamber of commerce, when Angela explained that most of Barton's Somali employees commuted from Waterloo. "Waterloo has a larger black population than the rest of Iowa. It goes back generations, since this was a stop on the Underground Railroad. Granted, there's a big difference between African-American Iowans whose families have lived here as long as any white Iowans and Africans who came as refugees in the last decade. But there's still a sizeable population that looks familiar. They have a religious community. Refugee resettlement services. Anyone would seek that out. We don't have anything close to Chinatown or Little Italy, but there are concentrations."

She'd thought Waterloo might be too different from Hammond to be relevant, but each meeting added important context.

Chapter 20

Late in the afternoon they made the easy two-hour drive down I-380 from Waterloo to Washington, where they had reservations at Cafe Dodici, a restaurant and B&B. Angela had stayed there once when she was on an assignment for the Iowa Economic Development Authority and looked forward to a return visit.

After they checked in, they agreed to meet in the lobby at seven for dinner.

With an hour to settle in, Angela shook the wrinkles out of the clothes she planned to wear the next day and hung them up. She threw her nightgown—actually an oversized T-shirt emblazoned with the words "I am woman, hear me snore"—on the bed. It wasn't sexy, but she didn't need sexy. On the other hand, it would be easy to take off if Alvaro wanted to try, she mused. In only six weeks, their relationship had gone from business to friendship, but there was no disputing that he was first and foremost a client. Though the idea of going farther was delicious, she wouldn't—couldn't—with a client, so the musing was harmless fantasy.

She opened her toiletry bag next to the bathroom sink, brushed her teeth, and touched up her lipstick. Despite her resolve, she spent an inordinate amount of time thinking about what Alvaro might be doing in his room. Was he the type who flopped on the bed, turned on the TV, and zoned out? Did he check out all the drawers? Read the literature inevitably sitting by the phone on the desk? Turn on all the lights? Was he thinking about her?

She replaced the khaki slacks she'd worn all day with black leggings topped with a simple tunic, and dressed the outfit up with a lightweight patterned scarf, hoop earrings, and a bracelet. She surveyed the effect in the full-length mirror on the closet door and nodded with satisfaction. Before she left the room, she'd put on heels. Perfect for Cafe Dodici, a restaurant with white tablecloths, candles, and impeccable service. A couple from Italy who landed in Washington through a family connection started the restaurant, the husband serving as chef and the wife as maître d'.

Downtown Washington, including the town square, had been an economic wasteland when the couple decided to buy and rehab the abandoned building. Their efforts inspired investments in other buildings on the square. The town applied for a Main Street Iowa grant, and in the process more of the town's business leaders came together to dream and plan for a more vibrant future. The results were tangible.

It wasn't as though Washington, Iowa, would ever be Iowa City or Des Moines or Chicago, but the town had become a vital center for southeast Iowa.

From all she'd heard, the people of Washington had welcomed the Italian outsiders coming in and taking over an abandoned building on their town square. Would they have been so open if the outsiders had been Mexican or Somali? Or was it the quality of the restaurant that mattered? Or was it that they bought the building and poured so much money and care into renovation?

The clock on the nightstand showed she still had more than a half hour before meeting Alvaro, so she opened her laptop and began to formulate a report on what she had seen thus far.

What seemed like moments later she heard a knock on her door and glanced at her computer clock. How could thirty minutes have passed so quickly?

"Just a sec," she called out. Peering through the security hole, she saw Alvaro had shaved and donned a sports jacket over an azure shirt. She was glad she'd dressed up a little, too. She fumbled with the lock, unhooked the chain, and opened the door.

"Are you ready?" he asked. "We can walk down together."

"Come in. I was making notes about today. Time got away from me. I'm almost ready." Quickly, she closed down her computer and sat on the end of the bed to slip on her shoes.

"I brought the notebook," he said.

She looked up. He'd stepped into the room but stopped within a foot of the door.

"Thanks." She pointed to the desk. "Leave it on my computer."

He did as she asked, then retreated at once to the door.

When she stood, she scanned the room. "Hear me snore" stood out on the T-shirt thrown carelessly against the pillow. She rolled her eyes, embarrassed he might have seen.

"OK." She checked her hair one last time in the mirror and grabbed her purse. "Let's go."

The host seated them at a small table in a quiet corner and handed them oversized menus in leather folders. The restaurant was every bit as elegant as Angela remembered from her previous visit.

"I don't eat in places like this often," Alvaro said.

"One of the perks of the job." She'd grown used to these kinds of restaurants when she traveled for business. One of the rewards of working for a big agency with top-tier clients. "It's not as expensive as it looks."

"More than Eduardo's." He read the menu. "Are you sure Mr. Barton is OK with this?"

"We've been frugal all day. You even supplied the coffee this morning."

But his questions triggered concern. Not about whether the place was too expensive. It wasn't particularly, and it would be part of a much larger report covering the whole trip. Her concern was for him.

"Are you OK with eating here? We can go someplace else if you'd rather."

"Are you loco? Only one time did I eat in a place so fine. At the ASEE conference, Mr. Barton invited me to lunch."

"Nice, huh?"

"At the hotel in Chicago, lunch cost as much as most people in El Salvador make in a year. This dinner we are having is another story I will tell when I go home."

It was all perspective. Growing up in southwest Iowa, Angela ate out often. Her parents belonged to the country club, where they liked to golf, but that country club was not much more than a dressed-up prefab building, and anyone in town could eat there if they made a reservation. The first time she set foot in the Wakonda Club in Des Moines, however, she felt she didn't belong there. The smell of old money wafted on the air as distinctly as the Chanel No. 5 worn by elegant women sporting professionally coiffed hair and designer dresses. Certain those women could spot an imposter in their ranks, Angela had bluffed her way through the cocktail party in her simple little black dress and strappy pumps. She learned the art of talking business, deflecting attention away from herself and onto her clients and their spouses.

Alvaro reached for the wine list. "Wine?"

"I like red wines," she said, "but don't know one from another. Will you choose?"

He studied the list, asking her questions about what she liked and didn't like in wines. When the server came, he ordered Malbec for them both. While they waited, he explained that he'd learned about wine through a student organization in college.

When the server returned with the wine, Angela followed Alvaro's example, swirling the deep-red liquid in the glass and holding the first sip in her mouth, searching for hints of the fruit he listed when describing the wine.

"What do you think?" he asked after she swallowed.

She ran her tongue over her lips. "I could taste plum. And pepper?"

His eyes reflected approval. "I had this wine at a tasting. It is as good as I remembered."

She lifted her glass in a small salute. "Thanks for introducing me to two great flavors. Eduardo's and Malbec."

"El gusto es mio," he said.

As they perused the menus, he asked, "Did today go as you hoped? Did you find out what you needed to?"

She gazed into the distance as she called to mind the day's meetings. "Seeing another plant was helpful, especially one that has so many locations. We could learn from them. Your thoughts?"

"I will dig into that research report. We have some practices to keep people from injuries, but maybe we can do more."

"Another thing is that in a larger town, ethnic groups can . . . not blend in exactly . . . but be more invisible." She sipped at the wine. "In Hammond, differences are visible everywhere: stores, churches, schools."

"I was surprised at the history of African-Americans in Iowa. They have lived here a long time, and there is still a divide."

"That's not encouraging, is it?"

They ordered and talked easily through the salad course. When their meals arrived—veal scaloppini for her and steak de burgo for him—they took a break from discussing work to savor the flavorful dishes.

After a few moments, she posed the question that had come to her about the owners of Cafe Dodici compared to people like Eduardo and Maria in Hammond.

"I am thinking of 'follow the money,'" he responded. "It must cost a great deal to buy this building and make this restaurant. I doubt Eduardo could afford such an investment."

"He could get a loan. I'm sure these people did—to afford this."

Alvaro shook his head. "Most Mexicans would not consider borrowing so much even if the bank in Hammond would give Eduardo the money. Besides, you say these people had family here to speak for them. Without that? I think it is doubtful."

She made a note to add financing to the report. Then she brought him up to speed on her conversation with the immigration attorney.

"I told Father Burke about the asylum and juvenile-status visa possibilities. And he said he'd talk with Emilio's uncle about getting an attorney. Do you know if Emilio had a deportation hearing yet?"

He shook his head. "I don't."

She buttered a piece of bread and said, "We need to find out. The attorney said it's important to make the case for either asylum or the SIJS visa right away. Emilio stays in the country until it is decided."

"How long does it take?"

"She said anywhere from a few months to a couple of years."

"I did not know it took so long. I will be gone from here before it is decided," he said.

There was that pang again. "We will both be gone," she said.

Alvaro drank the last of his wine, and they ordered two more glasses.

"It has to be unsettling," she said. "Not to know where your future will be."

He did not respond, and she realized she may have touched on a personal concern for him.

"Do you worry about yourself?" she asked.

He sat quietly for a moment. "Doesn't everyone?" he asked. Then he cut another bite of steak.

"Not in the way Emilio does. Not the way you must."

Then she turned to her own meal, and for a couple of minutes, they ate, lost in their own thoughts.

Finally, she broke the silence. "Did I ever tell you I talked to Gordon about the housing? He told me Barton Packing doesn't own those houses or manage them."

"No?" He was as surprised as she'd been when she heard.

"Huh-uh. There's a company in Chicago." She filled him in on what she knew. "Barton Packing really is doing a service to employees to pick up the cost for the first month."

Alvaro continued to eat in silence, then said, "They could do more."

"What do you mean?"

"They are a big company, and the rent isn't much for such a big company."

"That's true, but it's not their job to provide free housing for employees." She recalled Father Burke making much the same point the first time she met him. Truthfully, she felt as Alvaro did but considered it an obligation to support the company. "I guess you've heard Gordon harp about the thin profit margins."

Alvaro persisted. "They are a big company. They could make the Chicago company clean the places up. Make the rent lower. We are always keeping their houses full."

"You make a good point. I will ask if they've ever tried."

The wine had begun to have an effect, and Angela had grown weary of talking business. They had finished eating, and the server removed their plates.

"Tell me about your tat. When I first saw it, I thought it was a snake."

Alvaro rubbed the arm where the tattoo was hidden by his shirt and jacket. "It is a river and the mountains near my home in El Salvador. My family took picnics by the river many times.

Before I left, my mother gave me a picture so I would remember where I came from."

"How long have you had it?"

"Since I knew I would not return home after college. I wouldn't see my family for years, so I had the tattoo made."

"How far does it go? The tattoo. Is it just on your arm or over your shoulder?"

He looked at her for an extended moment. His right eyebrow arched. "You want to see it?"

His tone delivered such a blunt invitation that desire flooded in, driving out all reserve. She rested her cheek on her palm, looked deep into his eyes, and let a seductive smile touch her lips. "I would."

She spoke the truth of her body, and as soon as the words were out of her mouth, she realized she'd crossed a line. Averting her eyes, she sat up straight and struggled to regain her professional demeanor.

"Not now, of course." She wiped her lips with her napkin, painfully conscious of the lava of desire rising in her core, belatedly aware that in saying "not now," she'd implied later. She swallowed to release the tightness in her throat and checked the time on her phone. "I didn't realize it was so late. I have to finish the report for my boss on what we've seen so far." She flagged the server down and asked for the check.

"He expects it tonight?" Alvaro asked.

"He'll look for an update when he gets in tomorrow morning. And we'll have to check out first thing to get to Columbus Junction."

"We will work on it together, yes?"

Working in her room crossed her mind, but she knew that wasn't wise, for her or him, not in a room dominated by a bed with her insane nightshirt on the pillow.

"How about we work in the lobby?" she suggested. "It won't take long. I don't want the night to run too late. I'll run upstairs for my laptop and the notebook."

She signed the bill to her room and concentrated on putting the receipt in her purse.

"I will meet you there," he said, and left the table without waiting for her.

She watched his back for a moment. She'd upset him. Maybe insulted him. They'd both been flirting, and she let herself go to far. *Oh, god,* she thought. *What have I done?*

In her room she grabbed the laptop and notebook. Looking in the mirror, she saw her cheeks were flushed, her eyes bright. Wine did that to her. Wine and an attractive man. The lobby was definitely safer. For them both.

By the time she'd come back downstairs, Alvaro had staked out a quiet corner with comfortable chairs. A couch was part of the furniture grouping, but he'd taken one of the chairs. To ensure distance, she imagined. She took the other chair.

Opening her laptop, she jumped immediately into talking about the report as though the exchange in the restaurant hadn't happened. All the while, he remained silent. She felt his eyes on her, could sense he didn't want to let it pass. But she didn't allow herself to return his gaze.

After several moments, he cleared his throat. "Nothing about Postville?" he asked.

A tiny breath—relief or heartache?—slipped between her lips. "It wasn't on our list."

"But it was interesting. The two women at the shoe store. They made you mad. Why not?"

She finally raised her eyes from her laptop. Her personal emotional reactions weren't the point. "I'm supposed to be neutral," she said. She could have meant either the women in the store or her relationship with him.

"You said that. You also said you speak for everyone. What about those women? And the woman in the bank in Hammond?"

She pursed her lips and leaned back into the comfort of the overstuffed chair. *Out of the mouths of babes,* she thought. Or a babe. She couldn't stop thinking about how hot he was. *Shake it off, Darrah,* she ordered herself.

Leaning forward again, she slid the computer to face her. "OK. It's good point." She started typing up a list of all the various people involved at the plant, in the community, customers, media.

As they talked, he took off his jacket. The azure-colored shirt next to his umber skin reminded her of blue sky over red rocks in the western states. She kept typing.

Finally, she handed him the laptop. "Take a look. I added everything we talked about and a few more things those made me think of."

"This could be clearer," he said. He had his hands over the keyboard but paused. "May I?"

"Sure. But I want to see what you're doing." She moved to the couch. "Sit over here so we can both see."

"You're not afraid?"

"What do you mean, afraid?" she blustered. Of course she knew what he meant, but she'd succumbed to a wine-fueled flirtation that could go no further. She hoped she had cut it off cleanly enough.

"Of being with me?" He spoke without innuendo.

"Crazy man," she retorted. "It had nothing to do with being afraid."

"No? What then?"

"Too much wine." She skirted the real issue, that she was genuinely attracted to him. "Speaking of which, do you want another glass of wine or something else?" She looked across the lobby to the restaurant. Maybe she could flag a server.

"Something else," he said.

She glanced at him sharply. The glint in his eyes told her she once again said something he intentionally chose to misinterpret. She slapped a palm to her forehead. "To drink, I mean. To drink."

"I know." He grinned. "A Coca-Cola. I'll go to the restaurant."

"Get one for me, too."

Any hurt or anger he'd felt appeared to have dissolved, and for that she was grateful. He returned with the Cokes, and for the next hour they sat shoulder to shoulder sipping pop, brainstorming, and putting everything in the grid Alvaro devised to keep track of various interest groups and issues and how they intersected.

An hour later, she closed the computer and relaxed back into the corner of the couch. "I'm beat. Are you ready to call it a night? I can't believe how much we got done. You were as good as anybody at Sherborn-Watts."

"It reminded me of the study groups we had at ISU." He scrubbed his chin with his knuckles. "Different than working at Barton."

"No doubt." She studied him for a moment. "You know, I really don't see you working in a plant long term."

"I see myself in some sort of industry," he said. "Maybe not a meat-packing plant. But that has been good for me."

"Is it different than you imagined?"

"Harder work. Maybe I am getting soft?"

"I doubt it." She stopped herself from saying anything about his physique.

"Someone needs to do these jobs. They pay more than people could make in Mexico or Central America. But it is not easy to see people treated poorly."

"Why don't they say something?"

"They need the jobs. They cannot speak up or they get points and they may lose the jobs."

"Couldn't you speak up?"

"I, too, need the job."

"But you will be leaving soon. What would you have to lose?"

He regarded her silently. "There is always something to lose, Angela. I will need the recommendation from Mr. Barton and Mr. Ryker. If I cause trouble, they will make it hard for me in the future."

"Hmm. I could see Gordon doing that, but not Nick."

She thought about the vast difference between the two company leaders. As she covered her mouth to hide a massive yawn, she realized the long day had caught up with her. "I'm so tired, I'm losing it. Let's call it a night, and we'll take it up again in the morning."

When they returned to their rooms, standing side by side at their doors, what could have felt awkward did not. She had her key in the lock, her hand on the door handle, but stopped. "Alvaro?"

"Sí?"

"I'm glad we kept working tonight."

"Buenas noches, amiga," he responded.

"Buenas noches, Alvaro. *Duerma bien."*

Inside her room, she leaned against the door. He called her "amiga." She quite liked the sound of that.

Chapter 21

In Columbus Junction their first stop was the chamber office, where the receptionist put cups of coffee in their hands before she ushered them in to see the director of community development, an enthusiastic woman in her fifties.

"Tyson is a model," she said, "for how a company can work with the community, treat their team members, take care of their facility. One real good example of that was during the 2008 flood. When the river ran over its banks and flooded the town, we lost our water supply. Tyson ran a fire hose from their plant all the way into town and supplied the town with drinking water for three days."

When Angela raised the topic of diversity, the woman provided interesting historical perspective. "Most people don't know it, but our Hispanic roots run deep in southeast Iowa. Mexican immigrants came to Iowa after the Civil War to work on the Santa Fe railroad. Many stayed. In fact"—she riffled through the papers on her desk until she found a brochure—"These immigrants started Mexican Fiesta, the oldest ethnic festival in the state. It's been held every year for more than ninety years."

"We know that many, maybe all, packing plants are recruiting employees from out of state. Latino, Asian, African. How has the community responded to that?" Angela asked.

The woman sipped at her coffee, reflecting before she answered. "It's taken some adjusting, but overall pretty well. One thing that surprised me was that the Latino community here in Columbus Junction was most vocal in opposing the influx of immigrants. Said these new people were taking their jobs."

"That is surprising," Angela agreed. Father Burke had mentioned something similar when he talked about US immigration history. But he hadn't said the opposition to immigrants could stem from citizens who were part of the same ethnic group. She would add this tidbit to her continuing effort to tease apart the tangled language surrounding immigration.

"Are there programs to encourage minority businesses?" Alvaro asked.

"We encourage everyone who wants to start a business. You can look at our chamber member list and see from the names how diverse our business base is."

After a tour of Tyson from the friendly plant manager, Alvaro and Angela left bursting with ideas. One program that particularly interested them was the language-learning software the company provided through a grant to local schools. Hammond schools, churches like Saint Catherine's, and individual employees could all benefit from a program like that.

For lunch, they discovered a Mexican restaurant almost as good as Eduardo's. Residential neighborhoods included houses with multiple satellite dishes, in no better condition than the ones in Hammond, but no one they spoke with linked those houses specifically with the Tyson plant. *Interesting,* she thought, *that Barton's effort to do something good for employees could be a negative.*

After lunch, they pointed the car to Ottumwa, the final stop on the trip.

The JBS USA pork plant manager they'd arranged to meet with had been called away unexpectedly. In his place they were met by Manuel, a Latino supervisor who led them to a large break room. Angela noted that vending machines dispensing sandwiches and wraps, vegetables and fruit, yogurt, and soft drinks lined a full wall.

"That's a terrific variety of food to have available," Angela commented.

"It's a big benefit to have so much food here. JBS asks team members at least once a year what we want in the machines," Manuel explained. "They also subsidize the cost so it is cheap to eat here."

Angela caught Alvaro's eye. She could tell he was thinking, just as she was, that the vending machines Barton offered paled by comparison.

They chose chairs at a quieter corner table, and Angela led the discussion of JBS involvement in the communities around its plants.

"We're committed to the communities we live and work in," he said. "In each community where we do business, we work hard to meet local needs."

Angela probed for examples and learned about donations to the food pantry in one town, uniforms for the Little League team in another, and food stands at the county fair in a third. In each case the company encouraged employee involvement along with the donations.

"Barton Packing donates product directly to a local church that provides meals," Angela said.

"For us, the food pantry is an equitable way to provide service without having to coordinate with many individual entities."

"Good point. Hammond doesn't have a food pantry, but there is one in the county seat." She added a note to her already-long list.

When Alvaro delved into workforce diversity at the plant, they learned that overall percentages of various ethnic groups mirrored those at Hammond's plant. "Do you have translators on staff?"

"We couldn't work without them" was the response. "In addition, many supervisors are multilingual, as I am."

"Hammond does not have so many whites who speak Spanish, let alone the other languages."

"At least half of our supervisors are Latino or Asian," Manuel explained.

Alvaro quietly arched an eyebrow toward Angela.

When they returned to the parking lot, Angela asked about that. "You reacted to his comment about their diverse plant supervisors. Why was that?"

"I am the only manager in the Barton plant who is not white."

She had focused questions on how the plants interacted with communities and what programs they had to engage and support employees. She hadn't asked about management diversity. She had a sinking feeling Barton Packing was unique in that regard, and not in a positive way.

* * *

Back in her motel room in Hammond a few days later, the phone rang and Angela marked her place in the future-world novel she was reading, then swiped the screen.

"Hi, Dave."

Her boss came on the line, full of enthusiasm and compliments for the report she had just emailed.

"Thanks," she said. "What struck us both was how many programs the other plants had in place to support the communities and their employees. Frankly, Barton Packing is in the Dark Ages by comparison."

"Give me some examples."

"It starts with something as basic as terminology. In other plants they refer to employees as 'team members.' At Barton, they're 'workers.'"

"That's an easy enough change to make. And wouldn't cost anything."

"Alvaro thought it would be well received by workers," Angela agreed. "But I'm concerned that if we change the terminology without changing the way employees are engaged, it doesn't mean much. And pretty soon employees would see through it."

"What kind of changes are you thinking?"

She listed several possibilities, from expanded vending machines to an actual cafeteria, time off for volunteering in things like community beautification projects or town events. She hesitated.

"Those all seem like reasonable things to bring up. What aren't you saying?"

"It's a lot of little stuff." She relayed the things that had niggled at her since she learned about them. The shabby housing. Relegating Muslim prayers to a chemical-storage room. Then penalizing workers for using it. The points system in general. Lack of management diversity. "But if we bring all this up, they may take it as an indictment of the way they run things."

"And they'd be right," he said. "So we won't do it."

His flat-footed decision to not move forward on any of these points astonished her. These problems were core to the employees, to Alvaro. Each time she and Alvaro revisited one of these issues, she came away enthusiastic about going to Nick to fix the problem. These were the right things to do.

They wrangled back and forth for another half hour. Twice more, Angela tried to convince Dave to help her find a way to address some of the problems she saw as core to the Barton culture. Each time he resisted. Finally, they settled on an approach that involved laying out what other plants did and letting Nick and Gordon draw their own conclusions.

"To change behavior, change beliefs." Dave stated one of his oft-repeated principles. "If they come to believe that there are better ways, they'll adapt their behavior to achieve better results."

The truth of the axiom had never been so clear to Angela as it had been since being at Barton Packing. She could point to the poodle woman at the bank or the shopkeeper in Postville or even Gordon, but Angela had to admit she had been equally judgmental herself. In a thousand small ways she made judgments every day. She'd been hesitant about the biker tailing her to the church only to find he was the priest. She'd assumed Alvaro wouldn't speak English and he wouldn't be educated because he worked in a packing plant. It had taken personal relationships and personal involvement to change her beliefs.

Perhaps the axiom would also work with Nick, even on the deeper cultural issues she and Alvaro knew mattered deeply to the employees. She doubted any move from Gordon, but she acknowledged that hope sprung eternal.

"Figure out a couple of days to come to Des Moines," Dave said as their discussion wound down. "How about coming in Friday? You could spend the weekend in Des Moines."

She hedged. If the weather was nice, she and Alvaro planned to take a few of the kids to the park. "Is there something I need to be on site for?"

"It wouldn't hurt if you spent face time with the people you supervise."

"I'll make a point to ask them directly next time we talk if we need to be face to face. And if the weather turns bad, I may come home. But if it's nice, we're going to have a picnic."

"We?"

"Alvaro and I and some of the kids." She quickly returned the conversation to work. "What did you find out about the product-expiration question?" she asked.

"I checked with research this morning. They got called in to work on a new business pitch and haven't had time to do the digging."

Vexed, Angela sniffed. She didn't get why he was so laid back about this. "It can't be so hard to figure out. Do I need to do it myself?"

"They'll get to it. Don't worry."

"But I do. I really think I should let Nick know about this. Or see if he knows already. It isn't something we should let pass, Dave." He always had such drive for getting things done, particularly when it came to a big client. "Or do you think I'm wrong on this, too?"

He ignored the edginess in her voice. "We need to be sure of the facts. Since the donation was eaten without a problem, it's not urgent."

"But what if it happens again?"

"Angela, you're manufacturing trouble here. That's not the way to build client business."

"But what about—"

"You're not listening. I'm inclined to think the expiration-date issue was probably a one-time thing. Gordon's too smart to let product expire on a regular basis."

Dave's tone told her to drop it. Angela acknowledged Gordon was smart, but she wasn't at all convinced he wouldn't make a practice of changing expiration dates if he needed to. In fact, from what she'd seen, that was exactly what he would do.

Dave might think she was off base with her concern, but she didn't. After they disconnected, she started to research expiration dates on her own.

Chapter 22

Ten minutes before she'd told Cesar and Camila Muñoz she'd be there, Angela parked across the street, two houses away from the Muñoz residence. Their story-and-a half arts-and-crafts-style bungalow fit well in the neighborhood of older homes, all with carefully tended lawns. Toys, including a play kitchen set, a child-sized table and chairs, and a pink-and-turquoise Big Wheel, crowded the porch spanning the front of the well-maintained house. Two bicycles leaned against the porch.

Angela didn't know why it hadn't occurred to her before to see where Emilio lived. Outside the classes twice a week at Saint Catherine's, the kids went on with their lives, and she went on with hers. After Father Burke told her he'd spoken with Camila Muñoz and found out the hearing date was coming up soon, Angela decided to meet Emilio's family herself.

From where she sat, Angela could see only a sliver of the Muñoz' backyard. She spotted tomato and pepper plants in what appeared to be a large vegetable garden.

A white van bearing the Muñoz Plumbing & Heating logo took up most of the driveway. Propped up on blocks, the right rear wheel removed, the van looked as though it had bigger problems than a flat.

According to Father Burke, the Muñozes had lived in Hammond for nearly twenty years, and Mr. Muñoz had built a reputable business. Cesar and Camila were parents to five children. Seeing their house, which likely had three small bedrooms at most, Angela could imagine their living quarters had been cramped even before adding Emilio.

She got out of the car and climbed the steps to the front door. A Latino man in his late forties with neatly trimmed hair and a good-natured smile opened the door before she knocked.

"Good afternoon. I'm Angela Darrah."

"Cesar Muñoz," he responded, stepping back so she could enter. "This is my wife, Camila."

A short, plump woman, Camila Muñoz smiled as she balanced a toddler on her hip and extended her hand. "Hello. Come in."

Angela shook hands with them both. "I'm pleased to meet you." She smiled at the toddler, an adorable little girl with huge dark eyes, dressed in a pink Hello Kitty T-shirt and brown polka-dot leggings, her shiny black hair held back by Hello Kitty barrettes. "And who is this cutie?" she asked.

"This is Mary," Camila said. At the mention of her name, the toddler buried her face in her mother's shoulder. "She is . . ." She looked to her husband. *"¿Cómo se dice 'tímida'?"*

"Shy," he said.

"Sí." Camila said to Angela, "she is shy."

Angela noted that Cesar's words held barely a trace of an accent, while Camila's still carried strong Spanish overtones. Additionally, it appeared the woman might be more comfortable speaking Spanish. For a moment, Angela wondered if it would be seen as condescending if she spoke Spanish? After balancing on that fence for a second, she responded in English. "She'll only be shy for a little while."

Camila smiled. "For a little while. Yes."

"Please." Cesar gestured to the sofa.

"Thank you." Angela took in the tidy living room as she sat. A gallery of family pictures lined one wall. Worn yet comfortable-looking furniture was arranged for a clear view of a flat-screen TV dominating another wall. A jumble of toys filled two white plastic laundry baskets next to the TV. An arched opening separated the living room from a dining room crowded with a large oak table and chairs. The slice of a small kitchen visible beyond the dining room didn't appear to offer space for another table, at least not one large enough to hold eight.

"You have a lovely home," she said, turning her attention to Cesar and Camila. "I appreciate you talking with me."

"Father Burke said you teach one of the classes at church," Cesar said.

"Yes. Emilio is in my class. He is a smart boy. He is learning English so quickly." She heard herself speaking more loudly, more distinctly than necessary and with the same kind of simple subject-verb sentences she used with the kids in class. What was the matter with her? Such simplicity wasn't necessary for Cesar or probably even for Camila, who appeared to understand English well, even if words might occasionally elude her. Lowering her voice, she continued.

"The reason I wanted to talk with you is because I wanted to know more about Emilio. I was astounded to hear how he came here. I spoke with an attorney . . ." She stopped when she saw that Cesar appeared confused. "You are not an attorney?" he asked.

Angela raised her hands and shook her head. "No, no."

"*Lo pensé . . . ,*" Camila Muñoz said.

A look passed between the two, and she stopped.

"Father Burke told my wife . . . ," he began, and stopped. "We thought that you were an attorney."

"There's a misunderstanding," Angela explained. "Emilio is in my class, and I was concerned about him. So I *spoke* with an attorney to learn how the system works."

Cesar frowned. "We did not understand. We do not think Emilio can stay here much longer, and we thought you would tell us what to do."

"He can't stay here? Why not?"

Cesar glanced again at his wife before responding. "It is only that we do not have room." He seemed about to say more, but stopped himself.

Angela took a new tack. "How did it happen? That you brought Emilio here?"

"When Emilio came to Texas, he told the border officials I am his uncle."

"That's what the attorney told me usually happens. A relative in the States is expecting the child."

"When Emilio's mother wrote to us, we told her it would not work for him to stay here."

"But he was in danger in Honduras," Angela said.

"We know this. But we cannot keep him."

"Are there other relatives?" she asked, recalling the attorney's comment about children having a better chance in California. "Somewhere else he can stay?"

"We have written letters, but we have not found anyone."

"I see. But Emilio can continue to live here, at least for a while?"

"Yes. He can stay for now. His hearing is in two weeks. Then we may know what to do."

"The attorney told me the two most common options for children are asylum or a special visa. Have you talked with an attorney about which is best for Emilio?"

"We do not have an attorney. That is why we thought you are here."

They'd greeted her with the hope of a solution; instead, she'd arrived with empty hands.

"Have you heard of Standing for Justice? They provide free legal counsel. I have their address and number." She searched in her purse for the paper with the number. "Here it is," she said, handing it to Cesar. "They are in Des Moines, but they could help you. Children who have an attorney are much more likely to be successful in staying."

Cesar looked at the paper for a long moment, then laid it on the arm of his chair.

"Their attorneys work for free," she emphasized.

"They are in Des Moines," he said, as though the distance ruled them out.

"I'm sure they could do most things by phone," she said.

"The hearing is in Omaha, and my van is broken."

"Will it be fixed by then? The lawyer told me it is critical he not miss the hearing." Angela began to feel like a social worker, asking personal questions, offering information, encouraging but not solving.

"It is five hours from here. A full day, and that is only the first. A friend told me there are many hearings. There are things I must do here."

In a discussion filled with new terms and acronyms, Angela had not thought to ask the attorney about the entire process of gaining legal status. Naively, she had pictured only one day in court. As soon as he said it, though, she realized several court dates made sense. Delays and continuances were part of every courtroom TV show she'd ever watched.

"Could you find someone else to take him?"

"Is it allowed?" Cesar asked.

"I don't know," Angela admitted. It frustrated her to continually find she knew less than she thought. What she did know was she'd be talking with the attorney again.

The steady stream of excuses stymied her.

"Mr. and Mrs. Muñoz, I do want to help, but I'm not sure how. You said the hearing is in two weeks. Can you tell me exactly when and where?" Maybe the details would mean something to the attorney.

"I will go," Camila said. Still holding Mary, she started to get up, an effort that elicited a small sigh.

Cesar touched her wrist. "Let me," he said.

Camila sank back into the chair. *"Gracias, mi amor."*

Their sweet exchange made Angela smile.

Cesar returned with a paper that he handed to her. Angela noted the hearing was at 1:00 p.m., two weeks from yesterday. She jotted down the information.

"Thank you. I appreciate this. If I learn anything that could help, I'll be back in touch. Now, I've taken enough of your time." She stood.

"I will walk you out," Cesar said.

On the porch, he stopped her. "Ms. Darrah." His voice held a touch of frustration. "We took Emilio in. But we have five children. And my wife . . ."

Searching his face, Angela saw a tightness she hadn't noticed before.

"We took him in, but . . . ," Cesar began, but again stopped short. He looked out toward the van before saying flatly, "It is too expensive to keep another child. We cannot afford to keep him."

Uncertain what to say, she followed his gaze to the van.

"I have a thought," he said. "Perhaps you could take Emilio to the hearing."

"I'm in Hammond to work for Barton Packing, and I have to be at the plant every day. I couldn't . . ." She heard herself rushing to excuse herself from the same things she had wanted him to do. To take responsibility for a child. To reorganize her life to assume additional roles.

"Father Burke says we can trust you. You say you want to help."

"I do, but I presume the child's sponsor would have to be there, wouldn't they?"

Cesar shrugged. "I don't know."

"Please call the number I gave you. I know Standing for Justice will help." She shook Cesar's hand. "What you're doing for Emilio . . . is important."

By the time she slid behind the wheel of her car, Cesar Muñoz had gone back into the house. She sat for a moment, thinking about the conversation and feeling wholly inadequate. The Muñozes had been so generous in taking in Emilio. But when they had reached out to her for help, she had backed away.

Chapter 23

On Thursday, she went to the church early hoping to see Alvaro before classes started. But her kids arrived, and she was drawn into class without spotting him.

"Is good?" Maria's question drew Angela back to the room.

She felt eight sets of eyes watching for approval as she scanned the classroom. They'd done an admirable job cleaning up. "Well done." She smiled. "Go on to supper. See you next week."

Linda showed up just as Angela was collapsing the last folding wall. "Staying for supper?" she asked.

"I am. Let's get in line." Angela looked toward the sanctuary steps. "Maybe Alvaro will join us."

An impish grin lit up Linda's face. "You had a good time on that trip, didn't you?" Her lifted eyebrows waggled and issued a tell-me-more invitation as they took plates and walked through the line collecting chicken enchiladas, salad, and bread.

"We were on business," Angela reiterated. "Did you know he hasn't been home in almost eight years?"

"Maybe he'll stay," she suggested.

"Not likely. His visa is up this year."

Linda nudged Angela with her elbow. "Maybe he has a new reason to extend his visa."

Angela felt herself blush. "I'm sure I don't know what you mean."

"I'm sure you do." Linda leaned closer and spoke in a whisper. "Hey, you obviously like him."

Angela busied herself with dishing up salad. "He's a client, Linda," she whispered over her shoulder. "It's really not an option."

Though I wish it were, she wanted to add. She'd spent most of one night in a frustrating debate with herself, trying to argue that being intimate with a client was OK. Her professional self beat her personal self every time.

"If you say so." Linda's grin said she didn't believe that for a second.

Angela changed the subject as they picked up glasses of lemonade. "I have to tell you what happened in class. I passed out papers so the children could fill in the missing words in sentences. At one point, Emilio held up his paper and said, *'Mirada, mama. Está bien?'*"

"He called you mama. That is so sweet."

"He didn't even realize he'd done it. The kids laughed and that embarrassed him, but it *was* sweet. And sad. I wanted to hug him." Emilio's unconscious slip had triggered a mothering instinct Angela hadn't felt before. When she had kids, she hoped one would be just like Emilio.

By the time they were through the line, many of the kids had finished eating, so they had no trouble finding seats. Father Burke came through the line last. Wearing jeans and motorcycle boots, he looked ready to ride. Angela beckoned him to join them.

"Thought you were saving that seat," Linda said to Angela before the priest walked over.

"There's still room. Besides, I want to get Father Burke's thoughts—and yours, too . . ."

Just then, Angela spotted Alvaro coming through the basement door. "There he is," she said, waving him over.

"Hola," Alvaro said. "¿Que pasa?"

"You're just in time," Angela said. "I spoke with Cesar and Camila Muñoz yesterday. If you'd like to join us, I'll wait to share until you get your meal."

"I already ate," he said, and pulled up a chair. "Go ahead."

Her attention went to the chicken enchilada on her plate, and she wondered if he wasn't eating because this chicken came from Barton Packing. Did he know of more expired product? She'd ask him later. She slid her own plate a few inches away and focused on telling them about the Muñoz discussion.

"They seem like nice people, but I came away concerned," she summarized.

"Why's that?" Father Burke asked.

"Several things." Angela ticked off points in her mind as she spoke. "It's a long way to Omaha, so Cesar would have to be away from home and work for at least a day. That's compounded by his van. It's unreliable. Then, even though the hearing is in less than two weeks, they don't have an attorney. Finally, and this is maybe most concerning, a couple of times Cesar repeated that Emilio can't stay with them."

"Did he say why?" Linda asked.

"From what he said, it sounded as though much of the reason is financial. I also felt he wasn't telling me everything. But he doesn't know me, so why would he?" She turned to Father Burke. "Also, Camila misunderstood you. She thought I was an attorney. They were expecting help I couldn't give them."

The priest grimaced. "Mea culpa. I thought I'd made myself clear. We need to help, and I know people in the congregation who would, but I'm hesitant to offer an open handout. Do you know them, Alvaro?"

"We have met once."

"Would you talk with them? I don't know them well, and they might open up to you more."

"I could walk Emilio home tonight," Alvaro said.

"Could you call your attorney contact again?" Father Burke asked Angela.

"I already plan to. Talking with Cesar, I realized I still had lots of questions, so I set up a call for tomorrow afternoon." Angela reached into her purse for a paper that already included a half dozen new questions. "Let's make sure I get everything we need to know."

* * *

"I have questions that relate to the process the boy will go through," Angela said when she had Schiffler on the phone. "I had it in my head there was just one hearing. Probably naive."

Schiffler laughed. "It's far more complicated. Actually, it can take multiple hearings over several years."

"I had no idea," Angela said, already envisioning the challenge such a time commitment would be for Cesar. "Also, he doesn't have an attorney. I gave Emilio's sponsor your name and number, but he seemed reluctant to call. What happens if he doesn't have an attorney? How will they know what to do? Will he ruin his chances entirely?"

"There's a volunteer-attorney program to provide temporary help at the hearing for children without representation. The attorney explains the options and provides packets of information on asylum and the SIJS visa."

"That's helpful," Angela said, taking notes furiously.

"To a point. It's a lot of information, and it's not easy to understand. Even for native English speakers. And the lawyer is only with the child for that day, to help the child through the legalese-heavy hearing process."

"So what happens at the first hearing?"

"The first court hearing is called a master-calendar hearing, and it's like an arraignment. The child admits to being in the US without documentation. Then the judge sets a future court date—an individual hearing—to hear evidence for why the child should be allowed to stay."

"Would the child have to say right away whether they wanted asylum or special immigrant status?"

"No, particularly if the child doesn't have an attorney. The volunteer attorney would explain that the child hasn't had time to find an attorney and they need more time. Then the judge would set a new master-calendar hearing date, hoping the child would have an attorney by then."

"How long could this go on? Pushing it out?"

"Most cases have at least three or four hearings before they finally get to the individual hearing—the one where the child presents their case. The individual hearing might not be for three or four years."

Angela couldn't believe she'd heard right. "Three or four years?" By then, Emilio would be in middle school, a teenager. The sweet little boy coloring pictures of dogs would be tackling science projects and all the hormone-fueled challenges of adolescence. The thought dazed her.

"That's correct. These kids' cases have been prioritized by the courts, though, so there will probably be a hearing in a year or two."

Cesar had voiced concern about going to Omaha once. How would he manage multiple hearings over years? Where would she herself be in three or four years? Not in Hammond, for sure. She'd imagined getting Emilio's legal status fixed in months. Not years. She shook her head. Thinking about that solved nothing. She focused again on Schiffler. "If the child missed a hearing, could an attorney reverse the process somehow?"

"An attorney would need to file a motion to reopen the case. The judges have to follow strict rules, though, so there's no guarantee. But they'd have to try because it's the only chance a child would have."

Once again, Angela could feel herself suffering information overload. The complicated process made Emilio's situation feel even more tenuous. But then she remembered Emilio's smile, how eagerly he participated in every class, his home with the Muñozes. She had to help him.

"One last question. Can someone other than the sponsor bring the child to the hearings? It may not be possible for the boy's uncle to make the trip."

"Anyone can bring the child to the hearing."

"I could do it?"

"Yes. Anyone."

Angela imagined that after hearing about the puzzling process and extended time commitment, Cesar Muñoz would be even more reluctant to keep his nephew with him. But at least his suggestion that she take Emilio to the hearing herself wasn't as crazy as it at first sounded. Her concern eased on at least one point. But they still needed an attorney, and she hoped Alvaro would convince Cesar to follow through.

Chapter 24

"Buenas tardes, Eduardo,*"* Angela said as she stepped up to the counter to pick up her carryout order. *"Hola,* Maria." She waved to the woman she seldom saw anywhere except at the stove.

"Buenas tardes, Angela." Eduardo greeted her with a subdued expression. "Do you have a moment?"

Angela glanced at her watch. Alvaro was waiting and the food was ready—she could see the bags set by the stove—but she smiled and said, "Sure."

"Let's sit there." He pointed to a corner table as he poured two glasses of pop.

His request was unusual. They'd only ever had one extended conversation when she began gathering information for Barton Packing; otherwise they exchanged chitchat only about food and weather.

"Thanks." She accepted the glass he offered. "What can I do for you?"

A normally amiable man, Eduardo shifted uncomfortably after he sat, clasping and unclasping his hands. He looked back to his wife twice. Finally, he said, "I want to talk with you about Alvaro."

Concern flared in her chest. "What? Is something wrong?"

He lifted a hand as though to wave off her anxiety. "Not as you think. I must speak with you because Alvaro is like a son to us." He hesitated before continuing. "There are so few people like him, so few his age in Hammond. When you came to town, it was good to see him have a friend."

"I've enjoyed knowing him, too."

"But we have seen you become close." Again, he looked to his wife, who had moved nearer to the cash register, within hearing distance. Her face serious, Maria nodded at him to continue. "This concerns us. You are a nice woman. Maria and I agree."

He offered the comment without sarcasm, yet it felt anything but a compliment. Angela tilted her head and responded cautiously, "I'm glad you think so."

Eduardo balled his hands into fists, then stretched out his fingers again. She could see him struggling to speak. Finally, she said, "Eduardo, please. Say what's on your mind."

"It's better to just say things, right?" He took a big swallow of pop. "All right. You two are together often," he said. "First here. Now at his apartment. And we think it is too much."

"I don't understand."

"We can see what is happening. It is not good."

She stiffened, pulling back from the table with a frown. The time she and Alvaro spent together wasn't any of Eduardo and Maria's business. She reached for the pop, letting the condensation on the glass cool her down. These were Alvaro's friends. She needed to understand where they were coming from.

"If Alvaro didn't have friends here and now he does, how is that not good?"

"Alvaro should be with a woman like him."

"Like him?" Confusion deepened her frown.

"A Latina woman. When Latino men and white women get together, it is a problem for everyone. Alvaro has great potential. He needs the right woman beside him."

Angela actually felt her jaw drop. He didn't think she was good enough for Alvaro because she was *white*? She didn't know whether to be angry, to laugh, or to be embarrassed.

He continued. "It was OK when you ate together from time to time. But now we can see it is more. This can only hurt him, and he deserves better."

"Eduardo." She struggled for a way to respond. "Alvaro and I are friends. He is also a client. There is nothing more than work and friendship."

"Is that what he thinks?" The older man's eyes squinted with skepticism. "Is it what you think?"

His questions stopped her. OK. Yes, she'd had plenty of thoughts about Alvaro. But she conducted herself professionally. Mostly. Everyone flirted a little. She'd never flirted where anyone would see them. She flashed back to the meals they'd eaten in the restaurant. They laughed. From time to time, she might touch his hand, or he hers. But anyone did that. It didn't mean anything. If that was what Eduardo was talking about, he'd misunderstood.

He continued. "This thing you are doing, it may be nothing to you. But it is much to Alvaro. We see that he cares about you."

She felt herself flush. "Alvaro is important to me, too."

"But you will leave soon. And when he returns to El Salvador, he will find a woman to marry. Someone like him. We ask that you think of that."

Irritation took over, and she responded abruptly. "Of course I think of these things. I'm sure Alvaro does, too. But that is our business."

She needed to get out, get away, before she said something really inappropriate. She stood. "If my order is ready, I'd like it. Before it gets cold."

Eduardo stood but hesitated once more. Before he went for the takeout bags, he added, "We want what is best for Alvaro. We do not want him to be hurt by a relationship that can't go anywhere. That shouldn't go anywhere."

The man had said things Angela had never imagined hearing in her life. Maintaining as much composure as she could, she said, "I appreciate your concern, Eduardo. All I can say is,

Alvaro is a smart man. I'm sure he can decide for himself how he spends his time. And with whom."

Angela slid two twenties across the counter and left without waiting for change.

Outside the restaurant, she drew a deep breath and tried to shake off the conversation. Across the street, she spotted Gordon Ryker leaning against a red pickup, talking with a heavy-set man. She pretended she didn't see him, but he caught her eye and gestured to her takeout bags.

"Seeing Al?" he called out.

She fumed. What was it with these people? Couldn't any-one leave them alone? She pretended not to understand what he'd said. "Just getting supper." She leaned in to put the bags of food on the passenger seat. When she straightened up, she saw him back the truck out of the parking place.

"Tell him I said hi," he called out the window as he drove by.

Angela ground her teeth. As she crossed town, she faced the questions Eduardo's comments raised. Where was she, re-ally, in this relationship with Alvaro? If they were in Des Moines and he were not a client? Would she want to be with him? Would people react the same? Would she be proud to be seen with him? In front of her friends? At professional meetings?

Alvaro was everything she found attractive in a man. Except he was a client. He was a good, kind, decent person. Those were the qualities that mattered. And he was handsome to boot. It mattered to Eduardo and Maria that Alvaro was Latino and she was white, but did it matter to her that he was Latino? It did not.

She was still shaking her head when she climbed the stairs to Alvaro's apartment. The Barton plan she'd expected to review with him that evening was shoved to the back of her mind.

Alvaro opened the door before she could knock.

"Hola, amiga," he said as he reached for the food. "I thought you'd never get here. I'm starving."

"Buenas tardes, Alvaro." She slipped her computer bag off her shoulder, setting it on the floor by the sofa before following him into the kitchen.

"You look like . . ." He sized her up. "You look . . . unhappy. What's up?"

"You will not believe what just happened," she said.

"Tell me." Alvaro pulled two bottles of beer out of the refrigerator.

"I had the oddest conversation with Eduardo." She leaned against the counter. "When I picked up the order, he warned me away from you."

He stopped in the act of opening one of the beers. "What?"

"He thinks we spend too much time together."

Alvaro's eyes registered disbelief as he flipped the tops off the bottles and handed her one. "He said that?"

"Pretty much. Yes." She took a sip. "He said that while I'm a 'nice woman,' you will go home and find a woman who is like you."

He leaned against the counter, arms crossed, considering what she said. "What bothers you?" he asked. "That Eduardo assumes you are a nice woman?"

His humor generally disarmed her, but she didn't even try to force a smile. "He wasn't kidding, Alvaro." She picked at the label on the bottle. "He seems to think I'm toying with you."

Alvaro nodded thoughtfully. "You are that kind of woman. I can see why he thinks so."

"I'm in no mood," she grumbled in response to his second attempt at humor. "He said you should be with a Latina, that a white woman wasn't good enough for you."

Alvaro snorted as he shook his head. "Man, that was out of line. He and Maria have been like family to me, but he still shouldn't have said anything. I'll talk with him. What did you say to him?"

"I said you were a smart guy, and you could make your own decisions."

They stood side by side in the kitchen, their backs to the counter, their hands cupped along the counter edge. He extended his pinky finger, crossed the quarter inch between them, and grazed her finger, the touch sending a shiver through her hand, up her arm.

"What about when you go back?" she asked, glancing at him quickly and then away. If Eduardo had not said what he did, if she and Alvaro had not had this conversation, maybe she could have convinced herself these months in Hammond meant nothing more than the short-term assignment they started out to be. Instead, she was looking squarely at a relationship she'd been working hard to convince herself was only a working friendship.

"You will leave Hammond before then." He stated the fact as though her leaving would mean she would never think of him again.

"Will that bother you?"

"Sí, amiga. It will bother me." Abruptly he turned to the bags of food and began to unpack them. "Get plates. And a bowl." He pointed to the cupboard behind her.

She pushed away from the counter, crossed the two feet to the cabinet, and opened the door, taking down plates. Stretching to reach the bowl on an upper shelf, she felt her T-shirt ride up, exposing the skin above her yoga pants.

When she turned around, bowl in hand, she saw him watching her, his eyes deep pools of dark chocolate. Her senses flared with the energy sparking between them.

"Amiga," he said, his voice thick with desire.

In that single word, a nickname that had come to carry so much more than its meaning, she felt him ask and offer. Her lips parted. How easy it would be to cross the distance between them, to rest her hands on his biceps, to trace a finger up the river that began above his elbow and follow it until it disappeared in the mountains. His eyes told her all she had to do was make the smallest move toward him.

A breath caught in the back of her throat as she forced herself to remember the "why not" list she'd made not two weeks ago. She forced herself to look away, set the bowl on the counter, tugged her T-shirt back into place.

"You dish it up; I'll get the silverware," she said. Grabbing forks and napkins, she edged past him out of the kitchen, the sound of his breathing following her into the living room. The silverware arranged and napkins folded, she sat waiting at the end of the couch, wondering if she'd be better off leaving.

Moments later, he handed her a plate. Instead of joining her on the couch, he dropped to the floor, sitting cross-legged beside the coffee-table trunk. Without a look or smile in her direction, without even taking a moment to pray, he picked up his fork and ate.

After a few bites, she tried to break the uncomfortable silence. "Maria did it again. This is terrific."

He didn't respond.

A bit later, she tried again. "Father Burke says he's thinking of starting a soccer league. How many of your boys would join?"

Alvaro continued to eat methodically, staring at his plate. Finally, he got up and turned on the radio. Found a station playing hip-hop. Not his normal choice. When he returned, he picked up his plate and carried it to the overstuffed chair in the corner. He sank into the shadows of the room, away from her, the occasional scrape of fork against plate a discordant screech against the syncopated music.

Finished, he set his plate on the floor. When he spoke, his tone was grouchy. "I don't know what we are doing."

"What do you mean?"

"You and me. What are we *doing*? What do you want from me?"

"We are friends," she began.

"Sure, amiga. Sure. We are friends." He spoke with a hard edge of sarcasm. When he said "amiga" this time, he clearly meant friend. Nothing more.

The bitterness stung and she tried to explain. "I didn't expect to find someone like you on this job."

"Someone like me. What does that mean?"

"Someone my age, for one thing. Someone I have so much in common with. Someone I enjoy spending time with."

"Is that it? I am confused. I see you look at me and I think . . ."

Feeling a flush redden her cheeks, she stared fixedly down.

"Then, like now, you turn away. What am I supposed to think, Angela?"

Hearing him say "Angela" so harshly stabbed into her chest. His nickname for her—amiga—brought her close. Calling her Angela pushed her away.

"If you don't want me here, say so," she said.

"That is not it. I like you here. And for a while I think maybe you like me."

"I do like you, Alvaro."

"But not like I like you."

Angela pulled her legs up to her chest and wrapped her arms around them, putting a barrier between them. "I didn't say that. But I'm here to do a job. My reputation is on the line every day."

"Your reputation. It is spoiled if you are with me. Yes?"

"That's not what I meant. To get involved with a client. It would cause people to question my integrity."

"You see me as your client. Is that what you think when we are together? He is my client, so we can talk about this but not that? He is my client, so I can share this with him but not that? He is my client, so I can get information from him to use? Are you using me, Angela? Is that all?"

Each word he spoke pierced her heart.

"When you put it that way, Alvaro, it sounds horrible, but you *are* a client. Yes, we've been friends, too. At least I think we've been friends. I hope so. But it would be unprofessional for me to go further than that."

The sun had set, and the room was dark except for the glow of light from the kitchen. She looked into the dark corner of the room where he'd gone to hide, wishing she could see his face. "I don't mean to confuse you. But I'm confused myself. I didn't . . ." She closed her eyes, and her voice dropped to a whisper as she said something she'd never said to anyone before. "I didn't expect to like you so much. I didn't expect . . . to want you."

There. She'd said it. With her eyes closed, she didn't see him emerge from the overstuffed chair, but she felt the sofa move as he sat, and she opened her eyes.

He faced her, his arm slung across the back of the sofa. "Angela," he said, his voice serious. "We must talk of this."

"I don't know what to say."

"It is better we are honest with each other. No?"

"Yes. It is. But I feel I've crossed a professional line even feeling the way I do. Let alone talking to you about it."

"I have felt the same."

"You have?"

He got up from the sofa and went to the bookshelf, where he pulled out a notebook. "I made a list of reasons we should not be together."

"Really?" She laughed. "Really?"

"What's funny?"

"I made a list, too. My 'why not' list."

"I have seven reasons," he said.

"So like an engineer. So thorough. My list has only three reasons."

"Three reasons. Of course. You are a PR professional. You always have three."

It was true. She'd said to him many times that three was as many message points as anyone could remember. Until he pointed it out, she hadn't realized she'd absorbed the concept into her personal life.

"Will you share?" she asked.

"If you will."

She nodded. "You go first."

He looked down at the list as though considering where to start or whether to start at all. Finally, he rattled off three reasons as though they were all one. "It would make work difficult. If the men at the plant found out, they may not respect my authority. I could become a joke."

"So you also see the problem we just talked about," Angela responded. "This was at the top of my list, too. If Nick found out, I imagine he would see it as unprofessional. With Gordon, it would prove what he already thinks. I couldn't imagine what fun he'd have." She shrugged her shoulders, throwing off the image. "Another of my reasons is similar," she continued. "My company and my boss would see it as unethical. In our business, it would be seen as compromising the counsel I provide. So it would jeopardize the account. What else do you have?"

She watched him concentrate on his list, eyebrows drawn into a dark line. He finally spoke without looking at her.

"What I said before," he said. "I cannot tell yes or no with you." Then he raised his face and looked at her directly. "You must be all yes, or I would not touch you."

His comment left her breathless. "Why, Alvaro. You really are a gentleman." Truly, she'd never met a man like him.

He tapped a fingertip to his forehead. "My mother speaks in my head. Before I left El Salvador, when I was much younger, she said to me, 'Be the kind of man you want for your sister, Eva.'"

"Your mother sounds like a wise woman."

He consulted his list again. "Also, people may think I am trying to take advantage of you."

"Take advantage of me?" She frowned. "How could that be?"

"If we were together, it may be possible to extend my visa. Or get another."

"But wouldn't we have to be married for that to work?"

"Yes."

Reflexively, Angela edged farther into the corner of the sofa. Yes, she had compared him to the mental image of the kind of man she would marry, but the idea of actually getting married had not crossed her mind. She'd known him for only a couple of months. She found him attractive, but . . .

"I'd really never thought of marriage," she said. "You must have, though. To have it on your list."

"As you say, I am thorough." Alvaro took another look at the notebook, then snapped it closed.

"Aren't you going to tell me what else you have on the list?"

"It does not matter. They all come to the same place."

"And what place is that?"

He looked at her thoughtfully. "I like you too much."

"You like me," Angela repeated, returning his gaze and feeling this was exactly the reason they should be together.

"Too much," he amended. "I have been with other women for a night, and I do not like how I feel after. My mother speaking in me again, no?" He tapped his temple and grew pensive. "For me it would not be casual. I do not think for you, either. Since we will both be gone soon, it is better we do not get involved."

"Liking someone too much is a reason not to be together?"

"Yes."

She considered this. She had slept with a few men, mostly in college, but she'd found those casual liaisons unfulfilling. Without making a conscious decision to, she hadn't let a relationship become intimate in a long time.

"I think you are right," she said. Having said it, though, she wondered whether, with this man, she had the strength of will to abide by the decision.

"OK." Alvaro smacked a fist lightly into his palm three times as though sealing the conclusion in his own mind. "OK." He went to the radio, found a blues station, and returned to the couch. "Will we work on the plan now?" he asked.

"Do you still want to?"

"If you do." He waited for her response. Frankly, she didn't know if she did. When she finally agreed, he went to the kitchen. "Another drink?"

"Sure. A Coke."

While he was gone, she retrieved her computer bag and the hard-copy documents she'd prepared, wondering if "can't we just be friends" ever worked, wondering if the vast emptiness she felt would ever go away.

When he returned, he switched on the lights by the sofa, and she handed him a draft document of her report from the trip they'd taken to the other plants. Then she curled her legs up under her, glancing through her own copy as he read. From time to time, she peeked at him, trying to gauge how he felt about the end of a relationship before it really started. He betrayed nothing, which made her wonder if he really cared for her as much as he'd said.

She swallowed a sigh and focused on the document, which outlined their trip and presented some possibilities that Barton Packing might consider implementing, including expanded vending machines, language software for the school, an ethnic food festival at the county fair, and a seed fund for business start-ups.

"I think we've come up with some pretty good ideas," she said when she saw he'd reached the last page.

"Do you think they will do all this?" he asked.

"Highly unlikely. But seeing others in the industry doing things like this might spur Nick to action. The plan is comprehensive. We tried to address everyone's interests. If they bought into all of this, Hammond could be a showcase for the state."

She pulled out another document and handed it to him. "I also found this study done by the immigration experts at the university. It says communities that find ways to help immigrants settle in faster—find their own space, set up businesses, learn English, be successful—are far better off as a whole than those that view immigrants as a necessary evil or who put up roadblocks to immigrants getting ahead."

"Immigration experts." Alvaro practically spat the words.

The bitterness of his reaction jolted Angela. "What did I say?"

"These *experts*. They throw all this out like it is so easy. It is not." He dropped the report onto the floor.

"It isn't," she agreed. "That's what makes the opportunity in Hammond exciting."

"I have been lucky—to get an education—to get a management job. But I am the exception. Most of the others in the plant, they cannot get ahead, no matter how hard they work. They are always on the line. A *necessary evil.*"

"Do you believe that? Really?"

"I have told you already. There isn't a Somali, a Chin, even another Latino supervisor at the plant. I am the only one."

"Maybe there isn't anyone who is qualified."

He glared at her, waiting for her brain to catch up with her mouth.

The words had popped out, and in the spotlight of his judgment, she recognized the lame argument white men used to keep women out of the boardroom. Chagrined, she realized those were the same words Dave used to explain why Sherborn-Watts employed no people of color. And she'd accepted it. She felt like a fool. "OK. I get it."

"The experts, they don't have any idea. Gringos."

She retrieved the report from where he'd dropped it and sat back, taking in the authors' names: Smith, Atkinson, Wilson. White. All of them. "Look, Alvaro. I've made a ton of assumptions since I've been here, and many of them were wrong. I'm trying to do better." She held up the report. "But just because the people who wrote this are white doesn't mean the research is bad or the conclusions are wrong. You know this."

"Sí," he admitted. "I do. I also see what is real in the plant. And around Hammond. It is not so easy to change as they make it sound."

He heaved himself off the couch and paced around the room, a caged lion looking to escape, before he plopped down again in the corner chair. Seeing him so disturbed caused her heart to race. Was his distress because of the report or a hold-over from their personal conversation? Or was it triggered by their time in the other plants?

"I know change isn't easy. I've been struggling with my boss about some of these same things." Saying anything more about the report felt counterproductive. She set it aside. "Alvaro, this conversation really upset you. Are you OK? Did something specific happen?"

He picked up a weight and began a set of bicep curls. At last he said, "There was an opening for a supervisor. One of my best men applied because I told him to. I thought, why not? Other plants promote people like him. Like me. But he didn't get the job. A man not as long with the company, one who did not know as much, they made him supervisor. He was a gringo."

"It was Gordon's decision?"

"Yes."

She'd known the answer before he said it, actually before she asked. Never in her life had she hit someone, but she wanted to punch Gordon Ryker. Standing, she paced around the couch, finally stopping with her fists on her hips. "What was his reason?"

"He did not give one. He did not need to. Not to someone who is a necessary evil." He switched the weight to his other hand and continued doing curls.

She knelt in front of him. "I'm sorry, but that's not you. He likes you."

"He has to. It was Mr. Barton's decision to hire me. Do you think Mr. Ryker would have done it on his own? No. Besides. It's not just Mr. Ryker. Most managers in the plant are the same way."

For the first time, she understood the reality Alvaro and most other workers at the plant faced.

"Even when someone is trying . . . I hope you know I am trying." She looked at him for affirmation. "Even then, they can still make mistakes. I can only imagine how hard that is to live with. But we—you and I—have a chance to make a difference. Will you help me?"

He grumbled, but finally set the weight back on the floor. "So what happens next?"

She stood. "We'll write all this up and present to Gordon first."

"You mean *you*, right? You'll present it," he clarified.

"Actually, I hoped you and I would present this together. A lot of this is our joint thinking, and I could never have gotten all I did if you hadn't been along," she said. "You should be part of the presentation."

He leaned back and crossed his arms. "No. It is not for me to do."

"Why? What do you mean?"

"This is not my job. I don't know anything about it."

"Of course you do. You met with every person I did. What's in here includes your work as well as mine. I've already talked with Dave about it. He agrees." She looked at him, puzzled. "Do you think I am asking you to make up for Gordon being such a jerk?"

"Are you?"

"Of course not. Don't you think these are good ideas?"

"They are."

"Then why won't you present them with me?"

"I will be gone soon. It's better this does not depend on me."

"You're not concerned about presenting, are you? You're an accomplished presenter. Otherwise you'd never have caught Nick's attention. Besides, you wouldn't have to present. I can do it. You can be there to answer questions and fill in if I miss things."

"I was gone a long time. I have to be on my job."

"It'll only take a couple of hours to meet with Gordon. I've already made an appointment for Tuesday. Surely you can take that much time."

"No. I cannot do it. Stop asking."

The heavy black eyebrows hung low over his eyes, reinforced by the don't-mess-with-me tone of his voice. She heard him loud and clear.

"Well, if that's the way you feel." She slid everything back into her bag, trying not to show how much his refusal hurt. There was no point talking about it further; she'd go it alone.

They spent another half hour talking about Emilio and Saint Catherine's, and finally parted on a generally good note, but back in her room at the Cozy Inn, she lay awake for some time thinking about the barriers that kept them apart: professional positions, cultural differences, potentially thousands of miles. But all the rational thinking collapsed as she remembered his finger touching hers, his eyes watching her as she stretched for the bowl, and how her body responded. With a groan, she curled up in a ball, wrapped her arms tightly around her knees. What had the night done to their relationship? To her?

Chapter 25

Angela stood down the hall from Gordon's office, taking even breaths to calm her racing heart. Under other circumstances, she felt eager anticipation before presenting a plan. But anything to do with Gordon surfaced feelings of anxiety, even dread. Reminding herself she was well prepared, she took another breath, smiled, and went to his door.

He appeared relaxed when he greeted her, and she jumped in, explaining that in this meeting she'd share the most important results, get his input, then set a date to take a full recommendation to Nick.

She handed him a copy of the report, which he laid on his desk, barely glancing at the cover sheet. Most clients couldn't resist turning to the last page to see the budget. Annoyed at first, she took a breath and gave him the benefit of the doubt. Maybe he just wanted to hear what she had to say before digging into the report.

"Tell me what you've got." Gordon settled back in his chair, his cool gray eyes devoid of expression.

She marshaled her professionalism and began. "We visited the three towns we agreed on plus Postville."

He picked up a pencil and began weaving it through his fingers. "Why did you go there?"

Her antennae were up for judgment, anger, sarcasm. He sounded curious but she wasn't sure.

"Since we could stay on schedule and still go there, we went. We didn't get into the plant, but we were able to pick up on community dynamics."

"Anything interesting?"

"Yes. More than we set out to find," she said. "There's a chart on page three."

Finally, he picked up the report and leafed through to the chart.

"Alvaro picked up on approaches the plants used to minimize line speed and repetitive-motion injury." She made a point to keep her eyes on Gordon as she talked about Alvaro's contributions. Her skin burned even now as she remembered Gordon's nasty comments.

"We're aware of that."

"Yes. You mentioned it when we toured the plant on my first day. Alvaro thought some changes could be implemented here. Any cost of redesigning workstations or training monitors would be offset by early detection and treatment of injuries."

"I'll talk with him about it. What else?"

She laid out the findings from other plants, both what they did internally as well as how employees were involved outside the plant. Then she came to the point about calling employees "team members."

"Lipstick on a pig." Gordon drew out his words with a sneer. "Christ. Is that what we spent money to get?" He shook his head as he flipped her report to his desk and reached for a chart from a nearby stack.

A rock-hard knot of anxiety formed under Angela's ribs as she saw his interest slip away. He'd seen the title change as superficial, which it would be if they didn't back it up with substance. Fearful that he would pull the plug on the meeting, she scrambled to draw him back in.

"Our view on this—Dave's and mine—is that employees are your most important asset. We agree the terminology is a small change, but we'd only do it if we backed it up with concrete actions." Her heart raced as she described how other plants engaged with and supported their team members, watching for his reaction. The fact that other plants had moved ahead seemed to sway him.

"I'll think about it. Keep talking."

The knot of anxiety eased when he picked up her report again. As she outlined more ideas, he began methodical questioning. How did programs work? Who was responsible? How were the packing plants involved?

Finally, he laid the document to the side of his desk again. "More than I expected," he said.

His grudging compliment encouraged her. "There's still more," she said. "On page five—"

He interrupted. "I'm out of time now."

A glance at her watch revealed they'd been talking for nearly an hour. The longest exchange they'd ever had. Once they'd gotten past the initial rough patch, the meeting had gone well. "I can come back later this morning. Or this afternoon? I want to be certain I have all your thoughts."

"Give me a couple of days to look it all over."

Days? She was taken aback. He'd received the report so well she was eager to move forward. "I hoped you and I could agree on how to present this to Nick. Maybe we could even set a time for that meeting."

"I need to make a few calls. I already know some of this won't work."

She frowned. His earlier comments had not suggested problems. "Which areas concern you?"

He looked at the wall clock. "There's no reason for us to put money into that Main Street cleanup project. The chamber won't buy it, either. They won't give money to local businesses that don't take care of their properties already."

"The financial assistance would be an incentive for everyone to spruce up. Plus, we might get funding from a state grant. I've talked with the head of the chamber. I got the impression—"

"Jack was being nice. He called me after you left."

Jack Taylor had sounded sincere. She'd gone back to him for more information twice. Each time, the chamber director had not only provided what she asked for but also offered ideas of his own.

Gordon continued. "The housing. That's a problem, too. I told you we don't control that."

"I know, but we thought Barton Packing could have leverage since you arrange so many renters. Surely the management company can see the benefit of making places more livable." She pressed the point. "Dave and I know this isn't something the company wants to talk about with the media. But at least it's something we should try to do something about."

"Why? These guys don't give a damn where they live." He searched through a stack of papers.

Angela was aghast. "Everyone cares where they live, Gordon," she blurted. "But that's not the point. People think Barton Packing makes money off those houses. When I tell them a Chicago company is in charge, they're surprised." She continued, "Maybe you could require fixing the houses up as part of the deal for channeling people their way."

"They've always been hard to reach. We've tried before." Impatience ground through his voice.

"A housing program like this is an area where Barton Packing leads. None of the other companies are doing anything like this. Free housing for a month is a real benefit to new employees. It's unique—"

Gordon's feet landed on the floor with a thud as he leaned forward, his jaw jutting out with pit-bull force. "I thought I was clear," he said. "I'm out of time."

Angela jerked back, shocked at the intensity of his reaction.

He stood, glaring at her as she snatched everything into a pile, the papers a jumbled mess. Then he strode to the office door. "I have another meeting."

With her papers clutched to her chest, she tried to end the meeting with a semblance of professionalism. "Let me know if you have questions. I'll check back in . . . a couple of days?"

"I'll call you."

She edged past him, her heart in her throat.

* * *

Angela leaned against the door of the bathroom stall, her pulse racing. *You idiot,* she chided herself. *You idiot. You idiot.*

She'd let herself get caught up in talking rather than listening to what he was saying. He'd been engaged, and she'd pushed until he lost patience. What the hell had she been thinking?

It wasn't all her fault, though. She knew that. Gordon had all the subtlety of a steamroller. Anyone could have ended that meeting without a physical display of anger. He enjoyed overpowering people. He enjoyed showing his power over her.

Pressing her palms against the cool surface of the toilet-stall door, she forced herself to breathe steadily, in, out, in, out. Felt her pulse begin to slow. Damn Alvaro. If he'd been there, Gordon would never have done that. *Damn you,* she whispered to herself, annoyed she would fall back on having a man around to be in control of a meeting or to protect her from a bully. And that's what Gordon was. A bully.

She turned and put her cheek against the stall door, then her forehead. The cool metal calmed her, helped her put what happened in perspective. Except for those last moments, the meeting had gone well. He'd been engaged, asked questions, encouraged her to expand several elements. What she'd said about the housing all made sense, but he'd told her he had another meeting, that he didn't have time to talk, and she'd pushed anyway. *Idiot.*

She texted Alvaro. *Talked with Gordon. When can you meet?*
She needed to talk with Dave, too. She'd have to admit to screwing up the meeting. She texted him: *Met w/ Gordon. Some sticking points. Headed to another meeting. Talk this p.m.?*

She left the sanctuary of the bathroom stall and stood staring into the mirror. She ran her fingers through her hair, pulled herself back together. She'd survive this. She had to.

Chapter 26

"It was going well and then it wasn't." She concluded a play-by-play recap of the meeting with Gordon to Dave. It pained her to admit it, but she added, "I screwed up. I don't see any other way to look at it. He pushed the report aside, and I got the feeling he might never get around to looking at it. Now Gordon can quash everything by never sending the report forward."

"Enlisting Gordon first was the right approach." Dave exhaled audibly, and Angela knew he was out on the patio smoking. "Don't beat yourself up too much." She'd called him from her car, where she could speak openly.

Her boss's words were only moderate comfort since Angela had worked herself into a pity pit. "It was probably a worthless effort anyway. If Gordon is Nick's successor, sooner or later, he'd block what we recommend."

"It happens. New leaders, new directions. But we're not there yet."

She usually welcomed Dave's ability to keep her on a professional track, but this time he annoyed her. "This plan is the right thing to do. I know it. Nick would agree. Gordon is such a jerk. If he'd open his eyes, he'd see it."

"Don't go down that road, Angela. Gordon's a client. If what you're doing isn't working, it's up to us to figure out a better way. I thought Duarte was going to be with you."

"I thought I could convince him, but he wouldn't."

"In for the road trip, but not for the hard work, huh?"

"That wasn't it. He said he couldn't afford to take more time off."

"He has his job, you have yours."

"I suppose." She'd thought they were in it together, and it bothered her Alvaro might not feel the same way.

They were having supper at his place that night. She carried frustration, disappointment, and anger to Alvaro's apartment. Canceling crossed her mind. They'd both have been better off if she had.

* * *

Angela curled up in her usual spot on Alvaro's couch, her arms looped around her knees, a nearly empty bottle of Dos Equis in one hand. Plates streaked with dried bits of Spanish rice and refried beans littered the trunk-turned-coffee table.

"All I'm saying is, the work was as much yours as mine." She tilted her head back, finished off the last swallow of beer, and set the bottle on the trunk, a warm buzz relaxing her muscles and flushing her cheeks. It was the third time that evening she'd said something similar.

"You think what happened with Mr. Ryker was my fault." Alvaro leaned back into the other arm of the couch.

She shrugged. "You know him better. You'd have seen he was getting ticked off. You'd have stepped in. Or stopped me. Or something." Once she'd started down the path of trying to get him to admit he should have been there, she couldn't stop herself.

"You wanted my *insights* from the trip. You wanted me to help write the report. It was your job to present."

"I thought I could count on you." She looked away, shrugged again, and sighed audibly. "Guess not."

He stood abruptly and headed for the kitchen. Leaving the couch, she stood looking out the window. A red pickup truck like the one she'd seen Gordon drive was parked behind her car. Why would he be here? She snorted at the thought. How did she even know it was Gordon? Every other vehicle in Hammond was a pickup. At least half were red.

She heard the clink as Alvaro grabbed a bottle from the six-pack she'd brought over. He'd drink her beer, he was OK with that, she thought. The *ftssst, ftssst* as he opened two bottles sounded like him spitting.

He set a cold bottle for her on the trunk and instead of returning to the couch, settled into the overstuffed chair, in the corner yet again, as far away from her as he could get.

She turned from the window, picked up the fresh bottle, and took a healthy swig. One beer was usually her limit. She'd drunk the first one so fast it went to her head. Ignoring an already-buzzed feeling of recklessness, she took another big swallow.

"I think you should have stood behind your work." She threw out the words, knowing even as she said them how deeply they'd cut.

Until now he'd let her vent, keeping his responses brief. But this last comment found its mark.

He leaned forward, shaking his head. "You don't get it, do you?" he said. "I am not like you. I can't spend every day vacationing all over Iowa."

"Vacationing? Is that what you think?"

"Fancy restaurants. Expensive wine. Talk to a few people. Call it a day. I don't call that work."

"If that's what you think, then *you* really don't get it. I don't know why I expected you would."

"Yeah. A Latino could never understand. Right?" He glared at her. "Do you not understand? This job is the money for me to live here and help my family in El Salvador. I cannot afford to lose this job."

"You got paid for those days we were on the trip, so you didn't lose any money. You would have been paid for the time presenting to Gordon. He approved you going. You wouldn't lose your job." She dismissed his concerns with a hand wave.

"Of course you do not understand. You cannot understand. You are an American. You are white."

"You're joking. Right?" She almost laughed but stopped. She saw no humor in his eyes. "Is that what you think? Really?"

"You come in here and think you can fix it all so fast. Quoting your 'immigration experts.' Wave a magic wand and change everything. And you don't even see yourself. What people do for you because you are white."

His words hit her like a fist. "That's not true. And it's not fair."

"Wake up, Angela. Look at what happened when we traveled together. People assumed I could not speak English—like you did when we met. People expected I would try to steal shoelaces. Shoelaces! They say I am not *normal*, not like them." He rattled off a litany of incidents, then reached for the hand weight beside the chair. He rested his elbow on his knee and began to do bicep curls, each one methodical, purposeful.

"This would not happen to you," he said. "They assume you are honorable and honest and smart because your skin is white." He switched the weight to the other hand and continued the methodical repetition, a sheen of perspiration on his forehead reflecting in the lamplight.

His words triggered a pathetic defense. "It's not my fault I'm white. I can't help how I was born any more than you can."

"You think I don't know that? Even a stupid Latino knows that."

"You're here because you want to be. You got an education. You got a good job. Now you'll take it all back to El Salvador. Like you planned. No reason to stay here."

As she rolled out each attack, feeling petulant and a little mean, she watched for a response. He continued with the bicep curls and didn't look at her.

"Sure," he said at last. "I'll go back to El Salvador. It will be worth it to get away from people who are afraid when they see me on the street."

He'd held up a mirror showing her world, and what she saw both angered and shamed her.

"You obviously have things to work out. I'll get out of your way." She grabbed her purse.

At the door, she stopped and looked back, giving him plenty of time to tell her to stay, but he didn't. He continued the bicep curls without even a glance in her direction.

She slammed the door and ran down the stairs, wondering how the conversation had gone so wrong so fast. Already, she regretted her harsh words.

He'd made her feel bad about being white and being American. As if it were her fault. Was she supposed to feel sorry for him because he wasn't? It was his job to make the most of who he was as a Latino man. It was her responsibility to make the most of who she was as a white woman. She'd worked hard to advance her career, to be successful. She'd taken the right classes. She'd worked summers, nights, weekends to earn money for college. She'd applied for scholarships and earned them because she was qualified. She'd applied for internships and worked hard at every one. She'd gotten where she was because she'd earned it.

But he made her doubt. How much of her life—of her success—was a result of the accident of birth? Her gender was the challenge she focused on. Breaking the glass ceiling. Overcoming the wage gap. Leaning in to squeeze even more out of her personal and professional life.

Back at the Cozy Inn, she changed into sweatpants and secured her hair in a ponytail. After she spit her toothpaste into the sink, she looked at herself in the mirror. Auburn hair. Gothic pale skin. Green eyes. The same face she saw every day. She paid attention to errant eyebrow hairs, an occasional zit, the color of her lipstick. She did not think specifically about being white.

When Alvaro looked in a mirror, did he ever think consciously about being Latino? Or was that forced on him because his dark skin stood out in white Iowa and white Iowans made assumptions about him without waiting to learn the reality?

As she had done. As she continued to do. Time and again, she'd been forced to adjust her thinking about him. Or maybe he was simply becoming multidimensional the same way anyone you met did if you took the time to get to know them. Maybe he really had come from further behind. She had to admit she'd expected him, as a Latino working in a packing plant, to be less educated, less capable, less.

Of course he'd worked hard to be successful, as she had. Yes, he'd overcome more hardship to get here—being born into the poverty and violence of Central America, losing his father, leaving his family behind, getting an engineering degree, getting a job at Barton Packing.

There were some differences between them, sure, but not many. None that changed who they were. Yet because of skin color, he was treated differently. She couldn't deny that. With a sigh, she flicked off the bathroom light. Switching off her thoughts was not so easy.

Alvaro was successful and people judged him, expected negative things of him, because of his color. Angela was successful and people like Gordon judged her, expected her to do less, be less, because of her gender. Was her success simply a result of being white? She didn't believe it, yet her time in Hammond had shown her perhaps otherwise.

To be honest with herself, she had to admit she'd carried her own frustration about their personal relationship into that argument. Even though she believed they'd made the right decision to keep their relationship professional, that hadn't prevented her from feeling close to him. Closer than her Sherborn-Watts colleagues. If he'd gone to the presentation, it would have shown he cared, not only about the work they'd done, but also about her. She settled into the chair by the bed and picked up *The Ambitious*

Woman from the nightstand but snapped it shut without reading a word. Win by helping others succeed? She didn't need that message thrown in her face right now.

Abandoning the chair, she paced back and forth. As she stomped from the bed to the kitchenette, her righteous indignation peaked: she could not be blamed for that over which she had no control. Wheeling around and pacing past the bed, she knew fairness demanded: neither could he. She imagined him in his apartment, working out with his weights, and for the first time, it occurred to her he worked with the weights not to build up muscle but to tear down frustration.

She'd been petty and cruel to suggest that her failure in the presentation was his fault, that because he hadn't joined her, he didn't care. She knew him. Nothing could be further from the truth.

She took out her phone and dialed his number. The call went to voice mail. Fifteen minutes later, she tried again with the same result. He didn't want to talk with her. Well, fine. If that was the way he wanted it. She didn't need him, either.

Chapter 27

She was almost ready to leave the ladies' restroom when the door opened and Liz walked in.

"Hey, Angela, I'm glad I ran into you. Mr. Barton wants to see you," she said.

Angela pulled up her phone calendar, scrolling the screen as though looking for an opening. "What's his schedule?" She knew she was wide open all day, but she didn't like to go into a meeting with Nick without a well-thought-out plan. It had been three days since she'd given her report to Gordon, three days since her blowup with Alvaro. Both meetings weighed heavily on her mind. She looked up from her phone. "Would later this afternoon work? Or Monday?"

"Actually, he's available right now, if you are. He had a phone call cancel, and he's going to be out this afternoon."

"I can make now work if that's best. Did he say what he wants to talk about?"

"Just said to send you his way," Liz said as she looked in the mirror and pulled at her spikes of white hair.

Angela slipped her phone back in her pocket. "That's a good look for you." She indicated Liz's hair.

"Not too young?"

"Huh-uh." She shook her head. "I have friends who've tried to pull off that look and can't. And with your white hair, it's stunning."

"Maggie Barton was always after me to update my look. After she died, I figured I'd take the leap. As a tribute to her."

"It sounds like Mrs. Barton was a terrific woman."

"She was. We ran in different social circles, but she always made me feel welcome. Mr. Barton's had a tough time since. All the plans they had. It's been good to see him getting out more of late."

Angela took out a tube of lipstick and touched up her lips, hoping to extend the conversation. "It must have been awful. Nick told me he meant for Gordon to take his place."

"That was the plan. Once Maggie got sick, things changed. People changed. Now I don't know." She shook her head.

"People changed?"

"She got sick about the same time Gordon's son was injured in Afghanistan. The two top men in the company came unmoored at the same time."

"I've wondered about Gordon's son. How serious were his injuries?"

"Bad. He lost one arm above the elbow and is paralyzed from the waist down. There was also head trauma."

"How awful." The handsome, strapping marine in the picture clearly no longer existed. "Gordon told me his son lives with them now."

"He does. Gordon and Diane had major construction done on their house to accommodate him. Diane quit her job to be his full-time caregiver."

"Wow." Angela sucked in her upper lip as the implications flashed through her mind—a disabled son, lost income, increased expense. She couldn't help but think of her mother and father, and the emotional and financial hardship they endured because of the Alzheimer's. "Wow."

"Yeah. Wow," Liz agreed.

It might have been out of line to ask, but Angela took a chance. "You've known Gordon for a while. What do you think about him as CEO?"

Liz hooted loudly, then lowered her voice. "That wasn't appropriate, was it?" She giggled. "Gordon has some rough edges, but Maggie was working on that. And having some success. But when she got sick, the whole timeline was thrown out the window. Mr. Barton didn't retire as planned, and he hasn't said when he will. Then Gordon's son was injured, and the stress brought all Gordon's rough edges back. Like I say, both men came unmoored." Liz looked at her watch. "If you want to catch Mr. Barton, you better go."

Angela would have liked to hear more, but she conceded. "On my way."

"And you didn't hear any of that from me," Liz said.

Angela pantomimed zipping her lips and left. Moments later she rapped on Nick's office door. "Liz said you wanted to see me?"

"Come in, Angela," he said, gesturing for her to join him at the conference table. "I'd like to hear what you found out on your tour. Just the most important things."

As she took a seat, she looked out the conference-room window and mentally brought up the report, wishing she had it in hand. The view outside was calming. Such changes in only two months. Rows of corn that had been barely visible in the fields when she'd first gotten to Barton Packing were now grown and tasseling out. She felt she'd grown, too, in ways she'd never imagined.

"The people you put me in touch with were helpful. As you might imagine, a lot depends on the size of town."

She spent the next fifteen minutes hitting the high points of the trip and sharing the insights she and Alvaro gained. Nick asked a few questions but mostly let her talk.

When she concluded, he said, "I have to say, Angela, you've got my interest. We should have had Gordon here for this. So what's next? When will you have something ready for us to look at?"

She shifted uncomfortably. "Actually, I shared our report with Gordon three days ago. I thought if he saw it first, he could offer feedback to help us refine it before we showed it to you."

"Good idea. When will you get back with him?"

"He said he needed a few days to check on things."

Nick considered that. "I'll talk with him. I'm eager to get going. So what are three things that rise to the top as efforts we could do for maximum impact?"

She tilted her head back and thought hard.

"Gut instinct," he prodded. "I won't hold you to it." He waited, an expectant look on his face.

"OK," she said. "Here are three." She walked through ideas for more in-depth employee research, convening groups of diverse business owners, and working with social-services agencies to identify local needs.

"Wouldn't it work to have Gordon take the lead in some of the meetings you're thinking about?"

The question made her squirm. Everything Gordon had done, especially at the last meeting, screamed that he'd be terrible as a community leader. But her public-relations training wouldn't let her say that directly.

"People respond better if they know the effort is embraced at the highest level. Plus, the meetings will take a significant time commitment. Gordon would have to be away from the plant often. However, if you do it, that might not fit in with your intent to retire. So it depends on where you are with that."

"That's one I'll have to think about." He scraped his fingers across his chin as the corner of his mouth curved into a teasing smile. "What? No media?"

"You know me well." She smiled. It tickled her that he'd become so interested in the media. Their small successes with releases had piqued his interest. "The three approaches I outlined have media potential but not right away."

"Do you see near-term media opportunities?" he pressed.

Angela's lips pursed. Gordon's reaction made her hesitate to bring it up, but the housing subsidy was the only thing she could think of. "The one thing Barton Packing is doing differently than the other towns is the rent-assistance program. Housing in small towns is almost always an economic-development issue, and you've found a way to ease a regularly changing population into the community. There are problems with that, though. The media will want pictures, and the condition of the houses won't be positive."

Nick nodded. "Gordon might also have the same objection he had to the product donation. Give it to one, have to give it to all."

"Don't you offer the subsidy to all new employees?"

"Some don't need it. They move in and find their own housing. Or they find housing in other towns—like the Somalis."

"I see," Angela said, rankled that Gordon continually found ways to undermine her. Whether he acted by design or not. "I wish he'd just said that."

Nick shrugged.

"So how many employees use the program and how many don't? Could a rent stipend be given to every new employee no matter where they live? It could be a good idea for both employees and landlords. If it wouldn't break the company bank."

"To tell the truth, I have no idea. No harm in at least looking at the numbers."

"I'll get started," Angela said. "But in terms of the company that owns the properties. They really don't take good care of them."

"This annoys me." Nick grew uncommonly edgy. "Go through any town in Iowa, and you'll see houses that look exactly like these. No one says a word." He stood and paced from the window to the refrigerator and back. "Yet a company like us gets involved, and everyone gets all righteous."

"That may be true." In the face of his irritability, she spoke cautiously. "We saw similar houses in one town, but no one connected them with the packing plant."

"We could stop the program altogether and let employees fend for themselves. I wonder how everyone would like that?"

She assumed his comment was rhetorical but answered seriously. "Not well, I'm sure. The thing is, some think you benefit financially from the properties while your employees live in shabby housing."

He frowned as he sat down again. "It's not true. This program is completely out of pocket for the company."

"Even worse, there's a sense Barton Packing is intentionally taking advantage of people who"—she came close to repeating what Father Burke said about a company store—"may not know their rights."

The tic pulsed in his cheek. "Are you serious? Who said that?"

Liz tapped on the door before Angela could respond. "Jack Taylor is here to see you, Mr. Barton."

"Tell him five minutes."

"Actually, Mr. Taylor is one who voiced concern about the housing condition," Angela said.

"Then this meeting is timely." Nick stood and straightened his jacket, resuming his usual aura of calm control. "Thanks. I'll think about your big three. If Gordon can get some action on the maintenance issues, I'm OK with a release on the housing program. Can't hurt to get the background together."

She really, really hadn't meant to get into that last part about employee rights. But ever since she'd talked with Dave about the problems in Barton's plant culture, the issue had simmered in the back of her mind. Dave had insisted she not approach the issue directly. And yet she'd nearly done just that.

Despite this, Angela left Nick's office pleased. The discussion had gone in unexpected directions, all more interesting than anything she could have planned. This exchange had been real consulting, the kind she'd always imagined herself doing. She looked forward to telling Alvaro how receptive Nick was to their work. If only he were speaking to her.

* * *

In the days since the quarrel in his apartment, she hadn't seen Alvaro at work and hadn't thought of a reason to go wandering in the plant, where she might come across him. When he hadn't answered the phone, she'd tried texting. He hadn't responded. The separation left her with painful withdrawal pangs. She wanted things back the way they had been. It cut deep that he did not.

Rather than create a scene by confronting him in public, she arrived at Saint Catherine's that night seconds before classes started and slipped out as soon as she let her kids go for supper.

"Angela." The priest's voice reached her as her hand landed on her car-door handle. "Angela, wait."

Reluctantly, she turned to face him.

"I thought we would talk over supper," he said. "About Emilio."

She brightened her tone, making up an excuse on the spot. "Actually, I'm going to see the Muñozes now. With Emilio's hearing coming up on Tuesday, I thought I'd see if they're ready."

"Didn't Alvaro tell you he talked with Cesar?"

"He didn't." She looked away. Scraped a fingernail on the door handle. "We've both been . . . busy."

Father Burke searched her face. "Is everything all right?"

"Fine," she said, knowing her face contradicted her words. "What did he find out?"

"Quite a bit. That's why we need to talk. Cesar doesn't have an attorney yet for Emilio. And at the moment, he has bigger problems."

"Bigger than whether Emilio gets deported?" Indignation and dismay flashed like lightning through her already-overloaded emotions.

"To him, yes. The first is that Camila is ill." Father Burke's calm response held no judgment.

"Oh, no." Mentally, she kicked herself for her harsh response. "What's the matter?"

"It's not confirmed. The doctors are doing tests."

The gentle touch she'd seen between Cesar and Camila had been laden with meaning she'd missed. "I thought there was something Cesar wasn't saying. You said 'first.' Is there something else?"

"Cesar didn't say anything directly, but Alvaro thinks Camila may be undocumented. If that's true, they have many reasons for not wanting to be visible in the courts."

"Oh." Angela's mind spun through the news reports of people being picked up by ICE. Even as a mother of five kids, who'd lived in the US for twenty years, Camila would have no protection from deportation. "Wow. What do we do?"

"Camila sees the doctors again on Tuesday. Alvaro told him someone from the church will watch their kids, so that's taken care of. We're letting Cesar use the church van until his is fixed. What we haven't figured out is how to get Emilio to the hearing."

Angela didn't hesitate this time. "I'll do it." She realized she hadn't even had to think about the decision. With so many other things in Hammond, she was forced to find a balance between what was beneficial to Barton, what was legal, what was professional. Helping Emilio was simply right.

"You can get off work?"

She couldn't recall what was on her calendar for Tuesday, but whatever there was, she'd move it. "I will make it work."

"Come inside and we'll talk about it," Father Burke suggested.

"No. You tell Alvaro and Linda. I'll go talk with Cesar."

Chapter 28

The low gray clouds that had threatened rain all morning gave way to a blue sky dotted with puffy white cotton-ball clouds as Angela crossed the Missouri River, leaving Council Bluffs behind and entering Omaha. *A good sign?* she wondered, glancing at Emilio.

The GPS sent her north, away from downtown Omaha, where she'd thought a courthouse might be. With the river and an expanding tourist area to one side and an industrial area offering storage units and truck leasing on the other, she grew anxious about whether they were going in the right direction.

"Mira, mira!" Emilio shouted as they passed a cluster of bronze sculptures in front of a large modern building. She'd been concentrating so closely on the roads and the GPS directions that she hadn't noticed the park. Or the frozen-yogurt sign on a nearby shop.

"Cuando volvamos, nos detendremos," she said. *"Tendremos helado."* This looked like a good place to decompress after the hearing was over. Though, so far, he hadn't appeared the bit least worried about what the day might hold.

When she'd picked him up that morning, Emilio had been bouncing with energy, focused on the car and the trip, not on what might happen in court. Cesar handed over an envelope with the documents they'd need: Emilio's birth certificate, his card from the Honduran consul, the forms recording his history with US Citizenship and Immigration Services and stipulating this court date.

She didn't really know what to expect, even though she'd been briefed by one of Schiffler's Standing for Justice colleagues. By the time she'd volunteered to take Emilio to the hearing, Schiffler was away on business, and it was too late to arrange other legal representation.

In the car, she debated whether to speak English or Spanish with Emilio. They weren't on the road ten minutes before she decided putting Emilio at ease was most important, so she launched into Spanish. Conversing in Spanish for an entire day would challenge her, but Emilio actually made it easy. Everything along the way drew his interest, and he pointed and jabbered, giving her time to catch up as she formulated responses. Livestock, farms, semis crowding the interstate, towering white wind turbines. Only the turbines caused her to struggle for the Spanish words. Finally, she told him the English words, and he learned those.

Halfway to Omaha, they stopped at a Walmart, where she bought him slacks, a belt, and a button-down shirt to replace the blue jeans and T-shirt he was wearing when she picked him up. His tennis shoes were black and reasonably clean. Making a good impression on the judge couldn't hurt, and she hoped Camila would not be offended when he returned home in different clothes. Back in the car, Emilio tore open the package of Twizzlers she'd let him choose as a treat. Then she'd had to be the bad guy and take the package away before he ate all the red licorice and made himself sick.

Now Angela leaned forward as they grew closer to their destination, scanning every sign. Moments later she spotted the sign for the US Department of Homeland Security on her right. The buildings reminded her more of an industrial park.

"We're here," she said as she turned into the parking lot and chose a spot under a small tree. Some shade was better than none. Stepping out of the car, she was hit with humidity that wrapped around her like boa constrictor. Reflexively, she took shallow breaths to conserve energy. Within seconds she felt her blouse adhere to her back with the stifling consistency of plastic wrap. Emilio came to her side, his shoulder touching her hip.

"Let's get out of the sun." She gestured to a grassy area where a Latino family with two small children had also taken refuge. Focused on his phone, the man appeared not to notice them, but the woman smiled as they approached.

Emilio didn't leave her side, and for the first time, he didn't have anything to say. She rested a hand on his shoulder as she surveyed the scene.

The modern, one-story brick building was not at all what she'd expected. Trees around the building were little more than saplings, making her think the property was only a decade or so old, built since the 9/11 attacks. Trees, a large planting of red rose bushes, and ornamental grasses softened the industrial-park impression.

"Let's sit here." She steered Emilio to the curb, taking care as she sat to choose a clean area. She continued in Spanish. "Do you have any questions before we go in?"

When he responded, his voice was barely a whisper. "Will they make me stay here?"

She looked at him, puzzled. "But that's why we are here. So we can make sure you can stay."

"Is this a jail?" His lower lip quivered.

"Oh, Emilio," she said. "Did you mean, will they make you stay here at this building?"

Tears filled his eyes.

"No, Emilio, no." She turned to face him directly, choosing her Spanish words and phrasing to be as clear as possible. "We are here to help you stay in the United States."

On the drive to Omaha, she'd told him as much as she knew about what would happen. She'd explained that the judge would ask questions and he should answer. Then, as now, they'd spoken in Spanish. She was certain he'd understood. Yet clearly he had not.

She searched his face. He looked away, staring at the building for a long moment, and when he looked at her again, she still saw doubt in his eyes. "I would not leave you here. Never. Ever." She hugged him. "Do you understand?"

"Yes, teacher."

"I will not leave you here," she repeated. "Do not worry." She smiled. "OK?"

Finally, he smiled. A half smile. "OK."

It hadn't crossed her mind the court might keep him here, but now the idea was planted, and she found herself confronted again with how little she knew about all this. She rolled her head to loosen her neck. Until proved differently, she'd move forward with confidence. For Emilio's sake.

She stood and dusted off her skirt. Straightened her jacket. Then she made sure his shirt was tucked in and tidy. She brushed a small bit of Twizzler off his cheek.

"OK. Let's go," she said in English.

He slipped his hand into hers. "OK. Let's go."

A tall, black fence edged the sidewalk leading to the immigration court. Inside, they passed through a security checkpoint, then into a small waiting room with sixteen straight-backed chairs, all of them filled. She and Emilio joined others standing with backs against the walls.

Some fifteen minutes later, a tall, slender young woman dressed in a gray pantsuit and platform shoes that increased her height by another two inches walked into the room, studying a clipboard. Other than Angela, this woman was the only white person in the room. She guessed this was the pro bono attorney.

"If you do not have an attorney and would like one, I am here to help you," she said in English. She repeated the message in Spanish.

Angela raised her hand and stepped forward, introducing herself and Emilio. "We would like to talk with you."

She jotted their names on her clipboard, then pointed to a door labeled "Pro Bono Room."

"Go in there. I'll join you shortly." She addressed the room again. "Is there anyone else who needs an attorney today?" she asked in English and Spanish. "There is no charge."

As Angela led Emilio into the small conference room, she noticed a half dozen others raise their hands. Apparently, coming without an attorney happened with frequency.

"It's going to be a busy day," said the woman when she joined them and introduced herself as attorney Madison Blakely. She looked again at her clipboard. "Hello, Emilio." She smiled and extended a hand. *"Encantado de conocerte."*

"Mucho gusto," Emilio murmured.

The rest of their short meeting was conducted in Spanish and included information Angela knew from her talks with Schiffler. In short order, speaking directly to Emilio and only occasionally glancing at Angela, Blakely explained what would happen in the courtroom. She assured him Judge Helen Henderson was kind, and all he had to do was answer a few questions. The outcome would be to set another court date.

"That's everything. Do you have questions?" Blakely asked Emilio.

He shook his head.

"Do you?" she asked Angela as she handed over a sheaf of papers explaining Special Immigrant Juvenile Status and asylum.

Angela actually had many questions, but none had to be answered now and they would only tie up the attorney for time she likely didn't have. "We appreciate that you're here for Emilio today," Angela said. "Is it all right if we sit in the courtroom and watch until it's our turn?"

"Of course. The master-calendar court is the first room down the hallway." Blakely stood and opened the door. "I'll be in as soon as I talk with the others. You won't be called before three."

Angela looked at her watch. It was only 1:25 p.m.

Outside the courtroom, Angela reminded Emilio, "We need to be quiet in the courtroom. *¿Vas a ser bueno?*"

He grinned and nodded. *"Soy bueno."*

"I'm counting on it," she said, and raised a fist. He obliged with a bump.

They slipped into the farthest corner of the back row of wooden church-pew-type benches in the courtroom, where they could see but not be in the way. Judge Henderson was a plump woman with gray-streaked brown hair. Angela hoped the smile lines around the judge's eyes signaled kindness.

On either side of Judge Henderson's bench were three other court officials. Within moments, the roles of the first two became apparent. The clerk, a woman with limp brown hair, wearing a pale-blue dress printed with tiny flowers, sat to the left of the judge. All paperwork passed through her, and on her computer she kept the calendar schedule, a big deal, as Angela soon saw. At a small desk to the right of the judge sat the translator, a man with a brown crew cut, wearing a blue blazer, pink shirt, and plaid tie.

The third court official was a thin woman who kept a large wheeled filing system next to her desk. This person's role was unclear since she never spoke and no one paid any attention to her other than to hand her paperwork from time to time.

Cases were handled with such speed Angela began to keep track. Six minutes. Eight minutes. Five minutes. Nine minutes. Whole days were invested to be there for a process taking less than ten minutes. She could see why some might decide there were bigger priorities.

After a few cases, she understood the terminology. Emilio was the one the court called "the respondent." She bumped him lightly with her elbow, caught his eye, and smiled. Labeling him so impersonally made her sad. Emilio was not a featureless respondent. He was a child with a name, a human being someone cared for.

Soon it became apparent there was a script, a list of questions always asked and answered, that everyone appeared to know. Whether a respondent had an attorney or not didn't appear to affect the time it took for the judge to handle a case. It occurred to Angela that each case was rather like a one-act play. All the players knew their lines, delivering them with expertise and sometimes boredom. Only occasionally was there improvisation.

Angela felt confident Emilio would handle all the questions well. The one question they hadn't discussed concerned his education. The judge always asked if the child was in school. In almost all cases, the child responded they would start in a few weeks, many even giving the exact day.

Leaning close, Angela whispered in Emilio's ear, "Do you know when school starts?"

"Yes. August 25," he replied.

"Good." She patted his hand.

It was with the school questions that Judge Henderson became most personal, smiling, sometimes asking if the child looked forward to school. This question appeared to surprise the children and often elicited a giggle. One teenage boy did not laugh.

"You don't look happy," the judge observed.

"I am a little nervous," the boy responded.

The judge smiled. "I understand. You'll be fine."

Almost always, the outcome for each case was the same—a new date set for when the respondent would return. Though Angela could not be certain, it appeared respondents who were in court for the first time got a date that was relatively soon, maybe only a month or so out. Attorneys who asked for a continuance received dates much farther out. The longest rescheduled hearing fell almost two years in the future.

Beside her, Angela felt Emilio begin to fidget. She laid a hand on his leg to get his attention and put a finger to her lips. It had been almost forty-five minutes; he wouldn't last with nothing to occupy him. She pulled a small notebook and a pencil from her purse and handed them to him. "Draw a picture," she whispered.

As she returned her attention to the court proceedings, she heard the attorney for the next case on the docket explain that the respondent, a young man of eighteen, had not shown up and that the attorney had not spoken to him in some months. Furthermore, he said, the respondent's uncle didn't appear to know where his nephew was, either.

The judge addressed the thin woman with the files. "How does the government wish to proceed?"

The woman responded, "We file a motion to remove in absentia."

Angela looked at the woman with heightened interest. So she was The Government, and that was how it worked. A missed date, a few words, the government filed a motion, and the child would be deported. Instinctively, she put her arm around Emilio's shoulders as though doing so could keep him from such a fate.

Almost an hour later, the courtroom door opened and the pro bono lawyer Blakely came in, followed by a crowd of Hispanic adults and children who filled all the empty seats in the courtroom. These people, like Emilio, didn't have attorneys of their own. Blakely motioned to Emilio. Angela stood, too, but Blakely indicated she should stay back. Seeing that, Emilio hesitated. Angela offered him her most reassuring smile, even as she felt her own stomach twist into a knot.

"Let me hold those," she whispered, taking the notebook and pencil. "You'll be fine," she added, and squeezed his shoulder gently. "I'll be right here."

Blakely guided Emilio past the rail separating spectators from the court and pointed him to a seat beside her at the table facing the judge. Emilio's dark eyes clouded with uncertainty as he looked back at Angela. It was all she could do not to go sit with him. She gave him another smile and nudged a couple over so she could sit on the bench closest to him.

"These are all yours?" Judge Henderson asked Blakely.

"Yeah, I have eight of them," she responded. "And I wasn't even supposed to be here today."

"Let's get started," the judge said.

As soon as the judge began her list of standard questions, Angela heard the script change. Asked if the respondent admitted to the allegation and conceded to the charge, Blakely said, "Your honor, I'd like to ask for a continuance so the respondent can seek an attorney."

Judge Henderson slid into the new script without a hitch, setting another court date and relieving Blakely of attorney responsibility at the end of the case. Then she asked Emilio the same questions she'd asked the other children.

The judge looked at her paperwork. "Who is Cesar Vincente Ramos Muñoz?" she asked.

"*¿Quien es Cesar Vincente Ramos Muñoz?*" the translator asked.

"*Mi tio,*" Emilio said.

"My uncle," said the translator.

"Is he here today?"

"*¿Está aqui hoy?*"

Emilio looked back at Angela as though fearful his answer might be the wrong thing to say. Angela nodded encouragement. He turned to the judge and said, "No."

"Who brought you today?"

"*Mi maestra.*" He pointed to Angela.

"My teacher," said the translator.

Judge Henderson sought out Angela. "You're his teacher?"

Angela stood. "Your Honor, my name is Angela Darrah. Mr. Muñoz could not be here today. I'm a volunteer who teaches English at the church. I am Emilio's friend."

The judge made a note and addressed the rest of her remarks to Emilio. Angela sat down and only then realized the small notebook was still in her hands. Turning it over, she saw Emilio had drawn the courtroom. In his sketch, all the adults were giant sized. At the table where he sat now was a tiny boy. She looked again at Emilio, a catch in her throat.

Finally, the judge reached the final act of the script.

Speaking in English, with the translator following in Spanish, Judge Henderson explained that the government believed Emilio had entered the United States without legal documents. That a hearing would be held so the court could assess all the facts. That at the hearing the government would present papers and documents, anything to help make its case. Also at the hearing, Emilio would be able to present documents of his own and question the government about its facts. She explained that Emilio had the right to have an attorney and encouraged him to get one, but that the government would not provide an attorney nor would the government pay for an attorney.

All during this explanation, which took maybe ninety seconds, Angela watched Emilio's head swivel from Judge Henderson to the translator and back to the judge.

"Do you understand?" the judge asked.

"¿Lo entiendes?" asked the translator.

In a small voice, Emilio responded, "Sí."

"Yes," said the translator.

Even though Angela had listened to the judge's spiel intently through several cases, she barely caught everything herself; there was no chance Emilio understood.

Then it was over. Emilio had had his ten minutes in court. She met him at the rail with a hug and a smile. "Bueno," she whispered as she led him out of the courtroom.

Before they were out the door, another respondent had joined Madison Blakely to face the judge.

Angela knew one thing at the end of that day: she would not let Emilio miss a court date, nor would she let him come to court without his own attorney, even if she had to pay for those services herself.

Chapter 29

Angela was in the midst of working up a proposal for Nick when Gordon appeared in her cubicle.

"Come with me. Now!" he said, and headed for the plant door.

By the time she could say, "What is it?" he was already yards away. The word "accident" reached her ears, and her heart clenched. Slipping on the tennis shoes she kept under her desk, she raced after him. He didn't stop for a hard hat or smock, so she didn't, either.

In the plant she encountered an unfamiliar stillness, and it took a few moments for her to absorb that the line wasn't running. A cluster of employees formed a tight circle, falling back as Gordon approached. On the elevated platforms next to the line, workers stood completely still, their arms hanging loose at their sides as they stared down at the floor.

Angela trailed Gordon into the group and gasped as she absorbed the scene. Alvaro knelt next to a woman, his hands covered with blood. He pressed bandages against the woman's arm and hand to staunch a crimson flood spreading over the woman's canvas apron and pooling on the floor.

She felt her stomach heave, and she looked away, focusing instead on the circle of workers, their eyes wide, jaws slack.

"What happened?" Gordon barked over Alvaro's shoulder.

"We called the ambulance. Tom's outside waiting." Alvaro's voice balanced on the pinhead of calm urgency. Looking past Gordon, he caught Angela's eye, holding it for a split second before returning his attention to the woman moaning under his hands. *"Vas a estar bien. No se preocupe."* He repeated the words again and again. "You will be OK. Don't worry."

Angela hadn't seen Alvaro since she'd slammed out of his apartment more than a week ago, a week she'd spent cycling through endless loops of reflection and self-recrimination. The sound of his voice and his brief gaze flooded her with profound relief.

"Wilson." Gordon caught the attention of a middle-aged man Angela recognized as another floor supervisor. "And you." He included Angela. "Over here." He moved away from the group surrounding the injured woman.

She hesitated, her eyes locked on Alvaro, reluctant to leave him, hoping he would look at her again, wanting him to know she was sorry for being a jerk. He had more important things to do than think about her, but she couldn't help wanting to rectify her guilt over how she'd acted. She pulled away and went to Gordon.

Gordon pitched his voice too low to be heard beyond the three of them. "Tell me what happened."

"The first I knew something was wrong was when Alvaro hit the emergency stop," Wilson said. "It looks like one of the carts clipped her leg, and she fell into the machine."

Angela sucked in a sharp breath as the image of the woman stumbling into a razor-sharp blade filled her mind. She looked toward the work area. A cart loaded with tubs of chicken parts stood abandoned nearby. It would have been an easy thing to happen.

"Who is she?" Gordon gave the briefest nod at the woman.

"Lupe Perez. She came with that last group from Texas. She was competent. Worked that machine since she got here."

"Damn it," Gordon muttered.

Just then a door opened and EMTs rushed in, wheeling a gurney. One knelt next to Alvaro and in seconds took over the woman's care. Alvaro stayed at the woman's side, repeating reassurances.

As Angela watched, a mental list of the people who needed to be informed of the accident started to form. And the standard steps for communicating in any crisis began to scroll through her brain: Tell it all. Tell it fast. Keep on telling it.

"Does she have a family?" Angela asked.

"Her husband is on the next shift," Wilson said.

"Someone needs to tell him," she said.

"I expect someone already did," Wilson said. "I saw a couple of people on their phones."

"But someone from the company should—"

"HR will deal with it," Gordon interrupted. He spoke to Wilson. "As soon as they're out of here, get the mess cleaned up and everyone back to work. Tell Al I want to see him in my office in ten minutes."

"Got it," Wilson said, and was gone.

Gordon's callousness chilled Angela's bones. He was more interested in getting the line running than in what happened to that poor woman. What about finding out for sure her husband had been called? He shouldn't hear through the grapevine his wife had been hospitalized.

"And you." Gordon turned to Angela. "Make sure there's no media on this. Do you understand me?"

"If a reporter shows up, we have to say something," she protested.

"No. We don't." Gordon's tone left no room for discussion.

Why the hell did he bring her here if he didn't want her expertise? Her blood boiled. She wouldn't stand down on this.

"Wait a minute," she said as he turned to leave. "I understand why you don't want media coverage. But what happens if a reporter hears about it? From a hospital source or an ambulance buddy? Maybe someone hears the siren. It's better to be preemptive than caught with your proverbial pants down."

She had his attention. He eyed her with suspicion. "Go on."

"If anyone calls, we give a brief, honest comment, something along the lines of: 'One of our employees was injured in an accident and was transported to County Memorial Hospital for treatment. The safety of our employees is of utmost importance to us. We will be doing everything we can to understand how this accident happened and to ensure such an accident does not occur again.'" She cleared her throat. "It's simple. Factual. Shows concern for employees. There's no damage I can see in saying it."

Gordon studied her as though she were trying to pull something over on him. "OK. But let me be damn clear—nothing gets said unless I OK it. Do you understand?"

"Yes, sir." Her mind turned to other people who needed to know. "Who tells HR? And what about Nick? He should know."

"Leave that to me." Again, he started to leave but turned back, holding her with the steel in his gray eyes. "Are we clear?"

"Yes."

"We better be."

The threat in Gordon's tone barely registered as Angela's mind raced in crisis mode. She thought of other things she needed to know even if she never told a reporter any of it. How often were there accidents in the plant? When was the last one? What did the company do to prevent accidents? She'd talk with HR, but first she needed to talk to Alvaro.

By the time Gordon left, the EMTs were wheeling the woman on the gurney out of the plant. As soon as the door closed behind them, the processing line started moving again. A cleaning crew was already training pressure hoses on the floor, forcing the pools of blood down the drain.

"Alvaro," she called out when she saw him head for the employee locker room. He looked in her direction but didn't stop. She hurried her steps to catch up with him. Blood covered his hands, soaked his clothes. A streak of blood smudged his cheek. Was he injured?

She looked him over and asked, "Are you OK?"

His eyes followed hers to the bloody smears on his skin and clothes. "Yes. I am."

"Thank goodness. But that woman. It was horrible," she said. "How is she?"

"Lupe is not well." He stared at his own hands. "Her arm. Her hand. It is not good." He shook his head and continued toward the locker room. "I have to see Mr. Ryker."

She reached out, took hold of his arm, made him look at her. "Alvaro, I know it's not the right time, but I want you to know I'm sorry. I was wrong. I shouldn't have walked out."

"I'm sorry, too, amiga." Relief eased into his worry-strained eyes. "I did not say it right, either."

She squeezed his elbow. "I'll wait in the break room. I'm going to see Gordon with you."

* * *

Between the break room and Gordon's office, Alvaro convinced Angela that inserting herself uninvited into the meeting would serve no other purpose than to make Gordon angry.

"I'll tell you everything I know later," he said as she walked with him toward Gordon's office. "Tonight over supper?"

"Yes. Tonight." She wanted to hug him but knew she should not. Not here. Not now. "Promise you'll text me when you get out. OK?"

His nod assured her that even if all was not well, it could be. He disappeared into Gordon's office.

As soon as the door closed behind him, she pulled out her phone and called Dave. When he answered, she filled him in on both the accident details and the message for the media that she'd suggested to Gordon. She leaned against the wall so she could see if anyone came down the hall before lamenting, "They don't want anything sent out proactively."

Dave grunted. "That'll put them behind the curve if this gets to be a story."

"I know." She lowered her voice further. "Gordon's resistance has been a barrier the whole time I've been here. But he was adamant. Advice?"

"I don't get his problem. Whatever Gordon says, you need to talk to Nick. Keep me in the loop."

"Will do." She disconnected and headed toward the stairwell. She had her hand on the doorknob when the door opened and Nick Barton came through.

"Nick. Has Gordon talked with you?"

"Not since before lunch. Why?"

She debated for a half second. This was not a time to stand on chain-of-command formality. "There was an accident in the plant. A woman was injured in one of the machines."

Nick's eyes squinted with worry. "My god! Is she all right?"

"I don't know yet. She was taken to the hospital. Alvaro was there when it happened, and he's briefing Gordon now. I talked with Gordon about having a statement ready if the media gets hold of this."

"You know this is exactly the kind of thing we have *never* talked with the media about."

"I do. But there are good reasons why we should." She outlined the rationale and the rough messaging she'd shared with Gordon. "Plus, you're under the media microscope because of the recall. That reporter has been nosing around. He'll be sensitive to anything further he could put into print."

Nick listened attentively, then asked, "Gordon agreed?"

"As long as we only provide the information in response to media questions. And he approves what gets said. Nothing goes out otherwise."

"I concur. If we do get questions, we want to be careful how we answer them."

They continued to talk through the issue for a few more minutes. This was the first time Angela had seen Nick under real stress, and yet again he impressed her. He responded as well as anyone she'd ever seen. His thoughtful questions, his concern for the injured woman left her wishing yet again she could work only with him.

* * *

That night, Alvaro suggested they take a walk. Perspiration formed on her neck as soon as they stepped out into the muggy July air, but Alvaro clearly needed to move as he related the details of the accident. For a half hour, they walked and he talked. Only a few times did she make a comment or ask a question.

"Three fingers," he said, stopping in midstride. Until that moment, he had not really looked at her. "She lost three fingers," he repeated, his expression bereft.

"Alvaro, I am so sorry. Can they reattach the fingers? Sometimes they can."

"I do not know. I pray they can help her. She needs her hands for work. For her family."

"I am praying for them, too."

They continued walking for a while in silence. Then he said, "The machine. It was one I recommended to Mr. Barton." Guilt spilled out with his words.

She put her hand on his arm and turned him toward her. "You don't think this was your fault, do you?"

He didn't answer. The pain etched on his face told her everything. "Oh, Alvaro. It wasn't. You know that."

"I feel it is," he confessed.

"No." She wrapped her arms around him, holding him tight. "No, it wasn't your fault." She pulled back so she could look in his eyes. "These things happen. Even with the best equipment and working conditions. Nick knows it. You did nothing wrong."

He nodded with only half-hearted agreement, and for another half hour they continued to walk in silence.

Upon returning to his apartment building, she asked, "Do you want me to come up?"

"I'm tired. Maybe next time."

His words confirmed he'd forgiven her. For the first time in more than a week, she felt light in her heart. As he turned to go inside, she said, "Alvaro? Before . . . all this . . . we told the kids we'd do another picnic this weekend. Do you still want to? Are you up to it?"

"Sí, amiga. It will be good. For them. And for me."

"For all of us."

Chapter 30

Angela swept the last crumbs of hot dogs, chips, and fruit off the plastic red-and-white-checkered tablecloth. As she worked, she kept an eye on the half dozen boys who'd run off after eating and were now engaged in a fast-paced game of soccer in the grassy open center of the park. Stealing glances when he wasn't looking, she also paid attention to Alvaro. She needed to reassure herself that he was OK, that they were OK.

Casually, she asked, "How are you doing, Alvaro?"

"I am fine," he said. "You do not need to worry."

"I can't help it. I do worry. Seeing something like that, being the one who stepped in." From what she could tell, she was more traumatized by what had happened than he. Maybe because he'd been able to do something while she'd only watched. The image of blood on the floor around the woman and Alvaro came to mind too frequently. "Have you been to see Lupe?"

"Yes. Her husband was there last night. He is worried for her. For them."

"I can understand. Will she be able to come back to work?"

"The doctors say she will go home in a few days. But back to work? I do not know."

The doctors had been able to reattach two of the fingers, but how much motion Lupe would regain was yet to be seen.

"What about their children? Who takes care of them now?" Since the accident, she'd learned that Lupe and her husband worked different shifts so one of them could always take care of their three children.

"Neighbors are helping."

"That's good."

He grabbed the bag of charcoal and lighter fluid and carried it all to the car, then stowed everything in the trunk.

Sunlight and cloud shadows flitted across her face, and Angela tilted her head back, feeling little kisses of warmth on her face. A thunderstorm had passed through during the night, taking with it the high humidity and leaving behind a puffy-cloud, blue-sky day—the best of the summer so far.

It had been awkward, knowing he felt about her as she did about him, knowing that if circumstances were different, they might have moved their relationship in a whole different direction. But each time they talked cleared the air between them a little more, gradually restoring the friendship they'd had and she hoped to retain.

After returning from the car, Alvaro straddled the bench across the picnic table from her. "My family, we went on picnics often," he said.

"By the river," she said. Since he'd told her the story behind his tattoo, she'd imagined that family scene often.

"We always had many kids at the picnics. My aunts and uncles and cousins all came."

"So it wasn't only your mom and sister?"

"No. Every time, many people."

She looked across the park where Emilio and his friends were playing soccer. She imagined Alvaro's El Salvadoran family. A big family.

His voice interrupted her thoughts. "Someone is coming."

"Who?" She looked around and spotted Trevor McKay a few yards off, headed in their direction. He waved.

Her heart sank. On a weekend? Like the other media, he'd shown little interest in the accident even though an ambulance siren always got attention in a small town. She had been ready when the media called. With the statement both Nick and Gordon approved, she had "told it all and told it fast," but had no need to keep telling it because there were no new questions. The speed with which she'd responded to media calls reinforced that the company was being open, concerned, and cooperative. Even Gordon had admitted that the approach had worked.

Interest had faded fast when people learned the injured woman was not a longtime Hammond resident and the accident did not result in death. She didn't like to think the disinterest could also stem from the fact that the woman was Latina.

She couldn't imagine what was on McKay's mind now.

"I thought that was you," McKay said as he came closer. "Great day for a picnic, eh?"

Angela looked up, shielding her eyes from the sun. "Hi, Trevor. What brings you to Hammond on a Sunday?"

"Enjoying the nice weather," he said. "Mind if I join you?"

She could hardly say no. Maybe this was small-town life. You couldn't even go on a picnic without running into a reporter. Or maybe he'd come specifically to track them down.

"Trevor, this is Alvaro Duarte," she said. "He's a supervisor at Barton Packing. Alvaro, this is Trevor McKay, reporter with the *Elbridge Times*."

The two men shook hands. "Pleased to meet you, Alvaro," McKay said.

"I have read your articles. Eduardo and Maria Gonzales are friends of mine."

"They were a good interview. I plan to talk with them again sometime," McKay said. "You teach at Saint Catherine's, don't you? I'm pretty sure Father Burke mentioned your name."

"I work with middle school boys," Alvaro said. "We study money and budgets."

"Not English?"

"Everything is English, and financial management skills are important." He added, "Angela teaches English to younger kids."

"Father Burke mentioned it." He turned to Angela. "Do you teach in Des Moines, too?"

"No. It's a new experience for me."

"Since you're only here for a short while, what made you decide to take on such a commitment?"

This was beginning to feel like an interview. She caught Alvaro's eye. They'd talked often about the media and particularly about McKay. He lifted a barely perceptible one-shoulder shrug that told her he understood the situation.

"Father Burke and Alvaro can be persuasive." She laughed. "It's been fun. And rewarding."

"You know, I've been thinking about doing a story on Saint Catherine's. You've given me an idea," McKay said, reaching into his shirt pocket. "Would you mind if I take a few notes?"

And there it is, Angela thought. "Hold on for a minute." She lifted a hand. "What do you have in mind?"

He didn't open the notebook, nor did he put it back in his pocket. "I'm in the beginning stages of an immigration story."

"Oh. Well, if you call me at the office next week, I'm sure I could pull together something related to the Barton workforce."

"I think there's a better angle," he said. "You've no doubt heard about the unaccompanied children coming to the US. Some have tagged them 'border kids.'"

His words sent an electric jolt through her, and she knew at once he'd been after this from the beginning. "I have, but what's that got to do with us?"

"I think there's a good story in the kids who make it all the way from Central America to Iowa."

Certain she knew where McKay was headed with this, she played for time. "I'm confused. What has this got to do with Barton Packing?"

McKay said, "It doesn't. But I understand you have one of these boys in your class. A profile on him would put a face on the issue everyone is talking about."

"Really?" The laugh that came out of her mouth echoed tin-can fake. "I wouldn't know. I'm a volunteer helping kids learn English. I don't get into their backgrounds."

Her eyes darted to Alvaro. He met her gaze with a look of disbelief.

She'd talked with the attorney three times, yet they'd never discussed the pros and cons of media coverage. She had no idea whether a story about Emilio was a good idea or not. Without even trying, she could come up with as many reasons why a story could hinder Emilio's case as she could why it might be helpful.

"I understand there's a boy who recently came to Iowa. And he may be in your class." McKay checked his notebook. "Emilio Garcia. Is Emilio in your class?"

"Kids come and go all the time, Trevor. There's no Emilio in the class at this moment. I'm sorry, I don't think I can be helpful." She lifted her shoulders and offered a weak what-can-you-do smile.

She'd never in her life lied, or even thought about lying, to a reporter. It disturbed her how easily the false words came out of her mouth. Once they were spoken, though, she began to justify what she'd said. Technically it wasn't a lie. He wasn't in the class at this exact moment. There were no children at all in the class at this moment. Emilio was here. In the park.

"But even if there were," she continued, "I question whether disrupting the life of a child who has already been through so much is the way to educate people about immigration issues. Leave them alone. Let them live their lives."

As she talked, she avoided glancing at where Emilio was playing.

"No need to be touchy. I'm on your side in this, Angela."

"I don't have a side." There it was, another lie.

"Gee, Angela." McKay turned on his kid-brother charm. "You're giving your time to this boy. I thought you'd be interested in seeing that the best happens for him."

"Of course I care. And I'd like to help you, but I can't. I don't know the boy you're asking about." Having started, she couldn't stop herself; lies just cascaded out.

McKay turned to Alvaro. "Maybe in your class?"

"No." Alvaro shook his head. "There is no Emilio in my class."

The corner of Angela's mouth twitched. Alvaro had gone along with her fib, but his answer was actually the truth.

McKay scratched his scalp with the eraser end of his pencil. "Guess I misunderstood." He slipped his notebook back in his pocket and stood. "I'll leave you to your picnic. Good to meet you, Alvaro."

"Same here," Alvaro said.

"I'll be in touch, Angela," McKay said.

She nodded. At the moment she almost wished he'd wanted to talk about the accident. She could have handled that.

When McKay was out of hearing range, Alvaro's thick eyebrows knit together in a thunderous black line. "What were you doing?" he asked.

Angela's eyes locked on a small three-corner tear in a red square in the tablecloth. She picked at it with her fingernail. "I didn't know what to say. I know I'm supposed to be able to handle things like this on the fly, but Emilio is personal to me. I would never do anything to hurt him, and I know so little I'm afraid I could hurt him without intending to."

"But you lied."

Self-disgust puddled in her chest. She couldn't meet Alvaro's eyes. "He probably already knows that. I was caught off guard. Unprepared. I've never done anything like that before."

McKay wasn't stupid. If he didn't already know she lied, he'd find out soon enough. He might even track down Emilio. Or Cesar and Camila Muñoz.

"I should go after him." She watched McKay cross the park yet remained rooted to the bench. "But I don't know what I'd say."

Alvaro reached across the table and pressed her hands between his, his warmth grounding her. "Do the right thing."

His eyes told her he had all the confidence in the world in her, and she knew that meant everything to her.

"Thanks." She squeezed his hands quickly and stood. McKay was at the other end of the park, getting into a car. "Trevor!" she shouted. "Trevor, wait!"

She ran toward him, knowing she'd damaged her reputation, but more importantly herself, with the lie. She hadn't the least idea how she'd handle the story he wanted to do about Emilio, but if she didn't engage, Emilio could be even more vulnerable, and she couldn't let that happen. The only way to fix all this was with the truth.

"Trevor," she shouted again. This time he heard her, turned, and waited. She stopped in front of the reporter, breathless. "I'm glad . . . I caught you." She gulped a breath. "That . . ." She looked back toward the picnic table, where Alvaro stood watching. "What I said . . . wasn't . . . true."

Head tilted, McKay waited.

She looked toward the kids. She saw Emilio kick the soccer ball, then raise his arms, his laugh joyful, triumphant, carefree. He deserved that kind of life. She turned back to McKay, rooted herself solidly in place, and looked him directly in the eyes. "I lied." Knowing it was important to say the exact words, she repeated them. "I lied. Emilio Garcia is in my class."

"I figured," he said.

She flushed. "You took me by surprise. I wasn't prepared. I didn't know what to say, and I'm overly protective of him."

"And lying was what you came up with?"

"Apparently, yes." She dipped her head, contrite. "It was a first for me. I'm so sorry."

"I'm not surprised." He snickered. "You're not very good at it."

"Thank goodness." She laughed, feeling lightheaded from the helium of truth. "Do you have time to talk to us about it now?"

"For the record?" He tapped the pocket where he kept his notebook.

"How about a background conversation first? Would you agree to that?" She needed to find out what he knew and what he planned for the story, how far things had gone.

Irritation flashed across McKay's congenial face. Having just lied to the man, Angela knew she was pushing to ask for a background conversation. She banked on his wanting a story on whatever terms he could get.

"If that's what it takes," he agreed.

"Thank you, Trevor," she said, and they headed back to the picnic table.

"We're having this conversation on background," she told Alvaro. "Background means Trevor won't quote us, and he won't use anything we tell him without getting the information from another source." She would have preferred to plot a strategy with Alvaro before talking with the reporter, but she knew how carefully he would read her face and attend to her words. She trusted his caution.

"OK." Angela turned to Trevor. "Let's start over. I was flustered, and I don't even remember what you said earlier. Can you tell us how you got started on this story?"

"I'd been following the story of these unaccompanied kids coming to the US. When I heard some of them had made it to Iowa, it sounded like a story worth pursuing."

"How did you find out about a boy in Hammond?" Alvaro asked.

"An anonymous tip led me to Father Burke."

A tip? *What a coward,* she thought. "What did the tipster say?"

"He felt it was important for people to know 'these illegals' are here. He's been watching the town change and doesn't like what he sees."

"They're children, Trevor. Their families sent them here to get away from the terrible things going on in their home countries. We should be helping them, not trying to throw them out." Angela felt her emotions taking over, and she tried to dial it back, to move the discussion onto neutral, practical ground.

"I'm from El Salvador," Alvaro interjected. "My mother tells me what it is like with the gangs. She is afraid even for me to come back."

McKay jotted a note. "I heard the government in El Salvador had a truce with the gangs."

"They did. They made the deal in 2012. But the gangs do not keep the truce. It is worse now than it was then."

Alvaro's intervention gave Angela time to think. She said, "You mentioned doing a profile. Have you considered the ethics?"

"How do you mean?"

"These kids are here without their parents. It would be so easy for them to be taken advantage of. Even naming them could create problems."

"We'd be careful. I'm sure of that," Trevor said.

"And what about what happens as a result of an interview? What if the coverage brings the government down on them? Are you and your editor willing to be responsible if these kids are deported back to the life-threatening countries they risked their lives to escape? We're dealing with children, so we all have to be especially careful."

"And we would be. Besides, the government already knows about the kids," he countered. "They each have a date when their status comes up for review. As I understand it, if their refugee status is confirmed, their sponsors can be formalized and all is fine."

Angela realized Trevor was as ill-informed about the process as she'd been. She considered whether to tell him that she'd taken Emilio to his first court appointment, but elected to hold that information until the interview was on the record. If it got that far. In the meantime, she could at least steer him to good background information.

"From what I've learned, it's not so simple," she said. "I've talked with a lawyer for my own background. I can give you her name if you want."

"Contacts would help," he said.

She pulled out her phone and shared the contact info for Schiffler and Standing for Justice.

"I'll share what I know, but I want to emphasize I'm not an expert," she said. "Also, whether Emilio will be interviewed or not really isn't up to me, but if you do pursue the story and his family agrees, I'd be glad to be there as an interpreter. If you need one."

She doubted Cesar and Camila would consent to an interview, particularly if Camila was undocumented. But could they say no without creating a bigger issue? Angela could help with that. She could make certain there was no misunderstanding.

"Do you have a deadline on the story?" she asked.

"Not yet. I'll talk with my editor later this week about it."

So the story wasn't a sure thing. She'd email Schiffler that night and ask about the advisability of media coverage for Emilio's case. "How about this. If you and your editor agree to pursue this, we'll be helpful to the extent we can."

"It's a deal."

Angela felt the tension in her chest lessen. But when he flipped his notebook to a clean page, her muscles tightened again. Truly, a Sunday afternoon in the park shouldn't be so tense.

"Actually, there is something else I'm working on," McKay said. "I understand Barton Packing has a free-rent program for new employees. What can you tell me about that?"

She scrambled to think. While the rent program wasn't a secret, Nick had agreed that a story wasn't a good idea until the houses got some TLC. Plus, the memory of the chicken-donation story was fresh in her mind, and she wouldn't make that mistake again.

"Yes, there is a program," she confirmed. "But I'd like to keep this discussion on background for the moment, too."

He tilted his head, a slight frown wrinkling his forehead. "Is there a reason you want to keep it a secret?"

"Are we on background?"

"If that's the only way you'll talk. But it does make me wonder if there's a problem."

This was exactly the catch she'd warned Gordon and Nick about, when anyone said "no comment."

She persisted. "So we are on background?"

"All right," he agreed at last. "Yes, we're on background."

Reassured, Angela shared the facts of the housing subsidy and the advantages for employees, community, and company.

"It all sounds positive," McKay said. "Why can't you go on record about it, then?"

For a moment she gauged how blunt to be. The management company wasn't a client, but she didn't want to say anything that could get back to them. In fact, HR had only just told her the company's name—Lake Michigan Properties, or LMP.

She said, "Some of the houses are more run down than we'd like to see. We're trying to get the company that owns the properties to do some work, but we haven't got them to agree yet."

"So Barton doesn't own the houses?"

"No. They don't. That's a misconception we hope to clear up because we know people assume the houses became run down on Barton's watch."

"The building I live in may be part of the program," Alvaro said. "Mr. Ryker set me up there when I came here. He said the first month's rent was on him."

Angela looked at him with surprise. Given how well kept Alvaro's building was compared to the other LMP houses, she'd never have guessed. A discussion for later.

Angela said, "Alvaro can make his own decisions about being interviewed, but everything we're talking about this afternoon is background only."

"I hold to that agreement," McKay said.

The interview wrapped up shortly after. As they stood side by side watching McKay walk to his car, Alvaro bumped Angela with his shoulder. "Nice recovery."

She smiled. "Thanks. You never told me your apartment was part of the company program."

"Until today, it never occurred to me it could be. It is not like the others. But the company paid for my rent like everyone else, so it may be."

"Lake Michigan Properties. Does that ring a bell?"

"That's it," Alvaro confirmed. "That's the name of the company I send my rent to."

"Humph." Angela flashed her eyebrows and shrugged. "Well. It's a relief that all the properties aren't dumps," she said. "Now I need to send some emails. Even though it's Sunday." She sat at the picnic table and sent the same message to Nick, Gordon, and Dave.

Trevor McKay, Elbridge Times reporter, just asked about the free-rent housing program. I confirmed there is such a program, and we have concerns about the upkeep of the properties. Provided no details. ALL discussion on background.

She hit "send." "There. We're good."

Within minutes, she heard from Dave: *Well handled. Let's talk tomorrow.*

An hour later, she heard from Nick: *Thanks. Continue getting details together in case we move forward.*

Gordon's response arrived late that night. *Unable to reach mgt co.*

Chapter 31

When Angela went into the break room to get a bottle of water, Gordon and Alvaro were already there. The men acknowledged her and continued talking, making no effort to hide their words.

"That woman shut us down for most of the morning," Gordon said. "There's a cost to that."

"Lupe Perez." Alvaro spoke the name with a note of irritation as he stood straight and square, mirroring Gordon's military stance.

"What?" Gordon asked.

"The woman who was injured. Her name is Lupe Perez," he repeated.

They were talking about the accident, and she thought about leaving, but if they wanted a private conversation, the break room wasn't exactly the place. Besides, she was curious.

She fed a dollar bill into the dispenser. The machine promptly rejected it. She smoothed out the bill, creased it, and fed it in again. Slowly. All the while listening to the conversation that continued as though she weren't there.

Alvaro spoke without hesitation. "Mr. Ryker. It was not her fault. She should not lose her job because of an accident."

"She'd be out for weeks, and even if she could come back, she couldn't do the job anymore."

Lupe might lose her job? Angela took her water bottle and slipped into a chair in the far corner of the room, out of Gordon's line of sight, then pretended to check her phone messages.

"She was careless. We can't afford slipshod work. They all know the rules."

"Lupe was not careless," Alvaro said. "A cart pushed her off balance."

Gordon's tone grew lethal. "You're right. The guy who pushed the cart is responsible, too. I'll have HR talk to him."

Alvaro said, "Mr. Ryker. That is not right."

"It is. Whoever pushed the cart shares responsibility for shutting us down."

The longer she listened, the more incensed she became. From everything Alvaro had told her, what happened was an accident. No one should be punished for an accident. It wasn't right.

"We have procedures. We have rules. And that woman was negligent."

"To be pushed into a saw, it is not negligent. It was an accident."

"Do you think I don't know what the rules are? What the law says? Besides, it's done."

"How is it done?" Alvaro asked.

"The woman quit."

"Quit?" Angela spoke before she could stop herself, then quickly covered her mouth and coughed. *What about workers' comp?* she wondered. *Shouldn't Lupe get temporary disability, at least?*

Gordon jerked at the sound. When he turned toward her, she glued her eyes to her phone screen.

"Why would Lupe quit?" Alvaro asked.

"Probably because she knew she was at fault. But to show we're good people, we gave her a payout. More money than she's seen at one time before."

Angela peeked at Alvaro. Irritation radiated off him.

"It's done, and that's the last I want to hear of it," Gordon growled. "She should count herself lucky she got any money." He left the break room through the office-side door.

Alvaro fed coins into the vending machine, retrieved a Coke, and joined Angela. "Lupe did not deserve to lose her job," he said.

"I don't understand. Why would she quit?"

"She did not have a choice."

"Why?"

"After the last time, I tried to find out what the law said."

"The last time?"

"There was another accident. A pallet tipped and crushed a man's leg. He quit, too. They also paid him."

Angela frowned. "What did you find out?"

"Not much. The man signed a form to take the money. He agreed not to talk to anyone about it."

"How much did they pay him?"

"He was not supposed to talk, but it was the same as for Lupe—$5,000."

Angela's frown deepened. She didn't know anything about employment law, but this sounded wrong. A coworker of hers had been injured in a fall at the office. The settlement took months to work out, and when it did, the amount that her co-worker received was staggering.

"But she is getting workers' comp or disability payments, isn't she?"

"As far as I know, she gets only what the company paid her."

"She definitely should be. Could you confirm whether she is or isn't?"

"I will ask tonight when I go to the hospital."

Angela chewed on her lower lip. "Lupe and her family are from out of state. How about the man who was injured? Was he someone they recruited from out of state?"

He tipped his pop bottle, signaling she was correct.

It sounded wonky, but Gordon was a smart man. Surely he wouldn't do anything to put the company in jeopardy. But why would someone with a serious injury simply quit? And for such a tiny sum? Did Nick know what was going on? She didn't like to think so, but she couldn't deny the possibility.

"Have you ever challenged Gordon like that before?" she asked.

He shook his head, then gulped from the pop bottle.

"I hope he doesn't come back at you in some way."

"A few more points." He shrugged. "What will it matter?"

"What do you mean? A few more points? Why would you have points at all?"

"It is nothing." Alvaro drained the last drops from the bottle, then took it to the recycling bin.

In all the times they'd talked about the points, he'd never told her they'd been levied against him. She insisted, "It's something. Tell me."

"I have points from the days we went out of town."

His answer stunned her. "But he approved you going."

"Because Mr. Barton said so, yes. The points were to let me know he did not agree."

This explained so much. His unwillingness to present the plan with her. His touchiness in even talking about it. "Why didn't you tell me before?"

The break-room door swung open, and a group of men came in from the plant. He nodded at them.

"I need to get back to work," he said. "I did not tell you, because it did not matter. He made his point. I made mine."

Speechless, Angela watched him walk back into the plant. He'd stood up to Gordon and gone with her anyway, knowing he'd get points. *He did that for me,* she thought.

No. He'd done it for himself.

* * *

Angela reported to Dave that afternoon. "You know the woman injured in the plant accident? She's been fired."

"When did this happen?"

"I learned about it today. Gordon says she wasn't fired, that she quit, but I'm not so sure. It sounds to me as though they might have coerced her. And Alvaro says he knows of another employee, a man, who left in the same way. After an accident. From what Alvaro knows, Lupe isn't getting workers' comp or disability payments, either. Dave, I think the company is doing something really wrong."

"Take a deep breath," Dave said after she'd unloaded her concerns. "They offered a settlement, and the employee signed off on it. It doesn't sound as though Barton did anything illegal."

He so consistently walked her back when she expressed concern that it didn't surprise her that he was doing it again now. It didn't surprise her, but it did annoy her.

"But for such a small amount of money? That can't be right. Lupe doesn't speak much English, and she doesn't have an attorney. It sounds to me as though she was forced out."

"You're getting ahead of yourself, Angela. And this isn't your business. Or ours. What you told the media about the accident was accurate. That's all you need to worry about."

"But what if there were others? Before? Who were terminated in the same way?"

"There may not be any illegal action; this could be standard procedure in the packing industry. Besides, you're speculating. You'd never let a reporter get away with that."

That comment caught her up short.

"You're right," she admitted. "But even if it's legal, do they really want the world to know how little they care about their employees?"

"You're getting yourself wound up in this, Angela. It's not personal. Your job—our job—is to represent the client. Don't forget that."

He was right. Of course he was. But it felt personal. She'd come to care about the people working there. That was her job, too, wasn't it?

"I've let you talk me down from the product expiration, from the points, from the Muslim prayer issue, but this is getting to be too much," Angela said. "Should I bring this up to Nick? Do you think he knows how Gordon is handling things?"

"First off, you don't know Gordon is doing wrong. Beyond that, Nick trusts Gordon or he wouldn't have put him in charge."

She heard him exhale and could almost see smoke curling into the afternoon air.

He said, "On a practical level, Nick could be in a situation of plausible deniability."

"Plausible deniability?"

"CEOs put a buffer around themselves. Subordinates make decisions, and if the wheels come off, the CEO can say they didn't know. It doesn't make them look good, but someone else takes the heat."

"Nick doesn't seem the type."

"I'm just saying. Plausible deniability is a possibility."

Before they disconnected, he reminded her again of what was her job and what wasn't. Generally, talking with Dave made her feel better. This time the conversation left her feeling out of sorts.

He had an answer, a rationale, an excuse, for everything. Did that happen after you'd been in the public-relations business so long? Didn't you allow yourself to be fully invested in anything? Would she be that way herself someday?

She swept her hair—now eight weeks overdue for a cut—back and found a scrunchie to secure it. She'd been sent to Hammond to do a job and found herself wrapped up in a whole lot of things that weren't her job. Emilio. English classes. Alvaro. Those interactions opened her to unexpected and unfamiliar experiences that made her even more sensitive to her client's actions. She'd never had a client challenge her as Barton Packing did. Right. Wrong. Legal. Illegal. Always there was an "it depends" attached. Dave had convinced her to overlook these problems. Sometimes she convinced herself. But the more she knew, the more she felt . . . squirrelly.

Walking away from these problems made her feel as though even if it weren't her job, even if she was technically right, she was actually really wrong.

* * *

Angela called the immigration attorney. "Do you have time for another question or two?" she asked.

"You caught me headed out the door," Schiffler responded. "I've got about ten minutes. Shoot."

Angela jumped in, keeping one eye on the clock. "If someone has an accident on the job, is it legal for the employer to fire them?"

"It could be if the employee broke the law or showed blatant disregard for company policies. But I'd need more details."

"What if the person fell and was injured because a piece of equipment run by another employee forced her off balance?"

"It doesn't sound like the employee was at fault. I assume you're asking me this because the person who had the accident is an immigrant?"

"Yes. Would it make a difference?"

"Only in that immigrants are less likely to complain."

"Why's that?"

"Lots of reasons. Their English may not be as good. They don't understand their rights. They're grateful to have a job and don't want to jeopardize it. Those are a few. And if they're undocumented, it gets more complicated."

"The employer uses E-Verify, so that last point shouldn't be an issue."

"E-Verify isn't perfect. Immigrants get papers to satisfy the requirements. Employers may do only what they need to have cover if they're questioned. Even if they don't know exactly which employees have forged documents, they know some do, and they take advantage of that to keep everyone in line."

It was never as neat as it appeared. Angela had taken the information provided on the government's E-Verify site for granted, just as she had Gordon's assurance they were clean on the hiring front.

"I guess I was naive." Angela made a note to dig further into E-Verify, and asked another question. "What about the company compensating an employee who is injured? Maybe in exchange for the employee quitting instead of being fired? Is the company off the hook? Is there any recourse?"

"You've touched on a lot of intertwined points. Can you be more specific?"

"OK." Angela worked to take identifying details out of the story. "A woman who speaks little English recently moved to Iowa from the Southwest to work in a packing plant. Through no fault of her own that I can tell, she cut her hand and wrist in one of the saws, severely enough she can't go back to work at least for weeks, maybe at all. She lost three fingers, though they were able to reattach two. The company gave her $5,000; she signed a release and quit."

Schiffler exhaled a long breath ending in a thoughtful "tsk, tsk, tsk."

"Curious. Companies who hire undocumented workers generally just fire them if there's a problem. They know the employee won't complain. I've never heard of one who did it this way—make a nominal payment and get a release form. My guess is, the employee didn't consult an attorney before signing, did she?"

"Not that I know of."

"And I bet she isn't the only one to have left the company this way, is she?"

"I know of one other. I don't know if there are more."

Schiffler muttered, "I'm not sure what to make of it."

"Do you think what the company has done might have . . . crossed a line?" Angela had a hard time saying the word "illegal" when talking to anyone about her client, let alone an attorney.

"I'm saying packing plants have been known to operate on a thin line. Iowa has had a couple of high-profile incidents. Those companies rely so heavily on immigrant labor it's easy to take advantage. What do you want to do?"

"I need to think about it, and I'll get back to you."

After hanging up, Angela stared at the wall, lost in thought. Had Gordon hired people he knew were in the US illegally? If he had, how would anyone know? Was that how he got away with so much? If that were true, he put the whole company at risk.

The problem was that Barton Packing was her client. If she pursued this, how could she continue to work for them? If she didn't pursue this, how could she continue to live with herself?

Chapter 32

Angela spotted McKay at the back of the library. Sitting at a small corner table next to a window, he was bent over a sheaf of loose pages, elbows on the table, head supported by one hand. Next to him, the ever-present notepad and pencil lined up squarely beside a manila folder.

Since that day in the park—a week and a half ago—she'd talked with HR and pulled together some numbers detailing the history of the rent-subsidy program. She'd run those numbers past both Nick and Gordon and put together a fact sheet Nick OK'd sharing with the media. Whatever she shared with McKay now would be on the record.

When McKay had called, his request to meet at the library rather than the plant seemed odd. She didn't mind, though, since there was more privacy here than in her cubicle, and the library offered the added advantage that none of her sources would be at hand. She could more easily delay answering any sticky questions.

As she approached, McKay stood to shake her hand, an uncharacteristically guarded expression in his baby-blanket-blue eyes. "Good morning, Angela."

"Hi, Trevor." She smiled and sat in the chair opposite. "What's up?"

He didn't return her smile. "I've been doing some digging on the housing situation we talked about."

"Fire away."

"My editor's giving me more time for this one." He rested a hand on the file next to his notebook.

That was unusual. He usually worked up a story in a week.

"It can be a good story," she said. "From the research I've done, what Barton is doing is unique in Iowa—at least among the packing plants I've researched."

"It may be unique, all right." He spoke with a trace of what sounded like sarcasm, causing Angela's media senses to quiver.

"Lake Michigan Properties. What can you tell me about them?"

She hadn't told him the name of the management company; obviously he'd been doing his homework. She quickly recapped the basic idea of the program, emphasizing how Barton Packing rented places from LMP for new employees.

Trevor jotted notes as she spoke and asked his next question as soon as she finished. "How did this program get started?"

"From what I understand, the idea first came up before Mrs. Barton passed away. She was interested in programs like this."

"So it was Mrs. Barton's idea?"

"I don't think so. But it was the kind of program—something to help employees and the town—that she appreciated."

"I've been to all the properties, and I've spoken with a number of individuals around town about them. Many are unhappy with how run-down these places are. 'A blight on the community' and 'not the image we want to show.'" He air quoted the phrases. "Does Barton have any agreement with LMP about property maintenance?"

Before coming to the library, she'd swung by Gordon's office to see if he'd had any success getting in touch with LMP. He hadn't been in.

"No, they don't. Barton Packing doesn't own or manage the properties. It's not up to them . . ." She stopped herself on the verge of giving him something that could become a quote. "You need to talk with LMP," she said, then bridged to a positive message. "I do know employees find the rent assistance really helpful in their transition to Hammond." Alvaro had introduced her to a couple of single men and one family who lived in LMP properties.

"I've already talked with a few," McKay said.

"Oh? Do you mind telling me who? In case I've also talked with them?"

McKay ignored her question. "How many properties does Barton have people in?"

She had the bare-bones set of approved facts in her notebook, but McKay's question wasn't answered by those. "Barton pays for the first month's rent. After that, employees rent directly from LMP. I'm not aware that we know whether an employee chooses to stay or move to other housing after the first month."

The reporter opened the manila folder and took out a sheet of paper. "The Hammond tax rolls show ten properties owned by LMP." He slid the paper toward her and added, "It appears LMP wasn't on the tax rolls before Barton began this rent program."

She scanned the paper. "Supply meets demand?" she suggested. With each question, Angela's media senses jangled louder. McKay was building to something, but what?

"Maybe. It seems like more than a coincidence that Barton Packing comes up with this idea, and all of a sudden a Chicago company shows up in Hammond with a portfolio of properties ready to rent."

"I can't offer any insight into that, Trevor."

"I trust Mr. Barton will be able to."

His ominous tone made Angela bridle. "You're making a connection that isn't valid. Barton rents housing from LMP. That doesn't mean LMP is connected to Barton Packing."

"Are you sure? I talked with people living in nine of the LMP units. Everyone I talked with works at Barton Packing. They tell me as far as they know, all rooms are rented to Barton employees."

"Barton is a big company with a lot of employees. The rent program shows Barton's commitment to helping employees and the community. Besides, it's not true all units are rented to Barton. The property Alvaro lives in, for instance, has units rented to people who aren't employees."

"That property is unique," McKay agreed. "It's well maintained, for instance. And Duarte is the only Barton employee living there. Curiously, units in that property also rent for market rate. One might conclude it's an exception on purpose."

"What do you mean?"

"Are you aware that single men in these LMP properties, living eight or ten to a house, are paying up to $400 per month each?"

She responded cautiously. "I wasn't."

"Even taken conservatively, those ten properties bring in from $30,000 to $40,000 every month. Rich, don't you think? Even by Des Moines standards?"

Renting a house in Hammond for $400 per month wasn't out of line. Getting that amount from each person who lived there *was*. Angela's stomach began to cramp. "What I think is irrelevant. LMP sets those rates. You need to talk with them."

"I wasn't able to get anyone at LMP to pick up a phone. Finally, I drove to Chicago and learned that LMP is only a post-office box. I waited until a woman picked up mail. Nettie Pickering is her name. Nettie collects the mail, deposits rent checks at the bank, and pays bills—utilities, taxes, whatever. She told me as far as she knows, she and her boss are the only employees of LMP."

Every new point McKay made, Angela wrote down, so she could report back. Looking up from her notes, she responded, "That's not so curious, really, is it? I imagine there are a lot of small real-estate companies run by only one or two people."

"Maybe so," Trevor said. "But it gets more interesting. Nettie's boss is Nathan Cunningham."

The name meant nothing to Angela. "And?"

"Cunningham is a common name in Hammond. At first I thought it was an odd coincidence. But I checked around. I found a Nathan Cunningham who farms a few miles northeast of here."

She frowned. She didn't know where this was going, but she felt certain she wouldn't like it when they got there. "What are you getting at?"

He pulled another paper out of the file and slid it over so she could look at the copy of a page out of a high-school yearbook. His finger rested on the picture of a boy kneeling next to a hunting dog. "This is Nathan Cunningham's senior picture in the Hammond High School yearbook. Nettie confirmed he's her boss."

"I'm still not following you. If a local man wants to buy property and rent it out, why shouldn't he?"

"I stopped in to see Nathan Cunningham at his farm. Nice guy. A farmer, yes. A Chicago real estate magnate? No more than my great-grandmother. Once he found out what I was after, though, he stopped answering my questions. In a not-so-friendly way, told me it was none of my business."

"If it's a private company, he's right, isn't he?"

"Yeah. But here's the thing, Angela." McKay leaned forward, never taking his eyes off her. "Nathan Cunningham is Gordon Ryker's first cousin."

"He's what?" Angela was unable to contain her surprise.

"You told me Barton Packing had no connection to LMP. That they couldn't get them on the phone. That they had no influence on whether the properties are maintained or not. I tell you, Angela, I find that really hard to believe."

She struggled to absorb what McKay was saying. Gordon had lied to her, and as a result, she'd lied to the reporter. She'd lied, no matter how unintentionally.

"You didn't know this," he said.

Angela shook her head. "I told you what Mr. Ryker told me." She scrambled to recover. "Just because they're cousins doesn't mean Mr. Ryker knows anything about the properties."

Even as she said it, she realized how unbelievable that was. If Cunningham did run a property company and had a connection inside Barton Packing, why wouldn't he use it? Given Gordon's need to control every detail, how could he not know about this? At the very least, Gordon and Cunningham would have had to work out the details for Barton Packing to make rent payments.

McKay continued, "What I'm trying to figure out is, who exactly profits from these properties? It appears a lot of effort went into making it seem as though LMP and Barton Packing are separate entities."

Beneath the quiet seriousness of McKay's words, Angela heard excitement. He was onto something and knew it.

"Someone is making a lot of money off those apartments," he added. "I don't think Nathan Cunningham is the only one."

Angela forced herself to continue writing down what McKay was saying, using that excuse to avoid eye contact, to avoid letting her feelings show on her face.

He stopped talking and waited until she finally looked up before he asked, "What financial interest does Barton Packing have in these properties?"

She pursed her lips. The answer was, none that she knew of, but what did she really know?

"I'm sure there's an explanation, Trevor. I'll need to get back to you. That's the best I can do." Anxiety writhed under her skin. She hoped there was an explanation. There had to be.

McKay sat quietly for a while before he flipped to another page in his notebook. "Let's set the housing aside for the moment. I also want to ask about Lupe Perez."

Angela felt sick. That, too?

He didn't wait for Angela to say anything before continuing. "I talked with her a week after the accident. She told me she wasn't working at Barton anymore. She said she quit because she can't use her hand anymore."

"Trevor, I'm sure you know I can't talk about personnel matters."

"Mrs. Perez was reluctant to say much, but she said enough to make me curious. So I checked the ambulance-call records going back several years for other accidents at the plant. Then compared those records to the meat-packing industry as a whole. Barton Packing's safety record is on par with others in the industry."

Apprehensive about where he was headed, she listened in silence. At least what he was saying so far was consistent with what she'd been told.

"Then I tracked down as many of the accident victims as I could find, but only a few still live in this area. All but two quit after their accidents. The two who didn't quit received workers' comp until their injuries healed and then came back to work at the plant. The rest either received nothing at all or were paid somewhere between $5,000 and $10,000, no matter how severe the accident."

She felt the anxiety snake up her back. He had worked his way into exactly the questions she and Alvaro had talked about. The questions her boss had told her were not for her to worry about.

"I'm not sure I understand where you're going with this."

"All those who 'quit'"—his emphasis on the word signaled his skepticism—"were Latinos who came from outside Iowa. Those who did not quit were white or Latinos who've lived in Hammond for a long time. What does the company have to say about the fact that employees who experienced debilitating accidents, accidents causing injuries that might prevent them from working again, lost their jobs with little or no compensation?"

"You know I can't answer that."

"Angela, you've been straight with me. So I'll be straight with you. It may only be unethical for Barton Packing to take advantage of people who don't really understand the language or the culture. Or it might be illegal. The fact that people would leave with little or nothing made me wonder if there were something else going on. I can't help but wonder if some of the workers may be undocumented. And that the company knows it."

"Barton Packing uses E-Verify," Angela said. At last, something she could state with certainty. "Everyone the company hires has the right papers."

"So I understand. I also know papers can be forged."

"Are you accusing Barton of that?" Angela tried to be calm, but the metallic taste of fear made her throat close on the words.

"The packing industry in general isn't squeaky clean on the subject. Combine the housing situation with what I'm finding out about injured workers, and it's troubling. It's hard to imagine Nick Barton doesn't know this is happening. But whether he does or doesn't, if all this turns out to be true . . ."

McKay let his words trail off, leaving her to draw her own conclusion. Angela felt as though she'd been hooked to the assembly line at the plant and sent through the stunner on the kill floor.

"I'm sure there's an explanation for all . . . of this." The wave of her hand was weak, ineffectual.

"I hope you'll help me figure it out. When can I talk with Nick Barton?"

"Where are you on this story?" she asked.

"We'll take the time we need to get it right. But I need a response from the company on the topics we've talked about, and I want to speak directly with Mr. Barton and Mr. Ryker."

McKay gathered up his papers and slid them back into the manila folder. He stood, and she stood, too. Feeling numb, she responded out of her public-relations training.

"Barton Packing is a good company, Trevor. Nick Barton is a good man."

He looked at her with what was almost sympathy.

* * *

Angela sank back into her chair after McKay left. She'd always wondered if the reporter had his sights set on investigative journalism. Now he'd confirmed her suspicions. How much of what he told her was true? Was LMP doing something illegal or simply unethical? *Simply unethical.* Had she really just thought that?

And what was Gordon's involvement with LMP? He'd lied to her. There was no couching that any other way. Lies that put her in the worst possible position. Could she trust him about anything?

Then what about the injured employees—all Latino—quitting? Were they undocumented? Did Gordon know and take advantage? What did Nick know about any of this? There must be an explanation. There simply had to be. She threaded her fingers through her hair, grabbing handfuls tight enough to hurt.

Dave would know what to do. She texted him: *A reporter told me Gordon has been lying about company actions. I need HELP. ASAP!!* She waited a minute for a response. Two minutes. Three minutes. She texted again.

When the phone vibrated, she grabbed it, expecting to see Dave's name. Instead, a text from Gordon flashed on the screen. *Come to my office. Plan feedback ready.*

Now? Really? She called Dave's number; it went to voice mail. She called the Sherborn-Watts receptionist, who said her boss had gone out and didn't mention when he'd return.

Get a grip, Angela. Think. Think. Assuming her client was guilty wasn't a good place to start. Gordon had lied, but maybe he had a reason. Maybe he could explain everything, and it would all make sense. Barton Packing was her client. She repeated that reality to regain focus. *Barton Packing is my client.* She could handle it. This was what they'd hired her for. With Dave out of the picture, she had to.

She texted Gordon—*There in 10 minutes*—then headed for her car.

Chapter 33

The feeling of being hooked to the plant assembly line, moving inexorably toward dismemberment, persisted as she drove to the Barton office. In the past three weeks, Gordon hadn't found any time to give feedback on the report no matter how much she asked. The accident had diverted all of them, but still. Now he was ready. Now?

He'd been lying to her all along. How in the world could she make anything good of this?

She checked her phone every few seconds, expecting Dave to respond, desperate for him to do so. Outside Gordon's office, she checked the phone one more time. Then texted again: *Meeting with Gordon. Pls call.* Normally she muted her phone before a meeting, but this time she left it on. Nothing would be more welcome than hearing from Dave. She squared her shoulders and knocked on the door.

Gordon gestured her in.

Taking the best-defense-is-a-good-offense approach, she opened her notebook and jumped in.

"I'm glad you contacted me," she said. "We need to hold on the plan for the moment, though. I met with Trevor McKay this morning."

"That reporter? What's he want now?"

Gordon's tone was suspicious. Or maybe she only imagined it was. His steely eyes revealed nothing. Surely he knew. Surely his cousin contacted him after the reporter stopped by. Did he think the reporter wouldn't pursue it? Did Gordon think he could continue to lie and everyone would believe it?

Though she felt her heart pound double time, she spoke evenly. "He had more questions related to the housing program. Also about settlements with employees in plant accidents."

"Why is he asking about that?"

"He's been talking to people. We knew he was looking at housing, but his questions about accident settlements were out of the blue."

"We brought you here to fix problems with the media, not make them."

"I did not . . ." She stopped, realizing she'd begun to defend herself against a pointless accusation. "McKay got these stories on his own."

"I told Nick this would happen. We never had trouble like this before."

"I understand you're not a fan of public relations. But at the moment, McKay is working on a story that could have serious ramifications for Barton Packing. I need to get back to him with answers. Soon."

Gordon leaned forward, picked up a pencil, twiddling with it as he spoke. "Tell me what he said. In detail. Every word."

Angela did as he asked. Every fact. She considered sharing McKay's accusations, but did not; the company needed to respond to facts with facts. As she made a check mark in her notebook beside each point she'd covered so far, the pen slipped between her fingers, anxiety making her sweat in the air-conditioned office. She rubbed her fingers dry on her slacks and picked up the pen again.

Methodically, she covered McKay's points about tax records, the trip to Chicago, the information from Nettie Pickering. She explained how he'd tracked Nathan Cunningham through high-school yearbooks to the man's farm and discovered the family relationship between Cunningham and Gordon. She said how he'd talked with current and former Barton employees about both housing and plant accidents.

When she had checked off every comment, she laid the pen down. "That's what he told me," she said, flexing her fingers.

"All right," Gordon said in a tone that betrayed no concern. "That's what he told you. So what now?" He settled back in the chair, elbows on the armrests, the pencil balanced motionless between his fingertips.

"We have to respond, and I need your help to craft what we say. OK?"

"Shoot," he said.

She thought for a moment, searching for the clearest, least ambiguous ways to ask questions. To get answers that would allow her to build a credible response. She began.

"Does Barton Packing have a financial interest in LMP?"

"No."

"None?"

"Don't you understand English?" His tone was as ice cold as his steel-gray eyes. He began to weave the pencil through his fingers.

For a brief moment she fixed her eyes on the pencil. Was the action intended to distract? Or was it subconscious?

"I want to be certain," she said. "McKay made it seem like Barton Packing set up this program to look like it was helping employees but was really using it for financial gain." She repeated McKay's rent calculations once more.

"Someone's making money for sure." He paused the pencil under his middle finger. "But I can tell you it's not Barton."

"OK then. That's a good start." She wrote down his words and continued. "Nathan Cunningham—the man who heads LMP? Is he your cousin?"

"What if he is? Do you know everything your cousins do?" The pencil moved again, back and forth, finger to finger, left to right, right to left.

"No, I suppose not. But I can see why McKay would think you'd know what your cousin is doing with a company you run in a town the size of Hammond." She dared to look at him directly as she waited for his response. He gave her nothing. "Are you connected to LMP?"

"That's Nate's business."

"McKay didn't believe Cunningham could be both a farmer and run a property company."

"A man can do two things. No law against that."

"No," Angela admitted. "But one of the facts you approved for me to say was you hadn't been able to get in touch with LMP. McKay didn't believe that."

"Let me make it simple for you. We were getting pressure from the town about providing housing for the people we recruited. I told HR to come up with a plan. They connected with LMP."

"But you told me you couldn't get in touch with them. You told me you couldn't influence property maintenance."

"The program was up and running before I learned Nate was involved. I figured it was better I had nothing to do with it after that. The whole thing's been running through HR. After you and I talked last week, I went to HR and told them they needed to tell Nate we have concerns."

On the one hand, a separation such as he described made sense. Though it just didn't seem plausible. As far as she could tell, there wasn't anything at the plant Gordon didn't have his hands in. Would he actually let such a big program run without his touch? She didn't believe what he said for an instant, but she had no proof otherwise.

"We'll need to talk with Nick about this, too," she said. "I'll draft a response."

Gordon stared at her for a long second. "He'll agree with me."

"I wasn't implying he wouldn't."

She scanned her notes again. There might be things she was missing, but she couldn't think with him staring at her like that. "Now to his questions about the settlements with Lupe Perez and other employees who've been injured in accidents."

"What about them?"

"McKay was skeptical an employee would quit after getting injured on the job."

"They would if they were at fault."

"But I thought Perez wasn't at fault. It was an accident."

"After I talked with HR and legal, we agreed there was no point in arguing fault. The payout was a good deal for her."

"Is that standard . . . for someone who lost a finger and had a tendon severed?"

"It was her choice to quit."

"Gordon, I'm pushing on this because the media will. McKay's question was whether she really understood what she was doing . . . especially since $5,000 won't even come close to taking care of her and her kids."

He snorted. "The *fact* is, Perez signed a release and cashed the check." He switched the pencil into writing position and made a note. "I'm going back to HR. Perez shouldn't even be talking about the settlement. If she violated the terms, she'll have to give the money back."

"I don't know whether she shared any of the details. McKay's talked to a lot of people—other employees who left the company after accidents."

"They made their own decisions."

"That's not really the point. McKay suggested there's racial discrimination involved. That injured Latino employees—those recruited from out of state—are treated differently than white employees who live in Iowa. And even that the company hired people knowing their documents were fake."

"I don't know where he gets his information, but I can tell you every person we hire passes E-Verify. And we have signed papers from every former employee. We're covered. Airtight."

"Gordon, I'm not here to debate either the housing or the termination policies. I'm here because Barton Packing has to answer to the charges—"

He'd been speaking with the self-possessed confidence of someone who knew the company and his job back to front, which was why Angela jumped when he slapped his hand on the desk, breaking the pencil.

"No." Gordon rose out of his chair. "The *fact* is, talking about this is pointless because we are not going to give anything to that reporter. He can dig around all he wants, and he'll get nothing." He leaned across the desk and jammed a finger into the middle of Angela's notepad. "Nothing. You can take that to the bank."

Shivers vibrated through Angela's fingers and along the back of her neck. Even if she responded to the primal instinct telling her to run, she wasn't sure her legs would hold her. Her counselor training took over. "Gordon, the reputation of Barton Packing is at risk here."

He bent across the desk until his face, eyes narrowed, was inches from hers. "What I see is, you can't handle a simple situation with a reporter. Since you can't even do that, you're useless to us." He kept his eyes locked on her for a good three seconds. Then he stood straight.

Was he firing her? She tried to swallow but couldn't. She made herself stand so she could meet his eyes on the level. "I can help with this. Please let me." She hated that she sounded as though she was pleading, but she didn't know what else to do.

"No. You're done. Nick will agree. You can also count on that. Now get the hell out of my office."

He sat, grabbed a spreadsheet off the stack on his desk, and began to circle numbers. He didn't look up again.

* * *

Back in her cubicle, Angela collapsed in the chair, hands shaking. She rubbed her palms together hard as she tried to sort through the conversation.

Had he really fired her? He had threatened her job; that was clear. Would Nick support him? She checked her phone. Dave still hadn't responded to her texts, and she needed to talk to him. Where was he?

She reread her notes detailing everything McKay and Gordon had said. The facts and figures and conclusions McKay drew made sense. Even though Gordon denied it all flat-out, and even provided a plausible response to every question, there was no doubt he had lied before and might still be lying.

Overshadowing everything was Nick's role in all this. She believed he didn't know what was going on. But what if she was wrong? She hadn't asked Gordon outright if Nick was aware of the termination details about the injured employees.

She'd committed to helping the company, and that meant Nick. Yet why would Nick believe her? Gordon was his man.

Dave could help her figure this out. Once again, she escaped to the parking lot.

Chapter 34

Secluded in her car, Angela stared at the Barton Packing flag hanging lifeless in the muggy July air as she tapped Dave's name into her phone and waited for the call to go through.

When the call went into voice mail again, she wanted to scream. She keyed in a text: *Met with Gordon. He went ballistic. Says NO to responding to reporter. Haven't seen Nick. I need you ASAP.*

She stared at the screen, willing a response, but none came. She decided to begin drafting a statement. Whether she'd be able to actually give it to McKay was another matter. She sent another text to Dave: *Working on response for reporter.*

For a half hour, she scribbled and erased, scribbled and erased, crafting a response that would work for McKay. Finally, she had a draft she knew was sound, based on what Gordon had told her. The problem was, she didn't believe it at all.

Again, she dialed Dave. At last he answered.

"Where were you?" she blurted, feeling rushes of both anger and relief.

"My phone died. I had to get it replaced."

"Have you read my texts?"

"I did. What's going on?"

As succinctly as she could, Angela briefed him on her conversations with McKay and Gordon. She concluded, "Gordon said they wouldn't give anything to McKay. That Nick would agree with him. And he told me I was done here."

"You're overreacting," he replied. "Of course they have to respond to the reporter. Nick will see that. Get him to postpone the meeting until this evening. I can be there in three hours. We'll work out a strategy together."

"But Gordon basically fired me."

"That's not going to happen. It's Nick's decision, and Nick will know he needs help with this."

Her phone buzzed, signaling a new text. She read it as she talked. It was Liz. Nick wanted her in his office. Now.

"Nick wants to see me," she said.

"Tell him I'm on my way. Get a later meeting time."

Short as it was, the conversation with Dave restored her confidence. Clutching the notebook with all her notes and the draft statement, she hurried through the lobby and ran up the stairs to the executive offices.

Nick was sitting behind his desk, something Angela had rarely seen him do. Gordon stood square on his feet, his jaw clenched. As Nick stared at her with a blank expression, the fragile smile she'd forced to her lips disintegrated. She could only imagine what Gordon may have told him.

"Sit, Angela." Nick pointed to the chairs in front of his desk. "You, too, Gordon."

She took the closest chair, angling it toward both men. Gordon faced Nick straight on. An echoing silence filled the room in the seconds before Nick spoke again.

"Gordon gave me an update on McKay's story. He tells me you've been working with the reporter to bring down the company."

Angela was startled by the gross misrepresentation, and her eyes darted to Gordon. He'd lied to her, and now he was lying to Nick to make her look bad. She struggled to keep her voice calm.

"With all due respect, Nick, I haven't been working with the reporter," she said. "McKay came to me this morning with information and serious allegations about both the housing program and employee terminations. I brought everything to Gordon at once. What the reporter alleges is disturbing. Dave can be here in three hours. The four of us can work together on how to respond then."

"We have never given out this kind of information before, Nick," Gordon interjected. "And there's no reason to now."

"We must respond, Nick," Angela insisted. "McKay has enough to run an article without your comment, and that would be really damaging. The only way you can come through this with your reputation intact is if we tell our own story."

"We'll talk this through now," Nick said. "I have to get a better understanding of what McKay's after. He needs to know everything we do is legal. We can say that."

She hesitated. As their public-relations counselor, she had a responsibility to take what they said and put together a statement. But she knew Gordon had lied to her on some things, and she felt certain he wasn't ethical about other things. The man lacked integrity, but was she any better if her professional counsel wasn't true to what she believed? She'd been walking a careful line of neutrality so far. But she knew she couldn't go forward with a statement she believed to be false.

Nick waited for her to continue. Out of the corner of her eye, she saw Gordon watching her, too. She could defer, request again that they wait until Dave joined them. But she realized this wasn't about Dave; it was about her. She sat up straighter, looked Nick in the eye, and abandoned any pretext of making a public-relations-approved, client-acceptable comment.

"Are you certain everything is legal, Nick?" she asked.

"We have legal counsel on every termination," he reiterated.

"OK, let's say each termination is legal. Have you looked at the details of all terminations over the last few years? That's what the reporter has done." She laid out McKay's reasoning, concluding with McKay's suggestions of racial discrimination, possibly targeting people the company knew had documents that weren't legitimate.

"Suggestions." Gordon grabbed the word. "Does he have a single fact? Has he proved anything illegal?"

Ignoring Gordon, she focused fully on Nick. "I'm telling you where the reporter is headed. The implication that you knowingly hire and take advantage of undocumented workers is a huge problem, whether it's proved or not. We need to be prepared for whatever he might come up with."

Gordon interjected again. "We're solid legally, Nick. Count on it."

Nick didn't respond to either of them, and Angela felt as though she'd hit a brick wall. She pushed ahead on another front.

"There's more, Nick," she said, half expecting Gordon to cut her off.

"What else?"

"Did Gordon tell you McKay's information makes it look as though Barton Packing is making at least $30,000 per month off the worker housing? And that Lake Michigan Properties is owned by his cousin, Nathan Cunningham?"

A frown crossed Nick's face, and he hesitated, looking at Gordon and then into the distance. Finally, he responded. "It's simply not true we make any money on the housing."

"I told her that," Gordon said.

"We could share what the program costs us if we needed to," Nick added.

So Nick had known about the housing. Disappointment welled in Angela's chest. "Nonetheless," she continued, "it all seems like you're taking advantage of employees who don't speak English or understand the laws. The housing story looks bad, but it can be managed *if* the separation between Barton Packing and LMP is as clean as Gordon described. But I don't believe the separation is clean. Gordon protests he can't get in touch with

Cunningham, a relative who lives on a farm not five miles from Hammond. How believable is that?"

Gordon exploded from his chair. "That's enough." He turned to Nick. "She's slandering my name and questioning your leadership, Nick."

She wanted to object, to say Gordon was distorting her words. Before she could, Nick spoke.

"Sit down, Gordon." Then he turned to her. "Angela? Do you believe what the reporter said?"

She'd been keeping her focus on Nick, but now she looked at Gordon. She'd worked with the man as best she could because he was her client also. She'd never confronted him directly; she'd given him the benefit of the doubt. Now she knew for a fact he'd lied.

"I have been . . . I am . . . committed to Barton Packing. But . . ." Angela stopped. She knew that "but"' effectively negated anything that came before it.

She bit her lower lip. She was at a point of no return. Either she spoke the truth as she knew it or she continued to walk that line of uncommitted neutrality. In that moment it was as though all the people who had brought her to this point stood in front of her now. Father Burke with his optimistic commitment to do what must be done. The Muslims who honored their prayer tradition no matter the conditions or penalties. Friendly, painfully honest Maria and Eduardo. Lupe. Even the woman in the bank. Emilio's mother, whom she'd never met, who risked never seeing her son again to give him a chance at a better life. Emilio, a brave, funny, courageous child. A child she knew she loved. And Alvaro. The man anchoring her entire experience. She heard him encouraging her to speak the truth. She could not be neutral any longer.

She straightened her back again, looked at Gordon for a moment, then settled her eyes on Nick and spoke.

"I came to Barton Packing committed to doing the best work I could for you." Her voice wavered, then gathered strength. "Everything I've done was with that goal in mind. I hope you know that, Nick. But I've been so intent on preserving the client-agency relationship that I haven't been willing to tell you the truth." She paused to breathe in more courage, then continued. "This company is off track. What's going on may or may not be illegal, but there's no question it's wrong. And you need to know."

Nick didn't respond, but Gordon did. "That's bullshit. She's been working against us since the day she arrived. We specifically said no story on the product donation. She gets a reporter to do one anyway. I told her we don't control the housing. Next thing we know, a reporter's all over us. She even built a conspiracy around the accident." His voice rose with each statement. "She decides what she wants to do, and it doesn't matter what we say. Pathetic." He spit the word out.

Angela kept her response even and firm. "That's not true. I admit I question what the company is doing." She swallowed another hard knot of neutrality. "More specifically, I question what Gordon is doing."

"Gordon keeps me apprised of everything," Nick insisted.

"Does he?" She shook her head. "You've given him so much responsibility, I wonder how much you really know? Every action looks fine on the surface but is questionable if someone digs deeper, as McKay did. McKay will follow these stories until he has answers."

Gordon moved to interrupt, but Nick lifted a hand and stopped him. He nodded at Angela to continue.

"And there's more than the reporter knows. There's the points system. And the product donations to the churches. It all seems fine on the surface, but it's not."

"But the product donations are a good thing," Nick said. "All the reasons you told us to publicize the donations were on point. The reactions we've had from the community since the article ran have been good."

"I thought so, too. But then I found out some of the donated product was past the expiration date."

"Who told you that?" Gordon asked.

Angela noticed he didn't deny the allegation, and for the first time, she heard uncertainty in his tone. Nick's face told her he'd never heard about this before.

She continued, speaking directly to Nick. "Employees changed the use-by date on the packaging. On Gordon's order. And that brings up the points system."

Nick held up a hand to stop her. "Was the product expired, Gordon?"

"She doesn't know what she's talking about. She's making a big deal out of nothing."

"Was it expired?"

"There was no health hazard. It was always frozen, and the churches planned to use the product right away."

There, Angela thought. Without saying so, he admitted to changing the dates. She looked at Nick, expecting him to call Gordon out. Disappointed that he did not, she pushed on. "I know companies have discretion about expiration dates. But whether there was a health issue is not the point. After the recall, an action like this jeopardizes the Barton Packing reputation."

Gordon stated, "We'd never ship expired product to a client. Donating it was a good use of inventory. The crew in the storehouse didn't rotate the stock right. They won't make a mistake like that again."

"That's always how it works, isn't it?" She glared at Gordon. "The blame shifts to employees? Changing the expiration date wasn't an employee error. That's on you." She turned again to Nick. "Employees follow Gordon's orders because they're afraid if they don't, they'll get points on their record. The points system is a club he uses to keep people in line."

"Bullshit," Gordon said.

He pulled a pencil out of his pocket and began to fidget with it. Now she realized the pencil was an unconscious indicator of nerves. He was more anxious than he was letting on.

"He wields the club arbitrarily," she said. "One example is allowing Muslim employees time for prayer. Muslim employees used to be able to take the ten minutes for prayer once a day without a problem. Since the points system was implemented, supervisors can give points to those who leave the line to pray."

"It's fair, Nick. You know we can't have people off the line without making trouble for everyone. You pay me to run things efficiently, and I do."

"My guess is, you let people use the bathroom," Angela said. "Or do they get points for that, too?"

Gordon didn't respond, and Angela wondered if she'd stumbled on another way the man kept employees under his thumb.

"Or how about this," she continued. "After you approved Alvaro going on the research trip with me, Nick, Gordon gave him points for going."

"Al knows the rules. Those points were no surprise to him."

"Gordon has an explanation for everything. And he may be right—maybe everything Barton Packing is doing is legal, but even if it is, it's not right. And when this story comes out, legal won't be enough." Her focus was trained on Nick, but he'd stopped looking at either one of them. "You started this company intent on creating a business fair to customers, employees, and the community. But your vision has been lost. There's a different culture in the company now. And it's not good."

She waited for Nick to respond, but, again, he did not, so she asked the questions that had been weighing on her since the beginning.

"Did you know Gordon was doing all these things? Did you approve them? Each time I came across one of these situations, I asked myself that. And I convinced myself you did not know," Angela said. "If you knew all this and OK'd it—"

"There," Gordon interrupted. "You heard her, Nick. She's accusing you, too. She bought into McKay's argument hook, line, and sinker. Her loyalty is anywhere but with this company."

Nick removed his glasses and rubbed his cheek, massaging the muscle Angela hadn't seen twitch in weeks.

"Those are serious allegations, Angela," Nick said after he put his glasses back on. He turned to his right-hand man. "Has McKay said anything that's true, Gordon?"

"She's got it wrong. You know me, Nick." Gordon leaned forward, lowered his voice, softened the edges, speaking friend to friend. "I'm as committed to this company as you. You put me in charge of operations four years ago, and we've never been more profitable."

He spoke as if Angela weren't there. His voice wheedling. *Like a snake,* Angela thought.

Gordon continued. "We can't afford to have someone representing us who doesn't believe in what we do. And I hate to say it, but it's not only her. Since she's been here, Al's become a problem. I thought he was one of the good ones. But not anymore. I know you were thinking about how to keep him on. I used to hope that would work, too, but not anymore. We can't trust her. Or him. It's time for them both to go."

Furious at the attack on Alvaro, Angela broke in. "Nick, Alvaro has been nothing but loyal to this company."

Gordon smiled in a way that appeared anything but friendly. "No surprise you'd look out for your *friend.*" His lips curled around the word "friend."

Angela started to rise out of her chair. He'd implied sex as clearly as if he'd said it out loud.

Nick raised his hands again. "Stop." He swiveled in his chair so his back was to them, facing the picture his wife painted. The peaceful scene of a seagull perched on a piling at the end of a pier, the sun setting on the horizon.

Silence descended on the room. Out of the corner of her eye, Angela looked at Gordon. He stared straight at Nick, the pencil quiet in his hand.

She flexed her fingers. She felt like she'd been playing catch with a hand grenade.

After an eternity, Nick swiveled back to face them. "Angela, what seems clear is that you question the integrity of this company. I can't have someone working here who feels that way."

"Nick . . . I don't question you."

"It sounds like you do. And you certainly question Gordon. The only answer I can see is that you leave."

Angela was stunned. Dave had assured her this couldn't happen. "But the reporter. We have to respond. Dave will be here in a couple of hours. He's already on his way. I'm sure—"

Nick shook his head. "No. You need to go. You're done here."

* * *

Angela's first action should have been to call Dave, to stop him from coming to Hammond, but she couldn't imagine telling him what had happened. The adrenaline that had carried her through the meeting ebbed, leaving her feeling nauseated.

A text message sounded on her phone. Alvaro. *How did it go?* She responded: *Meet?* He answered: *15 min. Dock.* She confirmed: *OK.*

Back in her cubicle, she stared, unseeing, at the phone. She needed to think, but no clear thoughts came to her head. Her head was fuzzy, her mind completely jumbled. It took ten minutes to calm herself enough to call Dave, and when she did call, his line was busy. She left a message: "Trouble here. Met with Nick. Not good. Call me ASAP."

Finally, she slipped on her tennis shoes and headed for the loading dock, grabbing a hard hat and smock from the closet along the way. The last time she'd need them. Down the metal stairs, past the processing lines, past a cleaning crew scrubbing everything down before the next shift. She forced a smile for the workers she passed. She recognized several of them, could call them by name.

When she pushed open the heavy door between the plant and the storage room, the cold hit her hard. She entered the maze of pallets, threading her way toward the dock.

Frozen quiet blanketed the cooler. She wrapped her arms around her chest, rubbing her hands along her arms for warmth, walking fast to escape the cold. Her breath quickened, rising in clouds of ice crystals so brittle she thought she would hear them shatter if they fell to the floor.

"Angela!" Gordon's voice came out of nowhere, startling her, freezing the blood in her veins.

She spun toward his voice as he emerged from the rows of pallets behind her.

"Gordon," she said, gritting her teeth to keep them from chattering.

He stood so close she could feel heat from his body. Conscious that she was completely alone, she backed up but found herself trapped against a stack of pallets.

"He doesn't believe you," he said, the heat of his breath an unwelcome caress to her cheek.

Angela tried not to glance toward the dock, where she knew Alvaro waited. "He'll believe the truth."

She turned to go but he blocked her, a hand on the stack of boxes behind her, his arm a ramrod.

"He'll believe me. Like he always has," he said.

If she didn't show up soon, would Alvaro come looking for her? Or would he simply assume she'd been pulled into something more urgent? Her heart ricocheted. Never before had she fought so hard to keep her voice even and her face blank.

"Nick won't let you ruin the company he spent his life building."

"*I* built this company."

"And you're taking it down. Nick didn't know what you were doing, did he?"

"He wanted a profit. I gave it to him."

He hadn't answered her question. "Did he know you made the profit by abusing people who didn't know their rights? That you're stealing thousands from the company every month?"

She guessed he'd been in league with his cousin all along, that LMP was a shell to protect him. She waited, watching his eyes.

"He knew what he needed to know."

His answer was a relief. "I thought not. Nick's a better man than that. You, on the other hand, you're pathetic." She crouched to duck under his arm.

He grabbed her shoulder, pushed her back against the stack. She gasped. Fear-driven sweat froze on her neck, yet she locked eyes with him and spoke with a power that surprised her.

"Really? You want to add assault to the list?"

His steely eyes told her he was considering the possibility. Finally, he stepped back. Dropped his arms. "I've put my life into this company."

She looked at him with disdain. Then she walked away, not hurrying, yet putting as much distance as she could between them as fast as she could, listening for his footsteps, expecting to hear him, prepared to run if she did, grateful when the only sound following her was silence. When she pushed open the door to the dock and was greeted by the warmth of the afternoon summer sun, she almost threw herself into Alvaro's arms.

"I am so glad to see you," she gasped.

He gripped her arms to steady her and led her to a bench the workers used on breaks. "What happened?"

He listened intently as she related the conversation in Barton's office. *"Bastardo,"* he hissed when she told him about confronting Gordon in the storage room.

"I don't regret saying any of it," she said when she finished. "What I regret is hurting you. I never imagined involving you would jeopardize your job."

"It is all right. My time is almost done here anyway. If I leave a few months early, it is not a big deal."

She knew he was putting a good face on it. A strong recommendation, months of pay. These were things he'd counted on. Even worse, if he was forced to leave the country early, Gordon could make sure he had a bad mark on his visa. Gordon was vindictive enough to make it hard for Alvaro to come back to the United States again.

Her heart felt torn in three directions. A piece belonged to Emilio, the child she'd grown to love and felt responsible for. A piece belonged to Alvaro, the man who'd become her friend and maybe more. The remaining piece was her career. It was everything to her. Or had been.

"I don't know, Alvaro. I . . ."

Her phone buzzed with an incoming call. She pulled it out. "It's my boss," she said. "I need to take it."

"We'll figure it out," he said. "Come to my place." He disappeared through the door into the plant.

Chapter 35

Finally, Dave was calling back. He would know what to do.

She was unprepared for the barrage that hit her.

"What the hell, Angela? Nick called me."

Her breath caught. "I called to let you know."

"I'd been talking with Nick for ten minutes by the time you did. For god's sake, Angela, I should have heard from you first. I don't know what you think you're doing. He told me you accused Gordon of being a crook."

"I told you what McKay had—"

"A story you don't even know is accurate. You accused Nick Barton's right-hand man of being *a crook*. What in hell were you thinking? I could have fixed this if you'd waited for me to get there."

"I tried to get them to wait."

"You didn't try hard enough."

"Please. If you'll let me explain—"

"You'll explain all right. Tonight. Be in the conference room at 7:30."

She looked at her watch. That was only three and a half hours. "But I have to—"

He cut her off. "Nick wants you gone. He also told me that the fall ad campaign is canceled. Get your ass in the car and get to Des Moines. Alec and Jerry want to see you."

"Alec and Jerry?" The agency owners barely knew she existed. "Why?"

"Don't you get it? We'll be lucky if the only thing that happens is we lose the account over this. There's a good chance we'll be sued."

"I don't understand."

"Gordon is threatening a defamation of character lawsuit."

"But he can't. It's all true. I know it."

"Oh, for god's sake, Angela. What's true doesn't matter. The publicity on something like this will go on for months. The agency's reputation will be mud."

Angela was stunned. She hadn't thought that far ahead. In the face of Dave's barrage, she couldn't remember a single argument she'd made in Nick's office. "I can explain."

"I sure as hell hope so. Now get down here." He disconnected the call before she could say anything else.

Angela could barely think. There wasn't time to find Alvaro or go back to her motel room. She ran back through the plant to her cubicle to retrieve her purse and keys. Then she realized she had to take everything.

Luckily, she'd brought little. Her eyes darted around the gray-walled cubicle as she threw everything into her briefcase. The menu from Eduardo's. She ordered so often, she had it memorized. The prayer card for pets Father Burke gave her after she told him about her work with the animal shelter. Emilio's drawing of a chocolate lab signed by all the kids in her class. A half-used notepad. Two gel-ink pens. The last item she stuffed in her bag was her "integrity" river stone.

Fifteen minutes after talking to her boss, Angela tossed everything into the back seat of her car, buckled her seat belt, and pulled out. It would take every minute she had to get back to Des Moines.

As she drove west out of Hammond, the late-afternoon sun hit her squarely in the face. The visor provided minimal protection. She sat higher in her seat, twisting to the right and left as she tried to avoid the blinding rays. Ultimately, she could no more avoid the sun than she could avoid the shock of the day, which replayed again and again as she drove.

At the first stop sign, some twenty miles west of Hammond, she dug her phone out of her purse. She hadn't heard the ping from Alvaro's text: *where r u?* She responded: *on my way to DSM. Talk later.* She hit "send," but the message didn't go through. Rats. She was in one of the no-cell-service pockets that plagued northern Iowa.

McKay's revelations were a bombshell, but at their core, they confirmed her concerns that had built as the weeks went on. She'd given the company the benefit of the doubt, and why not? It was her client. Plus, Dave readily offered logical explanations for everything.

McKay had no reason to excuse the company. Her client didn't talk with the media. She did. Her anger flared. It was her reputation damaged, not theirs. She was in trouble, not them.

Knowing she wouldn't have to face Alec and Jerry alone provided some comfort. Angry as Dave had been on the phone just now, she knew he'd be in her corner when it came to meeting with the agency owners.

Her phone buzzed. Her mother's name showed on the screen. How could she tell her mother she'd lost the client? Her mother had been so proud to see her advance in her career.

She'd lost the client. She gripped the steering wheel so tight it hurt, blinked away tears that sprang to her eyes. She sent the call to voice mail.

After turning south on I-35, she didn't have to battle the sun anymore. Cornfields, soybean fields, wind turbines. She barely noticed them.

Without Barton Packing, she'd lose her supervisor title. And the extra salary that came with it. She wouldn't be able to send money to her mother anymore. She had failed her family.

Her phone buzzed again. Alvaro. Such a fine man. He had a good job at Barton. Great experience. Money to support his family in El Salvador. Until she screwed that up, too. She sent his call to voice mail, unable to talk with him any more than she could her mother. A moment later another call came from one of her team members at the agency. She turned the phone off.

Back and forth she cycled through her conversation with Nick and Gordon, going over and over every point, every fact, every piece of information. What she knew. What she believed in her gut. What she could tell Dave and the agency owners.

The exercise calmed her to the extent she could be calm. She knew she'd put herself out there with Nick and Gordon, put it all out there, because to do less would have been false. As a counselor, she owed honesty to them and to herself. She hadn't considered that being honest would cost her, and the agency, the client.

* * *

Angela made it to the Sherborn-Watts office in record time. When she opened the conference-room door, she found the three men already there. As Dave motioned her to a seat across the table, she searched his face, hoping for some encouragement. But he averted his eyes. She put her notebook and water bottle on the table and sat.

The presidents on Mount Rushmore had softer faces than the agency executives facing her across the table. A grim mask replaced the genial charm Alec Sherborn exuded in agency staff meetings. Jerry Watts, the agency's no-nonsense client-service leader, was equally dour. Dave still didn't look her in the eye, and his curt introduction gave her nothing.

"The floor is yours, Angela," he said. "Explain yourself."

Heart thudding, Angela laid out the information McKay had shared with her about the housing and the termination of workers. She explained the points system, the distribution of expired product. Periodically, one of them asked for clarification, but they mainly remained silent.

Finally, she told them about Gordon's sexist behavior and threats, not because she wanted their sympathy, but because it showed his true character. And because it wasn't enough to speak up for others if she wouldn't speak up for herself.

When she finished, Watts said, "As far as I can tell, this went off track when you forgot why you were there. You let your personal opinions get in the way of your responsibility to the client."

"I always tried to do my job, to give them good counsel. But what if the client isn't doing the right thing?" She sipped from the water bottle she'd brought with her, her throat suddenly parched.

"That's not for you to decide," Watts said.

"Isn't it?" She looked to Dave for support. "If they're doing things counter to the public good, don't we help them see that and move them in a better direction?" He'd made this point to her more than once.

Dave looked past her when he said, "We help clients develop programs that respond to public needs." He looked directly at her when he added, "We don't accuse them of being crooks."

She didn't understand what was happening. Dave had always been her mentor; she even counted him a friend. Now it felt as though she were on trial and they wouldn't believe anything she said. She tried again.

"I have to decide if the client is one I can represent and counsel, ethically." This was a foundation of the public-relations code of ethics.

"What Barton Packing is doing may be no different than any other packing plant," Sherborn pointed out.

"That doesn't make it right. Besides, I don't believe Nick— Mr. Barton—knew what Gordon Ryker was doing."

Sherborn said, "Since Nick Barton is OK with what his man is doing, you're out of line."

Dave asked, "Did you set Gordon up?"

"No!" The accusation felt like a kick in the gut. One Gordon himself delivered. "Did Nick say I did?"

"Among other things."

"That's simply not true. I did the job I was sent to do as well as I could. But the situation is complicated." She looked at Sherborn, then Watts, and finally turned her attention back to Dave. If anyone would understand, he would. "As a counselor, I'm supposed to see all sides of an issue." Even as she said it, the words felt weak and pointless.

"While always representing the client's interest," Dave said.

"I did. It was in Nick's interest to tell him about things going on right under his nose. Gordon was wrong."

"A judgment call," Watts said. "You don't know for sure."

She bridled. They were attacking her, and they knew nothing. Her cheeks burned with righteous indignation as she leaned forward. "I know Gordon straight-up lied to me. I know I told Dave about each issue as I learned about it."

"There were multiple ways to look at every situation we discussed, and you know it," Dave said. "It wasn't as clear cut as you're presenting it now."

Watts asked, "Where does Duarte fit in this?"

The rapid switch in topics nearly made her dizzy. She took another drink to settle herself. "Alvaro Duarte has been a company resource who's helped me understand the business and the diverse culture. He helped me develop sound counsel."

Dave said, "From what I understand, that's true."

It was the first time he'd said anything remotely supportive. Even so, his comment was hardly a ringing endorsement.

"Nick told Dave you're having an affair with Duarte," said Watts.

Her heart stopped. "That is not true." This was unbelievable. She'd told them about Gordon's sexual innuendos, about how he cornered her in the storeroom, and they hadn't voiced the least concern. Now they were accusing her? Her nostrils flared.

"Gordon says he knows it for a fact," Dave said. "He's seen you at Duarte's apartment."

Angela shook her head to clear it. She'd never told anyone she ate supper at Alvaro's apartment. If they'd asked, she would have. She had nothing to hide. Her mind raced as she remembered the first time Gordon came upon them having supper at Eduardo's and his subsequent tasteless comments and innuendos. She'd dismissed the red pickup truck outside Alvaro's apartment. But it must have been Gordon's after all. It hadn't been her imagination. He'd been following her the whole time. She felt her cheeks burn with embarrassment and anger.

"That man . . . ," Angela began, then stopped herself. She looked at Dave with a frown, holding his gaze for seconds. "If you don't believe me on this, Dave, then you won't believe me on anything else."

She felt certain he would tell her she was wrong, that he did believe her, that their years of working together meant something. But he didn't say any of that. He remained silent, eyes fixed on the table.

Then she had a moment of clarity as crystalline as the one in Nick's office. They said she should represent the client's interest. Barton Packing's interest. But no. They wanted her to act in Sherborn-Watts' interest so the agency didn't lose the business.

So this was how it would be. She was on her own. The realization made her strangely calm.

She looked each man in the eye, then said, "With all respect, you weren't there. I was. I had to tell them the truth, and I did."

"You should have cared more, Angela," Sherborn said. "About your job and your friends here. About your duty to the agency." He cleared his throat, looked at the other men, and continued. "Angela. We have to consider our employees, our other clients, the agency as a whole. Whatever happened at Barton Packing will take time to settle, and we think it best if you take some time off while we work it through."

"Are you firing me?" Disbelief struck her like a lightning bolt as she realized they'd made the decision before they'd even heard her side of the story.

"It would be disruptive for everyone to have you in the office," Watts added.

"What about my other clients?" She looked at Dave.

"They're not your problem anymore."

He didn't look at her when he said it. She would remember that forever.

As if on cue, the three men stood.

"Alice is waiting in your office," Sherborn said. "She'll help you get your things."

Angela made herself stand, but how she remained upright she didn't know. Dave didn't say a word or acknowledge her in any way as he walked her to her office and turned her over to Alice.

A half hour later, she left Sherborn-Watts with a box of personal effects in her arms, escorted out the door by HR.

She stood on the curb staring back at the building. She'd been on an endless loop throughout the day, one stunning shock after another, and now she had nothing left. She'd been stripped and gutted as cleanly as a chicken. Everything she thought she had, everything she thought she'd achieved—gone.

Chapter 36

Back at her apartment, Angela looked around at the familiar surroundings, trying to get her bearings. Disoriented, her eyes stopped briefly on the papier-mâché-and-wire sculpture of a fairy she picked up at an art fair, moved on to a collection of wood Balinese cat sculptures, took in a Brian Andreas print about the illusion of control. These were all things she loved, but she didn't feel love now.

She wandered into the bedroom. The Georgia O'Keeffe print of two red-orange poppies always made her feel warm and sexy. She sat on the edge of the bed feeling anything but sexy. After any other trip, she would have unpacked at once, thrown dirty clothes in the hamper, hung up her suits, returned shoes to her closet. But this wasn't a normal return home. This time she had nothing to unpack. She'd left Hammond without checking out of the motel.

On a normal day, she'd sit down with her laptop to work, often adding hours to the workday. But the agency had kept her laptop. What did it matter? She had no clients anymore. Without her job, she hardly knew how to think.

She wandered out to the living room. As she passed the kitchen island, she grabbed a handful of peanut M&M's and stuffed them all in her mouth. Fighting back tears, she called Alvaro.

He answered on the first ring "Where are you?" She envisioned the black slash of his eyebrows coming together with worry.

"In Des Moines. I got your messages, but I wasn't where I could answer."

"I worried if you were safe, amiga."

"I know. I'm sorry. I was with my boss. And with his bosses." She burrowed into the corner of her couch, her knees up to her chest. The sleek style of her modern couch wasn't as comfortable as Alvaro's leather sofa.

"How are you?" he asked.

"Numb. Just numb." She pulled her grandmother's multicolored afghan around her shoulders and tight up under her chin.

"You sound not so good," he said.

"You could say that. They fired me." She related the meeting with her boss and the agency owners. "The worst part is, my boss didn't support me at all. I've never felt so abandoned."

"We are birds of a feather, then."

"Why do you say that?"

"Mr. Ryker."

"Oh, Alvaro. He didn't fire you, did he?"

"Sí. But he had no one to take the shift on short notice. So he is letting me keep working for now."

"He is *letting* you continue to work. What a prince." Angry tears burned down her cheeks. "I'm so sorry. Everything was fine until I dragged you into this."

"That is not true. Everything was not fine, but I did not know what to do about it."

Alvaro's assurance didn't make her feel better. "What else did Gordon say?"

"Nothing. He does not explain himself to me."

"He didn't tell you he accused us of having an affair?"

An unexpected burst of laughter came through the phone.

"How can you laugh?"

"It is funny, no? Since we did talk of it?" Alvaro chuckled. "Too bad we didn't, if they are going to think of it anyway."

Still smarting from the accusation, Angela was not ready for humor, though his comment did make her realize there were no restrictions now. "It wasn't funny when my boss brought it up. Or when he didn't believe me when I told him it wasn't true."

"I'm sorry, amiga. I can see that would hurt."

"I guess we'll both have to figure out our futures," she said, mollified by his apology. "Have you seen Emilio? I know I've only been gone a few hours, but I'm worried about him. I'll call the attorney tomorrow. I hope Schiffler can take Emilio's case, but if she can't, I need to find someone else and start preparing for the next court date."

"He is a strong boy," Alvaro reminded her. "How can I help you?"

"Keep talking to me. It helps me to hear your voice. When I talk with the attorney, I'll find out what your options are, too. One thing she did tell me in her last email is she believes media coverage is helpful. That's something I know I can do."

"Will you come back to Hammond?"

She finally allowed herself to laugh. "I have to. I left my clothes at the motel."

* * *

The next morning Angela awoke disoriented, puzzled to feel a chenille bedspread against her cheek, to see orange poppies on the walls, and finally to realize she was in her own bed. It took a good thirty seconds for her to remember that she'd lost her job. She pulled the pillow over her head and screamed. A guttural, wounded-bull sound.

Feel better now, Darrah? she asked herself. Admitting she did, she propped up the pillows and reached for her phone.

"Mom, I have bad news," she said as soon as she heard her mother's voice. "I lost my job."

Her mother's love and support were so immediate and unconditional that more quiet tears streaked Angela's face. As a nurse, her mother possessed both sympathetic and practical characteristics, features Angela leaned on now. Over the next half hour, as Angela explained what had happened and how and why, her mother listened, questioned, encouraged. By the time they disconnected, Angela felt restored. And recommitted. To helping her parents. To helping Emilio. To finding another job, which would make all those vital things possible.

Another job. She couldn't get her head around the fact that she didn't work at Sherborn-Watts anymore. As happened so often these days, Angela's thoughts gravitated to Emilio. The challenge she faced in finding a new job was nothing compared to the tenuous circumstances he faced. Again and again, she pictured him in front of the judge. When Schiffler had first told her about the juvenile immigrant visa, it had felt like the right answer, but having learned more, she realized now it might not be. They'd have to make the case that Emilio's parents mistreated him. Emilio would have to tell the judge that his mother abused him. How could they ask him to lie in court? How did you do that to a child? She doubted his mother understood this was what would happen.

She scrambled out of bed, dressed, and pulled out the list she and Alvaro created the night before in a call lasting until almost midnight.

First she dialed Schiffler. The Standing for Justice receptionist made an appointment for the following day.

Then she called Father Burke to let him know that she wouldn't be able to teach anymore. She explained that her assignment at Barton Packing had ended, nothing more. He didn't pry. "Tell the kids I love them," she said, ending the call before she broke into yet more tears.

Knowing Alvaro would already be at work, she texted him. *Leaving soon. See you at noon.*

Finally, she called Trevor McKay. In the briefest, most neutral way possible, she explained she would no longer be his contact at Barton Packing and in the future he should contact the company for comment. He asked a half dozen questions about the housing and employee terminations, and she answered each one with the same "you have to talk to Barton Packing about that" response. At last, he gave up.

"You're the only contact I could count on to be straight with me." He sounded genuinely dismayed.

"I still can be, but on a different subject." Then she told him about her interest in the unaccompanied minors, still without mentioning Emilio specifically. She wanted the attorney to confirm that media coverage would help before going forward.

McKay jumped at the chance to have her full participation in a story. "I'm glad I can get on a story like this now," he said. "The way the news goes, in another year, people won't be thinking about these kids at all."

She knew that what he said was likely true, that public attention was fickle and short-lived. They agreed to meet that afternoon in Hammond.

It was only in the car, as she drove the three hours back up to northern Iowa, that she began to face her decidedly mixed emotions about Barton Packing and Sherborn-Watts.

She thought she'd established a level of trust with Nick Barton. It hurt he hadn't given her comments any credence. Granted, he'd known her only a short time, while he'd known Gordon Ryker for decades. Dave Wilstat inflicted a deeper wound. He was her mentor, her friend. At least she'd thought he was.

She'd spoken up because it was the right thing to do. She'd believed that at the time—and she still did. But look what being honest got her. A choking sob erupted from her throat. She pulled off on the shoulder as tears streamed down her cheeks.

There could be more casualties from her actions. If the agency lost the Barton Packing business, some of the ad team could also lose their jobs.

A lawsuit involving the biggest marketing agency in the state would be all over the media. She expected Gordon would get over his distaste for talking with the media long enough to smear her name from here to Chicago. Her career in public relations would be over, at least in Iowa. Would the agency provide counsel if there was a lawsuit, or was she on her own?

As always, her thoughts gravitated to the workers at the plant and to Emilio. Thinking of them affirmed the decision she'd made, the action she'd taken.

She stopped at the Muñoz home as soon as she arrived in Hammond. She took it as a good sign that the van in the driveway stood on all four wheels.

When Emilio raced out of the house toward her, her heart felt as though it would burst. She dropped to her knees and opened her arms. "Hola, Emilio. ¿Que pasa?"

"In English, please," he responded with a mischievous grin.

"You are so smart!"

"Sí, *maestra*."

Fortunately both Cesar and Camila Muñoz were at home. She explained her new situation to them and assured them they could rely on her as long as they needed. She would get an attorney to take Emilio's case and either drive him to hearings herself or go along for support. Whatever they wished. Cesar's gratitude was palpable.

She also told them about the reporter's interest in doing an interview. Cesar refused. "I cannot risk my family," he said. "I am sorry."

This refusal confirmed Camila's undocumented status, at least in her own mind.

"We will find another way," she told him. "Don't worry. We will not involve you and Camila." She didn't know how Emilio's story might still be told, but there had to be a way.

When she met Alvaro outside the restaurant, tears sprang to her eyes and she hugged him tight, not caring who saw them.

He held her for a long moment, but when he let go, they both stepped away into an awkward silence.

"You're on a lunch break," she said. "We better eat."

He nodded and held the door for her.

Having a meal with Alvaro at Eduardo's felt like going home. Eduardo's welcome was genuine. Maria even came out of the kitchen to greet her. Angela caught Alvaro's eye across the table, and he winked. He must have talked with them, though he'd never told her about it.

After the food arrived and Alvaro started to pray, she closed her eyes, too. She said thanks for Alvaro and asked for help for Emilio. When she opened her eyes, she was met with Alvaro's warm smile.

"What's going on at the plant?" she asked. She meant Gordon, and he knew that.

"It is all the same," he said.

She sighed. "I guess I shouldn't have expected anything else. At least you're still working." She poked at the carnitas, unable to enjoy the dish as she usually did. "I can't get his accusation of an affair between us out of my head. He told Nick he could prove it."

Alvaro shrugged. "He lied about many things. This is another."

"I suppose." She laid her fork down. "The thing that really bothers me is my boss accepted the accusation, accepted everything they said about me, as truth. He didn't believe me."

Alvaro reached across the table, covering her hand with his. His warmth sent comfort straight to her heart. "You did the right thing. That is what matters."

It was too early for her to feel good about what she'd done. Why did doing the right thing have to be so hard?

They spent the rest of their time together talking about Emilio, Saint Catherine's, his visa, and her unclear future. When they left the restaurant, they continued to talk as they stood on the sidewalk by her car.

"I must go," he said at last.

"I know," she said. "I'll call you tonight."

Then she hugged him again. And he hugged her back.

"Adios, amiga," he whispered. His lips grazed her cheek as he stepped away. "See you later."

"Absolutamente," she said. Then she teased. "I hope you understand my accent."

She watched his car as he drove away, touching her fingers to her cheek where she could still feel his lips. They'd been consciously, intentionally apart. Would that change? She didn't know. But she did know this was the first time he kissed her, and it felt delicious.

Chapter 37

A week later, she sat at her kitchen island digging into internet job sites when the phone rang. Expecting the caller to be the immigration attorney, she was surprised when Dave Wilstat's name showed on the screen instead. They hadn't communicated since the night she'd been ushered to the agency curb, her belongings in a box.

She answered without warmth. "Yes?"

"Can you come to the office?" he asked.

"Why?"

"I spoke with Nick Barton this morning. You're going to want to hear what he had to say. When can you get in here?"

Offended by the upbeat tone of his voice, her nostrils flared. She looked at the time. It wasn't even eight in the morning yet. He'd fired her. He didn't own her time anymore. Didn't he remember?

She responded with a voice as brittle as ice. "I have other things to do today."

"Please, Angela. It'll be worth your time."

He'd launched into the call as though she still worked for him, sounding as though nothing had happened, acting as though she'd be absolutely delighted to hear from him. What the heck? She had half a mind to hang up. He had, however, piqued her interest. What could Nick have said?

"I'll be there at 9:30." She didn't ask if the time worked.

"See you then." The line went dead.

She finished her coffee and headed for the bathroom to get ready.

Her days since getting the ax at Sherborn-Watts had been full, and today would be no different. After her meeting at the agency, she planned to use the public library's computers to research more on immigration issues. Spending money to replace the agency laptop felt like an extravagance she couldn't afford. Her iPad worked for searching for jobs, but she liked a bigger screen and keyboard for updating her résumé, writing application letters, which she'd done six of already, and doing long research sessions.

Schiffler's belief that media coverage could help Emilio's case had unleashed in Angela a flood of ideas for pitches she could make to her long list of media contacts. The opportunity to put her media skills to use on a cause that mattered to her filled her with hope. And excitement.

Also, she'd talked more with Schiffler about the options for becoming Emilio's legal guardian. As it seemed with everything related to these unaccompanied minors, there was a long, nuanced continuum of what guardianship meant, ranging from supporting him financially to taking him in and raising him as her own child. The real question was, what was best for him? Emilio faced a long journey, and no matter how it ended, she wouldn't let him face the uncertainty alone. She and Alvaro talked about it every night on the phone.

As much as she wanted to see Alvaro in person again, she hadn't been back to Hammond. Money for gas and a motel were other extravagances. Until she got another job, she resigned herself to being ultracareful with money.

Finished cleaning up, she slipped on khaki slacks and a sleeveless blouse and headed downtown to see what Dave thought was so important. She also wondered how he would handle this meeting. Would he acknowledge in any way that he'd failed her? Or would he still put it all on her? That was what really had her curious.

She'd been gone from Sherborn-Watts for only a week, yet sitting on the patio outside the agency offices watching Dave light a cigarette felt otherworldly. He continued to act as though the unpleasant meeting when she'd been fired had never happened. That surprised her more than hearing she'd been right about Gordon and Barton Packing.

Tilting his head back, Dave blew a cloud of cigarette smoke into the air. "Gordon's self-dealing on the housing was on point," he said.

"How do you know?"

"Nick talked to McKay and then verified it himself."

"He talked to the reporter?"

"Yep. Called him in."

Angela shook her head. All that time and effort she'd spent trying to get Nick to talk with reporters or shield him from the media—and then he turned around and called McKay in himself. Well, well, well. How about that?

"But why? Nick believed Gordon."

"What you said made him question what he thought he knew. He couldn't believe his trust in Gordon had been misplaced, but eventually he couldn't ignore what you said. He brought in McKay to hear the story firsthand. Then he talked to his HR people. And brought in the plant supervisors, Duarte and others.

"Turns out Ryker had been selective in what he'd told Barton. Enough to be credible, but not everything by a long shot. Barton didn't know about the expired product, as you said. He also didn't know Cunningham was Gordon's cousin. He didn't challenge him when you brought it up, because he thought it was possible Gordon had told him and he'd forgotten. He learned Gordon had been running the place with an iron fist. People were afraid to challenge him."

"What about the employee terminations?"

"That's a tougher one. When Gordon said they were legally airtight, he was actually right. But McKay's info puts it in another light. It appears Gordon contracted with a guy in Texas who recruited people to come to Iowa. The Texas contact made sure everyone had papers that would pass E-Verify, though some of the documents may have been forged. Nick has done enough digging into that to be concerned. It took a while to separate truth from lies, but in the end, Nick was convinced. He confronted Gordon. Boss to employee. Friend to friend."

It was strange, but Angela felt detached from everything Dave was telling her. Almost as though she were listening to someone recount the plot of a movie. Each revelation vindicated her, but none of it had anything to do with her anymore.

"Did Gordon admit what he'd been doing?"

Dave shook his head. "Not entirely. He continued to make excuses and justify his actions. Also, Nick doesn't know for sure that Gordon realized the Texas contact was sending people with forged papers. But he must have suspected. That's the only reason he would terminate people the way he did."

"Humph." Angela now realized that every single statement Gordon had made could have been the truth and a lie at the same time. The man was more devious than she'd imagined.

"This is the part you're going to like. Nick fired Gordon."

"Is that right?"

"He did. Then he called me. Nick says he won't have someone working for him he can't trust." Dave looked at her briefly and then away. "Ironic, isn't it? Gordon wanted you out, but he got kicked out himself. On the same charge."

It was ironic. But she couldn't see much difference in where they wound up. They'd both been fired.

"Even with Gordon gone, Nick's got a mess on his hands," Dave continued. "He owns that at least half of what went on under Gordon's direction was his own fault."

"How so?"

"He set the tone. Everything Gordon did—except the housing deal—was based in Nick's own actions. One example. Nick personally hired most of the managers in the plant. He hired and promoted the guys who'd helped him start the company. All white guys. Gordon took over hiring and promoting long before he took over the rest of the plant. He simply continued the bias Nick had set up himself. It was the rare person who broke through that color barrier."

"What about Alvaro? Gordon fired him right after I left."

"Gordon fired him but in name only. He's continued working right along. Maybe you knew that?" He looked at Angela.

Of course she knew that, but she gave him nothing. He could think what he liked. It was none of his business.

Dave shrugged. "Anyway, Nick will officially rehire Duarte today. He told me he also intends to talk with their lawyer about getting Duarte a permanent work visa. Nick needs someone like Duarte who has credibility with the workforce and who knows the business."

This was the first thing Dave had said that got her excited. If Alvaro knew about any of this new information, he would surely have called her. She couldn't wait to tell him, and she would. As soon as she left Sherborn-Watts.

"It had to be hard for Nick to have someone he considered a friend betray him," she said, opening the door for Dave to own up to his betrayal of her. He lit another cigarette and, once again, said nothing. Once again, she was disappointed. "Nick was trying to retire," she said. "And now he doesn't have the man he was going to turn the company over to. What's he going to do?"

"Who knows?" Dave shrugged. "Maybe he'll sell to another packing company. To make that happen, though, he has to have a solid company. That's where we come in."

"Does that mean Nick changed his mind about the agency? And what about the lawsuit? Do you think Gordon will go forward with it?"

"He could still sue, but he wouldn't have much credibility without Nick on his side. And he probably wouldn't want to risk even greater exposure of what he's done. And, yes, Nick's keeping the ad agency in place. He may even do more advertising and customer communication to rebuild the company's reputation."

"That's good. I'm glad it worked out. Thanks for telling me all this." She picked up her purse and stood. She didn't need to talk about it anymore, and she was eager to call Alvaro.

"Hold on. How soon can you get back up there?"

She cocked her head. "I don't understand."

"Nick wants to talk to you."

"He kicked me out."

Saying that hurt, but standing there looking at the man she'd admired so much, the one who'd let her down so badly, she realized other truths hurt more.

Over the last few days, she'd had ample time for reflection. In those many hours, she'd come to realize how frequently she walked that line—professionally but not personally committed. She succeeded, excelled even, at her job, most of the time without thinking about how the work affected her personally, but sometimes consciously burying her beliefs.

A few short months ago, she'd have been equally enthused at having Barton Packing as a client again, grabbing at the prize client assignment dangled in front of her. She'd have been so concerned about preserving her career that she would have let his silence pass. She couldn't be silent anymore. He'd let her down on the issues she'd discovered throughout her time at Barton. He'd betrayed her fully when he'd stood by and let her be fired.

"Nick kicked me out," she repeated. "So did you, Dave. I counted on you, and you let me down."

Dave took a good long time to stub out the cigarette butt before answering. When he spoke, he gazed into the distance.

"Angela, I know we acted fast. I'm sure it felt harsh. We needed to do it for the good of everyone."

"I understand about the agency. I'm talking about you."

"I haven't stopped thinking about it since we . . ." He picked up the cigarette butt and slowly shredded it.

"Since you fired me," she completed his sentence.

Finally, he looked at her. "Yeah." He stood up and faced her directly. "Since I fired you. It's hard to say that. I didn't want to lose the business, and I laid the blame on you, even though you'd kept me in the loop all along. Nick trusted Gordon too much; I didn't trust you enough. I let you down, and I let myself down. I'm sorry."

Angela considered what he'd said. She had relied on Dave as much as Nick relied on Gordon. She'd followed his lead without giving equal weight to what she believed. She had to learn a new way.

"I appreciate you saying that," she said.

"We want you—I want you—working on the Sherborn-Watts team again. You're a good counselor—even better for having worked with this client. Nick knows he put his trust in the wrong person. He wants to apologize face to face, if you'll let him. And if you accept his apology, he wants you to work with him to get things right at the plant." Dave pulled a piece of paper out of his jacket pocket and handed it to her. "We want you back here at the agency, too. This letter explains what happened and clears everything up for the personnel files."

She glanced at the document, then handed it back to him. "I don't know, Dave. I don't know if working for Sherborn-Watts is what I want to do."

"You could make a real difference."

"I could make a difference in lots of places. Top of my list is helping Emilio. If there's anything I can do to keep him in the States, I'll do it. And there are so many kids like him. We can't kick them back to their home countries. Not after everything they've been through."

"You can't take responsibility for all of them."

"No, but I can help this one. And maybe more. Those kids need someone looking out for them. If media coverage helps, I can do that."

"We can help with that here at the agency. We can take on Standing for Justice as a pro bono client. You could head the effort and have a team working to support you."

The proposal had some appeal. A continued connection to Barton Packing offered advantages. She could help achieve the best result for the employees, the community, and the company through a new company direction, fully supported by Nick now. And see Alvaro and Emilio every day.

Yet she regarded his proposal with skepticism. Keeping her at the agency was in his self-interest. It remained to be seen whether it was in hers.

"I won't commit to coming back to the agency," she said. "I need time to think about your offer. In any case, I'd have to keep enough flexibility to figure out how to best help Emilio."

"We'll do whatever makes sense," Dave said. "Can we count on you to work with Barton?"

"As a consultant. I'll contract with Nick directly."

Angela could see from the look on his face that Dave hadn't expected this from her. At the outset, he'd wanted her on the account because she was strong. In the past three months, she'd developed true strength. Finally, she knew it.

"I'll coordinate with you or whomever Sherborn-Watts puts on the account," she added. "I'll go to Hammond tomorrow. But right now, there's something I need to do." Suddenly she was wildly eager to get away.

"We'll talk this afternoon?" Dave asked.

"I'll call you," she said. She shook his hand and left.

Knowing Alvaro was at work, she texted him. *Call me, amigo. Great news.*

Chapter 38

"This is heaven." Alvaro sighed after swallowing the last bite of *pupusa* scraped from the cardboard tray.

"No, this is Iowa," Angela said, then laughed at her own joke. "That's a line from a movie," she explained. "We can watch it sometime."

The crisp, clear October air filled Angela with energy. When Alvaro had told her he could come to Des Moines for the weekend, she'd been elated. They appreciated every opportunity to be together, especially in Des Moines. First on their list, the farmers market. They'd arrived at the market in time to hear the opening bell and get a cup of Java Joes coffee before heading to the Salvadoran food stand.

Angela delighted in watching Alvaro take such pleasure in food from his homeland. Pupusas offered reason enough for him to come to Des Moines.

"I want another one before we leave today," Alvaro said as he wiped salsa from the corners of his mouth.

"For sure," she said. "The Salvadoran women would be disappointed if you didn't come back. I think they want to adopt you." She reached over with her own napkin and wiped a last bit of salsa from his cheek. "Missed a spot."

"Talking to them, I feel like I am home. Women like them made pupusas at the markets where my mother took me as a boy."

The wistful tone of his voice tugged at her heart. Maybe he would be going home in a couple of months. Maybe not. Nick had been true to his word. The company attorney was trying to find a way for Alvaro to stay in the US. But the quest for an extended visa or green card had anything but a certain outcome. Like so much in the immigrant world.

Alvaro was conflicted about where his future might be. He'd had his mind set on returning to El Salvador, on seeing his family. But that was when staying in Iowa wasn't a possibility. If he could remain in the US, he would. At least for a while.

Angela was torn on what she hoped for him. She wanted him to be happy, and she wanted him in Iowa. If only those desires could be met the same way. She chose not to dwell on the possibility that he might have to leave Iowa and never return.

Emilio's situation was no more certain, but at least she could do something to help there. She had already succeeded in getting two profiles on Emilio's case published, using a pseudonym for Emilio. An article profiling Standing for Justice was in the works. Alvaro had learned that, as Angela had suspected, Camila Muñoz did not have legal papers, so Angela was doubly careful to shield the Muñoz family from reporters. Camila's health had improved, and with the support of many in the community, the financial concern Cesar expressed about keeping Emilio with them had lessened.

Angela threw away their trays and napkins as they continued on through the market crowd, discussing work and life in between stops to taste samples and talk with vendors.

It had been three months since the blowup at Barton Packing. Angela had returned to Hammond as a consultant, spending some portion of each week working with Dave, Nick, and Alvaro to scope out a master plan for getting Barton

Packing back on solid footing. In his new role as liaison between Nick and the plant, Alvaro had become an integral part of the team.

Everyone agreed on the need to reestablish trust with employees. Promoting Alvaro, eliminating the punitive points system, and devoting a room for Muslim prayer demonstrated the company's goodwill. They continued to explore other long-term programs for the company.

Not as easy to change were entrenched attitudes among several of the supervisors. Nick met with each of them one-on-one to explain and lay out the new direction. He let them know that, while he hoped they'd stay with him, if they couldn't embrace the new plan, they'd need to find new employment. Most adapted readily; others he was sorry to see go.

Simultaneously, Nick reached out to city officials, the media, and the government. On Dave's recommendation, Nick alerted US Department of Labor officials about what had been going on and explained the company's plan to rectify any discovered wrongdoings. Such proactive steps on the part of a packing company were virtually unheard of. It seemed likely the company would still incur a fine. Possibly substantial. That decision hung ominously on the horizon.

As a team, they went round and round on the subject of what to do about the possibility that some employees might have forged documents. They decided to focus on the things the company could control in the future—how they hired, how they treated employees, and how they managed terminations. Since E-Verify had cleared everyone, they operated on the presumption that everyone worked legally. So far, ICE had not been in touch.

They had also begun to address the housing-subsidy mess. Barton Packing expanded the rent subsidy to all new employees and put pressure on Nate Cunningham to clean up the properties. Getting the rent rates lowered proved difficult since there were no regulations. It took Hammond business owners using their influence with Cunningham to make a difference.

McKay eventually wrote a series of articles on the plant. Though the articles were accurate and fair, Nick found it hard to see the company's problems laid out in black and white. Though Angela did her best to help him view the articles objectively, it was at this time that he especially missed his wife. The sting eased when many of his friends and business associates came to his defense.

Gordon had dropped out of sight. Liz heard that he had taken his family to stay with relatives in Alabama, escaping the inevitable scrutiny and judgment of such a small town. He had not filed a lawsuit, at least not yet. When Angela thought of Gordon, she felt sympathy, if not for him, at least for his wife and son.

Working as a consultant suited Angela well. Now, whenever she gave counsel, she asked herself if she truly believed what she recommended. As doing so became second nature, her confidence grew.

Her assignment in Hammond would not end anytime soon, which was valuable for many reasons, not the least of which because it reestablished her financial footing. As more programs moved to implementation, she adjusted her schedule to three days a week at the plant, choosing days that allowed her to continue to teach at Saint Catherine's. Alternating weekends she spent with her parents. On her days in Des Moines, she worked with Standing for Justice, where the financial reward was modest but the emotional reward was exceptional.

Gordon's accusation of an affair opened the door for her and Alvaro to revisit the "why not" conversation. She knew in her heart Alvaro was the right man for her. He felt the same about her. So they found a compromise that worked. They dated openly in Des Moines while keeping their relationship low-key in Hammond. Alvaro came to Des Moines whenever his work schedule allowed it.

She believed they could not in good conscience keep the relationship a secret from Nick Barton, especially given all that had happened. They went to see him together. The meeting was awkward only for a moment.

"Are you asking my blessing?" Nick asked.

"No," Angela said. "Letting you know so you aren't blindsided."

Alvaro added. "Tell us if it is ever a problem."

"And then you'd stop seeing each other?" Nick asked.

Angela saw the twinkle in his eye. "No, but you might cut us some slack."

Nick had laughed. There had been no need for discussion since.

Now Angela and Alvaro stopped at a stand sampling cheeses. Alvaro picked a half pound of aged white cheddar to go with the wine they were taking to a picnic later in the day. "Is it enough?" he asked.

"With the other appetizers I fixed, yes." She looked at him with affection. The end of the year loomed, and she could not keep the possibility of losing him out of her mind. But there was nothing either of them could do about it now, and she chose not to let the uncertainty ruin a beautiful day.

They moved on to a stand where Angela picked up a half dozen miniature decorative gourds and a pumpkin twice the size of a softball to decorate her kitchen.

"Emilio's next hearing comes up in a couple of weeks," he said. "Are we prepared?"

"I'm coordinating with Claudia Schiffler," Angela said. "She's coming to Hammond soon to talk with Emilio and the Muñoz family. We're exploring what level of guardian role I could have."

"I will go with you to Omaha for the hearing."

"Can you get off work?"

"Don't worry, amiga. I've already talked to Mr. Barton. It's OK."

"Emilio would like that," she said. Linking a hand through his arm, she leaned close and kissed his cheek. "So would I."

That morning after she'd dressed, she had run a finger across the integrity stone sitting on the bathroom counter. In the months the stone had sat on her desk at Barton Packing, the grooves of the word "integrity" had gathered dust. Now the black letters sparkled.

She still believed everything she had about integrity when she first went to Hammond. But her understanding of the word had become deeper, more nuanced. Now she saw that integrity included so much more. Integrated. Being whole. All parts together. She continued to explore the word. With more experiences, she imagined finding even more depth.

She'd thought she could live her life counseling her clients, understanding their audiences, working for the good of both, while never committing herself—her *self*—either way.

These past months had taught her that professional integrity must also include personal integrity. Both required courage, strength, and commitment. Qualities she would continue working to develop.

Next to the stone sat a card her mother had sent the day after Angela had been fired. Her mother had written, simply, *I'm proud of you, Angela.*

The End

Acknowledgments

From first to last, *Simple Truth* benefited from the input of many individuals. In its earliest stages, the story foundation took shape in Kelly Dwyer's plot workshop at the Iowa Summer Writing Festival. For insight into the legal challenges facing unaccompanied minors, I turned to immigration attorneys Lori Chesser, Ann Naffier, and April Palma. Francisca Bodensteiner and Dinora Amaya assisted with Spanish. Any errors in the novel related to immigration law or Spanish are entirely my own. Special thanks to my writing partner, Mary Gottschalk, who walked with me from the beginning, reading each version with patience and insight. The story improved significantly in the capable hands of editors Amara Holstein and Kirsten Colton, who helped me make the story the best it could be. Finally, I return endless love to my husband, David, a steady rock in the sometimes-turbulent waters of my writing life.

About the Author

Carol Bodensteiner grew up in the heartland of the United States, and she continues to draw writing inspiration from the people, places, culture, and history of the area. She is the author of *Growing Up Country: Memories of an Iowa Farm Girl*, a memoir about growing up in the middle of the United States in the middle of the twentieth century. Her first novel, *Go Away Home*, is set in Iowa in the years leading up to World War I. *Simple Truth* is her second novel.

She enjoys hearing from readers, so please keep in touch. You can reach her via:

- Her website: www.carolbodensteiner.com
- Twitter: @CABodensteiner
- Facebook: www.facebook.com/CarolBodensteinerAuthor
- Goodreads:www.goodreads.com/author/show/1323422. Carol_Bodensteiner

Reader Discussion Guide

1. From the outset, Angela finds herself judging and making assumptions about the people she meets in the packing plant. Often, those assumptions are inaccurate. Could you relate to her in this regard? Have you ever found yourself judging or making assumptions about people you meet? How does Angela grow in her openness to new people and cultures? What are some of your own discoveries regarding false assumptions?

2. When Angela shares the problems she's seeing at Barton Packing with her boss, he is not as concerned as she. What did you think about the way he handled those calls? Could Angela have presented her concerns more effectively? If she had pushed harder, do you think the outcome would have changed? Why or why not?

3. On several occasions, Angela is confronted with racist remarks. Often she doesn't challenge the person who says these things in the interest of maintaining good relationships or because, in the moment, she is too taken aback to respond. What do you think of the way she does or doesn't respond to these comments? When have you experienced a similar situation, and how have you handled it?

4. Angela struggles with whether to speak up or not in the face of injustice. When she does make a stand, the results are not at all what she expected. Were you surprised at her boss's reaction? The agency bosses'? Barton's?

5. Hammond is a small town, a significantly different world from the city of Des Moines, where Angela lives. Are the

racist situations she faces more likely to occur in a small town than a large city? Or are they simply more visible in a small town? Why or why not?

6. Angela is attracted to Alvaro, the Salvadoran plant supervisor. How likely do you think it is that their relationship could flourish when her assignment ends or that it could survive if he returns to El Salvador? What did you think about the way they address their relationship?

7. When Angela takes on a teaching assignment with immigrant children, she comes into contact with a child who came to the United States illegally to escape the violence in Honduras. Some people believe these children should be sent back immediately, yet once they are in the US legal system, it may take years to sort out their status. Was what you learned about these children in this book a surprise? How do you think these children should be treated?

8. As a public-relations person, Angela is responsible for representing her client while also taking into account the needs of others. How well do you think she balances this responsibility? Are there instances when you think she is less or more effective?

9. Angela holds herself to a high ethical standard of truth and honesty, yet at one point she finds herself lying— and then justifying her lies. What did you think of her when that happened? Are there circumstances when lying is justified?

10. A man tells Angela his niece could never be a public-relations person because she can't lie. He voices an attitude about public relations that many people hold. What are

your thoughts about public relations? Did reading this book affect your attitude about the profession or those who practice it?

11. "To change behavior, change beliefs." That is a basic premise of human behavior that Angela and her boss use when planning. What personal beliefs do you hold that affect your behavior? Can you think of instances when you changed something you believed and, as a result, changed your own behavior?

CPSIA information can be obtained
at www.ICGtesting.com
Printed in the USA
LVHW112341140119
603948LV00002B/312/P